To Ron and Annette

Merry Christmas!

From the Paradis Family

(Zach, Tammy, Dylan, Robyn)

Drathorn Hellbound

THE INAUGURATION

DY Paradis

Drathorn Hellbound

THE INAUGURATION

D.Y. Paradis

To order additional copies of this book, contact:
Xlibris Corporation
1-888-795-4274
www.Xlibris.com
Orders@Xlibris.com
71101

I'D LIKE TO SEND THANKS TO;

All of my family and friends for sticking by my side, even when others
did not, I also thank all others who have helped me through life such
as past teachers and mentors. If any of you are reading this,
know that I think well of you and that I hope the rest
of your lives are filled with happiness.

THIS NOVEL IS DEDICATED TO;

Mom, Dad, and Robyn for helping me become the person I am today.
Thank you for believing in me even at times when I did not believe
in myself. I love you very much and dedicate this work to you.

Colin, my best friend, you have always been there to lend a helping
hand and a word of advice to me. It was your unfailing loyalty that
inspired the character Troy Blaygard and some of our times together
that brought out the imagination I needed to complete this;
you are my brother in all but blood. Thank you.

"The best way to predict your future is to create it!"

-Abraham Lincoln-

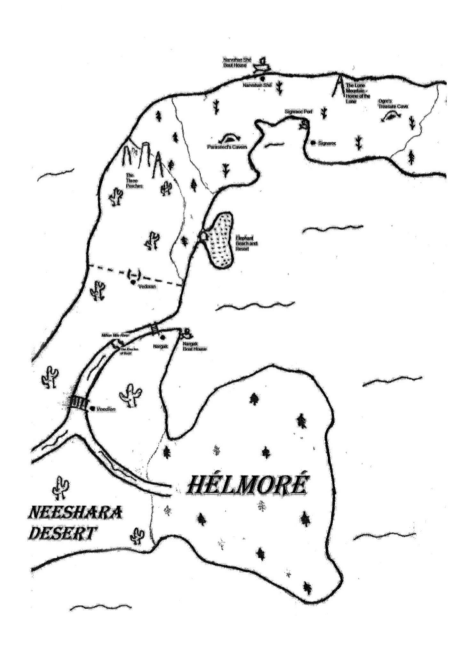

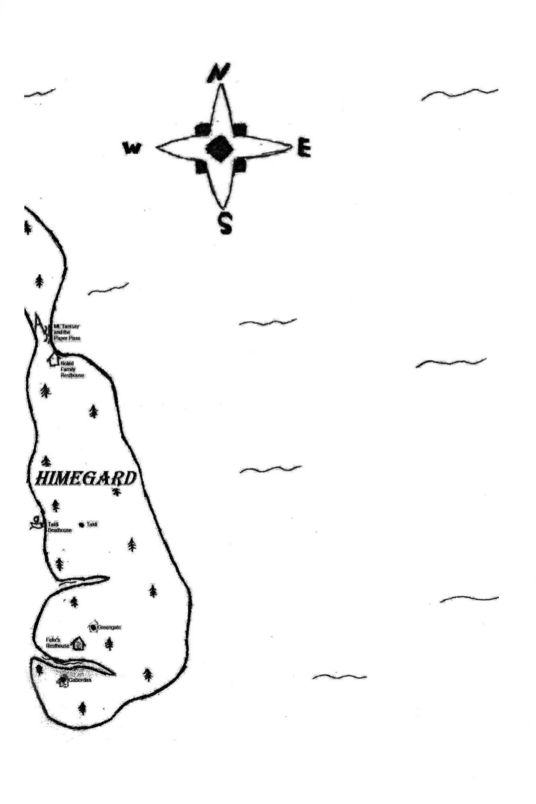

The Gods

ZATHIUS: (Zay-thee-us) the god of Life, and controller of love. He is the leader of the thirteen. He was the creator of humans as well as most others. His animal is the Dove.

DAVEAROUS: (Dave-are-ohs) the god of Wisdom, and controller of air. He is mainly worshipped by Chis and Dragonians and created them both. His animal is the Fox.

BORJIL: (Bore-jill) the god of Strength, controller of stone. He was the creator of the dwarves and is worshipped by all those who need strength emotionally or physically. His animal is the Bear.

MAGNIUS: (Mag-nee-iss) God of magic and controller of healing. He and Aleena created the elves and he is the source of all magic. He also helped make the mermaids. His animal is the Wolf.

ALEENA: (Ah-lee-nah) Goddess of beauty and controller of nature. Her relationship with Magnius lead to the creation of Elves and Mermaids. The Elves are a symbol of their love for each other. She is greatly worshipped by the Elves and parents of all races. Her animal is the Swan.

DELVANEROUS: (Del-van-air-us) God of discovery, controller of minerals. He is worshiped by scientists and researchers. He is the brother of Deandra and Dimanious. His animal is the Bat.

DEANDRA: (Dee-an-dra) Goddess of dreams, controller of water. She is a favourite of the merfolk and is sister of Delvanerous and Dimanious. Her animal is the Dolphin.

DIMANIOUS: (Die-mane-ee-us) the god of destiny, controller of lightning. He is worshipped by all heroes for his power over their futures. He is the brother and power-figure of Delvanerous and Deandra. His animal is the Eagle.

SELEEN: (Suh-leen) the goddess of hope and controller of light. She is the arch-enemy of Alexandria. She is in love with Sylvaston but he seems to pay her no attention. She is worshipped by those who fear the dark. Her animal is the Horse.

COLASPIS: (Call-ass-pis) the god of pain, controller of metals. He is brother to Sylvaston and married to Alexandria. He is worshipped by all of evil purpose especially assassins, bounty hunters, and necromancers. His animal is the Crow.

SYLVASTON: (Sil-vas-ton) God of anger, controller of fire. Little is known about this god. He is the brother of Colaspis but little else is known about him . . . he created the Gar, Dragonians, Hellbound and Dragons. His animal is the Snake and he controls all reptiles and creatures of fire.

DEHEANO: (Deh-hay-ah-no) God of time, controller of ice. This, the most mysterious god is said to have a chill that kills even those who are already dead. Few worship him, and even fewer would venture near his territory. His animal is the Tiger.

ALEXANDRIA: (Ah-lex-an-dree-ah) the god of Fear and controller of darkness. She is the enemy of Seleen. Her marriage to Colaspis is obvious and well known. She is said to be beautiful but the legends always talk of her as nothing but smoke and shadows . . . yet more about her past is known the Sylvaston or Deheano's. She is the creator of the Gar. Her animal is the Spider.

Contents

Prologue;

Hellen's Last Stand

Our story takes place on the solitary planet of Corrone. This planet is inhabited by thousands of creatures that we can only dream of yet it has only one plot of land; a great island on the surface known as Tanroe. Nearly four hundred years ago a war broke out on this island . . . it still rages. The war was started when the formidable forces of good invaded the renowned badlands of Tanroe, before this invasion the forces of darkness used the badlands as a place of refuge. The forces of darkness were angered by this attack and struck back . . . to this day the war over the badlands continues. On the far eastern side of this island (the part farthest from the fabled Badlands) our story starts . . .

May, 14, 18283; Hellen Hellbound had lost every family member she had ever possessed that night; all but her young nephew clasped safely in her arms. As she ran she looked back at the great Hellbound Mansion; it was her family's home. It was positioned right in the Imperial City of Veedion. The imperial city was where the emperor of Corrone resided. Hellen stared at her home; the great mansion was ablaze and two dozen figures ran from the flames. Five minutes ago her only living relatives had been her father, her sister and her husband and their child; Drathorn Hellbound. If it weren't for the fact that she had just witnessed the deaths of all but the youngest she would have foolishly run back to greet her family and their rescuers. But she knew that those two dozen figures were really an assassin and his minions.

As soon as those figures emerged from the flames Hellen ran faster, still holding the young Drathorn Hellbound in her arms. As she ran from her pursuers she thought of the night's events; her family had been throwing a house party for their friends in Veedion when a strange red haired man and two dozen creatures arrived and began slaughtering her family and the guests. *So the king of the badlands has finally managed to find the remaining Hellbound has he?* She thought. The Hellbound family was made of the world's greatest warriors, they were the darklord's greatest enemy and ever since Hellen's ancestor, Gradorn Lebasta Hellbound, had started the war with the badlands the darklord had been hunting down Gradorn's descendants. Gradorn had died nearly three hundred and seventy years ago but the fabled darklord still walked as though he were immortal.

Hellen spotted her escape route ahead; an alley way that led to another street that could take her to the imperial prison where the imperial guards could protect her and Drathorn. Hellen ran as fast as she could, she turned the corner and was at the end of the alleyway when she realized she had made a wrong turn. It was a dead end. She looked back. The way to the street was blocked by two dozen shadowy figures.

Hellen knew that the only way to escape was to fight but she knew that she would never survive. She placed her six-year-old nephew on the ground where he stared, unblinking, at the slowly approaching foe. "Drathorn . . . listen to me." Hellen spoke firmly to the young boy but he did not look up. "I need you to run . . . these people want to hurt you . . . I want you to run and hide in the market . . . do you understand?"

The boy finally looked away from the approaching enemies to look into his aunt's eyes. "Where are mother and father?"

Hellen looked down at the small child; he stared deep into her eyes without fear. He would get his answer; "They are dead." And Hellen felt no emotion but anger as she spoke but Drathorn allowed only a single tear to escape . . ."Don't cry Drathorn . . . that's not like us . . . we're the Hellbound . . . this is life for us. Now . . . do you understand me?"

The boy looked back at his enemies, anger and sadness flooding his heart, and nodded. Hellen handed Drathorn a small dagger with a greenish tint in the metal and Drathorn looked at it curiously. "If one of the monsters attack you stab it with that and it will release you . . . this is a highly poisonous dagger . . ." Hellen told the boy. Again he did nothing but nod; he was a warrior. "Hide in the market . . . you'll be safe there . . ."

"I love you aunt Hellen . . ." The boy said it very quietly but Hellen heard it and chose to ignore this comment as she looked to their enemy again; they were closing in.

"Tomorrow . . . if someone asks your name tell them you are Drathorn Teldaga . . . do you understand?" she asked.

The boy only nodded again.

Hellen drew the long sword at her side and faced her enemy. A crimson fireball blazed suddenly to life in her left hand, the flickering light glistened off of her sword. On the back of her sword hand was the mark of the Hellbound; three tears burned into the back of her right hand, almost flower like in appearance, they formed a triangle mark. They were the tears of a dragon.

"Put away your weapons fools . . ." said the lead figure. "You cannot hope to defeat us!" The voice was human . . . and young. A young man stepped into the fire light. Hellen was shocked by his appearance. He couldn't have been more than twenty. His hair was a crimson red, his eyes a startling blue. In his right hand was a long sword. Hanging from every clasp of his iron armour was either a short sword or a dagger. He was ready for anything a fight could offer but yet he looked as innocent as a newborn child. "I said put away your weapons, Hellen!"

"You know my name . . ." Hellen asked, confused. "How?"

"I am an Assassin . . ." The man stated. "I always know everything there is to know about my target."

"No matter," Hellen said, recalling her anger. "You cannot hope to defeat a Hellbound!"

"Really?" the assassin laughed. "I just killed your sister, your brother in law, and your father! Not to mention about fifty party guests!"

"You only surprised us . . . you shall not take my life!" Hellen prepared to attack.

"So be it . . ." the assassin stepped back, out of the circle of fire light and his strange followers closed in. "Destroy her . . ."

Hellen didn't hesitate. The fireball had left her hand before the creatures had gotten close to her. It hit one monster and exploded. The monster that had been hit died instantly and the explosion destroyed two others; only ashes remained.

"Run, Drathorn!" the boy hesitated for only a moment to watch his aunt decapitate a creature in the darkness and then he ran. The young boy ran as fast as his little legs could carry him, he wasn't afraid; he was just doing what he was told.

A long and non-human hand grabbed his ankle and he fell. Drathorn screamed in shock and stabbed at his attacker's wrist. The dagger collided and his enemy shrieked in pain as the poison immediately began its journey through his body. Drathorn stabbed again and was released. He scrambled onto his feet and ran from the alleyway, the greenish dagger still clutched in his tiny hands. "Get that boy! No fools! Kill the aunt! Kill her!" The assassin's voice rang through the air as Drathorn ran.

The sound of another fireball colliding rang through the air and then his aunt's scream of pain split the sky. Drathorn knew that the assassin was coming for him next but it was too late; he had already taken up his hiding place under a market stall that was holding oranges.

The assassin never found Drathorn under that stall, the next day Drathorn was found by an imperial guard and he claimed to be Drathorn Teldaga as Hellen had instructed. A week later Drathorn found himself in a public orphanage in the far away town of Greengate.

This is a tale of war, destruction, corruption, power and love . . . This is the tale . . . of the Hellbound.

I

On the Hunt

Families are separated by the millions every day on earth but it never happens to one boy as many times as it has to Drathorn. Drathorn was adopted three times since his tragic accident yet he still managed to find a way to spend more time in the orphanage than anywhere else. Drathorn was utterly destroyed when he lost his family but life continued for him. Our story continues over eight years after the death of his aunt; it's ten P.M. on Saturday, January 20th, of the year 18291. Drathorn is fifteen now and he still lives on, but not happily. We continue our tale while Drathorn Teldaga walks through the woods on this cold night; his aunt's dagger held safely at his side by his leather belt.

Drathorn wandered the icy forest alone that night but he didn't follow any paths. He had long, messy black hair and dark blue eyes. He was average height for his age of fifteen; the mark of the Hellbound was on the back of his hand, hidden in the darkness. Somewhere in this forest his foster brother was hunting.

He had been adopted after a month in the orphanage by the Peters family. The Peters cared for him for almost three months when the home caught fire and Drathorn was the only one to escape. After that he was sent back to the orphanage for two years. Then he was adopted by the McHaveman family. Unfortunately Drathorn was startled by his new brother from his sleep and punched him violently multiple times. The angry parents sent Drathorn back to the orphanage after only one night. When Drathorn was twelve he was adopted by the Flintclaw family. The father of that family went to war with the imperial army and was killed in battle a year after Drathorn's adoption. The mother died of shock a week later. Since then the older brother had been caring for Drathorn.

Elgard Flintclaw inherited the family business when his mother died. It was a world famous hunting company called 'The Claws of Hunting'. Now Elgard was twenty-three and Drathorn was fifteen. They traveled the eastern section of Tanroe on hunting business. They were currently in the great Gaberdan Woods. Drathorn was rather bored as he walked through the silent forest; he stepped lightly to avoid startling any lurking animals and thought of the nearby town of Greengate.

The place he'd grown up in for so long, the orphanage, he was glad to be away from there yet he was anxious to see his old home again. He didn't have any friends there but he still thought of the place as home; a place he hated but would never forget . . .

Drathorn stopped suddenly; right in front of him was a great mountain lion. Almost seven and a half feet long and roughly two hundred and twenty pounds, the mountain lion stared silently at Drathorn, unmoving and with a beautiful golden coat of fur. The January winds rustled the lion's fur with a peaceful grace. The lion seemed to sigh with relief at the sight of Drathorn. The mountain lion turned its head toward a small path on the other side of the bush.

The moonlight caught a spot on the mountain lion's face and for only a moment there was a flash of blue; a beautiful pearl blue underneath its acidic green eyes. "Elgard . . . is that you?" Drathorn whispered quietly to the creature. The creature looked at him again and the moonlight flashed off the same spot.

The mountain lion considered Drathorn for a moment and then, slowly, it nodded its great head. Drathorn relaxed and moved his hand away from Hellen's dagger. Elgard turned slowly to look over the bush and as it passed through the spot of moonlight Drathorn noticed that a great paw shape of pearl blue was tattooed to its forehead. That was Elgard alright.

The tattoo was the mark of an Ali-Manicota; a transformer of two lives. Years ago when magic was discovered anyone was permitted its use . . . but when dark wizards appeared it was made illegal to use magic unless you were an Ali-Manicota. You could only become an Ali-Manicota if you were pure of heart. Each Ali-Manicota could transform into an animal at will, a different animal for each one. In the animal or human forms you could always tell if they were Ali-Manicota or not for every one had a different symbol and there was only one Ali-Manicota for each animal in the world.

But the most amazing feature of the Ali-Manicota was their uncanny ability to live forever. They could only age until they were thirty and if they were killed in one form they would live on as the other. Elgard had never died in either form and still aged normally, for the time being. Drathorn suddenly imagined himself as an old man while Elgard was still looking to be around thirty years old; he shook the image from his mind and looked over the bush at the game path Elgard the puma was staring at.

A young male deer grazed silently on grass not far from the brothers . . . the mother and her infant trotted slowly along the game path and towards the clearing Drathorn had come from. "*Wait here . . .*" Elgard's voice echoed in Drathorn's head and he remembered Elgard's ability to talk with his mind. Drathorn nodded and waited . . .

"*Deer travel in strange ways to avoid predators.*" Elgard said with his mind. "*The mother and the babies travel ahead and the father stays hidden so that he can surprise any predators . . . so my job is to take care of the father so the hunters can deal with everyone else . . . Do you understand?*" Drathorn didn't know what to do so he just nodded. Elgard's laugh exploded inside of Drathorn's head like fireworks; "*You can talk to me through your thoughts too Drathorn . . . I can read your mind when I'm in this state.*"

Drathorn was surprised at that and forced himself to think; "*Do you do that often?*"

"*No . . . I give people their personal space . . . I broke into someone's mind before . . . I really didn't like what I saw . . .*" Elgard laughed again as the male deer drew closer. "*The mind is a truly strange thing . . . The strangest thoughts of a person are so exposed and yet so . . . unknown . . . Here it comes . . . don't move . . .*"

Drathorn stayed in a kneeling position and watched the male deer approach slowly; its eyes focused on the female and her young child in the clearing ahead. Drathorn didn't move as the young male passed the bush, it was almost ten feet away from Elgard when the great puma leapt suddenly out of the bush. The sudden attack startled Drathorn and he fell over but the male deer had no chance to warn its family as the great puma landed on its back.

The deer bucked wildly and tried to shake Elgard off but the more it struggled the deeper Elgard's claws sank into its skin. The struggle was quite interesting but Elgard seemed to get bored and ended it with a bone crushing bite to the neck. The deer fell heavily to the ground, dead, and Elgard looked at Drathorn lying in the grass with an inhuman smile. The puma stepped away from the dead animal and stared at Drathorn. A moment later the beautiful blue mark on his face began to shine.

The light grew brighter as Drathorn watched and soon Drathorn was forced to shield his eyes from its radiance. Then, just as suddenly as it had begun, Drathorn noticed the light stop. At first he saw nothing but darkness and the voice of his foster brother echoed loudly ahead of him. "Drathorn, my brother, stand up . . ." He laughed loudly as Drathorn struggled to his feet. "The blood of a deer is disgusting . . . you have no idea . . ." He laughed again and asked; "Are you alright?"

Drathorn laughed and said; "Yeah . . . just give me a second for my eyes to adjust . . ." There was silence for a moment and then Drathorn found that he could make out the body of the dead deer. He looked around and saw his brother standing in the middle of a great patch of moonlight. He was now a human.

Elgard was slightly taller than Drathorn and had wavy blonde hair. He stood casually waiting for Drathorn to say something. He wore a great assortment of leather armour and he had a long bow and a quiver of arrows slung onto his back. A short sword was sheathed at his side. "Ok . . . Now what?" Drathorn asked.

"What do you mean, 'now what'?" Elgard asked, "How long have we been doing this?"

"A long time . . ." Drathorn answered, "But I don't usually follow you in . . . I usually stay in the camp and practice my archery, remember?"

"Yeah I know but I thought you at least knew what was going on out here." Elgard said. Drathorn just shook his head. Elgard sighed and said; "Now I fire an arrow into the sky and make it light the sky with magic . . . this makes a flare that blinds the animals long enough to kill the mother and capture the baby. Do you understand now?"

"Yeah I get it." Drathorn said nodding, "but why do we capture the babies again?"

"They can't survive alone in the wilderness and don't have enough meat on them for eating. So we capture them and sell them in town. They can make good pets you see." Elgard prepared his bow and fished out an arrow. "Are you ready?"

Drathorn nodded. "*Efrall!*" The word escaped his lips with a thick accent of magic. Pure power flowed into the arrow in his hands and yet . . . nothing happened. He shot the arrow into the sky above the clearing and it disappeared into the night. Drathorn waited quietly. Then, very suddenly, the sky was lit with a fiery light. It covered the sky and lit the forest for miles around. Drathorn looked at Elgard and saw him staring out into the clearing. Drathorn looked out and saw what he was watching.

The deer in the clearing were going wild with fear at the sudden explosion of light. A few black lines suddenly flew out of the forest and struck the mother and she collapsed, dead, in seconds. Then a few hunters bearing a great black object ran from the cover of the trees and attempted to secure the baby. Weather or not they caught the baby, Drathorn didn't see because the light from the arrow suddenly went out. Before Drathorn could let his eyes adjust to the returned darkness another arrow erupted in the clearing. The light illuminated a scene in which the mother was already being dragged away by two men and the struggling baby was being dragged along behind it in a great black net by three others.

"How can you end the lives of so many animals each day, Elgard?" Drathorn asked, "Do you not feel their pain as they die?"

Elgard seemed caught off guard by that question. He considered the question as he took a step forward. "I used to feel the pain . . ." Elgard said as they walked out into the clearing. "But after every day on the hunt I pray to Dimanious and Zathius . . . I pray to Zathius, the god of life, for the forgiveness of my sins. And I pray to Dimanious, the god of destiny, as a thank-you for allowing my catch to fulfill its destiny in keeping my race alive. Over the years the pain has decreased for me . . . but I still feel it . . . I've actually thought of using an angelic symbol you know."

"Angelic Symbol? What's that?" Drathorn asked, trying to keep pace with Elgard's long strides.

"An Angelic Symbol is a scaring in your flesh; a symbol carved into a selected part of your body. It's a sacrifice of blood to the gods; every time a person with an angelic symbol commits a sin they feel the pain of the cut again. I heard that some sinners use it so that they will be admitted to heaven no matter how bad their sins may be during life . . . I tried it a few years ago . . . I had accidentally killed a man that had meant me harm . . . it pained me so much that I attempted an Angelic Symbol . . . but I nearly fainted from the pain and the sight of more blood . . . I just couldn't do it."

Drathorn had never heard the story about that man but he knew that it would be a bad subject so instead he asked; "What does an Angelic Symbol look like?"

"That wasn't the question I was expecting . . ." Elgard said; "It can be any symbol that means nothing about anything . . . it can't be a rune of magic or a letter . . . it has to be a random symbol that will mean nothing to anyone else . . . Other than that it can be anything. I was actually expecting you to ask for the story about that man . . . but I thank you for not asking . . . I don't want to talk about it."

"I know . . . that's why I didn't ask you . . ." Drathorn said.

"Elgard! Drathorn! Mission accomplished my friends!" A fairly large man in hard leather armour walked up to them with a wide grin and a broadsword at his side. "How was the hunt?"

"Ah, Regal, my friend! It was excellent!" Elgard hugged the man as he spoke then said; "The male is in the woods over there . . . he was a fairly tough one . . . should be some good meat on him. But he's a heavy one so I suggest you get Zorg to take care of him."

"Someone say Zorg's name?" An even larger man in leather armour with a giant war hammer on his back walked over and Drathorn recognized Zorgastoyil Barganzas, a strong but fairly slow-witted man that could carry a few hundred pounds on his back with ease. Drathorn suspected he was a half-giant. Despite his size and stupidity he was a useful member of the team.

"Yes, Zorg . . ." Elgard said; "There is a young male deer on the ground in the forest over there . . . I want you and Regal to go and get him and I want you to carry him back . . . you can follow Regal so you don't get lost, ok?"

"Uh . . . ok . . . can Zorg have dinner soon?" The large man asked.

Elgard laughed, "Yes, Zorg you can have something to eat when you've done your job, ok?"

Zorg smiled and then picked Regal up in a firemen's carry and began running to the young deer while Regal pounded on his back yelling; "Put me down you fool!"

When they were out of ear shot Drathorn asked; "Didn't we already have dinner?"

Elgard laughed again, he was a very cheerful person. "Yes, but with Zorg's total body mass and all the heavy lifting he does around here he gets hungry fast."

"I thought so . . ." Drathorn replied, "Why is he so big? I was thinking he might be a half-giant but is that even possible?"

Elgard didn't laugh this time. "Well you're right . . . he *is* a half-giant. Regal, Zorg, and I are the only ones who know . . . They are rare but yes they do appear. Giants are a twisted creation of the gods Sylvaston and Borjil . . . Anger and Strength . . . You add Zathius's power of love to get reproduction between humans and the giants and you get an even more twisted half-giant . . . It's horrible . . . yet wonderful at the same time . . ."

Elgard fell silent as Zorg rushed past, carrying the deer and the angry Regal back to the camp. "That's everyone . . . we can start heading back now . . . another big day of hunting tomorrow and it's nearly midnight . . . you should be getting to bed soon . . ."

"Alright, Mom!" Drathorn joked as they walked slowly back to the camp. Elgard pushed him jokingly and Drathorn returned the gesture.

Drathorn and Elgard walked alone for almost an hour before they finally reached the hill that hid their camp from view. They climbed the hill, still joking and pushing each other lightly and then the fun stopped very suddenly. Elgard stopped dead and Drathorn walked right into him. Drathorn looked at his brother to find a look of pure terror on his face, Drathorn's own smile faltered.

Drathorn looked down at the camp as well and all traces of his smile were wiped off his face in a matter of seconds. The great camp that once held thousands of hunters and their families was now burning before their eyes and no one seemed to be alive . . .

II

A Brotherhood Destroyed

"... Who would do such a thing?" Drathorn asked as he looked sadly down at a dead hunter's child.

"T'was the darklord's armies . . ." Elgard said. "Those are his warriors . . . They must have seen the camp and decided to raid it . . ." Elgard gestured to two dead men in iron armour.

"I thought the war was taking place farther west?" Drathorn replied, "They weren't supposed to pass the capitol!"

"They probably came through on a ship to try and gain supplies for one of their armies . . . it looks like they hit the jackpot, eh?"

"We should get out of here." Drathorn knew this scene all too well; the darklord had once again found Drathorn and was using his warriors to try and kill him, but again Drathorn had not been there at the time of the attack.

"No! We must look for survivors! Hopefully Regal and Zorg and the others got here too late to be killed."

"Look out! Behind you!" Drathorn yelled suddenly. Elgard unsheathed his short sword as he spun. The blade glinted in the fire light and there was a loud clang of metal on metal as sparks flew. Elgard's blade had collided with his attacker's blade and they were now battling fiercely over the bodies of the dead men and women. Drathorn was about to help by stabbing the attacker when he saw the shadows of three others moving in the direction of the fight. Drathorn readied himself for an uneven fight but he didn't need to worry. Regal ran suddenly around a burning wagon and beheaded one of the attackers with his broad sword. Zorg followed him and tackled one enemy while flattening the face of the other with his hammer. Regal finished them off with two fast sword thrusts and then turned to find Elgard staring at the body of the first attacker, also dead.

At first the reunion was quite silent but then Elgard asked, "Have you found any survivors?"

Regal answered, "Yes . . . we sent them away with the others to get help from the city of Gaberdan . . . It seems the enemy's main force has left the campsite but there are still a few warriors raiding the camp. Zorg and I were trying to remove them when we heard Drathorn shout. We came right away . . . have you guys found anyone yet?"

"No . . . we only just arrived . . ." Elgard replied sadly. "We should continue to search the area . . . let's go together."

"No . . . split . . ." Zorg spoke loudly.

"I have to agree with him on that, Elgard . . ." Regal added, "We are all capable of combat . . . Drathorn is no exception . . . though where you learned to fight I don't know." He added, looking at Drathorn in wonder.

"You've seen me fight before?" Drathorn asked, shocked.

"Yeah . . ." Regal replied, "a few drunken hunters last year some time . . . you showed them!"

"I never heard that story before!" Elgard laughed impressed, somehow reuniting with his friends had restored some of his good mood. "When do I get to hear that one?"

"When you tell me the story about the man you killed." Drathorn joked.

"Fair enough . . . we'll split up . . . Be careful, my brother . . ." Elgard said, his frown returning with the memory.

"No, you be careful . . ." Drathorn said walking towards the western side of the camp, "I've lost more than enough family in my time to loose you!"

Drathorn wasn't sure if Elgard or any of the others had heard that last remark as they had run in different directions only seconds before. He walked on with confidence. His aunt's poisonous dagger gripped tightly in his hand as he recounted the story in which he had wrestled two drunken hunters almost a year ago . . . He had been wondering the camp late that night when the hunters came out of their tent and saw him. They asked Drathorn a few ridiculous questions and he commanded them to return to their tent. They got mad at Drathorn for trying to tell them what to do; they had talked back and Drathorn gave them the command again. They had attacked him and he had defended himself . . . They were too bruised to hunt the next day.

Drathorn was quietly laughing at the thought of the bruised hunters when he saw a flicker of movement beside him. Drathorn stopped moving and stared into the shadows that were being made by the flickering flames. Had he imagined it? Was there a flicker of light in the shadows? A slight movement behind that tent? A grunt of pain near the flames? "Is someone there?" Drathorn asked the flaming tent.

"Help . . . me . . ." the voice was weak and fearful but it was there. Drathorn ran around the tent holding his dagger at the ready in case it was a trap.

It wasn't a trap. A young Chis boy was lying in the mud. A Chi is a human that is covered in fur like a cat and even has a tail and sandpaper tongue like one. They populated most areas of the world with their human counter-parts and favoured Davearous, the god of wisdom. Drathorn looked at the young Chis and noticed that three arrows stuck out of his body. Drathorn dragged him out of the mud and held his head up off the ground so it was easier for him to breath. "What happened?" Drathorn asked.

"Warriors . . . they came from the hills . . . lots of them in silver armour . . . they surprised us . . . and they were strong . . . we . . . couldn't fight them . . ." The boy's orange coloured fur was matted with blood and dirt and he gasped for each breath. But he continued, determined to live, "Eventually we managed to drive them back . . . but then a man in a black cloak came . . . he . . . used powerful magic to hurt us all . . . and they began to win . . . and then even more enemies came . . . we couldn't win . . . they were too strong . . ."

Drathorn made a silencing noise and said, "Stay silent my friend . . . save your breath . . . you can live through this. Stay calm." The boy looked at Drathorn sadly . . .

"You're Drathorn aren't you?" The boy asked, "You're Elgard's brother!"

"Yes . . . yes I am . . ." Drathorn said, "And what's your name?"

"Philip . . . My dad was a hunter here . . . It'll be nice to go and see him in heaven . . . and to meat our master . . . Davearous . . ."

"No . . . you can live! Fight it! Stay strong Philip!" Drathorn cried.

"There is no reason to live now . . . I have nothing in this world . . . what good is fighting when all it does is cause more harm?" The young Chis may have had a good point but that was no reason to die there in Drathorn's arms.

"No! That's not true! You cannot die!" Drathorn cried even louder but the boy slowly began to close his eyes. "Philip, No!" But the boy had gone limp and his eyes remained closed. "No . . . no . . . no . . ." Drathorn cried for the dead boy and all the others who had been lost in the fires of the darklord's armies; he cursed Dimanious, the god of Destiny, for allowing such a tragic event to occur on that night. He cried for almost ten minutes before he heard a scream from somewhere nearby. It was the scream of a girl in trouble and Drathorn knew he had to do something; he had allowed Philip to die in his arms and he would not let this girl have the same fate.

Drathorn placed the young boy on the ground and retrieved his dagger. Then he turned and ran in the direction the scream had originated from.

The scream echoed loudly again from the wreckage of a burning wagon up ahead. Drathorn ran towards it and stopped outside of the burning wreck. A bucket of warm water sat in the grass nearby. Drathorn sheathed his dagger picked up the bucket then ran recklessly into the burning wagon with his hand covering his mouth and nose. He ran into the wagon without fear; only determination. He didn't feel the heat of the flames as he ran across the wagon . . .

The girl was in the far corner of the wagon. The roof had collapsed around her and she was trapped behind the burning wreck. Drathorn ran across the wagon, still not feeling the heat, and threw the bucket of water on the wood separating him from the girl. He reached across the wood with his hand and yelled over the crackling flames, "Take my hand! I'll help you out of here and then we'll escape together!"

The girl reached out for his hand but the wood pile was too wide. "I can't reach!" the girl screamed.

"Hang on!" Drathorn yelled back. He climbed up on the wood pile and reached down, "Grab my shoulders!" The girl reached up on her tip toes and held tightly around his neck. Drathorn lifted her up by the waist and was surprised by her extremely light weight. He lifted her up unto the wood pile and then released her waist and took her hand. Together they jumped off of the woodpile and onto the wagon floor. The wood was burning fast and yet Drathorn, remarkably, felt no heat. But this girl was already choking on the smoke that Drathorn couldn't even see. He held the girl's hand and together they ran to the exit.

Suddenly the floor beneath them gave out and they both screamed as they fell the few feet to the ground below. Drathorn managed to keep himself from being hurt but the girl hit her head on the way down and was lying, unconscious next to him. He rolled her out, gently, into the moonlight and crawled out after her. The wagon was indistinguishable from the fire by now, it lit up the western side of the camp well with the help of the burning tents and smaller wagons.

Drathorn gently pulled the girl away from further harm sat down exhausted beside her. As he sat he examined her for further wounds. She had long, straight, black hair like the night that reached almost to her waist. When he lifted her lids to look into the eyes he saw they were a beautiful brown that seemed to shine in the firelight more than any human's should. Her skin seemed to be smooth beneath the ashes and burns caused by the fire and Drathorn thought she was extremely beautiful, even with the scratches and bruises of battle covering her arms . . . a large lump slowly formed on her forehead but it did nothing to tarnish the beauty. A golden chain was wrapped around her neck. On the end was a shining blue gem that lit up her sleeping face with a blue light to rival that of Elgard's transformation.

After a few moments Drathorn heard running footsteps coming from the center of camp. Drathorn unsheathed his dagger and waited; they cannot take her away now that she has been rescued. But he didn't need to have worried. Elgard, Regal, and Zorg all rushed toward him, tired but unharmed. "Drathorn! We heard the screaming and rushed here as fast as we could . . . are you ok?" Elgard sounded very concerned as he spoke . . . he didn't seem to have noticed the young girl lying on the grass beside his brother. Drathorn nodded and looked back to the girl.

"Who is she, Drathorn?" Regal asked, "Is she alive?"

"I don't know who she is . . . I've never seen her before . . ." Drathorn replied looking up at him, "But yes she is alive . . . just unconscious . . . she hit her head when I was helping her escape that burning wagon."

"She . . . beautiful . . ." Zorg noted as he looked down at the young girl.

"That she is, Zorg . . . that she is . . ." Regal laughed; humour returning now that Drathorn was known to be safe.

"And about your age too Drathorn!" Elgard joined in with a smile.

Drathorn rolled his eyes but agreed personally that she was the most beautiful person he had ever seen. "Did any of you guys find anyone?" Drathorn asked hopefully.

They all shook their heads. "But I did run into a few of those armoured figures . . . did any of you?" Regal asked.

Everyone else shook their heads. "This time we stay together, agreed?" Elgard said. Everyone nodded again and Elgard continued; "Drathorn, can you carry the girl?"

"Yeah," Drathorn said, "But why me?"

"We're better fighters so it's ideal that we have both hands ready to fight with. If you can manage her on your own it'll be better for us all." Regal answered like it was obvious.

"Ok . . . I'll carry her . . . she really isn't very heavy." Drathorn answered.

He walked back to the girl in the grass and knelt beside her. In that second hundreds of armoured figures suddenly appeared out of the darkness, separating Drathorn and the girl from the others. "What's going on?" Drathorn yelled.

"This time I've got you, Drathorn!" The voice was young but unfamiliar; the speaker may have been about thirty-five years old and sounded strong but it originated from a thin, cloaked, figure in front of him. "You have evaded destiny for far too long! Now you will die!"

"Back off you fiend!" Elgard yelled. Drathorn looked at him; he was being held back by four of the armoured figures, as was Regal. Zorg tried desperately to help his master by wrestling almost ten warriors. "Who are you?" He ended with a demand.

"I am he, whom you call, the Darklord . . . Ruler of all that is evil . . . your brother here is a nuisance to me . . . I have hunted him since the day my assassin failed to kill him over eight years ago! Now I have found him . . . and now I will kill him!" The shadowy figure laughed mockingly as he looked at Drathorn.

"Sir, is that what I think it is?" A large man with a bark-like voice asked pointing at what appeared to be the girl's necklace. There were whispers and mutterings among the warriors and many of them shifted uncomfortably.

"Yes, I believe it is . . ." The Darklord muttered, "We will be getting multiple prizes tonight my friends . . . I could not have hoped for more . . ."

"You can't have it!" Drathorn yelled. "Whatever you want it for, I won't let you take it! It is not yours to take!"

The Darklord and a handful of warriors, including the one who had first pointed at the necklace, laughed evilly and then the Darklord spoke again, "You do not know what you have there, Drathorn . . . That girl . . . and that necklace . . . I have searched for them for many years . . . and now they fall into my hands along with the last remaining Hellbound!"

"Hellbound?" Elgard asked, clearly confused, "Who?"

"Why my friend, Elgard . . . Drathorn here is the last remaining descendent of Gradorn Lebasta Hellbound!" The Darklord laughed again and said, "I had my assassin hunt him and his family down over eight years ago and he failed to kill only Drathorn . . . I have found him many times but he is never there when I arrived for the kill. But enough of this boring chatter . . . you must die!"

"No!" Elgard roared. But Zorg reacted first. His neck began to glow with a powerful orange light and the shape of a star was illuminated on the back of his neck. Many warriors shot arrows at the warrior but they shattered before they could hit him.

"Fools! He is an Ali—Manicota! As he transforms he is invincible!" The man with the bark-like voice yelled.

The light enveloped Zorg in a matter of seconds and a giant wolf ran from its brightness. It crashed through a handful of warriors and soon the blue of Elgard's puma and the green of Regal's rhinoceros were shining as well. The three animals charged forward on a rampage. The warriors were torn apart by the animals. The man with the bark-like voice threw a sword and it stabbed into Elgard's puma, killing it instantly. It took only a moment for the real Elgard to stand in its place and continue the battle with his sword. "*Esgatso Monakium!*" Elgard yelled and Drathorn felt his power blast forth as ten enemy warriors dropped dead but appeared unharmed.

"This ends here!" The Darklord yelled angrily. "I, *Icarus Maxwell*, the *Darklord* of the badlands, and owner of the *Icarus Maxwell Banking Co.* demand it! This spell will leave me too weak for combat for a few years but that is the cost of eliminating my enemy! *Elembrana Siscom Gratmorr Danalas-Vorg!*" The beam of light that radiated from the Darklord soared at Drathorn with immense speed; Drathorn watched it, intrigued and frightened, he saw his death coming forth but he seemed to want to embrace it . . .

"Noooo!" Elgard blasted out of the crowd of warriors and jumped right in front of the beam. The beam hit Elgard in the chest with a great bang . . . Elgard didn't fall . . . he just stood there . . . no one moved . . . not even the battling warriors around them. " . . . *Drathorn . . . I . . . want you to . . . run . . . ok? Take the girl and the amulet and run . . . Don't let my sacrifice be a waste . . . This Icarus character is too weak to pursue you and I have commanded Zorg and Regal to use their final breaths to protect you . . . Run . . . my brother . . .*" the voice of his brother rang through his head as if he stood there beside him. Elgard stood a little ways ahead of him where he had been hit. He had not yet fallen to the ground but Drathorn knew there was no hope; he felt the tears well up inside him . . .

Then his brother died in a most unexpected way . . . The Ali-Manicota tattoo on Elgard's cheek swam off his face and moulded into a small blue sphere that drifted into Drathorn's waiting hand . . . Then the clothes and items melted off of Elgard and the human he had once known became dust on the wind . . .

"Noooo!" Regal yelled it this time. "Run, Drathorn! We will protect you with our last breath!" Drathorn placed the Ali-Manicota sphere in his pocket and sheathed his dagger . . . then he picked up the girl and ran, unhindered by the enemy. He saw the Darklord teleport away from the fight with the man with the bark-like voice, he saw a giant rhino trample five warriors and yet none of it mattered now; Elgard was dead, Drathorn had to run . . .

Elgard died on January 21st, of the year 18291, at three A.M. Drathorn eventually found himself in the town of Greengate where he and the young girl were sent to the orphanage. Upon arrival the girl identified herself as Thira Usonki. After hearing Drathorn's story about the rescue (though he left out the part in which his true identity had been revealed) Thira and Drathorn remained good friends at the orphanage and Drathorn continued to go by the name of Teldaga and never removed the Ali-Manicota sphere from his pocket. The dagger remained safely hidden in the travel trunk in his room.

III

Searching For the Darklord

Drathorn and Thira appeared quite comfortable at the orphanage. Thira soon gained friends among the girls and Drathorn quickly gained admirers among all the orphans and homeless adults the orphanage supported. It was on April 29th, 18291, (over three months later) when Drathorn was out in the yard sitting in a corner working on homework for his geography class when he was confronted by three older boys from the orphanage.

One boy was a Dragonian; a human with large dragon-like wings coming from his shoulders and mysterious all-seeing white eyes. Dragonians were resistant to heat and cold so he wore only a pair of deerskin shorts. Drathorn immediately recognized him as Zargel Zorthagin, from his Mathematics class.

The second boy was obviously half-giant and had a build much like Zorg; he towered over Zargel and his leader. Drathorn knew him as Gunnel Harthbend.

The leader of these boys was a human. He was of an average build with black hair and dark blue eyes. Mardy Gonvalsen stood in front of Drathorn staring down at the work in his hands. Gunnel stood stupidly at the side and Zargel watched Mardy with interest. "Are you Drathorn Teldaga?" Mardy inquired.

"Depends why you're asking." Drathorn answered angrily, annoyed by the interruption.

"You should watch your tone boy!" Zargel said angrily, "You be smart like that again and I'll have Gunnel here squash you to jelly!"

"You wouldn't dare touch me here . . . too many witnesses . . ." Drathorn waved his hand around. His friends sat just out of hearing distance and Thira and her friends were watching the conversation with interest from slightly farther away.

Zargel looked around uncomfortably and snarled at him. "That's enough you two!" Mardy said with authority to Drathorn and Zargel. "I didn't come here for a fight I came here for a business offer."

Both Zargel and Gunnel looked at Mardy like he had said something ridiculous. "Really?" Drathorn frowned, "What kind of business?"

"I've heard your story, Teldaga . . ." Mardy spoke quietly. "About how you rescued that Thira girl from the burning wagon while the Darklord's warriors attempted to kill you both . . . If there's any truth to that then I suppose you're a good fighter . . . . Correct?"

"You're smarter than you look." Drathorn replied, this time Mardy snarled but he continued quietly.

"We run a small band of thieves through which we steal from large, rich companies in the city and hide our plunder here in the orphanage so that someday when we're old enough we can buy wonderful homes for ourselves. Tonight we're going to be robbing the biggest banking district on Corrone. The *Icarus Maxwell Banking Co.* I'm guessing you've heard of it?"

Drathorn's eyes had lit up at the name of the company; he remembered that night, three months ago when the Darklord had cast the spell; he had yelled his name; *Icarus Maxwell.*

"Answer him, Boy!" Zargel yelled suddenly.

Drathorn stood and looked Mardy in the eye; *If I go on this little mission there's a chance I will find and possibly kill Icarus while he's weak . . . If for some reason Icarus is not there then I can turn on Mardy and these boys and turn them in to the guards. Either way I'll do much good through this.* He thought.

"Fine, I will help you . . ." Drathorn stated, "But I want my fair share of the gold!"

"Well . . ." Mardy said, "With you there will be . . . seven of us . . . but only four of us will be doing this job . . ."

"So twenty five percent!" Drathorn stated the obvious.

"No!" Mardy said, "As leader I get more of the money than anyone else! The way this works is each of you three get twenty percent and I get forty! Deal?"

If Drathorn had planned on doing this for real he would have disagreed on the spot, but because he was only in this to put an end to evil deeds he agreed slowly.

"Good! Meet us here at midnight tonight and bring a weapon . . . we'll have masks and such to hide your identity with us. Understood?" Mardy stuck out his hand and offered it to Drathorn. Drathorn nodded and shook it roughly. Then Mardy and his friends turned around and walked away. Drathorn sat down again on the ground by the fence and opened his geography book again.

It was only a moment before the quiet footsteps of Thira Usonki were noticed. "What was that all about?" She asked gently.

Drathorn looked up and, as always, was immediately struck by her beauty. Her long black hair was almost waist length and the scratches and burns that had been there before had finally healed, perfecting her smooth skin. Drathorn could just see the gold chain of the beautiful necklace around her neck; the stone was hidden beneath her shirt. Drathorn thought about what he should tell her and then spoke slowly, "He was making a business offer. He's not really bright and he needed help on his homework . . . I told him that if I did his homework he couldn't pick on anyone I know . . . we agreed." It was the worst story he'd ever invented and he had spoke too hastily near the end but she accepted it with a disapproving shrug.

"What's that you're working on?" she asked.

"Geography homework . . ." Drathorn frowned as he looked back at his page. "I just don't get it . . ."

"Is this the fill in the blanks one?" She asked, taking the book. "Oh that's why, silly! The capitol of Tanroe region is Veedion! Not Vedoran!"

Drathorn looked back at his page, "Oh . . . yeah I knew that I just put in the wrong word is all!"

Thira laughed and said; "You're supposed to help him with his homework but you always seem to need my help at the same time don't you? How do you plan to help him?"

"I'm good at history!" Drathorn said, "And that's the one he needed help with!" Again he was lying horribly but what was he supposed to tell her? Again she shrugged.

"Oh, ok!" Thira laughed again, "Well the break is almost over and I still need to get to the gymnasium for my class . . ."

Drathorn stood and walked with her to the entrance of the schooling building and there they had to split up; Thira for gym and Drathorn for history. The rest of the school day passed by slowly and at four thirty he was released from the schooling building and he went to his dormitory.

When he arrived he found it empty but knew that it would not stay that way for long. He ran and unlocked his trunk. He fished through all of the clothing and eventually found his aunt's dagger. He hadn't taken it out of the trunk since he'd arrived and he suddenly remembered the runes on the handle. Drathorn opened his rune dictionary and translated them quickly only to decipher one word; *Venomstrike*. Drathorn supposed it was the name of the dagger; he shrugged and slipped it carefully into his pocket just as two more boys walked into the dormitory. Drathorn put away his textbooks, locked the trunk and went down to dinner.

Drathorn received his plate at the door to the cafeteria; on it were two chunks of bread and a little bit of stew. Drathorn looked at the pitiful meal and walked into the cafeteria. On one side of the cafeteria were the teenagers and on the other side were the homeless adults, young children were spread throughout the room, looking for crumbs that people might have missed.

Drathorn spotted Thira sitting alone in her usual seat and he walked over to meet her. Many people greeted him as he walked by but he barely heard them amongst the chatter of happy children. He sat down across from her and said, "Where are your friends?"

The sudden nearness of his voice startled her and she looked up, frightened. "Oh, Drathorn . . ." She sighed in relief, "They're eating elsewhere today . . . I saved this spot for you." She gestured to the seat he was already occupying and then asked, "Have a good day?"

Drathorn laughed, "It was as good as any other day in this place . . . how about you?"

"It was ok I guess . . ." she rubbed her stomach and looked at his food hungrily.

"Where's yours?" he asked, handing her a slice of bread.

"I already ate it but . . . the stew had meat in it . . ." Drathorn frowned; he had forgotten she was a vegetarian.

"You won't even eat meat if it means your survival?" Drathorn asked.

"No, I'll eat it if I really must but . . . I'm not gunna die here." Thira answered as she ripped a bite out of the bread.

Drathorn picked up his other piece of bread and took a small bite of it gratefully. Then he noticed a small child looking hungrily at him from the floor. The boy was a small Chis and was so thin that he might have been a furry coat rack. Drathorn looked sadly at the child then he placed his stew on the ground for him. The small boy smiled weakly and muttered a word of thanks before digging into the food gratefully. "You're so nice to the kids here . . . for most of us it's survival of the fittest but for you . . ." Thira seemed lost for words as she watched the poor child eat Drathorn's stew.

"We need to learn to work together in times like this." Drathorn said. "I can go days without getting hungry so I usually give most of my food away. Without me a lot of these kids would have died of starvation . . ." He frowned at the last bit of his bread and then gave it to Thira, who ate it thankfully.

"It's good that someone takes care of these kids . . ." Thira said. "That's what I should have done with my stew . . ."

"What did you do with it?" Drathorn asked, "You didn't throw it out did you?"

"No . . . I ate it . . ." She sounded disgusted . . ."I threw it up . . ."

"Oh . . ." Drathorn frowned . . ."Well you were hungry . . . it's to be expected that you at least try and eat it."

"Yeah . . ." Thira sighed . . ."I'm gunna get some fresh air ok? I'll talk to you later."

"Ok, feel better soon ok?" Drathorn said, worried for her health.

"I'll try." She said, and then she got up and walked out of the cafeteria.

Drathorn sighed, waited a moment and then followed her out of the cafeteria, more people waved and called out to him as he left but this time he ignored them completely.

Drathorn pretended to be asleep around nine P.M. that night. The other's in his dormitory fell asleep around ten. When they were all asleep Drathorn woke and did the last of his homework by candle light and then got up out of bed. He stood in the cheap dormitory and looked around for an easy, quiet escape. He checked the door but the headmaster seemed to have locked it already. So he went to the window. It was closed, but unlocked. He opened it as quietly as possible and slipped out. He walked across the lawn in the moonlight and soon he saw the dark shapes of Mardy and his friends. When Drathorn finally arrived Mardy spoke. "We have your costume here."

Drathorn suddenly noticed that they were all wearing black leather armour as clothing. The leather caps had slightly see-through black veils that could be draped over their faces. Drathorn took his from Mardy and put it on. It was quite uncomfortable but he would get used to it. "How are we getting there?" He asked.

"We're gunna hop this fence and walk there . . . It's not far . . ." Mardy said as Gunnel started climbing over, and Zargel started flying over, the fence. "It's only on Seventeenth Street . . . about five minutes away from here." He turned and followed his friends over the fence and Drathorn climbed it beside him.

Once they were on the other side of the fence they walked quietly down the cobblestone streets. They didn't speak as they walked but they eyed each other accusingly as if they thought one of the others would suddenly rat them out, which was exactly Drathorn's plan.

They walked on for about five minutes before Drathorn found himself standing in front of a thirteen story building made of bricks. The west wall on the thirteenth floor was made entirely out of glass and Drathorn guessed that was where Icarus Maxwell would be. "Lead the way new guy!" Mardy said suddenly.

They all pulled down the cloth veils and walked into the bank. All of the customers were immediately silent and the bankers stopped moving immediately at the sight of the invisible warriors. When none of them made any sign of movement Drathorn stepped forward, "We'd like to open an account?" he asked a banker. The banker sighed in relief and the customers returned to their business. The banker began to lead Drathorn over to a desk as Drathorn whispered to Mardy. "Wait for my signal . . ."

Drathorn followed the banker and they began to talk about the company's banking abilities. Mardy, Zargel, and Gunnel spread out throughout the area, pretending to be interested in paintings and manuscripts on the walls but their hands were hidden underneath their cloaks, most likely clutching their weapons and awaiting his signal. Drathorn decided to get things over with.

As the banker shifted through his papers he jumped over the bank desk in a single, quick, motion and *Venomstrike* flew to the banker's throat just as Mardy and the others revealed their weapons. Gunnel pulled out a giant war hammer and smashed two fleeing customers with it. Zargel drew out a short sword and stood defiantly in front of a group of bankers. Mardy wasted no time in shooting a crossbow bolt across the room and killing a banker who had tried to reach a megaphone through which he could alert the whole building of the danger.

The room went deathly silent and Drathorn felt the fear in the room escalate as he looked at the unconscious customers and the dead banker. He couldn't believe what these boys had done . . . they were murderers! "No body move!" Mardy yelled to the room at large as he fitted his crossbow with a new bolt. "We don't want to hurt anyone . . . we're just looking for some easy money!"

As Mardy ordered the bankers to fill leather bags with gold Drathorn released his hostage and snuck away up the staircase. He climbed to the thirteenth floor and saw one door standing ajar at the end of the hall way. He snuck over to the door and peered through the opening cautiously. As he expected he was looking into a room with a west wall made entirely of glass. The black-cloaked figure of Icarus Maxwell sat on a neatly carved wooden chair beside a strange figure, also in black, who stood with a black top hat angled to hide his face and a black cloak covering his body. In one of the second man's hands was a small briefcase, in the other was a wooden healer's staff topped with a blue orb.

They seemed to be deep in conversation with an unseen character. "To what do I owe the pleasure of your summoning, my lord?" The unseen man spoke loudly and Drathorn recognized the voice of the man with the bark-like laugh that had been present at the time of Elgard's death.

"I have . . . called . . . you . . . here for two . . . reasons, Cherry." Icarus gasped. "As you see . . . I am . . . still weak . . . from the . . . spell . . . I cast . . . three months . . . ago . . . I must return . . . to . . . my tower . . . I need you to . . . take care . . . of the . . . company . . . for me . . . in my . . . absence . . . is this . . . acceptable?"

"Of course my lord!" The unseen man named Cherry said, "It is my honour to be of service again!"

"Good . . . and . . . there is . . . one other matter . . . I need . . . your help . . . with . . ." Icarus spoke between gasps and coughs.

"Anything, sir!" Cherry said happily.

"My . . . assistant is . . . a master . . . at . . . healing arts . . . but he does not . . . posses . . . the power . . . to cure my . . . weakness . . . but if . . . he had . . . the city of . . . Signaroc's . . . fabled . . . book . . . he

may . . . be able . . . to . . . speed up . . . the . . . recovery . . . process . . ."
Icarus paused with a serious coughing fit and went on, "I . . . wish for . . .
you . . . to . . . secure . . . this . . . article . . ."

"The Journal of the Great Thirteen?" Cherry exclaimed in awe. "The
only known relic of the gods' magic?"

"The very same . . . if you will . . . lead . . . my forces . . . I will
supply . . . an army . . . Three thousand gar . . . from the swamps . . . ten
thousand . . . Vikorgan . . . a hundred . . . Ogres . . . and two hundred
and . . . fifty Trolls . . . are ready . . . to be . . . shipped to . . . the city . . . of
Narvahan . . . Shé . . . They will . . . also . . . be joined by . . . a force of . . .
one thousand Gar . . . fighters . . . from the . . . swamps of the . . . west . . .
to help breach . . . Signaroc's . . . first . . . line of . . . defence . . ." Icarus
hesitated a moment then, "No . . . reinforcements will . . . arrive for . . .
Signaroc or Narvahan Shé . . . because the . . . roads . . . will be held . . .
by the bandits . . . The Orange . . . Riders will be helping . . . you . . .
in . . . your conquest of . . . Narvahan Shé . . . but they . . . won't . . . be
there for . . . the battle of . . . Signaroc . . ."

There was a moment of silence and then, "I accept this task, my lord!
I will also supply a few of my own." Cherry said thankfully.

"Very well . . . we must . . . return . . . to the tower . . ." Icarus
disappeared with his "assistant" in a flash of light just as he broke into
another coughing fit. Cherry seemed to still be in the room as Drathorn
could hear him moving around. *I might not have been able to kill the
Darklord, especially not with the others here, but I at least know his plans
and can stop them from taking action.* He thought.

He ran into the room with *Venomstrike* in his hand. The room was
beautifully polished and contained only a fine oak desk and chair by the
window and the other chair that Icarus had just vacated.

Cherry was a very strange man indeed; he sat in the desk comfortably
but was obviously too large for it. His body was covered in scars. He
wore chain mail leggings for pants and a leather vest as a shirt. His boots
were made of black leather and his head was bald except for a fine brown
Mohawk cutting across the center. He wore leather gloves that were cut
off at the finger tips to expose his trimmed nails. Around his neck was
a fine chain of silver with a violet rune hanging on the end of it. At his
belt was a large dagger that was labelled with runes much like Drathorn's
Venomstrike but they were slightly different.

Cherry stood up fast and caused his chair to fall back. "I never thought I'd see you just walk through the door, Mr. Hellbound!" Cherry laughed and pulled his dagger from his belt. Drathorn eyed the dagger cautiously as Cherry in turn eyed *Venomstrike*. "This is *Flamestrike,* your dagger's counterpart if you'll believe it!"

Drathorn removed his eyes from the dagger and watched Cherry. "I am Cherry Weldum! The king of thieves! I will bring your head to my master!" Drathorn and Cherry both lunged forward at the same time. Drathorn's *Venomstrike* glanced off of Cherry's chain mail leggings and Cherry's *Flamestrike* missed Drathorn completely.

They both backed away and prepared to strike again, Drathorn prepared to charge but Cherry lunged first and Drathorn was forced to jump to the side. Cherry's dagger struck the door and dug in deep. Drathorn saw this as an opportune moment to strike Cherry and prepared to attack but the door was suddenly engulfed in flames. The flames swallowed the door in less than a second and the dagger was released. All that remained of the door was a pile of ashes on the floor yet none of the surrounding area had been damaged by the flames in any way.

That's a powerful dagger Drathorn thought . . . *If it really is* Venomstrike's *counter part then I wonder what* Venomstrike *can do to a person . . .*

Drathorn dodged another attack from Cherry and was forced back. Then they both lashed out at the same time again. The daggers collided and both were sent flying out of their owner's hands. *Venomstrike* stuck harmlessly into the wall and *Flamestrike* skidded across the ground and stopped near the oak desk. Cherry ignored the daggers and leapt at Drathorn; his fist collided with Drathorn's cheek and Drathorn was forced to recoil again, there would be a bruise. Cherry attacked again but this time Drathorn side stepped him and punched with all his might. His fist collided with the side of Cherry's face in mid-tackle. The force of Drathorn's punch sent Cherry in a new direction. He landed on the oak table and it split in two beneath him.

As the astonished Cherry struggled to his feet Drathorn backed slowly away. Cherry picked up *Flamestrike* off of the ground and turned to face Drathorn again. Drathorn swung Icarus's fine wooden chair at Cherry's face as hard as he could. The chair shattered on impact and Cherry was forced backward. He stumbled through the glass wall and somewhere between the shattering of glass and splintering of wood was the thief's cry of pain. Cherry fell through the window and a cracking noise was heard as he landed on the dark pavement thirteen floors below.

Through this whole fall, *Flamestrike* never left Cherry's hand. The dagger and the thief disappeared in the darkness and Drathorn stood, looking down after them. Drathorn finally retrieved *Venomstrike* from the wall when alarms were sounded from the floor below. He looked around and left the building by using a fire escape rope beside the broken window. He quickly looked for Cherry's body but had no luck. So he ran on, dreading the confrontation with Mardy that was sure to come, back to the orphanage . . .

IV

Could Have Been Friends

When he finally woke he felt restless, paranoid and sore from his fight with Cherry. It was April 30th, 18291, when he made his miserable way to breakfast and looked constantly over his shoulder for Mardy and his gang. He arrived in the cafeteria and there was more scattered waving and calling. He walked to the back of the cafeteria; giving his whole plate to a young girl he passed without looking at it. He sat alone in a dark corner in silence for nearly ten minutes.

"Rough night?" Thira's voice erupted right across from him. Drathorn immediately felt safer and happier in her company. He looked up and was again immediately calmed by her beauty but he obviously didn't *look* calm. "You look horrible . . . Did you get any sleep last night?"

"Maybe an hour or two . . ." Drathorn said as he frowned.

"What did you do all night?" Thira asked, looking at his bruise.

"Oh, this?" Drathorn pointed at his face, "Somebody opened a door as I was going down the hall last night and I walked right into it."

"Then why didn't you get any sleep?" Thira sounded concerned and her face showed confusion.

"Nightmares . . ." He replied truthfully.

"About what?" Again she sounded concerned, but when Drathorn did not answer she frowned and touched his hand. "It's okay, you can tell me."

"My brother . . ." Drathorn finally answered. This was indeed true for hearing Cherry's laugh had awakened memories and he had again seen Elgard's death played over and over again in his head that night. He had also dreamed of Cherry chasing him with the dagger *Flamestrike* yelling 'You killed me! Murderer!' as well as screaming vile curses.

"Oh . . ." She looked at him sadly and then said. "Sorry for bringing it up . . ."

"It's fine, don't worry about it."

"Well, I've gotta go to class ok?" She said after a moment of silence. "I'll talk to you at lunch or during break." She got up from the table and walked away, her long hair flowing like a cape behind her; his hand immediately felt colder without hers resting on it.

Drathorn followed her out of the cafeteria after a moment and went to the gymnasium where his team easily won a game of dodge ball.

When the break finally arrived Drathorn walked out into the yard and to the very back of the field; he knew Mardy and his gang would soon be there so he waited patiently. It was only a moment before Mardy's voice erupted somewhere nearby. "Teldaga! Where were you last night?"

"What do you mean? I came all the way there with you!" Drathorn pretended to play dumb as he noticed that the whole gang had come. Not only were there Mardy, Zargel, and Gunnel; but there were also three others. Calvin McBride (A tall, thin boy with lots of leg muscle), and the two dwarf twins Don and Drog followed the first three men. Don, Drog and Gunnel all held large clubs, Zargel and Calvin both held long wooden quarter staves and Mardy seemed unarmed.

"As soon as the money started getting shoved around you disappeared! And then there was an explosion of glass on the top floor and a bunch of alarms went off! We only got half the money we wanted before the guards arrived! So I say it again, where the hell were you?" Mardy was obviously furious.

"Well I was the one sounding the alarm obviously!" Drathorn laughed and stood calmly. By now there was a large crowd around them and he doubted Mardy would try anything here. He stood in front of Mardy and watched as he stared angrily at him.

"I'm sorry to hear that then." Mardy said, "We could have been good friends . . . partners . . . But now we must show you our wrath!" Mardy looked at all the excited spectators, Drathorn noticed Thira watching both fearfully and curiously near the back. "I'm gunna give you a beat down right here in front of all your admirers, get him boys!"

Drathorn was surprised that Mardy would attack him here with so many witnesses; he was so surprised that he only barely dodged Calvin's attack with surprise but managed to snatch his quarter staff away. In a matter of seconds he smacked Calvin across the face with his own quarterstaff and he fell to the ground, unconscious. "Fight, fight, fight, fight, fight, fight!" The chant echoed from all the onlookers except Thira who seemed to be struggling to get closer to the commotion.

Drathorn blocked Drog's club and then kicked the little dwarf in the face. Zargel's quarterstaff collided with Drathorn's ribs and Drathorn backed up. Then he was hit again by Mardy's fist. As he recovered he hit Mardy with the quarterstaff and then swung at Zargel. Zargel blocked and the two of them were suddenly sparring with the staves. He barely blocked Don's attack and then blocked seven of Zargel's strikes. As Don struck out again, Drathorn ducked and spun with the staff and swept Zargel and Don's legs out from under them. By now Drog was standing again and Thira had managed to squeeze into the fight. She picked up Zargel's dropped quarterstaff and was immediately chased by Drog and Don with their clubs. Drathorn blocked an attack from Gunnel and the quarterstaff snapped in half from the blow. Drathorn was surrounded by Mardy, Gunnel, and Zargel. Calvin was still unconscious on the ground and Drog and Don were attacking Thira.

Thira blocked Drog and Don's attacks for about thirty seconds and then took her turn on the offensive; she wasn't going to let Drathorn fight alone. Drathorn was surprised by her skill but could not admire her for long.

Drathorn blocked Zargel and Mardy's fists with his sword sized sticks but was hit from behind by Gunnel and his giant club. He stumbled for a moment and then as he turned to counter Gunnel's attack Zargel's fist caught him in the back of the head. Drathorn couldn't keep up with all three of them. He launched one stick through the air and it collided with Zargel's face; he joined Calvin on the ground. With the remaining stick he struck Mardy on the chest and kicked Gunnel between the legs. Gunnel crumpled to the ground in pain with tears in his eyes and Mardy backed off for a moment allowing Drathorn to notice Thira having troubles with the twins.

Drathorn leapt over the twins and landed between Thira and the dwarves. He blocked two attacks from Don and one from Drog and then he attacked. His stick slapped Don across the chin and he spun like a top before tripping over Gunnel's giant form. Then he struck Drog in the stomach area; the blow knocked the breath out of the tiny dwarf.

Drathorn looked around. Calvin seemed to be regaining consciousness. Drathorn threw the stick at him. It caught him in the head and he fell again. Mardy looked at his fallen comrades and then at the now unarmed Drathorn. "You'll pay for that Teldaga!"

Drathorn pushed Thira away gently and stood fairly still as Mardy ran forward, fist at the ready. Drathorn ducked under Mardy's fist just in time and punched him in the stomach. Mardy keeled over and Drathorn ended the fight by kneeing him in the face. Mardy did a small flip and landed on his back in the grass, blood dripping from his broken nose. The crowd cheered for Drathorn and he turned slowly away. "Watch out!"

Drathorn looked at Thira and saw her launch the quarterstaff like a javelin right at him! He ducked and rolled over just in time to see the quarterstaff hit Don square in the forehead. He watched, surprised as Don fell to the ground. The crowd cheered as Thira ran over to Drathorn's side. "Are you ok?"

Drathorn looked up at her and said "I'm fine, how about you?"

"I'm fine; if you hadn't come when you did the twins would have got me though."

"If you hadn't arrived when you did I would have been pummelled!"

"What did you do to make them so angry?" She finally asked the question Drathorn had foreseen.

"I'll tell you later, I promise." Drathorn was going to tell her why they were angry, he owed her that, but he wouldn't tell her about Cherry; that was his own problem. He would wait until they were alone and he would tell her all about the robbery. He eyed the cheering crowd meaningfully. "Did they hit you?" he asked as he stood.

"Drog got my elbow, but barely . . . the hits you took were worse I can see that from here." Thira looked at him as he walked closer to her. "That big one got you good."

"Gunnel? Yeah he was a though one . . ." Drathorn laughed, feeling the pain from every hit individually as though taking them all again. "But he'll be sore for a while."

Together they walked to the school building and then into Mathematics together. They sat on opposite sides of the room so they didn't talk throughout class but Drathorn *did* have a fun conversation with his friend, Billy, who sat right next to him. At first all Billy wanted to talk about was the fight but then Drathorn reminded him of the test that they had and he began asking questions on how to solve certain math questions.

After explaining most things to him the test started and Drathorn was immediately bored. The test would last the whole period and Drathorn knew that it was not going to be fun. Two hours later there was a great disruption; Billy fell out of his chair on the side opposite of Drathorn and a few kids laughed. The teacher, Mrs. White, was furious. She walked over to Billy and was ready to beat him for causing this disruption when she gasped. "Someone get the Headmaster!" she screamed. Mrs. Bellvin, Mrs. White's assistant, ran from the classroom in search of the Headmaster without asking any questions.

Billy was lying on the floor, writhing like a mad man. He shook uncontrollably like a miniature earthquake. Drool dripped from his mouth, an endless fountain of spittle. "Everyone, get away!" Mrs. White yelled. "Get away! He's having a seizure!"

Drathorn didn't move as the class all backed against the walls. Mrs. White's body was now blocking Billy's body from his sight but it was obvious that whatever this might have been, it was worse than a seizure; the class gasped suddenly and Mrs. White screamed hysterically. They all seemed to see something that Drathorn could not. It was only a second before Drathorn did see it though; Mrs. White and the nearby desks were suddenly launched through the air and a great monster turned to face Drathorn and Billy was gone.

The beast wore Billy's clothes but they were torn and strained over its bulging body. Billy's shoes were no longer on his feet they were in a small pile of ruined fabric near where Billy had been laying before. The beast's feet were five times their original size with yellowing claws on the tows. Billy's eyes had melted together to form one giant eyeball in the center of his head. There was no hair on its head and there was a gaping hole in one side that showed the exposed skull. His teeth were sharp in his wide mouth and his ears were just tiny holes in its head. Its right arm was cut off at the elbow and in its place was a wicked, long, sharp blade that could most likely cut through anything it crossed paths with. The other arm was also removed, this time from the shoulder, but it was replaced by a great green tentacle with odd suction cups on one side.

The students screamed in fear and tried to escape but Drathorn and the monster blocked the only exit from the room. Mrs. White landed on the other side of the room, a desk landed on top of her, trapping her and leaving her alive but exposed as an easy target for the monster. Billy turned towards his teacher and eyed her hungrily. It took a step forward and Drathorn yelled, "No Billy!"

The creature looked up at its name and stared angrily at Drathorn. "Leave her alone!" The creature ignored him and slowly moved toward Mrs. White. Drathorn snapped the leg off of a nearby desk and ran forward. He hit the creature on its head and it roared angrily and threw his tentacle arm out at Drathorn. The arm hit Drathorn in the stomach and threw him across the room. Drathorn landed on a desk and it broke under the impact. He got up and ran at the monster again, desk leg still in hand. He jumped between Billy and his teacher and struck it across the face with the table leg. Before the monster could attack again Drathorn struck it in the stomach. He hit it again and again, driving it slowly away from Mrs. White. But finally it flung a desk at Drathorn and he fell over it. He stood and corrected his footing then looked around for the monster. It was now ignoring the trapped Mrs. White and had been drawn by Thira's beauty.

"I worked hard to save her life, Billy!" Drathorn yelled as he ran at the monster, "You're not gunna end it!" He jumped between Thira and the creature just in time. The blade on its arm had thrust out at Thira, ready to pierce her chest. Drathorn had jumped in front of the blade at an odd angle and it pierced his left shoulder. Drathorn screamed in pain and stabbed out with the chair leg in his right hand. It went into the hole in its head and pierced the skull. It sunk deep into the creature's brain and it fell; its blade exited Drathorn's arm. The students were still screaming uncontrollably and Thira was staring at the monster, paralyzed with fear. Drathorn watched as the Headmaster ran into the room, Mrs. Bellvin close behind and a nearby girl fainted. Drathorn sighed and closed his eyes, peace taking the place of the pain. He fell, beside the defeated monster, and was soon unconscious on the ground.

V

Knowledge of the Headmaster

"He has shown remarkable recovery from the wound, Headmaster." The voice of a caring woman floated into Drathorn's mind. "He heals extremely fast for a human . . . It is surprising really."

"I see . . ." The voice of an old man followed, "How long before he will be able to move again?"

"If he continues to heal at this rate he could be back on his feet and into classes in another two days . . . But what surprises me is that he lost so much blood . . . He should have died from that wound . . ." Said the woman.

"I see the reason for your concern, Lenora . . ." The man said again, "But this boy is just remarkably strong . . . nothing unnatural . . . Actually he's a hero in the making! While the fight took place I had a family in my office interested in adopting . . . They have seen what happened to Drathorn and are extremely impressed by his bravery. So is Captain Xavier of the Greengate guards. Both wish to see him upon awakening . . . Also . . . how is Justice?"

"Mrs. White?" Said the woman, "She is in shock . . . she was launched about fifteen feet and then crushed by a desk . . . she is bruised and has a few broken bones but she will heal. As will poor Patricia Parkinson . . . the sight of blood has rendered her speechless . . . but she will get better . . . I recon that all who were in that room should be fed extra and permitted excuse from all their classes today and tomorrow."

"I agree" the headmaster replied "And I believe there is one other visitor for Drathorn when he wakes . . . Young Thira . . . the girl he saved in that class room . . . She wishes to give her thanks."

"I don't want anyone in here to bother him until I've had a proper examination of him, headmaster!" The woman sounded stern now.

"I understand, Lenora . . ." The headmaster said again, "When you've finished with him allow Xavier to see him . . . and then the family . . . I will observe both meetings . . . How does that sound?"

"Acceptable . . ." The nurse said, "What about the girl?"

"After the first two meetings I must visit the prison with Xavier . . . Thira may visit Drathorn after that . . . I see no reason for which that conversation must be observed." There was a silence and then the headmaster spoke again, "I will leave for now . . . Have someone come for me when you've finished running your tests . . ." There was the sound of the door opening and then closing. Then there was silence.

Drathorn lay still as he tried to understand the conversation . . . but his head spun painfully. There was the sound of footsteps and then gentle fingers touched his shoulder. A small twinge of pain escaped Drathorn but the nurse never noticed. She undid the bandage around his shoulder and the smell of rotten flesh and healer's cream filled the room. The nurse's gentle hand touched the wound and Drathorn sat up and gasped in pain.

He forced his eyes open to look at the astonished nurse. Her white dress had small blood stains on it and her hands were a mess. Her curly blonde hair was in a hairnet and her face was etched with worry. "I'm sorry, did I wake you?" She asked quietly.

"No . . . I was already awake . . . it just hurt . . ." Drathorn relaxed a little bit and placed his head back on the soft white pillow. "What day is it?"

"It's April 31st, 18291 . . . The blade of that beast pierced you well, Drathorn . . . It's a miracle you are alive!" Lenora Hemlock looked at him gently and then took another step toward him. "May I?"

Drathorn looked at his wound and frowned. The flesh was blood stained and rotting, but quickly re-growing. It was obviously deep and Drathorn thought the blade must have pierced the bone. He nodded slowly and she moved forward again. She held her hand over Drathorn's wound and seemed to pray. The twinge of pain that he had felt was suddenly gone, the wound did not heal but it went numb. "What did you do?" Drathorn asked curiously.

"I prayed to Deheano and asked that he numb your wound so I may work with out you feeling the pain. I am a cleric, I use the elements of the gods to help heal the world, but I am not an Ali-Manicota . . . Clerics are the one exception to the law of magic only because our deeds are done through prayers, not the ancient language. Since my energy is brought through prayers directly from the gods there is no law against what I do." She answered simply and began rubbing healer's cream around the wound. She felt his head and then peered deep into his eyes and ears. "How do you feel?" she asked.

"Horrible . . . I feel like my head is ready to explode . . ."

"That's because you obtained a concussion when you fell . . . Here, let me help." She placed her hand on his forehead and prayed again. But this time Drathorn heard the words, "Magnius, God of magic and patron of healing . . . Help this boy, a hero among the children, recover . . ."

Drathorn felt the swelling in his forehead go down and the pain seemed to stop immediately . . . but instead of thanking her he said "I am no hero."

She laughed and said, "Oh, yes you are! This is the second time you've saved that Thira girl from the forces of darkness! And you put your own life on the line to do it! Every orphan in Greengate knows what happened! This will be the talk of the century!"

Drathorn groaned with the thought of all the questions he would get from his peers when he returned to class in a few days . . . but instead of denying his heroism again he asked "So Thira is ok then?"

"She is unharmed . . . in deep shock though . . ." The nurse frowned as she continued to work on his arm. "She wants to see you . . . along with about a thousand others . . . If it was up to me I wouldn't let anyone in here until mid-afternoon next Friday . . . but the Headmaster insists."

"What about Billy? Is he . . ." Drathorn stopped as she looked at him.

"Billy . . . is dead . . ." Drathorn closed his eyes to hide the tears as she continued, "He was dead before you killed him to be truthful . . . Undergoing that kind of transformation immediately kills the human counterpart and leaves only evil in his mind . . . There was nothing left of the Billy you knew when you stabbed him, do not feel bad."

Drathorn said nothing as he looked around the room. Mrs. White was lying on a bed nearby; she was in a full body cast but seemed to be awake and alive. There were two sick boys nearby as well who were examining him closely. There was also a girl named Patricia Parkinson sitting alone in the far corner and looking away from Drathorn, she was shaking violently even though she was covered with three or four thick blankets. The rest of the beds were empty but two assistants stood nearby, one examining a sick boy, the other trying to calm Patricia. "Can one of you go get the headmaster?" the head nurse said to the assistants, let him know that Drathorn is awake and seems well." The assistant who was caring for the sick boy got up and left the room. Drathorn watched quietly as Lenora spread additional healer's cream and bandaged the wound again and then left to find Drathorn a glass of water. She returned with a full goblet and handed it to Drathorn. He took it using his good arm and sipped it slowly, and then he set it on the bedside table.

After a moment the door opened and two men stepped into the room led by the nurse's assistant. The first man was tall and thin, he had a great white beard and a cheerful smile. His long white robes dragged behind him slightly on the floor. The man behind him was young and strong. He walked with a long sword at his side and a shield on his right arm. His Iron plated armour was tinted silver and bore the red symbol of the Imperial guard. A red cape flowed steadily behind him as he walked with the Headmaster, trying not to step on his robe.

"He is ready, Headmaster." Lenora said and then she and her assistants returned to caring for the others.

"Hello, Drathorn! I trust you remember me?" The old man smiled at Drathorn and Drathorn recognized him as Bronc Silvermask, the headmaster and founder of the orphanage. "It has been a while since I last spoke to you . . . And I trust you remember Xavier as well? He was the captain you spoke to the night you arrived here with Thira a little over three months ago."

Drathorn nodded in recognition to both of them and Captain Xavier stepped forward. "I want to give you my thanks for slaying that beast; it was a powerful creature that would have taken many of my men to kill. It is a surprise that you even harmed it, but to kill it? Every monster in the area will fear you by the time the word spreads!"

"Billy was no monster!" Drathorn said angrily, "He could have been saved!"

Xavier frowned, "No he could not, young one . . . When a human goes through the transformation from man to beast it dies. There was nothing but monster left in that one."

"That's not true!" Drathorn stated angrily, "I said its name and it seemed to recognize me for a minute! He could have been saved, I know it!"

Both the headmaster and the captain were surprised at this, "Are you sure?" Xavier asked.

"Positive!" Drathorn stated.

Xavier frowned and then shrugged, "It is rare, but not unheard of. There's nothing we can do now, if you wouldn't have helped many others would have died as well . . . you did what was right."

"No I did what was easy, I may have saved many lives but I ended a good one, there is always another way . . ."

"Xavier, you best hurry this up, it is obvious Drathorn hates the idea of killing." The headmaster said.

"I understand . . ." Xavier said to the headmaster, and then to Drathorn, "I was going to offer you a position on our elite force in the imperial army, with a little bit of training and a bit more age you could have been a good member of the team. But I see you hate killing so instead I will award you with this coin . . . The creature you killed was evil and would have destroyed many lives, my commander sees it fit that you receive an award. You will be allowed to enter the city in two day's time to spend it as you will." Xavier placed a small pouch of gold on the bedside table; he looked disappointed in Drathorn's choice but said nothing else as he turned to leave the room.

"Captain!" Drathorn called out. Xavier stopped and looked back. "What caused Billy's change?"

"We don't know," Xavier stated, "But we plan to find out . . . Is there anything else?"

"Yes . . . I may not approve of killing the innocent . . . but the Darklord is far from that . . . isn't he?"

"Yes he is . . . why are you asking?" Xavier seemed slightly confused.

"He killed my brother, captain, and if I ever get the chance again I will kill him . . . anyone who can cause such pain and devastation for so long deserves to die . . . as do all who serve him . . . I decline your offer for now . . . but in the future I may still join your forces."

Xavier smiled and said "My master will love this news . . . I understand that you are not ready for the commitment and responsibility being an

Imperial Guard takes but we will forever welcome you. But for now I must go, my power is needed to search for any more of these vile creatures in the area." Xavier then left the room and the door snapped shut loudly behind him.

"That was unexpected, Drathorn." The headmaster said. "But why would you ever go near the darklord again?"

"I never said I would, I just said *if.*" Drathorn replied . . ."Is there anything else?"

"Actually yes, another family may be interested in adopting you. They have seen your skill and want to meet you . . . They would be extremely happy to take you into their family." Bronc looked at him calmly, "They live in Gaberdan, the city on the other side of the woods in which your brother was slain. They wish to meet you if that is ok?"

"Where are they?" Drathorn asked.

"They are in the library, if you accept their company then I will have Mrs. Hemlock get her assistant to fetch them. Is that acceptable?"

Drathorn nodded and the headmaster walked over to the nurse. Mrs. Hemlock herself then went to get the family. The pain in Drathorn's arm slowly began to return and he shifted uncomfortably. He reached for his goblet and drank deeply before shifting again. "Is something wrong, Drathorn?" Bronc asked gently, "Are you uncomfortable?"

"A bit . . ." Drathorn admitted, "The pain in my arm is coming back now . . ."

"Do you want me to do a prayer to Colaspis?" He asked, "The god of pain may have pity on your case and release your pain." But the Headmaster sounded quite doubtful.

"And if he has no pity for me?" Drathorn asked.

"It is likely that there will be no effect . . . but . . ." The old man shook his head sadly. "The god of pain is the brother of Sylvaston, God of anger . . . Colaspis' anger may not be as powerful as his brother's but if we pester him with a petty prayer he may grow angry and decide to increase the intensity of the pain instead. Are you willing to take that chance?"

"No that's ok . . . I'll be fine." Drathorn didn't want to anger the brother of his birth god. Sylvaston was the god of Anger and the patron of flame. He was the creator of the ancient Dragons and the god who combined the power of the Dragons and the will of humans . . . Therefore he was the creator of the Hellbound.

"I do not understand your fear of the pain . . ." Bronc said quietly, "You will jump in front of a sharp blade to protect this girl, you'll fight against impossible odds in my field and yet you fear the pain that follows?"

"I am not afraid!" Drathorn said, angry at this remark, "I just do not want to anger the gods! And how do you know about that fight?"

Bronc frowned at him. "You wisely avoid angering the gods . . . I know that you have some reason for doing so but I will ask no more. As for the fight in the courtyard; I know about everything that happens within these walls . . . I also know why you weren't in bed a few nights ago. It was unwise of you to wander off into the darkness to rob a bank . . . But I know why you went . . . the name of Icarus still fresh in your memory, the image of your brother's last moments . . . The truth about who you really are . . . great secrets that I alone can know and keep for you."

Drathorn lay absolutely still now. He had tensed at the robbing a bank part, he had gasped when he heard Icarus's name and now his right arm was beneath the sheets, hiding the mark of the Hellbound that remained engraved on the back of his hand. There was silence. The other patients had heard nothing of this conversation but they still seemed quite silent; as though they were desperately trying to hear the conversation. Drathorn was very angry at first but then the surprise of being discovered hit him. "I thought I was being so careful . . . How did you learn this?"

"Actually just a few hours ago." Bronc frowned again. "When I first saw the mark on your hand I thought it impossible . . . but after linking the death of your brother and all the other family deaths you've experienced and realising that your mysterious appearance in Veedion eight years ago happened the day after the Hellbound mansion was destroyed and Hellen's body was found . . . well the story spelled itself out for me. And you've hid hear all these years . . . and never found by the darklord . . . amazing!"

"The darklord found me many times . . . it was only by chance that I avoided him . . . but he knows I'm here and after killing his associate it won't be long before he comes to collect me. By then I plan to be gone . . . do you understand?"

"I understand better than you think, Drathorn." Bronc smiled slightly as he spoke, "I think it works well in your favour that this family is coming to visit you . . . . If all goes well you may be taken away from here. They live in Gaberdan . . . on the other side of the forest . . . after a few days there you can flee and begin your journey . . . unfortunately Gaberdan is in the opposite direction of Signaroc . . . If that is indeed where you plan to go?"

"You know a lot for a normal headmaster . . ." Drathorn answered, rather annoyed at this point. "But yes, Cherry may be unable to take action but I have a feeling the darklord will find someone else to lead the assault. If I can get there before Narvahan Shé falls that will be best but I doubt my speed and I may not reach Signaroc in time to give them much warning."

"Then I will meet you in Signaroc." The Headmaster decided. "After your departure I will begin to take the road to Signaroc . . . If you take a faster passage . . . Across ocean and into Hellfire Bay for instance, we may meet on the road!"

"Why do you wish to go to Signaroc?" Drathorn asked curiously.

"I am a master wizard . . ." Bronc informed him. "I am undefeated in the arts of magic and I am also gifted in the arts of the Cleric . . . though not as well as Mrs. Hemlock . . . Speak of the Angel!" He looked up just as the young cleric entered the room. "Where are the Blaygards?"

"They are waiting just outside the door so you may have a word with them before they enter." Mrs. Hemlock looked at Drathorn as he attempted to rearrange his sheets again. "Are you uncomfortable, dear?" she asked as Bronc left the room.

"No . . . it's my arm . . . it's bothering me slightly . . ." Drathorn groaned as his arm sent a spark of pain through his body.

"Here . . ." She said, leaning over his wrapped arm. "Let me help . . . Deheano . . . Patron of ice and commander of time . . . numb the wound of this child so he may have peace on this day . . ." Her palm shined and the pain in Drathorn's arm ceased immediately. "When you are done speaking to the Blaygards I want to take another look at your arm. And then I want you to sleep."

Drathorn nodded thankfully though he regretted not being able to see Thira. "Are the Blaygards the family who has come to see me?" Drathorn asked.

"Yes . . . They have had slight disasters in their life and probably think that you will bring them better luck . . . They are fools in my opinion." Mrs. Hemlock said with distaste.

She walked away and Bronc returned a moment later, followed by a short, plump woman with red-brown hair. In her arms was a baby boy. Beside her walked her husband; a tall, strong man with brown hair and wrinkles on his face that showed, not age, but years of happiness and laughter. And at the end of the party was another boy. Drathorn guessed him to be about fifteen. He had fairly long blonde hair and blue eyes. His hair hid his ears and needed to be pushed out of his eyes constantly, just like Drathorn's black hair. But he walked with a great limp and Drathorn noticed that his left leg was made of wood.

Their clothes seemed frayed and loose with patches here and there but still fairly clean. The older boy's left pant leg was cut off at the knee so his wooden leg wouldn't be tripped by the fabric. Drathorn supposed they were one of the poorer families who needed a hand around the house. Drathorn noticed, although they seemed poor, that they all seemed fairly well nourished and quite strong as far as he could tell; even the baby. "Drathorn, this is the Blaygard family." Bronc said, "But I'll let them make their introductions."

It was a moment before Mr. Blaygard stepped toward Drathorn. "Hello, Drathorn . . . I am Mark Blaygard." He said as he shook Drathorn's good hand and Drathorn smiled at him.

"I'm Drathorn Teldaga . . ." Drathorn thought it was pointless to introduce himself since they obviously already knew his name but Mr. Blaygard nodded and gestured to his wife.

"This is my wife, Nikkoli." He said moving over to her.

"You can call me Nikki or Nicole if you want, Drathorn." She said gently.

"This little guy is Timothy . . . but we just call him Timmy, ain't that right, little guy?" Mr Blaygard tickled the baby in Mrs. Blaygard's arms and he made a small gurgling noise and giggled loudly. "And this, my young man, is Troy." Mr. Blaygard said finally gesturing to his oldest son.

Troy didn't make much effort to add anything to the introduction, he acknowledged Drathorn with a nod and Drathorn returned the greeting. Mr. Blaygard waited for one of them to say more but after a moment in awkward silence still nothing came. So Drathorn decided to fill the gap.

"What is it you do, Mr. Blaygard?" He asked innocently. Mr. Blaygard seemed to find it odd that he was being addressed by his last name but he answered normally.

"I'm a miner in the iron mines on the northern region of Tanroe. It's dangerous work but it keeps me fit and feeds my family so I keep at it. And Nikki is a house mother; she stays home and cares for Timmy while Troy goes to school. Troy also has a part-time job at Hall's Garden; it's a grocery store in Gaberdan." Mr. Blaygard seemed to take pride in his job as a miner and seemed proud of his son's job as well.

Drathorn faked interest and asked Troy a question, "What is it you do at Hall's Garden, Troy?"

Troy seemed surprised that Drathorn was speaking to him but recovered quickly and answered, "I'm a Transporter; I ride in a wagon to the edge of town and load up the fresh vegetables in crates onto the wagon. Then we take them back to the store and I move them into storage to be put up for sale. It is heavy work carrying those boxes around but I don't mind it . . . Though I guess if I were doing it full-time I would have troubles with my leg. I already do sometimes . . . I'm a bit slower than the others but I still do my share."

Troy fell fairly silent after that but he seemed more interested in the flow of conversation now and was watching the other patients like they were the most interesting thing he'd seen for many years. Conversation moved on to living conditions and interests. Drathorn didn't say much about interests but made the point that he loved to travel and was trained well in multiple forms of combat.

It was almost another hour before Timothy seemed to be getting restless. "Well Timmy needs a nap and I've gotta get ready to go back to the mines in the morning and Troy has school and everything too . . . We really should be going."

"What? It's still early!" Drathorn said. Drathorn and Troy had finally begun having a proper conversation while Mr. and Mrs. Blaygard spoke with the Headmaster about when they would be able to adopt Drathorn.

"Yes it is still quite early but by the time we get all the way to Gaberdan it will be quite late . . . Its many hours of Traveling along the road . . . not as long if you cut through the forest but our wagon is too large for those paths."

Mr. Blaygard seemed reluctant to leave as well but his better judgement eventually lead the family out of the orphanage and left Drathorn in the hospital area.

Mrs. Hemlock unwrapped his shoulder and rubbed on the cream again before placing her hand on his forehead and muttering the following prayer, "Deandra, goddess of Dreams . . . allow this boy to sleep comfortably and without dreams starting now and lasting throughout the night, may any pain be vanquished in the deepness of such peaceful sleep . . ." The last thing Drathorn saw was the softly glowing light from her palm before he fell asleep.

VI

The History of Gorganite

On May 1st, 18291, Drathorn didn't wake until morning of the next day. It was a bright and cheerful day outside and Drathorn felt well rested and strong. His arm hurt terribly but it seemed to have healed greatly over night. He was now the wonder of the orphanage; to recover so fast from such a deadly wound was nearly unheard of. After examining the wound Mrs. Hemlock decided to keep the bandage off of it. After a well prepared lunch Thira was finally brought in.

She seemed uncertain of where to go. At first she stood around uncertainly at the door. "It's ok, dear, you can come on in." Said Mrs. Hemlock. Thira then moved over beside Drathorn.

"Hello, Thira." Drathorn said.

"Hi . . ." Thira said quietly. She shuffled her feet and looked at his arm. She seemed sad and Drathorn knew exactly what she was about to say. "You shouldn't have done that Drathorn, (in his mind he laughed; this was exactly what he had been expecting) you could have been killed by that thing."

Drathorn frowned again; he was annoyed by people referring to Billy as "That thing" and "Monster". He spoke calmly though. "I could have . . . but I wasn't; that's what matters. I still breathe, which is more than I can say for poor Billy." He laid his head back on the pillows but kept his eyes on her.

At first she seemed ready to argue again but instead she said, "Thank you . . . This is the second time you have saved me, Drathorn." Drathorn had not been expecting this at all but before he could reply she reached down her shirt and grabbed the golden chain. She pulled it out and showed him the glowing crystal. "This was my mother's . . . It is supposed to bring good luck and protection . . . It gave me both, for your finding me on that dreadful night was only by chance, and as you continue to save me it also seems to give me protection."

Drathorn didn't know what to say. The crystal was shining slightly in the room and was both beautiful and mysterious, much like the girl who held it. "I . . . I guess it did . . ." was all he could say to her.

She closed her fist around the crystal and the light was gone. Drathorn looked back at her and saw that she seemed to be fighting some urge. Drathorn briefly wondered what it was. Then she pulled the chain from her neck and opened her hand again. The crystal shone brightly again as she brought her hand over to him. "I want you to have it."

"No!" Drathorn exclaimed, "This crystal is of a beauty that I cannot even begin to understand. It was your mother's and it was passed to you, you must not give me this, I will not accept it."

"I want you to have it; it is rightfully yours now, as is my life." Thira ignored his protesting and began to fasten it around his neck.

"Neither this crystal or your life is mine. They both belong to you and you alone."

"You have saved my life twice now, I owe you my life, twice, and therefore I give you my most prized possession and my life."

"I would accept this charm as very generous thanks, but I refuse to say that you owe me your life. Your life is yours and yours alone to control."

Thira looked at him sadly now. She finished with the charm and sat up again. It glowed brighter than ever around his neck. "Thank you." She said suddenly.

It was silent for a few moments, both trying to find a new topic of conversation. "I'm going to be adopted . . ." he finally said. "I thought you should know."

Thira looked at him sadly. "I know . . . the Headmaster told me yesterday. I came to visit you but you were asleep. I sat down for about an hour beside you . . . and then he came in and told me . . . I cried."

"You sat by me that long?" Drathorn was touched. "What else did you guys talk about?"

"He just told me that you were being adopted . . . then he saw me crying and he said that you were lucky to have a friend like me . . . I told him that if you were so lucky you wouldn't be in the hospital. He frowned and then left and I stayed here till about bed time."

Drathorn was lost for words; she had sat by him for so long and he had never known? She had cried? Drathorn lay motionless for a long time before an idea struck him. "I'm going into town tomorrow." He said to Thira. "I got some coins from the Captain for killing Billy yesterday. I'm allowed to enter the city to spend it and buy new belongings for my new home . . . I want you to come with me."

She looked at him happily, "I'd love to! I haven't left this place at all in so long . . . I'll definitely come." Then she frowned again, "But I haven't got much money of my own . . . just a few coins that I've saved since the day you first rescued me. Will I even be allowed?"

"That doesn't matter, if there's anything you want I'll get it for you, I just want you to be with me." Drathorn said with a smile. "As for permission, I will talk to the headmaster."

"Then yes I will come!" She was in a much better mood as they talked throughout the rest of the afternoon. They exchanged news and talked about the city. It was only when bed time came that Thira finally left. One of the last things they talked about was the night of Elgard's death. He asked about the crystal and why Icarus would want it. She said that its magical powers were wanted by him and she knew not where it had come from but that her mother had received it from a stranger long ago. They had been talking all day and it was getting late so Thira finally stood and said good-bye. She left slowly, still in a good mood and unwilling for the day to end as Drathorn lay back on his pillows again. He reached down his shirt and pulled up the brightly shining crystal; weather it was magic or superstition he would forever wear it, at least to remember her by.

"Drathorn?" Drathorn looked back at the door to see the Headmaster standing there. Drathorn had been staring at the mysterious crystal for some time now.

"Yes, sir?"

"What is that you have there?" He asked.

"It's Thira's good-luck charm . . . she gave it to me today." He answered.

"May I?" he asked, walking over and holding his hand out for it. Drathorn removed the amulet and placed it in Bronc's hand. As soon as it left contact with Drathorn the glowing seemed to stop but it seemed just as beautiful.

Bronc looked closely at the crystal and then gave it quickly back to Drathorn . . ."That is no good luck charm." He said fearfully. "Put it away, fast." Drathorn stuffed it into his shirt again, confused.

"What's wrong, sir?"

"Have you ever heard the story of the Gorgan wars?" He asked. Drathorn shook his head. "I suppose not . . . It is not often covered in history class. Are you awake enough for a story, my child?"

Drathorn nodded. "The story of the Gorgan Wars starts almost ten thousand years ago, before the Elves took refuge in the forests of Hélmoré . . . The free races of Corrone were under threat then as well. A race known as the Gorgans were conquering the world and destroying its people. They used the Onyx tower to command their forces. They were a power greater than any. Inside the Onyx tower was a great crystal made of what they called Gorganite. It prevented the gods from interfering on Corrone. Without the power of the Gods to help them magic and prayers had no effect and the free peoples were being defeated. The Gorgan's were indestructible it seemed. The remaining armies of the free people gathered in the Dwarven city of Dargurmén in the year 8291, two years after the old capitol, Marthandel, was overrun by Gorgans. There they selected a hero from each of the races. Elémond Rainingstar of the Elves, Zark of the Gar population, Lorford Jacques of the Draconian mountains, Mordan of the King's Hammer tribe from the Dwarves, and Drathorn Sky (your name sake) of the human kingdoms. These heroes were to infiltrate the Gorgan's Onyx tower and destroy the Gorganite Crystal. If they failed, the remaining people of Tanroe would fall. If they succeeded then the peoples of Tanroe would battle in their honour."

"Wait I'm confused." Drathorn said. "What about the Mermaids of the ocean? And the Chis? And Isn't the Onyx tower where the Darklord is hiding?"

Bronc nodded, "We did not know of the existence of the Merpeople at this time and yes the Darklord does currently reside in the Onyx tower. The Chis were busy fighting their own battle elsewhere . . . may I continue?"

"Yes sir . . . I apologize. Continue." Drathorn said.

"No apology necessary." Bronc continued. "After selecting the Heroes the people returned to their homelands. The Heroes left for the Onyx tower alone. They infiltrated the tower easily and were in the throne room with the crystal when it all went wrong . . . But maybe it's better for you to see what happened?"

"It would be but that's not possible is it?" Drathorn said.

"Yes it is. I can have Deandra make you dream of it. If that's ok?"

"Yes I would like that." Drathorn said.

Bronc placed his hand on Drathorn's forehead and began a prayer. "Deandra, Goddess of Dreams and Patron of Water . . . let this boy see the battle for the Gorganite Crystal . . . A dream that will allow him to see the truth but awake in its end."

Drathorn saw his hand glow but nothing happened. "What's going on?" Drathorn asked.

"It's the amulet . . . it doesn't let the power of the gods affect you. Take it off." Drathorn placed Thira's necklace on the table and Bronc repeated the prayer. The light flowed from his palm and then it was gone.

"Sky!" Zark said suddenly in the quiet of the Tower. "Is that the Crystal?" Zark stood in his leather armour, waiting for an answer.

"I believe it is, my friend." Drathorn Sky said with a smile.

They were in a large room at the top of the Onyx Tower. Zark's red lizard head was pointing directly at the great crystal. His narrow eyes fixed by its beauty, his sword hanging loosely at his side.

Drathorn was in iron plate mail armour with his long sword sheathed at his side, a large iron kite shield on his arm. He, too, looked at it admiringly. Mordan of the King's Hammer tribe entered the room with his great hammer on his back, his thick Dwarven armour slowing him down, followed closely by Lorford Jacques, his staff in his hands. "Where is Elémond?" Lorford asked, "That Elf is always running off." But Lorford was getting old and his eye sight was not as it had once been.

"I'm over here you stupid Dragonian!" Elémond Rainingstar stood at the far side of the room, looking out of the tower window. His honey coloured hair flowed down his back, his elfish armour sleek and shining. His oak long bow was polished in his hand and his Elvin short sword was sheathed at his side.

"Don't start you two!" Drathorn said. "Let's just destroy it and go."

"I agree!" Mordan said taking his war hammer off of his back.

"Alright, do it King's Hammer." Zark said, already bored.

The dwarf walked forward and raised the hammer but then he tripped. The hammer hit the ground loudly and so did the Dwarf. The sound ran throughout the entire tower. They all stood still, hoping against hope that no one had heard the disturbance.

But the sound had been heard. The cries of the Gorgans could be heard, "Intruders! Intruders in the throne room!" the voices were inhuman, unlike anything ever heard before.

"Great going you stupid Dwarf!" Lorford yelled, "We're dead now!"

"Relax! We are Heroes for a reason!" Drathorn yelled. "Everyone get ready, they're coming and we must fight them!"

"I agree, Sky!" Zark said, he stood beside Drathorn and was soon joined by Mordan and Lorford. Elémond got behind them and strung his bow. The Gorgan's burst into the room and Elémond released an arrow, killing one instantly. The other's charged forward and began attacking their foe. The battle lasted long. Drathorn slashed ferociously, easily the best fighter of the five heroes. Mordan bashed three Gorgans aside with a single blow of his hammer. Zark stealthily sneaked around stabbing enemies that were not paying attention to him. Lorford battled furiously, keeping the Gorgans from getting near Elémond as he shot arrows. Together the five warriors were an amazing team. But it wasn't long before Drathorn, Mordan and Zark were separated from Lorford and Elémond. Lorford was over powered by his enemies and Elémond was forced to abandon his bow and fight beside Lorford with his sword.

Even with their combined efforts Drathorn was forced to rush to their aid. But he was too late. Two Gorgans struck Lorford at the same time and he fell to the ground, dead. Out of anger Mordan knocked fifteen Gorgans across the room with his master weapon. He rushed over to Drathorn and Elémond and together the three of them battled bravely. Zark dropped suddenly from the roof and struck two Gorgans that had nearly killed Drathorn. But as he did so he was hit by a third Gorgan. Zark fell and lay dead as well on the other side of the room. Mordan screamed out in anger as the Assassin fell and he rushed into a large group of Gorgans, his war hammer held high. He blasted Gorgans around the room with a tear in his eye. Before Drathorn or Elémond could save him he was beaten to death by the unending enemies. Drathorn and Elémond battled together, defending themselves as well as each other from the unending foes. Their swords were stained with the blood of the Gorgans. They fought alone for many minutes, neither giving in. But Elémond tripped over the body of Mordan and hit the ground hard. A Gorgan stabbed him through and he lay on the ground choking on his own blood. Drathorn quickly sheathed his sword and took up Mordan's fallen hammer.

He swung the hammer in a wide arc and sent the Gorgans flying. "Drathorn . . ." said the elf, "Tell my sister . . . I love her . . ." Drathorn fell to his knees beside his fallen companion. "End this now, my friend . . ."

"You would have made a great Elf Lord, Elémond Rainingstar, brother of the queen . . . I will give your message, my brother." Drathorn picked up the war hammer but instead of striking the enemy he spun and smashed it against the Crystal. The Crystal and the hammer exploded and so did the entire tower. Gorgan's were slain by the explosion and Drathorn Sky was launched from the tower. He fell miles away, into the heart of the Hélmoré forests.

Elémaren, Elémond's brother, found him moments later. A fair sized shard of the Crystal was stuck in his stomach . . .

Drathorn woke suddenly in the hospital lying beside Bronc who sat calmly in his chair. "Did you see it?" Bronc asked.

"Yes . . . I saw Drathorn Sky destroy the Gorganite Crystal. He landed in Hélmoré forest . . . he had a shard in him."

"That was the only shard of the Gorganite Crystal that was ever found . . . the rest was utterly destroyed."

Drathorn suddenly realized something . . . something he should have noticed during the dream but realized only now. "Those Gorgans! They-"

"Yes . . . they are the exact same race of creatures as what Billy turned into."

"But . . . how?" Drathorn asked, surprised. "The Gorgan's were destroyed!"

"Not all of them. A few escaped and found each other . . . They have hidden themselves for a while. They have children with Humans and then leave so that their population may thrive . . . the emperors of Corrone have been hunting them down for a long time . . . Billy was the first one we've found in many years."

"What happened after Drathorn Sky was found?" Drathorn asked, trying to get the subject away from his dead friend.

"Drathorn Sky gave his message . . . he told Elémond's sister, the Elf Queen, that Elémond was dead. And he told her that the Crystal was destroyed. Drathorn Sky died from the shard and Elémaren removed the shard from his body. She named it Dranémor, which means Sky Star, in honour of Drathorn's memory. She told the other people of the victory and they hunted down the remaining Gorgan armies. The Gorgan Wars ended and the Elves went into hiding in the Hélmoré forests. They told the Human Emperor that they had the shard but refused to give it up.

"They fought for a year over the shard and that's why the Elves went into hiding and are the only race not part of the Empire. And now you know the story of the Gorganite Wars."

"Is this crystal the Dranémor?" Drathorn asked.

"Yes." Bronc stated. "Not only does the Darklord want you dead but he wants Dranémor. With his power he could not only stop the gods from controlling him but *he* could control the gods!"

"But how did it come to Thira?" Drathorn asked.

"That I don't know . . . but I think it is best you keep it. She may not even know what it is." Bronc said thoughtfully.

"I doubt she does . . . but the Darklord knew she had it . . . the night we were attacked he tried to kill me and take the necklace." Drathorn said.

"I think there's more to this that we do not yet see." Bronc said. "But now it is time for bed . . . it is extremely late and you've got a big day in Greengate with Thira tomorrow . . ."

Drathorn again found himself shocked to find that he knew this piece of information. "How do you do that?" He asked but then he rephrased the question quickly and instead asked, "You mean she can come?"

"Yes." The Headmaster laughed before uttering his prayer of sleep and Drathorn was lost in an endless black void, dreamless as far as he could remember.

VII

In Greengate

Night seemed to pass slowly in the black emptiness but Drathorn finally woke, on May 2nd of 18291, to the bright sunshine as Mrs. Hemlock examined his arm again. "Sorry dear, did I wake you?"

"No, no." Drathorn said, sitting up, "It's ok . . ." Drathorn looked at his shoulder. There was barely anything there now. It had nothing but an extremely thick scratch on it now, not even a scar. "Is that normal?"

Mrs. Hemlock looked at what was left of the wound and shook her head. "Gorgan's blades are made of Strominite; a metal that burns the flesh and prevents healing. It's impossible that it can heal like this."

"But it did . . . I don't understand . . ." Drathorn said. But then an idea struck him, maybe the Headmaster knew? Did this healing have anything to do with him being a Hellbound? The headmaster knew so much about so many things was it possible he could help Drathorn? "Where is the Headmaster?"

"He is in his office . . . but he doesn't know either." Mrs. Hemlock said.

"I know I just wanna talk to him." Drathorn lied, "It's about the Blaygards."

Mrs. Hemlock nodded and said; "You can speak to him before you leave today . . . I want you to eat first."

Drathorn had a good breakfast and left the Hospital later that morning. He crossed the yard and knocked at the door of the Headmaster's lodge while the others were still in class. He waited for a moment and then the door opened. Bronc stood in the door way, still in his bed clothes and looked quite tired. "Ah, Drathorn." He said, "Is there a problem?"

Drathorn shook his head. "I wanted to talk about the Gorgans . . . just a question." He asked hopefully.

Bronc looked around and allowed him to enter. The lodge was quite small. The west wall was made of a book case covered in ancient volumes. The northern wall was hidden by a bed and a small window looking out onto the field. The eastern wall was bare. In the middle of the floor was a large wooden table. "I've been packing my belongings . . . I'm leaving for Signaroc soon." Bronc stated. "Now what is it you wish to talk about?"

Drathorn sat down in a chair at the table and looked at the Headmaster. "Why am I healing so fast?" he asked, "Mrs. Hemlock says it shouldn't be healing at all . . . The metal the blade was made of is cursed with fire. It burns the wound, keeping it fresh and open until you die from it . . . but I'm not dying . . . why?"

Bronc smiled and sat down across from Drathorn. "Strominite is a metal creation of not only Colaspis but Sylvaston as well. The fires of Sylvaston and the metal of Colaspis combine to create the ore. But as a Hellbound you have Sylvaston's fire within you. Sylvaston made the Hellbound immune to fire." There was a moment in which he thought before adding; "Actually you absorb the power of flame and use it to heal yourself. The Hellbound have always healed fast . . . it is their most natural ability. By using the power of fire you can heal many times faster than without the fire . . . hundreds of times faster than any normal human. You also can see clearly through smoke and smog when you are surrounded by them as well as breathe without interference."

Drathorn was amazed by this fact; this was why he hadn't been burned by the fire when he rescued Thira and why he could see so clearly and breathe so easily in the wagon! "So what you're saying is, I can walk through a wall of fire and not feel a thing?"

"No. You will feel the flames . . . their warmth . . . but it will not harm you. All Hellbound could even harness the fire within and use it in a pure form . . . like throwing fireballs without actually praying or using magic. If you were seconds from death and you crawled into fire you would have a great chance of surviving."

"Why didn't you tell me this? You act like you don't know anything but when I ask you, you know all the answers!" Drathorn demanded, slightly annoyed now.

"I am a seeker." Bronc said, "I seek answers to every problem and problems to every answer. But I do not reveal my knowledge unless I am asked to do so . . . and the one problem with my gift of knowledge is this; I can never lie . . . it doesn't matter how hard I try, every word I speak is the truth." He frowned slightly and then said "Why don't you go and get Thira from the cafeteria? You two can meet me at the front gate and I'll let you guys go on out and have some fun."

Drathorn nodded then got up, left the lodge and began to make his way slowly to the cafeteria where the orphans were eating their breakfast. Drathorn realized that it must still be early when he noticed few people were inside. Mardy, Gunnel, Dorn, and Calvin were sitting together and talking quietly at the far side of the cafeteria. On the other side was a small group of kids trying to finish last minute homework assignments. Thira, again, sat alone near the entrance. She was picking slowly at her food, not entirely interested.

"Am I early?" Drathorn asked. Thira started and looked at him.

"Yes actually, but not by much." Thira said, but she seemed happy to see him again. Drathorn noticed how much her face lit up as she smiled . . . her beauty was astounding and he wondered if anyone else noticed but him . . . surely this unnatural beauty wasn't just his imagination?

"I didn't want to be in here while it was full." Drathorn said. He looked around and noticed that the nearby children that had been doing homework were now watching him admiringly, as were Mardy and his gang with angry glares. "Do you wanna leave now?" He asked.

Thira looked at the kids too and said, "Yeah, I guess we should." She got up and they walked together out of the cafeteria. They walked across the field and toward the front gates just as a large group of people exited a nearby dormitory to head down to breakfast. Bronc could already be seen standing at the gate.

Thira and Drathorn walked up to the Headmaster. He was properly dressed now and stood with a ring of keys in his right hand. As they approached he fiddled with the keys, apparently searching for a specific one.

"Hello, Headmaster." Thira said politely.

"Good day to you, young Thira. How are you this morning?" Bronc seemed in a better mood now.

"I am quite well actually, and you?" She asked.

"Quite well." Bronc said. He selected a rusty old key from the key ring and placed it in the gate's keyhole. "Aha! Finally found the key!" He turned the key and unlocked the gate and then removed the key from the ring and handed it to Drathorn. "Go on into town and have fun. Be back before dinner time. Unlock the gate with this key, lock it upon entering, and give the key to Mrs. Hemlock when you return."

"Yes, sir." Drathorn said. He and Thira walked out of the orphanage together, waving at the headmaster as he locked the gate with another key that had been beside the first. "So . . . Is there anywhere specific you wanna go?" Drathorn asked.

"Well . . . I've never really been into town . . ." Thira said, "And I don't really have much money . . ."

"Well how about we walk around and we'll stop anywhere that seems interesting?" Drathorn asked. "And if you see anything you like let me know and I'll help you buy it."

"Okay . . . but I'm not letting you spend your money on me!" Thira said.

Drathorn just laughed as they walked around the city. Greengate was full of happy people and shops of every size. They walked past Icarus' Bank and Drathorn didn't even give it a second glance, he was too absorbed in watching Thira's smile. Thira eventually found a fancy clothing shop on Thirteenth Street. "*Madame Silverwater's Clothing and Accessories*?" Thira read the sign aloud as they passed. She stopped outside and gazed into the window. Many fancy dresses and other forms of clothing were set up neatly in the window. "Would you mind if I took a little break from walking and looked for a new blouse?" She asked.

"Not at all!" Drathorn said. He looked around and saw an armoury across the cobblestone street. "I'll just be browsing the armoury until you're finished . . . women's clothing isn't my favourite shop. Let me know if there's anything you want."

Thira went into the store with another smile and Drathorn crossed the busy cobblestone street. A large bald man stood behind the counter of the armoury. In the wall behind him was a doorway into the smithy. Hanging on the wall were several displays of weapons and armour. "Sorry friend!" Said the man in a thick accent. "We just don't have da man power ta finish somethin' like that in such a small amount o' time." He seemed to be talking to another man at the counter.

"Fine . . . I'll try somewhere else." The man turned and walked away from the armoury. Drathorn caught a glimpse of the red lizard's head of a Gar but that was all. He was puzzled for a moment but then he walked over to the counter and looked up at the man.

"Hello there son!" Said the man with a thick accent. "Bit young to be purchasing weaponry ain't ye? But oh well, business is business an' in times like these 'tis only natural to want da proper protection!"

"What do you mean, 'times like these'?" Drathorn asked.

"Well da bandit problem o' course!" He laughed. "Da war may be takin' place farther west but we've bin havin' big problems wit' bandits in this area."

"I see . . . well I'm just browsing today, I'm not allowed any weapons." Drathorn said. "They interest me though . . . and this seems like a good place for me to come if I were to purchase them."

"Aye, we carry da largest stock o' weapons an' armour in da Himegard region!" the man said. "But da thing with dat is; we don't have enough employees ta keep dat reputation."

"I'm sorry to hear that." Drathorn said, "I was actually wondering about your sword prices."

"Ah, you're the adventuring type are ye?" he asked. "Rather run through da wild with a sturdy blade o' steal, making da region a bit safer than be stuck up in yer home prayin' dat those damned guards can protect ye! Well it all depends on what type o' blade you're lookin' fer my friend! If you be lookin' for a sturdy blade to protect yer family with than try a short sword, lookin' to be a grand adventurer o' da sorts? Try a long sword! They quick and strong with a good reach. But better yet is the Hand-an'-a-half sword. Can be used with one or two hands and are great if you're lookin' to be da one doin' da damage."

Drathorn thought for a moment then said, "I'm thinking of doing a bit of adventuring in the near future . . . how much do you charge for a simple long sword?"

"Just a simple one?" The man repeated, "Well . . . I think I could make you an offer o' fifteen coins. We need better equipped adventurers out there. I'd be out there meself if me Pop weren't sick. I need to take care o' da shop for him 'till he gets better."

"Well I hope he does get better, maybe we'll meet on the road in the future." Drathorn said. "I like your prices but like I said; I'm not allowed a weapon . . . yet . . . when I am I will return."

"I thank ye for da good tidings friend . . . an' I do so hope we meet again . . . may ye travel safely."

Drathorn crossed the street again just as Thira exited the shop. "Did you get what you were looking for?" Drathorn asked.

She smiled and pulled a beautiful blouse from a brown paper bag she was carrying. "Seven coins." She said as she slid the blouse back into the bag. "I have three coins left, how about you?"

"I was just exploring, I can't buy any weapons while I'm still in the orphanage . . . but I've still got about a hundred coins." Drathorn said. "How about we get some lunch?"

Thira agreed and they walked to a small restaurant and Drathorn bought lunch for the both of them. After eating their fill they began walking around again and spoke in high spirits. Near the end of the trip they decided to stop into 'Gallop and Trot'; a well known store where steeds and riding equipment could be purchased and traded. They both knew that they wouldn't be able to afford any horses but they agreed that it would be an interesting visit.

It wasn't long before Thira had made good friends with a white stallion. It had beautiful white fur and a perfect pearl coloured mane. As she patted the young Stallion and had her face licked, Drathorn found a strong brown horse in the next stall. Its body was of the deepest chestnut brown colour and it had a black mane of hair. Its eyes were a deep green and a white mark that resembled a star sat on its forehead. "That there is Starcruser." The manager said. "He's our pride and joy."

"What breed is he?" Drathorn asked.

"He is a Red-runner." The manager said. "The only one we've ever had in stock. They make excellent companions on the road. Great for traveling, they can carry great weights of luggage and are natural war-horses. He's seven hundred coins."

Drathorn sighed and left the horse Starcruser alone in his stall. He walked into Thira's stall to see her giggling and playing with a young white stallion. He smiled at her laughter and looked to the manager, "How about this one?"

"That there is a stallion . . . quite common in this region but she's a beauty that one is . . . a fair speed-horse, but much more child friendly than the Red-runner. They are fit enough for carrying a person and a few supplies and are also fair war horses . . . a great choice . . . worth about three hundred coins."

Drathorn frowned; he wanted to get this horse for Thira. He looked at Thira as she played happily with the young horse. He knew she would be upset to leave such a beautiful and friendly animal behind and he would hate to make her sad . . . but he just could not afford it. He took a step into the stall toward Thira.

"Freeze! No body move!" Mardy's voice rang like a bell throughout the stables. His muscular figure was standing near the door, holding a large crossbow and pointing it into the shop. The thin form of Calvin and the winged form of Zargel were seen in other spots of the shop. And a short figure moved throughout the shop with his club . . . probably one of the twins.

"As long as everybody co-operates no one will be hurt! I want everyone to step slowly out of the stalls with their hands raised! Dorn! Check all the stalls! Make sure no one is hiding!"

The figure of the Dwarf walked slowly from stall to stall. Drathorn held Thira back and whispered quietly, "Stay here . . . It's Mardy . . . I'll take care of this . . ." Thira's eyes grew wide with fear as Drathorn hid himself in the shadows of the stall. All was quiet as Dorn walked through each stall, looking for anyone who was hiding. His small body appeared suddenly in the stall Thira and Drathorn were hiding in. He saw Thira immediately.

"Oi!" The Dwarf yelled. But before he could say anything else Drathorn had hit him over the head with a heavy broom. Dorn fell, unconscious to the ground. He took Dorn's club and threw it straight at Mardy. The club knocked the crossbow from his hands before he could shoot. Drathorn jumped out of the stall and into the open.

"Everyone get out!" Drathorn yelled. The people in the shop panicked and ran for the door; the horses panicked as well and began galloping wildly around in their stalls and around the shop. Zargel and Calvin began fighting their way to Drathorn, adding to the confusion even more. Calvin jumped high above everyone and Drathorn saw that he held a short sword in his right hand. Drathorn side stepped Calvin and punched him in the face as he landed. Calvin recoiled and Zargel flew high above the others, a quarter staff in his hands. Drathorn picked up a bag of money that the manager had dropped and threw it through the air. It hit Zargel hard and he fell out of the air and landed on his back. Calvin got back up and ran at Drathorn with his sword. Drathorn flung open a stall door and Calvin ran straight into it. At the same time the frail form of Thira leapt from the stall colliding with Drathorn. They landed on the ground together. It was just in time; Mardy had found his crossbow and shot a bolt directly at him. If Thira had not come out at that exact moment the bolt would have pierced his forehead. "Thanks, Thira!" Drathorn yelled. But before she could say anything he threw her off to the right and rolled immediately to the left. A horse stomped with his front hooves right where they had been laying just seconds before. Out of the corner of his eye he could see her trying desperately to get back to him. But Zargel flew at him again and stabbed at him with his quarter staff. Drathorn rolled and avoided one strike, and then another.

Thira yelled suddenly and Drathorn looked over at her. She had knocked Calvin unconscious and had thrown his short sword to Drathorn. Drathorn rolled right and caught it. As Zargel's staff came down on him a third time he rolled right and cut the staff in half with the blade. Zargel snarled in anger and Drathorn hit him with the hilt of the sword first in the knee and then in the head as he fell. Zargel too, was soon unconscious. Drathorn looked up to see Mardy aiming his crossbow at Thira. Drathorn yelled but it was too late. He saw in slow motion as the crossbow bolt began to fly towards Thira. He threw the sword and watched as it soared across the store. The sword arrived just in time; it slapped the bolt right out of the air only seconds before it would have it Thira. The clang of the metal bolt striking the sword ran throughout the store.

Thira screamed and Mardy gazed, amazed at the still living Thira. Drathorn swerved in and out of the panicking horses and leapt at the still astounded Mardy. Mardy had no time to react as Drathorn landed on him. All Thira saw between the passing horses was a flail of fists and legs. A moment later Drathorn stood and Mardy lay unconscious on the ground. He swerved his way to Thira and they left the store together, hand in hand.

It had been an hour since the brawl in the store. The manager and his assistants had finally calmed down the horses and the guards were able to arrest Mardy and the others. Thira and Drathorn had been forced to answer many questions by Captain Xavier, who rushed off shortly after to arrest the others in Mardy's gang, and then when things had finally calmed down again the manager of the store had come out to see them. With him he brought Starcruser and the white stallion; both were saddled up and ready for ridding.

"Hello, my name is Edward . . . I'm the manager of *Gallop and Trot*." He said. "I have spoken with my assistants and we have all agreed that you should be awarded for what you have done here." He looked at Drathorn meaningfully. "We want you to have the red-runner, Starcruser, and our best riding equipment."

Drathorn couldn't believe it; a seven hundred coin steed and three hundred coins worth of equipment were being given to him free of charge! He shook is head and said simply, "I couldn't have done it without Thira . . ." he looked at Thira with a smile "I would rather you gave her the stallion."

"That is quite noble of you, Mr. Teldaga. But we knew you would say this. We also know that Thira indeed helped you in there." He smiled at Thira, "We are giving both of these horses to you; you may do with them as you please. In this way, you will have the steed you rightly deserve for your actions and you will make your girlfriend happy as well."

"She's not-" Drathorn exclaimed.

"We're not-" Thira followed.

"I'm-" Drathorn blurted out.

"We're just friends!" They chanted together.

The manager laughed and Thira and Drathorn both blushed deep crimson. "Very well . . . You will make your *friend* happy." The manager said, still chuckling at their red faces. "Now, if you will excuse me, I must return to the store. We need to clean up the mess so we can open again for tomorrow."

Thira and Drathorn mounted their new horses to small applause and they rode down the street together. The beautiful Thira rode upon the beautiful stallion that had yet to be named and Drathorn rode beside her on the powerful red-runner, Starcruser, still blushing slightly. As they neared the orphanage for dinner they began talking again, their happiness returning now that the embarrassment had passed. He was slightly annoyed that Edward had jumped to such a conclusion about them but as they rode Drathorn couldn't help but wonder, *What if?*

VIII

The Ride South

At dinner a dozen guards showed up and arrested the rest of Mardy's gang based on Drathorn and Thira's knowledge. With the bullies removed the two were happier then ever. But the next day was the day of the Blaygard's return. May 3rd, 18291, Drathorn had returned to the hospital for the night. Upon awakening Drathorn went to his dormitory and packed his meagre belongings. He brought his trunk to the hospital and allowed Mrs. Hemlock to examine his arm for the last time. It was now almost fully healed and no longer pained him.

Drathorn then walked yet again to the cafeteria to say goodbye to Thira.

It was quite full today. No one called out to him, nor waved but they all watched him; the hero of the children, the protector of the orphanage, walk towards Thira. Many children stood on benches to get a better look at him and others had no idea what was happening but watched eagerly anyways. Muttering and whispers filled the cafeteria as he walked slowly to Thira.

Thira looked up at him. She sat alone in the far corner, and she appeared to have been crying. Drathorn walked straight to her and they stood face to face for a moment before Thira said, "I guess this really is goodbye then, huh?"

Drathorn frowned. They had shared much together in the last few months. Would it really end here? Would they ever see each other again? Drathorn supposed they would. If Icarus wanted him bad enough he suspected the Blaygards would not live long in his company. He expected to be back within the month. "Only for now." He said, smiling wryly, and trying to make her feel better. "With my luck, I'll be back soon."

Thira began to cry slightly and the smile disappeared from his face. Drathorn wasn't sure about this; it was certainly a hard way to say good bye but . . . after only three months? Drathorn didn't know what else to do; he took a step closer and put his arms around her. Her arms rested on him, her face hidden in is shoulder. They stayed that way for a little while, unaware of the many people crowded in the cafeteria. After a moment they walked out of the cafeteria together; Drathorn's arm still around her shoulders, Thira's face still tear stained. When they finally stopped outside of the headmaster's cabin they saw a small group of people awaiting them by the open gates.

Bronc and Mrs. Hemlock stood beside Drathorn's trunk. Mrs. Blaygard and Troy stood together near them, Troy held onto the reins of Starcruser for him. Captain Xavier stood in his armour with the company of two other guards and a tall man with his sword sheathed at his side held onto the reins of two other horses on Bronc's other side.

"Good morning Drathorn!" Captain Xavier said. "I heard you were leaving today and I figured I'd come to say good bye. I want you to know that you are always welcome in Greengate and still have a place reserved among the guards for when you choose to take it."

"Thank you sir." Was all Drathorn said to the captain.

"And I also want you to know that Mardy and his friends are going to serve a long time in prison before returning to the orphanage, hopefully that will change their tune." At those last words Xavier waved goodbye to the group and lead his men away from the orphanage.

"I'm not sure if I like that man yet . . ." Drathorn said. "He seems pretty sure I'll join the guard."

Bronc chuckled slightly at this comment. "He is a good man, but his personality is often confusing . . . and yes he's quite controlling . . . it's natural not to be sure."

"Okay." Drathorn said, unsure of what else to say. He tightened his hold around Thira, letting her know she was not forgotten.

"Hello, Drathorn." The man with the two horses said. "I am Eldrath." Eldrath was a Gar. His lizard face was a green colour, unlike the man in Greengate he had seen. He was quite old by the look of him, and he was quite short as well. His sword was a curved scimitar. "I am Bronc's travel partner." Eldrath stuck out his human hand and Drathorn shook it politely.

"Eldrath and I are going to travel to Signaroc . . . we start shortly after your departure." Bronc said.

"What are you going there for?" Mrs. Blaygard questioned, curious.

"We've heard that there are slight problems concerning their crops . . . something has been poisoning them or some such trouble. We are going to see if we can find whoever is behind it and put a stop to it." Bronc answered.

"My sister lives in Signaroc . . . she was telling us about it last night . . . apparently it's just locusts." Mrs. Blaygard said.

"Odd . . . that area has never had locusts before . . . perhaps something in that area is doing it to terrorize the people . . . something that has control over the locust population."

"Well I have no idea what could control the locusts but I wish you luck . . . and I hope you have no trouble with bandits in your travels, but we must be going if we plan to arrive before dinner." Mrs. Blaygard now looked awkwardly to Drathorn and Thira; Drathorn still held her tightly. He was worried that if he let her go she would begin crying again; she looked ready to start even now. "Umm . . . are you ready to go, Drathorn?" she asked uncertainly.

Troy stood, watching the conversation with little interest. Thira had to be the most beautiful person he had seen in his entire life; her hair was straight and black and was nearly hip length, her eyes were of the most beautiful brown. She wore the new blouse she had bought when she had been out with Drathorn the day before. She was clearly the most perfect girl on the island and she stood in Drathorn's arms, ready to cry. He couldn't take his eyes off of her but she didn't seem to notice for she didn't take hers off of Drathorn. Troy only vaguely heard the words being said.

Drathorn turned his head and looked down at Thira; she looked gently back at him and for a minute nothing could be said. Then she took a single step away from Drathorn, his arm falling from around her and staying limply at his side. She stood slightly off to the side, the tears ready to fall again, and looking even more beautiful while surrounded by the shabby Blaygards. Drathorn looked at Mrs. Blaygard and nodded slowly; "Yes, now would be best."

Mrs. Blaygard looked between Drathorn and Thira with worry for a minute and then said "We had to park the wagon on the outskirts of town . . . it is too large to take down these busy cobblestone streets. I hope you don't mind the walk?"

Drathorn shook his head and began walking beside Mrs. Blaygard, Troy limping as fast as he could beside them. "I love to walk." He answered. "Troy . . . you can ride Starcruser if you want." Drathorn said. And that's how they started. The trunk and Troy were loaded onto Starcruser and Mrs. Blaygard and Drathorn walked beside the war horse without saying much. They had just passed through the gate when Thira's voice rang out.

"Drathorn, wait!" Drathorn turned around just in time to see Thira running toward him. He had only a second to brace himself before she gave him another enormous hug that could very well have knocked him down. She looked up into his eyes and whispered, her breath falling pleasantly on his face; "Let this not be the last time we see each other." She let go with one arm and touched the Gorganite Amulet beneath his shirt; "Wear this to remember me by . . . and take this as a promise that we shall meet again." She stood up on her toes and kissed him. Her lips gently touched his. He felt her breath upon his lips and it had a strange but familiar smell. It was pleasant and beautiful yet mysterious and unrecognizable; it was *her* breath. Drathorn held her tightly as she kissed him. He suddenly wanted to let her go less than ever.

Drathorn stood there, shocked, even after she had escaped his arms and began making her way back to the orphanage. Drathorn could hear her weeping as she walked away but there was nothing that he could do; for a moment later the gate shut behind her. Drathorn wanted nothing more than to scale the fence and rush back to her side but he knew that he could not. Instead he stared after her, tears now welling in his eyes as well. He felt Mrs. Blaygard's soft hand on his shoulder and he turned to face her.

He wiped his eyes on his sleeve and then muttered; "Let's go." in a hoarse whisper. He greatly feared the thought that this might be one promise he might not be able to keep; would he *ever* see her again?

Mrs. Blaygard did the best she could to try and cheer him up and made constant attempts at conversation. Drathorn did not expect it to work but by the time they had crossed town and reached the Blaygard's immense wagon Drathorn was in a slightly better mood and was deep in conversation with Troy.

When they arrived at the wagon it was to meet another portion of the Blaygard family waiting for them. A large, muscular boy with a buzz cut sat on the driver's seat of the wagon, a long sword tied to his belt. A girl about Drathorn and Troy's age sat on the ground beside the single horse, patting the old grey mare that was supposed to pull the wagon. A large woman with curly hair and a small dagger sat just visible in the wagon and Drathorn supposed she was Mrs. Blaygard's sister. She sat holding the sleeping young Timothy in her arms.

"Ho, there Drathorn!" yelled the older boy in the driver's seat. He jumped acrobatically from his perch and landed in front of Drathorn. "I'm Ben!" He stuck out his hand and shook Drathorn's firmly. "I apologize for not being able to meet you the other day but I had to work." He smiled at Drathorn and Drathorn guessed he was about twenty years old. "I'm your cousin." He added as an after thought.

Before Drathorn could say anything the woman in the Wagon and the young girl had wondered over to them. "Hello, Drathorn. It's nice to meet you!" said the woman, "I'm Nikki's sister. And I guess I'm also your aunt Pat now!" she said happily. "And this is my daughter, Hailey." She gestured to the girl who stood back slightly. "She's rather shy . . . I would have come to meet you the other day but I stayed home with Hailey . . . She was sick in bed. And Ben here is my older son. Ben lives in Gaberdan with his wife Linda . . . he lives just down the street from you!" She smiled and then added, "My husband would be here but his ship was late coming from Signaroc to Taldi. I have no idea why two of the best ship yards are owned by those Tribesmen . . . Why the Emperor doesn't have them removed I will never know."

"Now, now, mother!" Ben said, "The Tribesmen play an important role around here. They may not follow our laws but they allow us to do as we please and cut across their lands. We don't need to start a war with those who are letting us live peacefully when we are already at war with those who are not."

"And you should all hush before you wake Timothy!" Mrs. Blaygard said quietly.

"Of course . . ." Ben bowed respectfully. "We are ready to go when you are!"

"Starcruser can help pull." Drathorn said. "That wagon looks like a hard job for just one."

"That is very kind of you Drathorn." Pat said, "Ben can you remove the trunk and tie him up to the wagon?"

Ben nodded and helped Troy off of the horse. Then he moved Drathorn's trunk into the wagon and began tying Starcruser to the front. Troy, Drathorn, Hailey, Pat and Mrs. Blaygard climbed into the back of the wagon. "Where's Mr. Blaygard?" Drathorn asked.

"Mark is working in the mines in the Neeshara Desert . . . he'll be home in a few days." Mrs. Blaygard said. The wagon was indeed quite large; benches were on both sides and Drathorn suspected that the giant wagon could hold multiple families. It looked like the group could probably all sleep quite comfortably in here. Ben jumped in and looked at them all.

"Ok . . . y'all know about the bandit problem going on around here so I'm saying this now; It's a long ride to Gaberdan by road and anything can happen. If we are attacked I want y'all to run while I hold them off. Drathorn, we have some spare weapons here . . . if something happens I want you to grab one and use it for your own defence." Ben said.

Drathorn suddenly realized that everyone was armed. Ben had a long sword at his waist, Hailey, Pat and Mrs. Blaygard all had daggers at their hips and Troy supported a small crossbow. "You really think we'll be attacked?" he asked.

"We've been lucky so far but anything can happen." Ben said. "I'm not sure what kind of weapon you're used to but all I brought was a spare blade." Ben handed Drathorn a simple short sword in a small wooden scabbard.

"A sword is best for me." Drathorn nodded. "I trained constantly with my brother before he was killed in January." He tied the scabbard to his belt and looked up at Ben. "I can fight, and if we are attacked, I'm not gunna run." Drathorn finished.

"Neither will I." Troy said unexpectedly.

Ben smiled at both of them and then left to start driving. It was only a moment before the creaking of the giant wheels and the steady *clip-clop* of the horses' hooves on the dirt path were heard. Mrs. Blaygard insisted that everyone in the back remained quiet so Timothy would not be woken so Drathorn climbed up front and sat beside Ben.

"Well hello, Drathorn." Ben said.

"Hello," Drathorn said. For a moment that was all that was said. The only sound was the soft whispering of Troy and Hailey in the back. Drathorn decided to start a simple conversation. "So . . . uh . . . where is it that you work?"

Ben laughed. "Here and there and a little elsewhere." He said. "I live in Gaberdan with my wife Linda but I'm not home all that often so she usually stays with Troy at your mum's place. I was hired as a peace keeper. The emperor has me try and keep the peace between the people of Corrone so that we can stay united against the Darklord's armies. It's an important job and all but it makes me angry when I'm away from Linda for so long."

"Sounds harsh." Drathorn said.

"Nah," Ben said, "As long as you're a fast thinker and a smooth talker you can get out of most fights and get home in one peace. Linda and I wanna have us a baby but we can't because I keep getting called in to all the hotspots where fights are ready to break out. Lately I've been working closer to home because of the Bandit troubles but I still don't like it . . . I'd hate to be an adventurer in these times."

"I want to be an adventurer." Drathorn said suddenly. "I have always wanted to travel Corrone and protect the regions. I know it's a big job and incredibly dangerous but it's what I've always wanted to do."

"Well don't listen to what others tell you, Drathorn. You follow your dreams. I wanted to be an adventurer too when I was young. But when I met Linda I wanted to settle down with a home and just stay with her . . . so I turned to peace keeping instead. Unfortunately I'm not home much more often than any of the adventurers these days. I think I should quit, and get a job as a smithy or something."

"I think you should follow your dreams too." Drathorn said. "Dreams are an important part of everyday life, without a dream to look forward to what is the point of looking forward? What is the point of life if there is no future?"

Ben smiled at Drathorn's unexpected wisdom. "Yes . . . My dream . . . I think I will quit . . . And I'll stay home and we'll have a baby . . . and I'll start my own armoury or smithy in town. Gaberdan doesn't have one you know . . . We can be a proper family." Ben smiled at the thought and didn't say anything else. He drove the wagon forward in silence, daydreaming of his possible future . . . After an hour or so of silence Drathorn climbed into the back.

Timothy was awake now and playing happily with Hailey on the floor. "-and maybe a bit of that fish Ben and I caught yesterday!" Troy was saying happily to his mother. He suddenly noticed Drathorn and said "How does that sound, buddy?"

Drathorn looked around and realized that Troy was speaking to him. "Sorry . . . I wasn't paying attention . . . something about fish?" he said.

Troy, Mrs. Blaygard and Pat all laughed slightly. "He was just trying to decide what to make for dinner." Pat said. "He's an amazing cook. He wants to make a special dinner as a welcome home gift."

"Yeah!" Troy said. "I was thinking; rye bread and butter with beans and some fresh fish, just caught yesterday. Oh and I could squeeze some orange juice or lemonade to drink!"

"Sounds great!" Drathorn said. It indeed sounded like a great meal; Drathorn hadn't tasted fish for almost a year now.

"What's for dessert Troy?" Hailey asked from the ground where she tickled the squealing Timothy.

"I was thinking I could try and whip up a batch of pudding or maybe get some of them sugar biscuits from Isaac's bakery." Troy said.

"Sugar biscuits! Definitely sugar biscuits!" Hailey and Pat said together.

"I guess sugar biscuits are the choice then." Troy laughed. "We'll need to stop into Isaac's on our way home then."

"No that's fine." Ben yelled from up front. "I'll take y'all home so we can get out of this wagon and give the horses a break from the day of traveling. Linda and I will take a walk and pick them up."

"Perfect! That way I can start dinner while you guys are out and it'll be almost ready by the time you get back!" Troy said. "And we'll do the pudding and turkey on the night before Aunt Pat and Hailey go back home!"

"Sounds like a plan to me." Said Pat happily.

"Yes it does . . . but all this talking about food is making me hungry . . . How about lunch?" Hailey asked.

"I agree." Mrs. Blaygard said, "Ben, how far are we from Felix's?"

Ben's voice yelled again from the front. "About ten minutes."

"Okay," She called back, "We're gunna stop there for lunch and then I'll take over the reins for the rest of the ride."

"Sure thing!" Ben answered.

Ten minutes later they stopped at a large wooden cabin on the side of the road. It was Felix's Rest House; a place for adventurers and travelers to stop and rest. It sat on the edge of the Gaberdan woods with a view of the Gaberdan River.

"We're about five hours from Gaberdan." Ben informed Drathorn. "If the Bandits hadn't cut the bridge across the River we could have crossed from here and been there in an hour but they did so we have to take the long way around the Gaberdan woods. Not that this goliath could have crossed that tiny bridge anyways."

"When was that cut?" Drathorn asked as they walked into the cottage. The lobby was littered with dinner tables and a few small sets of people who were traveling between Gaberdan and Greengate.

"About a month ago . . ." Ben answered as he and the others took a seat at one of the largest tables. Drathorn followed. "But it isn't Felix's job to fix it and the Gaberdan construction company refuses to leave the city until the Bandit problem has stopped."

"These Bandits are really giving everyone hell, aren't they?" Drathorn said.

"Yes . . ." Ben said. "They aren't actually as bad here though . . . the area between Taldi and the Paper Pass is apparently really bad for it though, the Taldi area especially."

"'Allo there Ben!" A middle sized man with a scratchy blonde beard said suddenly. "Is this here the new man?"

"Yes, this is Drathorn." Ben said to the man. "Drathorn, this is Felix. He runs this rest house."

"Aye, I do." Felix said with a nod. "Them bandits came through 'ere earlier today. Scared off a bunch 'o mine customers they did!"

"Was any one hurt?" Ben asked, surprised.

"Well one man was hit in the shin by a crossbow bolt but everyone else is alrigh' . . . them bandit's are trouble and I don' like 'em one bit!" Felix said.

"Are they still here?" Ben asked.

"'course not! They shot that man and scared all me customers! I threw 'em out by the collars! Damn bandits! I barely get enough folk comin' through here without them meddlin' with it! Anywho . . . what can I do for ye?"

"Sorry to hear about your luck, Felix. We're just stopping in for lunch on our way back home with the newest member of the family." Ben said.

"Ah o' 'course!" Felix said. "How could I have forgotten about ye? Drathorn was it?"

"Yes, sir." Drathorn said.

"There'd be no need for sir's and ma'am's in this cottage." He laughed. "I'm Felix. S'all you need to say. T'is a pleasure to meet you."

"It's a pleasure to meet you too." Drathorn said shaking his hand.

"Now my friends, I'm a busy man, is there anythin' I can get fer ye?"

Ben ordered a large lunch for the group and they soon sat, ate and talked happily together. After the meal Felix returned to bid them farewell.

"Y'all can come more often ye know." He said as they walked to the door. "I won't forget what Mark did fer me in the past. Y'all can drop in fer a bite anytime ye wish. It's on me!"

"Well if that bridge was up I'd come much more often but it's much too long of a ride around the forest." Ben said.

"Well I've got a raft out on the river righ' now . . . ain't big enough for a wagon but if ye all came through on foot ye would fit comfortably." Felix stated.

"Well I'll keep that in mind." Ben said. "But in the mean time we shall stick to the roads and the wagon . . . we must leave now if we wish to be home at a reasonable time for dinner."

"Fair thee well!" Felix called after them.

"Same to you!" Ben answered.

They climbed into the wagon and Mrs. Blaygard started the horses. In a moment the sound of the horse's hooves could be heard. "Felix said he would never forget what Mr. Blaygard did for him in the past . . . what did he do?" Drathorn asked.

Everyone was suddenly quite silent. No one said anything. "What? What's wrong?"

"Uncle Mark . . ." Ben said, "and Felix are old friends. They have known each other for a very long time. A few years ago Mark was part of the guard. Mark and his unit had been out patrolling near Felix's cottage for a group of murderers. They stopped in at Felix's place and sat for a bite to eat. While they were there a couple guys from the unit did a search of the place. They found the dead body of a missing man in the cellar. When Felix found out he tried to kick the guards out. The guards put up a fight. So Felix and his brothers fought Mark and his unit. In the end Mark and Felix were the only ones left fighting, everyone else had died.

"Mark cornered Felix and forced him to reveal the truth. Felix and his brothers had been the murderers . . . But it had been a misunderstanding. Felix's brothers blackmailed him and forced him to commit the murder. The brothers may not have done the killing but they were responsible. So Mark decided to help his friend. Instead of turning in his friend he and Felix buried the bodies and all the evidence. Felix was a free man. He hasn't killed since." Ben told the story sadly. "Afterwards Mark left the guard and joined the mines."

"So . . . Felix was a murderer?" Drathorn asked.

"Yes . . . but he was blackmailed by his evil brothers. They tortured his wife until he killed the man. When the guards had attacked the brothers a crossbow bolt from one of the guards accidentally killed Felix's wife. Ever since then we have kept this secret in the family. Felix eventually remarried and was happy. We never speak of it . . . but we are proud of Mark. His actions saved Felix from the pain of execution and he has proved a valuable friend."

"Enough of this!" Pat exclaimed suddenly. "Today is supposed to be a happy day! We should not speak of the horrors and mistakes of the distant past!"

"I agree . . ." Drathorn said.

The rest of the trip to Gaberdan was finished mostly in silence but Drathorn continued to think. He was not the only murderer; both Mr. Blaygard and Felix had killed before . . . just as Drathorn had killed Cherry *and* Billy.

IX

The Blaygard House

They finally passed through the gates of Gaberdan. It was nearly six o'clock. Drathorn sat up front with Mrs. Blaygard, looking around at the buildings and shops they passed. Gaberdan was obviously one of the poorer towns on Tanroe. Its houses were old and dirty. The shops were small and quite empty. There was more yard space than house space in the town. The few people who were walking around were shabby and ragged and most were in poorer condition than the Blaygards.

The giant wagon pulled into the dirt driveway of a small house with an enormous yard. The house was old and falling apart in places. A giant oak tree stood at the end of the driveway, its branches started so close to the ground that they could be climbed like stairs or a ladder in places. Drathorn could clearly see a way up to the top of this fifty foot tree. "We're home!" Mrs. Blaygard said as she untied the horses from the wagon and tied them instead to a wooden pole where four other horses were already tied.

"I'll run down the street and get Linda." Ben said. "Then we'll take a walk to the store and pick up the biscuits from Isaac's. We'll be back before dinner hopefully." Ben then ran off and left his long sword in the wagon.

Troy picked up the sword and led the way into the house. The hallway was small and crowded as they went in. Stairs were at the immediate left, leading to the first floor. Everyone removed their weapons and handed them to Troy. Troy began to slowly struggle his way up the stairs with the heavy pile of weapons as everyone made there way across the ground floor.

Drathorn stood in the hallway, not sure what to do with himself. He decided to follow Troy up the stairs for he had not thrown his weapon on the pile. Troy was only halfway up when Drathorn caught up and took the long sword and a dagger off his hands. "Thanks." Troy said.

"No problem." Drathorn said. At the top of the stairs were three doors.

"That one," he said, pointing at the door on the left "leads to mom and dad's room. The one in the middle is Timothy's room and this one on the right is where we keep the weapons." They entered the door on the right and Drathorn saw a room full of old weapons, armour and trophies. A set of heavy iron plate mail was hanging on the wall beside the door. On the far wall was a large assortment of weaponry including crossbows, swords, maces and axes. The wall on the left was supporting multiple sets of old leather armour. The wall on the right was covered in trophies, awards and shields. Troy walked over to the weapon wall and hung up the crossbow. Then he hung the three daggers from nails sticking out beside it. He then hung the long sword beside the Iron plate mail. "And yours?" he asked.

Drathorn untied the short sword from his belt and Troy hung it beside three others on the weaponry wall. "There are a lot of weapons in here . . ." Drathorn said.

"There's a lot of everything in here." Troy laughed. "The long sword and the plate mail were dad's when he was a guard. And the awards and trophies and such were his from then as well. The rest are weapons and armour he's purchased and found that we've used to protect ourselves. Everything in here, every individual sword has a story to go with it . . . I can't really remember most of them . . . but that two-handed sword was used to kill an ogre that was terrorizing Gaberdan a few years ago, it's his favourite. Dad's a big hero in this town, he would never leave it. But come on, they're waiting for us downstairs."

Drathorn followed Troy out of the room and Troy locked the door behind them. They walked down the stairs slowly and Troy handed the key to Mrs. Blaygard. Then Troy went into the kitchen. In one corner was a cooking range. Along the far wall was a counter where the food could be prepared. Cupboards hung above the counter. In the other corner was a washtub for washing the dishes. Drathorn thought this had to be the cleanest room in the house.

"This is the kitchen . . . my favourite room in the house, my pride and joy, and mom's greatest fear." Troy said.

"Why her greatest fear?" Drathorn asked.

"A few years ago a fire demon erupted from the range." Troy said with distaste. "It killed her brother and nearly killed her . . . Destroyed most of the kitchen before dad killed it. Ever since then mom won't go near a fire of any kind. She would rather freeze to death. Since then I have taken over the kitchen and the slightest mention of fire demons will make anyone in my family angry enough to kill."

Drathorn could already hear the anger in Troy's voice; he left the kitchen hurriedly as Troy slashed the head of a large trout. Mrs. Blaygard was in the dining room setting the table for a large amount of people. "Drathorn, dear, your aunty Pat is in the living room with Hailey and Timothy if you'd like some company while Troy and I get everything ready. Oh and do you know if he's started the fish yet?"

"Yes, Mrs. Blaygard, he just started a minute ago." Drathorn answered.

"Well it's a good thing we keep the utensils and plates in the dining room instead of the kitchen ain't it?" She said rushing over to a small dresser filled with cutlery and plates in the dinning room.

Drathorn didn't say anything as he walked into the living room. A sofa of wood and sheep wool was along one wall. Two rocking chairs and one hard wood chair were also in the room. On a woollen rug on the floor was Timothy, playing happily with a ball. Hailey sat in one of the rocking chairs reading a book and rocking steadily back and forth. Pat sat on the sofa reading a letter that had been left on the dining room table.

"What's that Aunt Pat?" Drathorn asked.

"It's a letter from Robby . . . my husband, your uncle." She said. "It just says that he's really sorry for not being able to make it. The bandits have taken control of the boat houses in Signaroc and Taldi . . . he had to travel to Veedion and pay for a griffon ride at the airport. He'll be here the day after tomorrow."

"That's good! At least he didn't have any trouble with bandits!" Drathorn said.

"Yes . . . That's what I was afraid had happened. I can sleep peacefully now." She said happily. "And Mark will be here the same day . . . they'll probably meet at the airport in Greengate and come home together."

"How are they getting here?" Drathorn asked.

"They'll walk." She said. But she didn't seem happy of the idea, "When Felix tells them about the raft they'll probably cut through the forest. Meaning they'll get here just before school lets out."

"School?" Drathorn said, shocked.

"Yes, Troy will still be going to school on Monday. Hailey's going to spend the day as a guest there. And you can either go with them or stay home for the first week."

"Um . . . I think I'll go . . ." Drathorn said.

"At least you'll have something to do when they're not here." Pat said, "That way you're not bored senseless the whole time."

Drathorn just shrugged and then there was a knock at the front door. A minute later Mrs. Blaygard had lead Ben and Linda into the living room. Linda was thin, blonde and good looking. She flashed a charming smile and sat down on the sofa beside him. Although Linda was incredibly good looking she was still nothing compared to Thira, at least in Drathorn's eyes.

The thought suddenly created a new pang of pain in his chest. Already he missed her greatly. He wondered what she was doing now; probably eating dinner in the cafeteria. How was she doing? Was she still crying? Or was she fine now? And would they ever see each other again, after that surprising goodbye and the time they had spent together? There were no answers. But Drathorn would not stay long, he *would* return to the orphanage.

He would stay for roughly a month and then he would leave the Blaygards and head north. When he passed Greengate he would stop in and visit her, maybe even take her with him . . . no . . . that was a bad idea . . . it was too dangerous. But could he really leave her again?

"What's on your mind, Hun?" Drathorn looked up at Linda. "You haven't said anything for ten minutes . . . What are you thinking about?"

Had it really been ten minutes? She had only just walked in hadn't she? "Uh . . ." Drathorn didn't know what to say. "I . . . uh . . ."

He tossed randomly through his mind for something to say, but before he could think of anything Troy called from the dinning room; "Dinner's ready!"

Hailey, Pat and Ben all stood up and rushed to the dinning room leaving Linda and Drathorn standing together in the living room. "Is something wrong, Drathorn?" She asked him.

Drathorn sighed and decided to just tell the truth. "I was thinking about my friend back at the orphanage." He said. "I miss her . . . And I am afraid that I will never see her again."

"Hmm . . ." Linda said, "It was a she? Was she your girlfriend?"

"No." Drathorn said, a little faster than he meant to, he sighed. "No." he said again, slower this time. "We're just friends . . . really good friends . . ."

"Well you can still write to her . . . and maybe visit now and then." She said. "Ben and I often go to Greengate to visit my sister . . . maybe we'll take you with us sometime."

Drathorn nodded sadly and then smiled. "I would like that a lot . . . If you wouldn't mind the company of course?"

"Of course we wouldn't mind!" She laughed, "Now let's go eat."

They walked together into the kitchen and then separated to sit at different spots of the table. Drathorn sat between Troy and Pat. On the other side of Pat was Hailey. On the other side of the table were Linda, Ben, and Mrs. Blaygard. Everyone ate a large amount and talked happily. It was decided that Drathorn and Troy would share Troy's room in the basement, Hailey would sleep on a spare bed in Timothy's room, Pat would sleep on the couch, and Ben and Linda would stay at their own home.

After dinner they had the sugar biscuits from Isaac's Bakery. They were quite sweet and were a perfect finish to the meal. After dessert Troy lead Drathorn down the basement stairs. The basement was just as clean as the kitchen above. Beside the door was a dresser with a small assortment of books on the top. Troy's bed was pushed up against the far wall and a small bed roll was already rolled out on the floor for Drathorn to sleep on. A small desk and chair was on the wall to the right, Troy's homework lay on top of it. The other wall was covered with old pictures of the family and pictures of Troy and his school friends. The room was fairly large; the only light source was a small fireplace next to the desk. "Welcome to my humble room." Troy said. "It ain't much, but I survive."

"It's great." Drathorn said. He walked over to the bedroll on the floor and put his trunk at the foot of it. Then he wandered over to the wall of pictures and looked at them all. Troy walked over and stood beside him. "There are so many . . . who drew them all?"

Troy laughed and said; "I did." Drathorn stared at the artwork on the wall. It was extremely detailed. A picture of Hailey and Timothy playing on the floor was slightly covered by a picture of Mr. Blaygard battling a great ogre. A small picture of Mr. and Mrs. Blaygard holding hands while they walked down the street partially hid a drawing of a team of crossbow wielding young men all standing together in a field. Drathorn scanned through all of the pictures but couldn't see Troy in any of them. After a few minutes his eyes rested on the portrait of a girl their age. She was quite attractive, her long hair blowing in the wind. Troy seemed to have taken extreme care on this particular piece.

Troy noticed his interest in the picture. "Girlfriend?" Drathorn asked.

Troy laughed, "No," he said, "That's Emily. I drew that about two months ago . . . before she moved to Veedion with her Dad. He won the lottery and moved away immediately."

"So she *used* to be your girlfriend?" Drathorn pressed.

"No . . . we were just friends." Troy said. But he walked away from the wall and his face showed much more care than what normal friends would have between each other. He wondered if Troy and Emily were as close as him and Thira.

"What about this one with all the crossbow guys?" Drathorn asked, "Who are they?"

"That's last year's Kami team." Troy said. "I draw one for every team."

"Kami?" Drathorn asked, "What's that?"

"It's a game played with crossbows." Troy explained. "There's the team leader and usually nine other team mates. But most of the kids are afraid to be hit and won't join . . . so our school is always a few players short."

"Well I don't blame them . . ." Drathorn said. "I wouldn't wanna run around shooting each other with crossbows and call it a sport." Drathorn said.

Troy laughed, "We don't shoot to kill." He said. "We place little balls of white paint in the crossbows and shoot. If you get hit you're out. The team with no players left standing loses." Troy looked sadly at the picture now. "We haven't one any of the games yet . . . Our players are horrible . . . My friend Karl and I are the only good ones on the team. We never leave the school. All the players suck. The Greengate Serpents always defeat the Gaberdan Stallions and we get eliminated from the competition . . . we only keep the team because the principal thinks that we might get better . . . we just laugh . . . but we keep going with it, makes him happy and gets us bonus marks in phys. Ed."

"So why are all the kids afraid of it? Does it hurt?" Drathorn asked.

"Stings worse than a bee." Troy said with a wry smile. "But after getting pelted by them so often you get used to it. The Imperial Guards use the game as a military training program." Troy turned back to his homework and stopped talking.

Drathorn continued examining the drawings on the wall; a sketch of Ben holding a fish that he'd just caught, a family portrait containing a few people Drathorn didn't recognize, a sketch of the house, and then Drathorn *did* find a picture of Troy. It was the only one containing him on the whole wall. Troy was walking happily down the street, the girl Emily on his back, both were laughing happily and had a strange gleam in their eyes. Troy's leg was still wooden in this picture but he was happy and he seemed strong. Like the portrait of Emily, this picture was extremely well done and much more concentrated than the others. If this had been in colour Drathorn would have thought that Troy and Emily were happily walking towards a window. Instead of asking about the picture Drathorn instead asked; "Who taught you to draw?"

Troy looked up from his work at Drathorn. He eyed the picture of him happily carrying Emily and then said; "No one . . . I taught myself. Come look . . ."

Drathorn walked over to the desk and Troy pulled out a spare piece of paper. His hand flew across the paper with the grace of wind, the pencil made no noise as it sketched a light outline of a body from a side view. In a matter of seconds the upper torso was finished. It was only a moment before Drathorn's head appeared, apparently in conversation with someone else. Drathorn watched, amazed as the drawing darkened and grew before his eyes. After only ten minutes of sketching Drathorn and Ben could clearly be seen, exchanging greetings outside of the giant wagon, Hailey in the grass with the horse and Pat with Timothy inside. The drawing was filled with detail not too much later; even down to the single hair on a head and leaf on a nearby tree. After adding a bit of shading on the scabbard of Ben's sword Troy looked up at Drathorn; "Have you really been standing there this whole time?"

Drathorn looked around as though he expected to see someone else standing there; "I don't appear to have moved do I?" he said.

"Do you mean you've been standing there looking over my shoulder for the last half-hour?" Troy laughed.

Drathorn shrugged, "Does that bother you?"

"No not really . . . I'm just surprised you could stand still so long." Troy said. He turned back to the drawing and tilted his head so that he could see it from a different angle. "Forgot Pat's dagger . . ." he muttered. In only a moment a realistic miniature scabbard, belt and dagger had appeared on Pat's waist.

"That really is amazing . . ." Drathorn said. "Even my art teacher at the orphanage couldn't capture an image of perfection such as this, even in an entire week. You cook like a master chef and draw better than anyone I know . . . it's amazing . . ."

"You should see my aim." Troy smiled at him. "My dream was to travel around Corrone and master the recipes of every culture while drawing the great landscapes of the world and helping the regions with their troubles." He said, "But because of this blasted leg I am far too slow and weak for any adventurer to pair up with. And the regions are far too dangerous for me to travel alone."

Drathorn looked at Troy critically. But Troy did not notice as he darkened the wood of the wagon. "I would take you with me." Drathorn said before he could stop himself. Troy had trained his hand with the pencil and his memory with the recipes for many years so that he could follow his dream. He had practiced the art of firing a crossbow as a sport to prove he was a worthy fighter. But because of his leg no one would take him. His dreams were stopped because of an accident long forgotten, possibly the same accident that had clamed his mother's brother and scared his mother so greatly. Yet he shed no tears. If Drathorn were to take anyone with him on a journey across Corrone it would be him; a boy who had had his dreams shattered by some fiend of the Darklord. "You shouldn't give up on your dreams."

Troy looked at him sadly, "You would take a cripple into the dangers of the world?" Troy said, "You would take me, a slow and weak mover among anyone, to battle monsters and demons when it would likely only endanger you more?"

Drathorn thought about this for a moment. But in the end he answered truthfully; "Everyone should follow their dreams, weather they must do so alone or not. We both wish to travel to the far places of Tanroe and beyond . . . when the day comes, we will do so together!"

It had been only a short while since they'd met, but already a bond of brotherhood was growing rapidly between them. And as Drathorn lay in the darkness of his bedroll that night he swore to himself; he would not let Troy die like Elgard . . . he would not let the Blaygards be massacred for giving him a roof over his head . . . Drathorn would battle the Darklord's entire army alone before he allowed that tragedy to occur again. And although the god's had no power over him with the necklace around his neck, he swore to Dimanious, god of destiny and patron of lightning, that he would stop the Darklord; for Troy's sake. And so Drathorn slipped into dreams.

The king stood in the manor, his Dwarven assistant stood beside him; muttering curses about the enemy and swearing loudly as he twirled his axe in his hands. "Argoss, calm yourself." The king said. "The Dragons have never failed us before . . . and they won't."

The dwarf stopped pacing for a moment and snarled angrily; "Aye, it's not the dragons I'm worried about! It's the boy! I'll not trust him with my life!"

"It is not for your life that they have come, Argoss, son of Alanrok." The king said, tightening his belt. "It is for the journal; though they will take your life as well if they can. If the boy is truthful then the Darklord needs only to seize the journal and unlock its secrets to destroy the Hellbound legacy and seal Corrone's fate."

"Then let us hope the old man and his mumbling thin-talkers can keep that damned book safe." Argoss growled. "I ain't here to risk my skin for a bunch of mages who might not be able to keep the bloody thing safe."

"There will be two battles on this night." The king said. "The battle for Signaroc will take place on the ground, while the battle for the journal is fought in the mage's tower. If Signaroc falls the outcome of the tower's battle will not matter. The mages cannot fight the entire army alone. But if Signaroc is saved and the book is taken, we still have the boy."

"Or so we hope." Argoss muttered.

Suddenly the image changed and a great dragon soared high above an army of foes. It breathed fire upon them, killing by the hundreds. An arrow pierced the dragon's wing and a young warrior jumped from its back. He fell gracefully and struck the ground with the force of a hammer to an anthill. Foes were blasted in every direction. After a moment the warrior was again surrounded by foes. "Take no prisoners!" the scream came loudly. The gates of Signaroc spilled out with men and the two armies collided, sparing the young warrior from the wrath of his enemy's army.

The image changed again, the warrior was backed against a corner; a familiar face pressing him against the wall of the wizard's tower. In only a second the warrior transformed into a giant tiger and lunged at the face of his attacker.

X

Good Ol' Boys Playing With the Bullies

May 4th, 18291; Drathorn sat up suddenly, a scream of anger and fear blasted from his lips. He lunged randomly foreword and struck the trunk at the foot of his bed roll. "What is it? What's wrong?" Troy's voice pierced the gloom of the basement like an arrow pierces flesh. Drathorn's hand made a cracking noise in protest of being hit so hard against the wooden trunk. Drathorn gasped in pain and held his arm. He looked around the dark basement. He was sitting in the bedroll; he had lunged at the trunk like he was trying to stab some imaginary figure. Troy was standing up at his desk, his homework open in front of him. Drathorn supposed it was morning.

"Are you okay Drathorn?" Troy asked, getting up from the desk.

"I . . . I'm fine . . . Bad dream." Drathorn said, laying back down on the bedroll.

"Yeah . . . I can tell . . ." Troy said, but he sat back down. "How's your hand? You hit it pretty hard."

"It hurts." Drathorn said. He looked down at it; it was already beginning to bruise in the darkness of the basement. "What time is it?"

"I don't know . . ." he answered. "I made breakfast a while ago . . . we all ate . . . mom said not to wake you up . . . You had been muttering about an army and something about a tiger . . . what was that about?"

"I don't know . . . it was a really strange dream . . ." Drathorn said. He had seen Cherry Weldum . . . he had seen himself on the back of a dragon . . . he had seen a Dwarf and the King . . . in the city of Signaroc. But was it even possible? Cherry was dead wasn't he? Drathorn shook his head slowly and sat back up. He opened the trunk and changed his clothes quickly. Then he wandered over to Troy's desk to see him starting a new drawing. But Troy had only just started the drawing and the only thing distinguishable was the sturdy legs and torso of a fairly tall man.

"Let's go see what time it is . . . and maybe get some lunch . . ." Troy said. He stuffed the drawing underneath his homework and began making his slow way up the stairs. Drathorn followed him slowly, doing his best not to bump into him or rush him. He finally made his way up the stairs and limped out the front door and examined a sun dial in the yard. "One o'clock . . ." he said, "You want a sandwich?" Troy asked, now limping back into the house.

"Um . . ." Drathorn didn't want to make him work but he was quite hungry. "If it's not too much trouble . . ."

Troy laughed; "Of course not!" he said, "If you would have said no then I would have made soup."

They made their way inside and Troy ushered him into the living room and then went to make sandwiches. Drathorn sat alone on the couch, looking around the room without much interest. His eyes lingered on a hand-drawn portrait of the family (Troy not included). Suddenly Drathorn's head seemed to split.

Pain and vision flashed before his eyes. *Thira's face was suddenly clear as day, surrounded by great flames; an evil, bark-like laugh filled his mind. "Drathorn!" someone screamed from far way. Thira was suddenly running away from an enormous burning building, the flames licking at her heels as she ran, a great white stallion right behind her.*

Drathorn fell off the couch and hit his knee hard, but his mind was still trapped in the vision. *Smoke rose from the building and shadows of many people fighting and screaming inside could be seen and heard. Thira disappeared into the woods near the burning building, another laugh erupted, followed by the sound, "DRATHORN!" and then the immense, hideous face of Cherry Weldum appeared again.*

"Drathorn!" Troy yelled again. Drathorn suddenly opened his eyes again. He was lying on the floor of the living room, Troy stood over him. Cherry's face vanished from Drathorn's view and the vision was over. "Are you okay? I heard you scream and I came to see what happened . . . and then you laughed and then you screamed again and fell off of the couch . . . and then you laughed and screamed even more . . . I was terrified!"

Drathorn looked around the room. It was quite empty, no fires or laughing dead men of the past, and least of all; no Thira . . ."I . . . I'm fine . . ." Drathorn muttered. He struggled to his feet but found that his legs would not support him. He lunged out at Troy, trying to catch his balance. But Troy lost his and they both fell hard. "I'm . . . I'm so sorry . . ." He stuttered. "I . . ."

A flash of blazing flames went across his eyelids again, for a moment illuminating the face of a dead orphan lying on the floor of the burning building. Then he saw Troy again, struggling to his feet. "I . . ." Troy finally managed to get to his feet and looked at Drathorn. "I . . . I saw . . ." The image flashed again, surprising him greatly. *Thira stood now in the burned ruins of the orphanage . . . a tear in her eye.* Then the image was gone.

"What was it?" Troy asked, "A vision? Hallucination?"

"Nothing . . ." Drathorn said, "Just a flash of my nightmare coming back." He lied. He didn't know why he should hide this . . . but it seemed the right thing to do for the time being.

"Hmm . . ." Troy examined Drathorn carefully as he struggled back onto the couch. Drathorn was suddenly weak and shaky but he made it back to the couch this time. "Are you sure you're okay?"

"Yes . . . yes I'm fine . . ." Drathorn said, "I just need a glass of water . . . that's all . . ."

"Yes . . . And a good sandwich . . ." Troy limped slowly back to the kitchen, still throwing worried glances at Drathorn over his shoulder.

Drathorn closed his eyes and saw Thira even more clearly now. *The remains of the Greengate Orphanage were just piles of rubble and burned carcasses. Their home was gone, but Drathorn just watched Thira; she stood, her beautiful, tear-stained face, looking at the wreckage.* "Drathorn?"

Drathorn opened his eyes again to see Troy standing there with the glass of water and the sandwiches. "Are you sure you're okay?"

Drathorn just nodded and took a sip of water. The cold rushed over his entire body, vanquishing the pain in his head and stopping the visions. He sighed in relief and looked about the room. "Where is everybody?" He asked.

"Mom took Timmy to the grocery store with her . . . and Hailey and Pat are over at Ben and Linda's place." Troy answered. "Have a sandwich."

Drathorn took a bite of a sandwich and immediately recognized the meat as chicken. He tasted the perfect amount of pepper and variable amounts of salt. There was also butter on the slices of bread. He took another bite and another sip of water before saying; "So what's the plan for today?"

"We can do pretty much anything we want right now . . . as long as we're home by five to start making dinner. But tomorrow we go to school." Troy said, "And on Tuesday Dad and Uncle Robby will get home! Just after the Kami game finishes they should arrive. And then Wednesday morning Aunty Pat, Uncle Robby and Hailey are going to take their wagon back to Signaroc."

Drathorn said nothing for a moment. He wondered what schooling was like outside the orphanage. He decided not to ask questions about school and instead said, "Let's go outside and do something or something."

Troy laughed; "Wonderful word choice Drathorn, that'll get you an A in English." Drathorn laughed too. "We'll go outside *after* you've had a proper lunch."

They had lunch and then Drathorn got to his feet. The food had brought back his strength so he closed his eyes and saw no vision. He smiled and said; "Let's go."

Troy got up and limped slowly behind him to the door. Drathorn opened the door and let Troy go through first. "Are you sure you're okay now?" Troy asked. Drathorn laughed.

"I'm fine Troy!" He said. "I just needed some good food is all."

"Where to then?" Troy asked.

"Anywhere . . . I just wanna get out and do something." Drathorn said.

"Let's climb the tree around back." Troy said. They walked to the end of the over sized drive-way and Drathorn stopped, wondering how Troy could possibly climb this tree with his condition. But Troy limped right to the tree and began using his arms and his good leg to pull himself up the tree with surprising speed. "C'mon Drathorn!"

Drathorn shrugged and took an almighty leap into the tree. His hands grabbed around a thick branch underneath Troy and he pulled himself up easily. Troy scrambled up and Drathorn followed him from below. After a few moments Troy's injury began to take its toll. He stopped suddenly on a thick upper branch and waited for Drathorn. Drathorn sat on the branch beside him; it had been a nice climb. Troy was panting and sweating a lot. "You go on . . . I can't . . . breathe . . . catch up in a . . . few . . ." Drathorn patted him on the shoulder and climbed up a few more branches. But he went slower now, hopping not to leave Troy too far behind.

Finally Drathorn got so far up the tree that he could go no further. He looked around him. Troy was quite a ways down but he seemed to have moved up a little bit since they had last spoken. Drathorn could see the whole town of Gaberdan around them. The old buildings were falling apart and the people were few but those he could see seemed happy.

He sat on that branch for a long time. Eventually Troy climbed up and sat with him. "That was a . . . long . . . climb . . ." He panted.

"Are you ok?" Drathorn asked. Troy looked ready to pass out.

"I'm fine . . . I just usually don't come up this high." Troy said. "Too much climbing . . ."

"You could've told me not to get so far ahead, I would have waited." Drathorn said.

"Nah, I'm fine." Troy said. "Getting down will be fun though . . ." he said looking down the immense tree trunk.

"We'll be fine." Drathorn said. "I'll give you a piggy back ride if I need to."

Troy laughed. "I'd like to see that." He said.

"C'mon! Let's try it!" Drathorn said.

"Isn't that dangerous? What if we fall?" Troy asked.

"We won't fall, I promise!" Drathorn said. "Now hold on!" Troy grabbed tightly onto Drathorn's shoulders and wrapped his good leg around his waist, a hint of fear in his eye.

Drathorn began climbing quickly down the giant tree. He took a few dangerous jumps but Troy didn't complain or scream. In fact he was yelling; "Wahoo! Do it again!" by the time they reached the bottom.

Drathorn laughed and stretched. "I would but I have a feeling that going up the tree is more work than coming down. And my back is sore."

"Ok, maybe another time then." Troy said with a smile. "But you're really athletic. You should join the Kami team at school with us! Maybe with your help we'll win a match or two!"

"Sure I'll try it out." Drathorn replied.

Troy's face suddenly went from a full smile to a half frown. "But if you join you probably can't participate in the first match. You wouldn't have been part of the team long enough. Then if we lose and get eliminated it won't matter. But maybe if you're really good the principal might pull a few strings."

"Hopefully." Drathorn said with a nod.

They walked slowly back to the house, Drathorn keeping Troy's pace. Out on the road there was a group of ten kids. They were walking slowly down the street and talking loudly.

"I don't even see the point of facing this town's school. Their so weak and poor that they don't last a minute in any of their matches! This is such a waste of time!" The leader of the kids said loudly.

"It's worth coming just to laugh at the place though . . . look at the houses! They're ready to crumble!" Said another boy.

"Still, Gaberdan's filth is making me sick . . . I wanna leave . . . It's too bad the tournament ain't 'till Tuesday." The leader said.

"I'm afraid to sleep in their hotel rooms, I might catch a disease!" One of the kids said. They all laughed.

"It's a little late for that!" Troy yelled at the kids. "Your face is so messed up even the crows wouldn't kiss you!"

Drathorn couldn't help but laugh as the kids looked at them. "You think you're so funny, eh, you pathetic Gaberdan worm?" The leader said, walking towards them with the others right behind him. "It's obvious you're from around here. Only your kind can stand to live in this dirt mound of a city!"

"You're calling him dirty?" Drathorn laughed, "Well that's fine. I'd rather be down right filthy than have a face like yours."

"Oh and you too huh?" The kid said. "How about I stick you one? No one insults me!" The kid reached into his pocket and drew a knife. Troy faltered and stumbled back a step. Even the other kids stopped laughing. Drathorn didn't even flinch.

"Sorry but you can't spread a man onto a piece of bread with a butter knife." Drathorn said. "You should save it for the jam."

"This isn't a butter knife, fool!" The kid said. "This dagger will put a hole in you the size of that over-large mouth of yours!"

"Try it!" Drathorn said. "Maybe a second mouth will allow me to say all the perfect insults that come to mind when I look at that face."

"Drathorn! Stop it! I know you're just playing around but this kid is serious!" Troy said, trying to pull Drathorn away.

"And so am I." Drathorn said. It went deadly silent now. "I dare you to strike me with that knife. I *dare* you."

"Well," The leader said, looking back at his friends; "He dared me!" He turned back to Drathorn and lunged.

Drathorn pushed Troy aside and spun. He kicked in mid-spin and the dagger flew from the kid's hand. Drathorn kicked upwards and caught the boy in the chin. In only a second Drathorn had leaned sideways and caught the dagger before it could hit the ground. He jumped on top of the kid and put the dagger to his throat. "I dared you." Drathorn said simply. The kid looked fearfully up at him, his friends stood helplessly, watching with fear. Troy sat on the ground, mouth open in shock. "Now, I'm gunna let you up. I want you to leave."

Drathorn tossed the dagger to Troy, who caught it easily, and stood up. He helped Troy to his feet and turned away. There was suddenly an angry scream. Drathorn jumped and did a spin-kick in mid-air. His foot collided hard with the boy's face. He fell right to the ground, unconscious.

"Let that be a lesson to you all." Drathorn said. Then he turned and walked away with Troy. They walked into the house and Troy began to walk up the stairs.

"I'm putting this dagger in the trophy room. I want to remember this day forever." Troy said beaming. "And you are *definitely* gunna sign up for the team."

Drathorn laughed and went to sit on the couch.

That night Drathorn lay down on his bedroll, thinking about his day. His mind wandered constantly to Thira and the dreams. It was only when Troy got up from his desk and walked over to him with the new drawing did his mind fully turn to Thira's unique good-bye.

The drawing was of Drathorn and Thira. Drathorn was standing outside the orphanage; Thira was kissing him. The drawing was done in great detail but the beauty of Thira was not nearly as close to the real thing. "Who is she, Drathorn?" Troy asked.

Drathorn looked at the picture and then turned away. "She was a friend of mine at the orphanage." He said.

"Girlfriend?" Troy asked, repeating his earlier question.

"No." Drathorn said. "We were just friends."

"You must've been pretty good friends for her to be so upset . . ." Troy said. "That was quite the goodbye."

"It was nothing." He said. "She was really upset and wasn't thinking straight. That's all."

Troy walked to the wall and put up the picture.

"What you said last night . . . About traveling the world . . . did you mean it?" Troy asked suddenly.

Drathorn looked over at him. He was staring at the portrait of Emily. He remembered that she had moved to Veedion, the capitol city of Corrone and of the Human race. Drathorn supposed he was imagining seeing her again. Drathorn thought of Thira as well. "I know why you ask . . . And yes. If we ever travel near Veedion we will stop to visit her . . . maybe even offer for her to join us. As long as we can do so with Thira as well?"

"Of course!" Troy said happily. "It has been many days since I last saw Emily. I want nothing more than to see her again. I would leave now if it were possible!"

Drathorn smiled as Troy climbed into bed; they would be leaving sooner than Troy expected . . . or at least Drathorn would . . . Troy would need permission from his parents first.

XI

Kami, the Game of Crossbows

The next day Drathorn woke in a much better manner. It was Monday, May 5th, 18291. Mrs. Blaygard had awoken Troy and Drathorn gently in the darkness of the basement. "Wake up boys. It's time to get ready for school."

"Bu' I don' wanna get up . . ." Troy groaned with his face in the pillow.

"Up!" Mrs. Blaygard laughed. "You need to make breakfast for you and Hailey and Drathorn! You have school!"

"School?" Troy muttered. "I don't like school . . ."

"Get up, Troy." Drathorn mumbled. "We need to get there early so I can sign up for the team!"

"The team?" Troy said, sitting up straight. "Yeah of course! The team!" They dressed in a bit of a hurry and Troy stumbled up the stairs to begin making eggs and toast on the range. Drathorn, Troy, and Hailey were the only ones eating at the table. Mrs. Blaygard had gone back to bed after ensuring that everyone was awake.

After breakfast they all set out together. It took ten minutes to walk to the old school. Upon arriving the three of them entered the building and went straight to the principal's office. "Mr. Principle?" Troy called, knocking on the open door. A small, bald man appeared at the door.

"What?" he asked in a squeaky voice. "Oh! Troy! My favourite student! What can I do for you?"

"Umm . . ." Troy said. "I just need you to sign a paper that allows me to bring a guest to school for today and tomorrow. My cousin Hailey wanted to see what the schooling was like here."

"Of course! Anything for the number one student in Gaberdan!" The principal said.

"Thank-you sir." Troy said. "And this is Drathorn, my new brother."
Drathorn shook the principal's tiny hand. "He was wondering if he could
join the team and take part in the match tomorrow."

"Join the team; yes." The principal said as he began an awfully long
and unreadable signature. "As for playing . . . I'm not supposed to let
anyone play until they've had a full five practices . . . but if he's good
then we may be able to pull some strings. I'll see how he is at practice
tonight." He handed Troy the signed piece of paper and bowed them out
of the office making himself even shorter.

Troy, Drathorn and Hailey then walked to Troy's first class together.
Drathorn had decided to take all of Troy's exact classes and since Hailey
was their guest she came to the same ones as well.

They first went to math. Hailey and Drathorn seemed to be equal
in this class but Troy was easily the smartest there. Then they went to
science where Troy astounded them with his knowledge of chemistry.
After science they went to History where Troy and Drathorn were actually
pretty close in marks. Hailey afterward proved her worth in language with
Troy while Drathorn struggled with the basic Dwarven runes.

They had lunch in the school cafeteria. The three of them had sat
together, away from Troy's usual friends to discuss their day so far. As
they sat, talking casually, a pretty young girl came up to them. She had
honey blonde hair and sea green eyes. She blushed brilliantly when
she approached them. Troy sighed as though he was tired of a boring
conversation and Drathorn raised an eyebrow while Hailey giggled. The
girl blushed deeper and then said "Hi, Troy."

"Hullo, Rose." Troy said politely. "How are you today?"

"I'm . . . very good thank you . . . how are you?"

"I'm very good too . . . just sitting with my cousin and my brother
today." He said, still polite and calm. "How was the talent show last
week? I'm afraid I missed it."

"It was good. I won second this year in the singing championship
and first in the dancing."

"Didn't go for anything else this year?" Troy asked, raising an
eyebrow.

"No . . . the only other thing I was interested in doesn't happen till
this Friday and I was hoping to have plans." She said, blushing again,
deeper yet. Troy frowned. "I was wondering what you were doing this

Friday . . . if you're not too busy I was wondering if maybe you'd like to go out . . . for a little bit?" she continued.

Troy's frown turned into a sad looking but sincerely apologetic face to go with his next words. "I'm so sorry Rose . . . I already have plans this weekend, from Friday right till next Tuesday in fact. I'm so sorry . . . I would have loved to go out, but my brother just moved here from Greengate and the two of us are going fishing for the weekend as a sort of get together." Drathorn was surprised; he really did sound sincerely sorry.

"No, no. It's fine." Rose said, blushing deep and looking severely disappointed. "Maybe another time?"

Troy nodded, "I'll try and keep a clear schedule for you." he said with a smile.

Looking a lot happier she smiled and said "I'll see you later Troy!" before skipping off happily to join her friends. As soon as she was gone his face turned into embarrassed annoyance.

"They don't let me have any peace do they?" he said, rolling his eyes.

Hailey giggled and Drathorn looked at him confused; "We're going fishing this weekend?" he asked.

Troy laughed, "Only if it gets me out of having a date."

"Oh, Troy." Hailey laughed, "I don't understand why you don't just accept one of them instead of turning them all down so politely. There has to be someone who interests you here! Rose was really pretty, why didn't you say yes?"

"I don't date." Troy said simply with a shrug as he turned back to his food.

"You don't date or you don't want to date anyone around here?" she asked with raised eyebrows.

Troy didn't answer and Drathorn had a vague suspicion that they were all thinking of Emily in Veedion. "I don't get why they all like me." He muttered.

This time Hailey's laugh was louder. "You're smart, handsome, polite, funny, caring, strong . . . need I go on?"

Troy frowned and shook his head. Drathorn looked at him for a minute and realised for the first time that his foster brother was indeed a handsome young man compared to most fifteen year olds in the area.

After lunch they went to Troy's baking class. "The afternoon is my favourite part of the day!" Troy informed them, happier now that the awkward cafeteria scene was done. Troy made a double batch of cookies and shared them with the rest of the class (he was the only one successful in this). After that they went to the gymnasium. The gym teacher decided to give them an easy day by playing dodge ball. Drathorn proved his aim and skill by helping Troy, Hailey and the rest of their team win seven out of nine games.

After gym they went to Troy's final class; Art. The art class was actually taught by Troy himself! The true art teacher was nowhere near as skilled as Troy was. She allowed Troy to teach the class while she did the marking of the last week's assignments. Drathorn and Hailey were absolutely miserable at art. But by the end of the lesson Drathorn had a simple sketch of a sword and Hailey had drawn a simple rose. Troy had drawn a beautiful hilltop, its grasses moving with a western wind, a small flower on the one side, with a sword sticking out of its top. The sword reflected the colorless rays of a black and white sunset.

At five thirty the day ended and everyone was free to go home. But Troy, Drathorn and Hailey walked down to the Kami stadium. The stadium was filled with sand. Great stones stuck up from the sand providing cover. A metal tube was along one side and a great stone pedestal with a ladder to the top was at the other side. The pedestal was forty feet high and twelve feet in diameter. Drathorn supposed this was a good advantage point.

The place looked like a desert. "Is this the stadium?" Drathorn asked as he examined the stands and seats around the desert environment.

"Yep!" Troy said. "This is probably the most expensive part of Gaberdan! We actually have one of the best stadiums in the Himegard region! We've had offers for Greengate to buy the stadium for their team. The highest so far was close to a million in coin. But we refused. Gaberdan stadium is the pride and joy of Gaberdan. It's also where we practice."

"Where's the rest of the team?" Drathorn asked, looking around.

"They won't be here for about a half hour. Practice doesn't start until quarter after six." Troy said, "But I like to come early and warm up a little."

"Where are the crossbows?" Hailey asked.

"This way." Troy said. He led them to a small tool shed beside the judge's seats. Using a key in his pocket he unlocked it and opened it.

Drathorn expected to see a bunch of crossbows hanging from the back of the shed but there was just a large hole in the ground inside. A thin wooden ladder reached down the hole. "C'mon!"

Troy began slowly climbing down the ladder, his wooden leg making it hard for him to get a grip. They reached the bottom of the ladder and there was another wooden door. Troy unlocked this one with another key. The door was thrown open onto a great changing room. The wall along the right was covered with old drawings of the old teams. Some of them were obviously Troy's. The left wall was lined with benches for the players to place their things, and sit, on.

The wall right across from them was covered with crossbows, small brown bags and sets of strange, black furs. Troy walked over to the wall. "Here, try these on." He said, pulling down a few select pieces of fur. As Drathorn began slipping the fur on over his clothes he realized that they were a form of armour. "You're not supposed to wear clothes under them in a real game but its fine in practice." Troy informed him.

"Why can't you wear clothes in a real game?" Drathorn asked.

"It interferes with the fur and can affect your movement." Troy said. "But we wear it in practice so we know what it's like. These little bags hang at your waist. They are your Kami balls. You load them into the crossbow and fire them like normal bolts."

"What are the rules again?" Drathorn asked as he slid the fur shirt on.

"Each team has a leader and nine players on the field." Troy stated. "If one of the normal players cannot play, or is too tired to continue in the next round, the team is allowed to bring up to five substitutes to replace them. There are three rounds and you can only substitute at the start of a round. If you get hit you sit out. When all the players of one team have been hit or when the twenty minute timer ends, the round is over. Best two of three wins. Simple enough?"

"Yeah . . ." Drathorn said. He pulled on the heavy fur gloves, strapped the Kami balls to his waist and said; "Let's shoot something."

Troy laughed and opened a trunk beside the bench. "I have my own special gear." He said. "Not only does it have the captain's badge and nametag but the leg is cut so my peg-leg doesn't trip up."

"Why do we have to wear such heavy armour again?" Drathorn asked; feeling stuffed as he tried to move in the suit.

"You'll get used to it." Troy said, pulling on his pants with some difficulty. "We need them because the force of the crossbow's shot is enough to bruise, break bones, and even kill if you get hit in certain spots. So we wear this so it's not as dangerous. The Kami balls won't kill us but they will still bruise and hurt a lot."

"I see . . ." Drathorn said. "So what do you usually do to 'warm up'?"

"Take some practice shots." Troy said. He finished putting the armour on and grabbed a crossbow and led Drathorn and Hailey out of the change room. "We just pick a random spot and try to hit it from a spot in the stadium. Well that's what I usually do . . . but we can take shots on each other now that there are two of us."

Drathorn and Troy split up and then Hailey blew a whistle. Drathorn ducked behind a stone as Troy shot a ball at him. The ball exploded on the rock. Drathorn jumped up and shot at Troy while he was reloading. The shot whizzed by his cheek and hit a rock behind him. Troy dived behind another stone and vanished from sight. Drathorn slipped another ball into his crossbow and locked it in place. He peeked over the rock but could see nothing. Suddenly Troy popped up and fired the crossbow again. Drathorn fired at the same time. The balls passed in mid air; Drathorn's missed Troy by only inches. Troy's hit Drathorn in the chest. The force of the ball caused Drathorn to stumble in surprise.

The hit stung greatly but Drathorn immediately reloaded his crossbow. "Are you alright Drathorn?" Troy called. Drathorn could just see Troy's body on the other side of the rock. Drathorn jumped up and shot. Troy yelped and ducked.

Drathorn laughed as Troy said, "Hey! I got you!"

"Yah but we're practicing! We don't stop right away!" Drathorn yelled. He reloaded and took another shot.

They shot for about another twenty minutes. After Drathorn had been hit three times and Troy had been hit twice the rest of the team and the principle arrived. There were seven of them. "We *almost* have a full team now!" One of them joked. "One more player and we will have a full team!"

"Minus the subs of course!" said another.

"Drathorn's pretty good guys." Troy said. "Let's give the principal a good practice and maybe he'll be able to play tomorrow." The principle went and sat in one of the judge's seats.

Troy started off by getting everyone to change and get their gear on. Then they had to do a large amount of stretches and running exercises. After the exercises everyone was already tired and sweaty. "Alright now let's practice." Many others groaned but Drathorn loaded his crossbow, wanting to prove his worth.

Troy and Drathorn took two others and went to one end of the stadium where they tied blue flags around their wastes and the other five went to the other end and tied red flags. The match turned out even and Drathorn's team won nine out of fourteen matches. After practice everyone returned to the change room and changed quickly. They were sore and tired but moved quickly with the idea of food waiting for them at their homes.

As they began to leave Troy, Drathorn, and Hailey were approached by the tiny principal. "Drathorn correct?" he squeaked. Drathorn nodded. "I was watching you out there, son. You did well. I think with your help we may win at least one of our three matches tomorrow. You can play but I expect you to follow the rules and be here on time." Drathorn nodded again gratefully. "Tomorrow you will not be participating in last period . . . instead you will come down to the stadium and get ready. Is that understood?"

"Yes sir." Drathorn said.

"Ok . . ." The principle said. "Get on home . . . it's very late . . . I think . . . Well its getting dark . . . be safe . . ."

The three of them walked home together, the tiny principle still trying to figure out the time.

Linda had made stew for dinner. The three of them ate gratefully and then Hailey went to read her book and Troy led Drathorn down the stairs again. "That was a really good practice." Troy said happily as he threw himself into his desk chair. "I think everyone's spirits have been raised by having such a good new player. You might be able to take over as captain for me so I can keep up with my school work!"

Drathorn laughed. He knew Troy was joking about becoming captain but he agreed that everyone seemed to have played very well today. "Tomorrow's the big game . . ." Drathorn muttered.

"Yeah . . . We get to pound the Greengate Serpents!" Troy said excitedly. He pulled out his history homework and began going over the questions. "Damn . . . There are questions on the ancient Gorgan wars on this page . . ." Troy frowned. "I'm good at history but the Gorgan wars aren't often studied and I was away for the week we were learning about them."

"I can help!" Drathorn said, remembering his night with Headmaster Bronc. "I know a large bit about the Gorgan wars!"

"Really?" Troy said. "Well I'm pretty sure the free people met in the Dwarven city of Marthandel . . . Is that right?"

"No . . . Marthandel was overrun by the Gorgans in the year 8289 when Lord Formangor was slain. They met in the new Dwarven capitol; Dargurmén." Drathorn said, impressed by his memory.

"How do you know that?" Troy exclaimed. "I didn't know they taught that in the orphanage!"

"They don't." Drathorn said. "I found an old text in the library and read up on it. It was interesting."

Together Drathorn and Troy finished the history worksheet and Troy helped Drathorn memorize the recipe for sugar cookies, only that bit didn't go so well for Drathorn.

Drathorn, Troy and the rest of the team stood out in the stadium. They were in full gear and were all hiding behind a large metal pipe. The Greengate Serpents were hiding somewhere on the other side of the stadium. The whole school and many visitors were in the stands, watching and cheering, waiting for the whistle.

Drathorn held the crossbow like a life line. The whistle sounded and the crowd roared as the teams immediately fanned out. Drathorn and one other stayed behind the pipe. Besides Troy, it was impossible to distinguish who was who. The only way of knowing friend from foe was the coloured flags around their waists. Drathorn waited until he could no longer hear the sound of his team's feet before he moved. He peeked around one side while the other team mate peeked around the other. There was one team member hiding inside the pipe. One team member was already lying on the ground massaging his leg and trying to crawl off of the field without being hit again.

Drathorn heard the team mate on the other side of the pipe yelp in pain. He looked at him quickly and saw that he had been hit square in the face by a ball. The shooter was on the tall pillar on the other side of the stadium. Drathorn took aim but he was suddenly hit by a ball in the

114

chest. Drathorn recovered and walked to the bench. The match lasted only a few more minutes. They had removed three of Greengate's players by the time their whole team was wiped out. The last man standing had been shot by four different people and was now sitting on the bench, refusing to join in the next match.

The second match started with seven on ten. Drathorn watched one enemy fall and two allies walk off to the benches. After only a minute Drathorn, Troy and Troy's best shooter; Karl seemed to be the only one's left on Gaberdan's team. Drathorn shot a Greengate player in the chest and reloaded. There was another player on top of the pillar and Karl and Troy were pinned. Karl was trapped in the pipe with two foes aiming at the entrances, waiting for him to come out.

Troy was hiding behind a rock, just out of the player on the pillar's view. While Troy tried to stay that way he was also having a shooting match with another player on the ground. Drathorn didn't know where the rest of the enemy team was but he would take his chances.

He jumped out from behind cover and was immediately face-to-face with another player. The player shot and Drathorn rolled to the side. The ball missed and Drathorn took his shot. The player fell; the ball had hit him hard on the knee cap. Drathorn took cover, hiding from the pillar and reloaded. Drathorn moved from cover to cover until he had a clear view of a player who was keeping Karl trapped. Drathorn shot him in the back of the head and began to reload. The player's partner turned toward him but Karl shot him from behind before anything could happen.

"Help Troy!" Drathorn yelled. Troy was now hiding from the pillar and three others on the Greengate team. Karl nodded and reloaded. Then he joined the shooting with Troy. Drathorn continued hiding from the pillar and listening to the battle by Troy and Karl but he kept his eyes open for the last Greengate player. Drathorn finally reached the pillar without any further problems. He climbed the ladder and peered over the top. The leader was sitting with his crossbow aiming at Troy's hiding place. Drathorn heard him talking to himself and recognized the voice of the bully from outside Troy's house. Drathorn snuck up and shot him in the lower back. As the enemy captain dropped his crossbow Drathorn reloaded and took aim on one of the enemies who had Troy pinned.

He noticed that there were now only two of them down there. Troy and Karl had managed to take one of them out. Drathorn took a shot and finished off another player. Troy and Karl now had the remaining enemy pinned. But only eight were on the Greengate bench. He looked around cautiously for the last one. Suddenly he heard something behind him on the pillar. The remaining player had snuck up the ladder behind him and had his crossbow pointed at Drathorn. And Drathorn had no where to run. Drathorn didn't think twice. He jumped off the pillar soaring high and falling fast. He took a shot at the enemy as he fell. The enemy was too shocked to move out of the way and was hit in the chest. Drathorn fixed his fall and landed hard on a rock. The last player saw him and took a shot. The ball hit his shoulder and Drathorn felt a sharp pain. But the player had moved from cover to do this. Troy and Karl both shot at once and the player was hit in the side of the head as well as the hip.

Every Gaberdan supporter cheered at the team's unexpected victory. Drathorn was out but the team had won! Troy and Karl leapt with joy and congratulated him on taking out the enemy captain. With renewed spirits the team went all in to the next and final match. Since they had won they got to choose their starting position. Troy immediately chose the pillar end. "Ok." He said. "We won one match. But to move on we have to win this one too. I'm going to take the pillar spot. I want two people up there with me to make sure there is someone to protect me if someone comes up the ladder, and someone to take over if I am hit. Sound good?"

Everyone nodded and Karl and one other volunteered to be his protectors. "Drathorn you're in charge of everyone else." He finished as he moved behind the pillar.

Drathorn looked at the rest of his team. "Alright." He said. "I want everyone to follow me exactly. We are going to stick together. It's harder to take out a constantly shooting group than one player who can only shoot once. We need teamwork guys!"

Everyone nodded in understanding and followed him behind the pillar. The whistle sounded and Karl began climbing the ladder fast. The other player followed just as fast and Troy struggled up slowly after them. Drathorn kept his team at the foot of the ladder until he was sure Troy had made it all the way up. "Alright c'mon." he said to his team. Drathorn ran out from behind the pillar. He was impressed to see that one enemy was already out and was surprised when three balls streamed towards his team. One team member took two hits and the third ball

116

missed completely. Drathorn yelled "Take cover!" And his whole team dived behind rocks.

Two enemies were behind one large rock, one was behind a small rock. "Alright!" Drathorn called to his team. "On three everyone stand and fire on the lonely one! One . . . Two . . . THREE!"

Drathorn's whole team stood and opened fire. Three shots hit the player behind the rock. He fell down in pain. Troy and his guards opened fire on a second player behind the larger stone and he was removed as well. But the third player shot down one of Drathorn's team mates. The shot had been meant for Drathorn but had missed just enough to hit the other member instead.

Drathorn's whole team took cover again and began to reload. All of a sudden another ball took out the player on Drathorn's other side. Drathorn looked up. The enemy was trying to run past Drathorn and get to the tower. Two players shot at this enemy but both missed. Drathorn shot and missed as well. Troy shot and hit him in the knee. Karl shot again for good measure. Drathorn now only had two members with him and Troy was still on the pillar with his two guards. Drathorn reloaded and looked at his team mates. "Cover me." He said. They reloaded and Drathorn ran from cover. He rounded a rock and found himself charging at an enemy. He shot and the enemy took the hit. The enemy who had lost his partner behind the big rock not too long ago shot at Drathorn. But Drathorn's team shot him as well. The enemy was taken down but his ball was still in the air. The ball missed Drathorn's head by only inches.

Drathorn panted and began to reload behind a new rock but he was on the wrong side of the rock. He was hiding as if he was hiding from Troy. An enemy on his way away from the pipe shot at Drathorn. The ball missed again and Drathorn jumped over the rock and hid on the other side. The enemy was shooting and reloading with rapid speed. In only three shots he had hit Karl up on the pillar and one of Drathorn's team mates. But Troy got his revenge with a well aimed shot. Drathorn held his position and was soon joined behind the rock by his last team mate and Troy's last guard. "Why aren't you with Troy?" Drathorn asked.

"He sent me down. The enemy captain and his last two are inside the pipe. They can't get out because he's got his crossbow on the pipe but he can't see them at the moment. He sent me to help you scare them out." The guard said.

"Ok here's the plan," Drathorn said. "We'll go to the left side of the pipe and then charge them together. That should force the enemy out into the open for Troy to shoot."

"That's a dangerous plan . . ." said the guard.

"It's takes risks and teamwork." Drathorn said. "We can still win this if we work together."

So together they crawled toward the pipe, inching forward and not being seen. They all hid together behind a rock, with the pipe in view, and waited. "Let's go." Drathorn finally said. They all jumped up. The guard took a shot and missed the captain by inches. Drathorn and the guard ran forward. One enemy panicked, shot, missed and ran out into the open. Troy shot and hit him in the side of the head. The leader and the other player held their ground and shot. Both hit Drathorn's team mate. Drathorn took a shot and hit the last enemy player. The enemy captain realized he was alone and ran while reloading. But Troy was too busy reloading to shoot him. Instead, Troy's guard, who had stayed outside of the pipe, shot his newly reloaded crossbow and hit the enemy captain with deadly accuracy.

There was a shocked silence for a moment and then the whole stadium seemed to erupt with the victory. "We have a winner folks!" yelled the principal running forward and shaking Troy's hand. "It's all thanks to our new captain and his excellent training programme!"

"No." Troy said. "It's thanks to Drathorn and our team's teamwork!"

"Well, Troy, it seems I was right to make you captain after all! And Drathorn is now a permanent member of the team!" The principal said. "And I think you should have more tryouts next Monday. There are going to be a lot more people wanting to join the Stallions now that we have actually won!"

"We definitely will!" Troy said. "But we must hurry home. My Dad and uncle will be there any minute!"

Drathorn suddenly remembered that their Dad and uncle were on their way. "Let's go, we're gunna be late!"

Drathorn and Troy ran into the stands and got Hailey and together they went home.

XII

The Fires of Icarus

"They're not here yet . . . But it shouldn't be long." Pat said. "How was the game?"

"We won!" Troy said excitedly to the group in the living room. Linda and Pat clapped happily and Mrs. Blaygard cheered.

"First victory ever!" called Ben. "How did you pull that off?"

"Well they totally hammered us in the first game. They got a guy up on the pillar and he shot us all. But in the second match Drathorn managed to sneak to the top of the pillar and take it over. He got shot but we managed to scrape a win. And then I took two guys to the top of the pillar and Drathorn got the rest to stay in a group and we took them down with some serious team work! You should have seen the captain of their team's face!" Troy was over excited. He realized the consequences when his wooden leg caused him to slip and he fell hard on his backside. It hurt even more because that's where he had been hit in the first game.

Drathorn helped him up while the others laughed. Slightly embarrassed, Troy went to the kitchen and began prepping a late dinner in hopes that it would be ready soon after the men arrived.

It was nearly an hour later that the men finally arrived. Dinner was out on the table, waiting to be served onto the plates of the hungry family. The men walked in and there was a great deal of hugs, kisses and an introduction between Drathorn and Robby. Then they all sat down. Ben was the first to start a conversation between the hungry people. "Well, father." He said. "I've decided to quit my job in Signaroc. I'm going to start an armoury here and I'm going to stay and raise a family with Linda."

"That's great, Ben!" Mr. Blaygard said. "And I have news for you all! I quit the mines! I couldn't stand being away for such long periods of time! How about we start a father-son business?"

There was lots of cheering when Mr. Blaygard and Ben agreed to become partners. "But first I will be returning to Signaroc with Robby and Pat tomorrow so that I can quit up front. It's the only way I can. It's not legal for me to quit by message." Ben added.

"Well I suggest you bring weapons. The bandits are great in the north. They have taken the city of Taldi and are in control of the Signaroc and Taldi boathouses. And we don't have the money to use the airport." Mr. Blaygard said.

"They've taken the city of Taldi?" Ben exclaimed.

"Yes . . ." Mr. Blaygard said sadly. "They massed up and attacked the village. They are apparently holding the elders and a large number of villagers as prisoners for their leader but the Imperial forces cannot reach them. If they were to attack the Taldi bandits they would kill all the citizens. And I also heard a rumour that they set up a toll on the paper pass."

"On the paper pass?" Mrs. Blaygard questioned. "That's the only other route to Signaroc! How much do they demand?"

"Ten gold pieces for each head to pass through or you lose your heads apparently." Robby cut in. "You can still go to the Greengate airport and take a griffon to Veedion and then travel to Signaroc like we did but that's a lot of money that we just don't have. I think the toll is the wise choice."

"Yes . . . but I don't like it at all . . . I would rather you all waited here until this bandit mess is cleared up." Mrs. Blaygard complained.

Drathorn listened to this conversation with interest; he needed to know how things were going outside Gaberdan if he was going to be traveling again before the end of the month. "We need to get home." Pat said. "We have everything there. And shouldn't the kids be doing their homework and getting ready bed? They have school in the morning!"

"Yes they should. Hailey you can stay for now because you don't have school tomorrow but Troy and Drathorn need to get ready." Robby said.

"Actually while we're on the subject of going to Signaroc, I'd like to come." Linda said. "I want to stay with Ben."

"Fine . . . we'll need fifty gold pieces . . . but we only have thirty between us all . . . so this isn't going to work . . ." Ben said.

"Here . . ." Drathorn untied his money bag and handed him the coins. "I don't need them at the moment so you guys take them. I want you guys to be safe. I'd rather that than to have this money."

"Drathorn there's at least a hundred coins in here!" Ben said. "You shouldn't give us all of this."

"Just take it and give the bandits what they want. Hopefully they'll leave you alone that way." Drathorn said.

"Drathorn . . . thank you . . ." Linda said.

"Just don't forget." Drathorn said. "I want to go to Greengate next time you go. Not tomorrow but next time."

"Of course." Linda said with a smile.

"Why do you wish to return to Greengate?" Mr. Blaygard asked.

"I want to visit Thira at the orphanage." Drathorn said.

Mr. Blaygard and Robby both went deathly still. Everyone looked around at them with worried expressions on their faces. "What's wrong?" Drathorn asked.

"Drathorn . . . Robby . . . can we talk in the living room?" Mr. Blaygard said.

"Yes, that would be wise." Robby said, nodding.

Drathorn followed them into the living room quietly. "What is this about?" Drathorn asked, looking from one to the other as they closed the living room door behind them.

"The orphanage is gone, Drathorn." Robby said slowly.

"What? That's not possible!" Drathorn exclaimed. "How?"

"It burned . . ." Mr. Blaygard handed him a small news scroll as he spoke.

Drathorn unrolled it and read the title; "*Local Orphanage Burns Down.*" "No!" Drathorn cried and he read the slip fast, remembering and dreading his dream.

No matter where they were born on the island of Tanroe, all orphans and homeless adults stay at the Greengate orphanage. Or at least they did. Sunday May 4ᵗʰ, 18291 the great Greengate orphanage burned down in a horrific fire. Reports say there was much screaming and multiple lights of teleportation within the building. It is believed that the Badlands' King, The Darklord, may have ordered an attack to capture, or even kill, famous wizard and scientist; Bronc Silvermask. However Bronc was reported to have left on an important business trip to Signaroc only a short time before this attack. His current location is unknown and he is currently unavailable for questioning. Many thousands of orphans and adults were killed in the blaze but closer examination shows sword and arrow marks upon their burnt flesh. This further concludes the idea of the Darklord's involvement. Many Orphans and adults did escape and they do encourage this rumour. After identifying the bodies of the dead and the living we have discovered that one orphan is missing, neither known to be dead nor living. Tracks lead from the burning building into the Gaberdan woods and they are believed to be those of the missing orphan; Thira Usonki and her personal white steed. But heavier tracks of armoured men follow hers into these woods and she is now presumed dead. No search will be conducted for this girl because all of Gaberdan's forces are currently being used to try and stop the current bandit crisis that can also be suspected of this attack as they are rumoured to have already taken the city of Taldi. Weather she was chased by the Darklord's men or bandits we pray for the safety of this young girl and if anyone knows anything we ask that they please step forth.

"Thira!" Drathorn gasped, "Thira where are you . . . please be safe . . ." he closed his eyes, wishing he could see her again as a solitary tear slid down his face.

"They still haven't found her . . . but if the bandits or the Darklord's forces are in those woods with her then she's most likely dead, captured, or about to be one of those two . . ." Mr. Blaygard said. "There's nothing you can do. It's not your fault . . . it just happened . . . they were after Bronc."

"No they weren't . . ." Drathorn said quietly, the orphanage's destruction had finally triggered his decision; it was time for action. "They were after me . . . Get the others . . . there's something I should have told everyone a long time ago . . ."

It was only a moment before everyone was settled in the living room. But they were all tense. Everyone sat except Drathorn, who stood by the window. "The Greengate orphanage was burned by the Darklord in search of me." He said to the room at large. "I am *not* Drathorn Teldaga. I am Drathorn Hellbound, the last living descendant of Gradorn Hellbound." There was a sharp intake of breath from many members of the family but no one spoke. "When I was young the Darklord burned the Hellbound

Mansion in Veedion. My aunt and I escaped. But the Darklord's assassin cornered us. He killed my aunt but I escaped.

"I was moved to the Greengate orphanage." He continued. "Every time one of my families dies I am sent back to the orphanage. But that is because the Darklord continues to strike only moments too late. So far he has missed me every time, but only barely. He finally struck the orphanage to get me and again missed. But it won't be long before he finds me here. So I'm leaving.

"I will travel to Signaroc and meet Bronc there. He is the only one who knew about me. We are going to Signaroc. We believe the Darklord will strike there next. I plan to take the fastest route possible to Signaroc and battle there. I want you all to leave home. Stay with Felix, you'll be safe there; the darklord will not expect it. And of course those who are going to Signaroc can still do that because Signaroc's walls will protect you better than Gaberdan's. I'm leaving Thursday, that should give me time to prepare."

"Drathorn . . . that's a lot for you to handle on your own. Why not go to the guards?" Mr. Blaygard asked.

"The entire city of Veedion could not protect the Hellbound mansion eight years ago. There is no way Gaberdan will be able to protect us against the might of the Darklord when his forces have spent these last eight years multiplying." Drathorn shrugged. "I must go."

"I'm coming too!" Troy said, standing up before anyone could say anything.

"No." Drathorn said simply. "It's too dangerous."

"You said it the other night! You said you would take me with you if you ever left! And that I had to follow my dreams and we would see our friends again and-"

"Thing's have changed Troy." Drathorn said. "The orphanage is gone, Thira's gone, I'm leaving earlier than I had hoped, the bandits have taken Taldi . . . Things have changed."

"I don't care!" Troy said. "Haven't I proved my skills? Kami isn't just a game! It's also a program used to train archers for the Imperial Guard! Haven't I proven that I can help?"

"He has a point, Drathorn." Mr. Blaygard said. "I don't like the idea of sending my son away but you need help. Let him go."

"Yes, Drathorn." Mrs. Blaygard continued. "Your name may not be the same but you're still our little boy and we care about you. And your father will go with you!"

"As will I!" Said Ben.

"And me!" Said Robby.

"No!" Drathorn stomped his feet. "Dad, you're staying! You will take the wagon and bring Mom and Timothy to Felix's. You will stay there until I send word and then you will come home and start your business!" Drathorn rounded on Ben. "And you will go to Signaroc tomorrow with Pat, Linda, Hailey and Robby and you will quit your job and come home with Linda to start your business before any of the fighting starts! And Robby and Pat and Hailey will take their wagon so that they move faster. They will go to Signaroc and then they will evacuate when the drums of war are sounded."

"And what about Troy?" Mr. Blaygard asked, "You didn't include him in those plans."

"I did promise . . . as long as he tries his best and has your permission I will take him with me." Drathorn said, seeing no way of avoiding Troy's company. "A promise is a promise. And I have a promise to fulfill to Thira as well!"

"Then Troy will go." Mr. Blaygard said. "Are there any other plans?"

"Yes. Tomorrow after Pat, Hailey, Robby, Linda and Ben leave I need you to go and spread the news that Drathorn Hellbound has returned. The fires of the Darklord must end!"

XIII

The More the Merrier

The next day, Wednesday May 7th, 18291, Drathorn and Troy woke up early. There was a very sad and fear filled good bye, made all the worse with the knowledge that every Blaygard had a target on their back. Hailey, Pat, Ben, Linda and Robby took the larger of the two wagons and left the smaller one for the Blaygards to use to get to Felix's cottage. Afterwards Mr. Blaygard took one of the horses and went to the post office to relate the story of the Hellbound's return. Drathorn began making a list of things they would need while Troy began writing up a list of ingredients and recipes they would need to purchase to keep up their strength as they traveled.

Mrs. Blaygard was attempting to prepare for their trip to Felix's house but was constantly interrupted by the attention seeking Timothy. Mr. Blaygard returned after almost three hours of being away and brought good news with him. "They are sending the story around in the news scroll tomorrow!" he informed Drathorn happily. "But may I ask why you inform the world that you're leaving for Signaroc when you should just leave in secret?"

"Because this will let the Darklord know I'm not with you, therefore you can return home a lot sooner and not need to worry about the Darklord. And just in case I'll be sending word to Felix's after I arrive in Greengate. I will send a dozen guards to protect you for a while at home and then they will return to Greengate. Just in case the Darklord comes after you anyways. That way you stay safe long enough for him to start giving chase to me." Drathorn said.

"A brilliantly daring plan!" Mr. Blaygard said. "Is there anything else I can do for you?"

"Yes actually . . ." Drathorn said looking at his list. "We still need protection for this journey; armour and weapons . . ."

"That I can do." Mr. Blaygard said, "Troy, Drathorn, follow me to the trophy room."

They followed Mr. Blaygard up the stairs and into the trophy room. "Take your pick." He said. "I will of course be taking my old guard armour and two-handed sword so that I can defend my family. But you can choose anything else you want."

Drathorn began taking down short swords and feeling them in his hands. He favoured one of them but then noticed the long sword. Mr. Blaygard wanted the two handed sword; not the long sword. Drathorn took it off the wall and felt it in his hands. It was almost perfect. Heavy, but still good. "This one." Drathorn said.

Troy looked around the room. He took down a heavy crossbow and the dagger Drathorn had taken from the Greengate Serpents' leader. Then he took down a fine set of crossbow bolts as well. "I'll take these." He said.

"Ok, put them over by the door and come try on this armour." Mr. Blaygard said. Troy and Drathorn piled their weapons by the door and began trying on different sets of leather armour. Eventually they both had proper fitting leather. Mr. Blaygard cut Troy's leggings off at the knee on one side so that his wooden leg wouldn't get caught. "There you go, all set!" he said. "Now you guys bring those down and put them in your room."

Drathorn and Troy had to make two trips each to bring everything down. By the time they had finished dinner they had packed almost everything. Troy sat at his desk and pulled out his sketch book. "I'm going to bring this so I can sketch the most exciting part of our journey each day. And so I can sketch the landscapes. Just like my dream. And I'm going to take all my drawings with me . . . For memories." Troy began taking his sketches off of the wall and putting them into the sketchbook.

Drathorn opened his trunk and removed *Venomstrike,* he walked over and added the poisonous dagger to the pile. Then he returned to the trunk. He pulled out clean clothes for the trip but that was all. "You're only bringing one set of clothes?" Troy asked.

"I want to travel light and fast. We leave everything we can spare behind." Drathorn said.

Troy then went to his bag and removed three sets of clothes and a spare cooking pan he had decided to bring in case something happened to the good one. He replaced all of these with his little sketch book. "Should we bring *any* spare clothes? Or just the clothes we start in?" Troy asked.

"As long as they won't slow you down it doesn't matter." Drathorn said. So Troy left the last change of clothes in the bottom of the bag and closed it with the drawstring. Drathorn didn't pack a bag at all. Troy's horse would carry his sketchbook and the food and tools, such as a small hatchet and tinderbox for lighting fires. Drathorn's horse, Starcruser, would carry the sleeping bags. Troy and Drathorn would each carry their own weapons and armour along with their canteens and the small amount of gold, enough to rent a room in Greengate, Mr. and Mrs. Blaygard were able to spare for their journey.

Once they were fully packed and ready to go Troy, Drathorn and Mr. Blaygard sat at the kitchen table with a map of the Himegard region. "What path do you plan to take, Drathorn?"

"We're going to go through the Gaberdan woods. It's faster than taking the road. While we're in there I want to look for Thira. We're going to cross the river with the raft and go to Felix's cottage and spend the night there. Then we'll leave and go along the road to Greengate. By the time we reach Greengate you should be at Felix's. We'll stay a night in Greengate and send guards to Felix's in the morning. While the guards are traveling we will take the forest paths toward Taldi. But we'll go around most likely and head to the paper pass. We'll either sneak through or pay the toll. Once we're done there we will turn west to Signaroc. If we're lucky we'll be there before the end of the month."

Mr. Blaygard traced the path with his finger and stared at the area between Taldi and the paper pass. "This will be very dangerous." He said.

"We'll manage." Drathorn said. "But we need sleep. We're getting up very early tomorrow because I wanna be at Felix's by tomorrow night. Will you be up to see us off?" Drathorn asked.

"We both will." Then Mr. Blaygard asked, "Now you want us to leave on Friday morning right?"

"Yes." Drathorn said. "And remember to bring protection. The bandits are still out there."

Thursday May 8th, 18291, Troy and Drathorn stood at the front door of the Blaygard house. The two horses were loaded for travel and Drathorn and Troy were armed for battle. Mr. and Mrs. Blaygard stood outside, saying their good-byes to Troy. A small crowed had already noticed the weapons and the sad goodbyes. And a few seemed to have already read the day's news scroll. The word was spreading fast; Drathorn Hellbound was leaving today!

Troy finished his good-byes and limped over to his horse. As Troy began to mount Drathorn said good-bye to Mr. and Mrs. Blaygard. He hugged Mrs. Blaygard and turned to Mr. Blaygard. But he was watching his son. Drathorn followed his gaze. "He will come back." Drathorn said. "I will bring him home safely if it is the last thing I do. Your son will not die while he travels with me." Drathorn was determined to make them stop worrying.

"That is not my fear." Mr. Blaygard said. "I pray to Borjil, god of strength, that he has the strength he will need on this trip. And even more I hope he doesn't slow you down."

"At the rate he is moving now," Drathorn laughed, "I may be slowing him down." Drathorn shook his head and walked over to Starcruser. He patted the horse on the side of the neck and whispered, "This is going to be a long journey . . . are you ready?"

The horse didn't seem to understand but it licked Drathorn's face and he smiled. He mounted Starcruser and together Drathorn and Troy began a trot out of town. Troy constantly waved back to his family and his home, and to people in town that he recognized. But he wasn't sad; he was following his dream. And he would return . . . some day. It finally struck Drathorn that Troy was leaving a lot behind; not only his family but school, friends, the team, and a part-time job as well.

They exited the town from the north and entered the light woods around Gaberdan. They followed the road until they saw a path branching off toward the Gaberdan River. They took this path. After a while the path slanted steeply upwards and was covered in stones. Drathorn and Troy dismounted and lead the horses up the rocky slope on foot. The rocks caused them to slip multiple times and even fall.

They finally reached the top and crossed on Felix's raft with ease after that. They filled their canteens while they floated across the river and allowed the horses to drink from its cool flow. Once on the other side they mounted the horses and began a steady walk through the forest.

Drathorn had wanted to move fast but they were in no rush today; they were examining the scenery of the Gaberdan Forest. The light roar of the nearby river, the calm twittering of birds . . . Troy's laughter as Drathorn told him of fun times with Elgard in these woods. They planned to stop at the wreckage where Elgard was slain for lunch. They rode on for many minutes. Troy finished an amazing drawing of his parents standing on the porch of his house, Mrs. Blaygard crying slightly while Mr. Blaygard waved good-bye at the unseen Drathorn and Troy.

The two of them had been laughing merrily at a ridiculous story of Troy's childhood when a clear voice rang through the woods around them. The voice was familiar and near but seemed far away to Drathorn. "Stop!" It said. Drathorn and Troy brought the horses to a sudden stop. Drathorn drew his sword and Troy readied his crossbow. "Is that a way to treat a friend, Drathorn?" A figure dropped from the trees and landed lightly on the path ahead. It was Thira.

Thira stood on the path, staring at Drathorn and Troy. She wore the blouse she had bought in Greengate. Her pants were torn and dirty from being in the forest. She had no shoes and her beautiful hair was tangled, knotted and filthy. A handmade sling hung at her waist and her ammunition was in a small money pouch beside it. A large quarter-staff was in her hands. It seemed to be slightly blood stained and she had a large piece of her pant leg wrapping around her forearm that seemed to be drenched with blood from the inside.

"Thira!" Drathorn exclaimed. He jumped off of Starcruser and rushed at Thira, stabbing his sword into the ground as he went. Thira ran toward him as well. He hugged her in a great bear hug and she hugged back, not letting go of the quarter staff in her good hand as he lifted her right foot off the ground. "I took this path as soon as I heard about the orphanage. I remembered the promise we made before I left. And it has been fulfilled. We have seen each other again!"

"Yes," she said, stepping back to look at him.

Drathorn suddenly looked at her injured arm again. "Thira . . ." he said, "What happened?"

Thira grasped her arm. "They came during the night." She said. "They teleported in with swords, axes, bows . . . You name it! They even had tons of mages. They killed everyone they saw. Even the babies . . . I escaped. I ran from the orphanage and I was followed by three of them. I escaped on my horse . . . the one they gave me in Greengate . . . I escaped into the woods but they followed me. I hid my horse and waited for them. I ambushed them when they came underneath me. Their swords were no match for my staff. But one of them did get my arm. I got back to my horse and ran blindly through the forest. I found the wreckage of Elgard's camp! I stayed there with two other survivors of the Darklord's attack."

"They are at Elgard's camp?" Drathorn said. "We should meet them. We can all travel together to Greengate!"

"Did you really come all the way here for me?" Thira asked him, examining his weapons and armour and eyeing Troy who still had his crossbow raised.

"Troy, its fine . . . she's a friend." Drathorn said to him as he noticed Thira's gaze. Troy lowered his crossbow and dismounted the horse. "Actually I heard about the orphanage and the thought of you possibly being dead made me reveal who I really was. I am Drathorn Hellbound."

"I know." Thira said. "I figured it out shortly after we met. I saw your mark and after seeing you fight Mardy in the store that one day . . . it kinda all fit together."

"I guess I didn't do a good job of hiding it then . . . Bronc figured it out too." Drathorn muttered. "Are you okay?"

"I'm fine, Drathorn . . . it just burns . . ." Thira said, still clutching her arm.

"Is your horse nearby?" Drathorn asked.

"It's just beyond those bushes . . ." She said. "Will we be returning to the camp?"

"Yes." Drathorn said. "I want to meet these survivors. Can you go get your horse?"

Thira nodded and ran into the bushes. Troy and Drathorn remounted (after Drathorn collected his sword) and waited for Thira. She returned on the back of her horse only a minute later. "Which way?" Drathorn asked with a smile. Both he and Thira were extremely happy now.

"This way." Thira said smiling as well.

But before they could start moving the earth shook and a group of trees fell over. The creature was huge! It was a giant beetle, capable of placing an entire set of buildings on its immense back. The shell was thicker than Drathorn was tall. Its legs were the size of elephants'. It had eyes the size of houses. Its face was a great opening in the shell; a dark hole with nothing but two giant red eyes. It was a Hell's Door Beetle. It was believed that anyone who ventured into the hole that was the creature's face would be sent directly to hell. This creature was a *door* to hell . . . Except it was *alive*.

"RUN!" Drathorn yelled. They all reared their horses around and towards the river. The creature screeched loudly from an invisible mouth and gave chase. Troy shot his crossbow into the creature's face but the bolt disappeared and did no visible harm. "Get back to the raft!"

"There's no way!" Troy yelled. "That thing will get us before the raft can start moving!"

"Run there! I'll hold it off!" Drathorn called. He stopped and turned left and off of the trail.

"No! I'm not losing you again!" Thira yelled.

"Let him go!" Troy said to her. "He knows what he's doing."

The beetle ignored Troy and Thira and went after Drathorn. Thira and Troy rode back to the raft, dismounted and untied it.

Drathorn suddenly appeared again with the beetle right behind him. "Go!" he yelled.

Troy and Thira kicked off with the two horses on board and prayed for Drathorn's safety. Drathorn charged at the river, the beetle staying close on his tail. Starcruser jumped onto the raft from a great distance and then off it onto the opposite bank of the river. "Jump! Fast!" Drathorn yelled.

Thira and Troy remounted and forced their horses to jump off the raft. They did so just in time; the beetle attempted to jump as well but it was far too large for the raft. The raft collapsed and the beetle became part of the flow. Since it was hollow it wasn't heavy enough to sink all the way so the water rushed beneath it and it soon got stuck when the river narrowed. The creature now formed a bridge of what seemed to be solid stone from one bank to the other when it suddenly got stuck. Drathorn, Troy and Thira turned to face this new bridge. The beast screamed and wiggled its legs but could not move an inch. Drathorn dismounted and lead Starcruser carefully across its slippery-wet surface. The bridge was large enough for even the giant Blaygards' wagon to cross and was impossible for any bandits to remove; that was one of this area's problems solved. "It's secure . . ." Drathorn called when he was halfway across. "Come on let's cross!"

"Do you think it will die if it stays here?" Troy asked, carefully following Drathorn.

"If the rumours about them are true; then no." Thira said. "The creatures are apparently monsters of indestructible power."

"That's not true." Drathorn said, shaking his head. "They are just stone tubes sealed at one end with eight-foot shells and giant legs whose insides are made of magic. I bet a few shots from a catapult could break one."

"Maybe . . ." Troy said. "But we don't have one of those on us do we?"

"No . . . but if he stays there he will make a good bridge once he's dry." Drathorn said. "Let's go to the camp."

They steered the horses back along the path and toward the camp. Troy reloaded his crossbow as they rode and began a sketch while Drathorn held his horse's reins. "How have the last few days been, Drathorn?" Thira asked, her happiness returning.

Drathorn looked over at her and then at Troy. Troy seemed preoccupied. He filled her in on the events of the last few days (but he skipped the part about the strange dreams and visions) and then gave an explanation of what he had overheard at the Icarus Banking Co. not long ago.

"Icarus Maxwell . . . is the Darklord?" Troy muttered, unable to wrap his head around it.

"It actually fits." Drathorn said. "The Darklord has access to great amounts of money to pay his assassins and feed his troops. But more importantly; if Icarus gets his hands on the journal he will have access to every secret the gods have ever left behind. Including how to kill me without battling . . . how to reverse or speed up time . . . to heal his poor health . . . to ensnare the minds of the free peoples' leaders . . . everything."

"So we must stop him from getting that book!" Thira said.

"You mean to come with me then?" Drathorn said, not entirely surprised. "It will be a long and dangerous journey."

"I have fought beside you more than this boy," Thira said, gesturing to Troy, "If he is coming I am too!"

Before Drathorn could say another word Troy said something; "I am not just 'this boy' as you say."

"No he isn't . . . he is my brother." Drathorn said.

Thira looked from one to the other and then; "But," She said, "You look nothing—Oh . . . I remember you now . . . you're that boy who was there when Drathorn was picked up . . . Troy isn't it?"

Troy nodded, "Yes, I am Troy Blaygard." Troy said, "I am Drathorn's brother." With that he returned to the sketch, he seemed slightly shy and afraid to look at Thira. Drathorn looked over his shoulder to see the outline of Thira landing gracefully in front of two horses, each bearing a warrior on its back. Troy continued to add detail for the next hour while Thira and Drathorn talked about happy days at the orphanage.

It wasn't very long before they rode slowly into the ruined camp. One man sat beside a warm fire near the entrance to the ruins. He was large and had a very ridiculous expression on his face. "Zorg?" Drathorn exclaimed as they drew near.

"Someone say Zorg's name?" the half-giant asked. His voice had not changed and he seemed to have been through a great ordeal since the attack over three months ago.

"Yes, Zorg!" Drathorn said, dismounting and walking towards him. "It's me, Drathorn! Your old friend!"

"Regal Rhino! Regal Rhino! Drathorn here! Drathorn here!" Zorg shouted.

Suddenly the voice of Regal entered Drathorn's head. And based on the expressions of Troy, Thira and Zorg, it was heard in their heads as well. *"I know, Zorg . . . Drathorn has arrived . . . And he brings friends . . . Welcome back, Lady Thira . . ."* A great Rhinoceros stepped out from behind a burned wagon.

"Regal!" Drathorn exclaimed. "You're alive!"

"Only in this form I'm afraid . . . The warriors of the Darklord destroyed my human form as we battled for your safety, but they left almost immediately once you escaped . . . And they destroyed Zorg's wolf form as well. Tell us, Drathorn, how have your duties as a Hellbound progressed?"

"Unfortunately they have only begun now." Drathorn said. "But it is thanks to your actions that they may start at all."

"True that may be . . . but I regret that Elgard's life was sacrificed in order to make this so. Why is it you return to this place?"

"We are heading to Signaroc." Drathorn replied. "This is my new brother, Troy Blaygard. And you already know Thira . . . she was that girl I rescued that night! We are heading to the City of Signaroc together. We believe that the Darklord will strike there next."

"*Then allow me to lend you our services. Any bandits that we may encounter stand no chance against my skin and Zorg's hammer. We can take you as far as the rest house . . . Then we must return. We have been hired by Felix to protect this forest from the bandits. We're fortifying this wreckage to use as a defensive outpost.*"

"The Blaygard family is on good terms with Felix." Troy said. "He will allow us to rest there, free of charge and give us protection until we are ready to leave."

"Yes," Drathorn said nodding. "And we also expect Troy's parents to be traveling along the road by wagon. They should be near Felix's place by early noon tomorrow. I ask that you escort them there safely and inform Felix that they need only a few days of his protection before returning home."

"*Give us a moment to prepare and we will set out for Felix's cottage. Know that what you ask of us will not go undone.*"

Drathorn nodded but was slightly preoccupied. As they rode Drathorn had a battle of the wits with himself; that had been an extremely dangerous foe and he was afraid that Troy and Thira could be hurt. He fought with himself; unsure weather they should really come along. But in the end he decided to ignore his worries.

XIV

Assassin

The group set out; Thira, Troy and Drathorn rode horses while Zorg rode on Regal's back. They traveled at a fast pace now for Regal didn't want to be away from the camp for too long. They rushed to the cottage and Regal stopped suddenly at the end of the line of trees. "*We will leave you here. Stay with Felix. He will protect you throughout the night. Zorg and I will await Troy's family and protect them without their knowledge. I promise that they will arrive safely.*"

Drathorn nodded. "I thank you for your help. May the day come when we see each other again in the future and perhaps fight side by side."

"*Let us hope that we both live long enough to see that day.*" With that Regal and Zorg turned back into the forest.

The trio guided their horses around to the front of Felix's cottage and tied them to a wooden pole as Troy examined a sun dial. "We made excellent time!" Troy said. "It's two o'clock now!"

"Yes we made perfect time . . ." Drathorn said. "How long do you suppose it would take us to reach Greengate if we left now?"

"Now?" Troy said, his smile turning to a frown; "Assuming we stop to sleep, we would probably arrive early tomorrow. But you don't really want to leave now do you?"

"No . . . I want to avoid spending this night in the wilderness." Drathorn said. "If we leave early tomorrow morning and we ride fast will we make it to Greengate for dinner?"

Thira spoke first. "Yes we would." She said. "We would actually make it for a late lunch if we left at approximately six in the morning. But what is your hurry to leave Gaberdan behind?"

Drathorn turned in the direction of Greengate. "The longer we take to reach Signaroc the more time that we waste when we should be preparing the city's defences. I grow worried that we may not make it on time."

"We will be fine." Troy said reassuringly. "We'll ride fast tomorrow, stay the night in Greengate and set out again in the morning. We will waste as little time as possible."

The trio walked into the cottage's open door in agreement. They stood at the entrance and looked around. A small family of Travelers sat at a large table near the middle of the restaurant area. A man in a silver cloak was hiding in a lonely corner. A waitress was taking the orders of two guards who had been patrolling the forest for bandit activity. Suddenly the most bizarre person they had ever seen walked over to them. His face was that of a fox. His torso seemed to be that of a man in a fancy shirt. His right leg was human and had a thick boot on it; his left leg was not a leg. It was another arm; a third arm in the place of a leg that remained human. His two arms were not human; one was a cherry red with a great pincer on the end and the other was like a large, pointed blue torpedo. He wore a green top hat on his fox head; a yellow feather stuck out of the hat. "Hello, young sssir!" The creature said its voice like a snake's hiss as it bowed low in front of Drathorn.

"Be gone you blasted Hergapy!" Troy said angrily. "Keep your hands in your own pockets or I'll be forced to cut them off!"

The creature turned his head to Thira as she spoke. "Troy! How can you speak to this creature that way? Have you no respect?"

"Of coursssse not, milady," The Hergapy said, his voice still a hiss but now with a woman's kindness. "Men are ssso arrogant and rude to usss women. I don't know how you can ssstand to travel with them."

"Well excuse me if trying to keep my friends safe from a filthy pickpocket is called rude!" Troy said.

"Filthy pickpocket?" the Hergapy squealed.

"Hergapy's are trained pickpockets and thieves." Troy said to Thira and Drathorn. "Why Felix would tolerate the presence of such a disgusting creature is beyond me. But I warn you again; keep your hands to yourself or you'll lose them!"

"I'd like to sssee you try and hurt me!" The Hergapy laughed, all womanly kindness gone. "The guardsss will protect me no matter what I am! It'sss their job!"

This time Drathorn stepped forward and drew his sword. In one motion he stepped around Troy and knocked the Hergapy onto a table. The blade swung down but stopped at the creature's neck. Out of the corner of his eye Drathorn saw Troy step forward and stomp on the creature's hand shaped foot. "I'd like to see them try anything!" Drathorn said. He saw the guards stand and draw their swords but they offered no further movement. "Be seated!" he commanded. "I am Drathorn Hellbound. All I wish is to eat and rest with my friends in peace. This little thief means to steal what coin we may possess and I shall not allow it." The guards looked at each other and then sheathed their swords.

"Sorry, sir." Said one guard. "We did not recognize you. Do what you will with the thief." The guards sat down again but stayed facing Drathorn.

Drathorn turned back to the Hergapy. "What now?" he asked. "These guards will not protect you!"

"Hellbound?" The Hergapy shrieked in surprise. "I am truly sssorry sssir! I would mean no harm to sssuch a hero and hisss friendsss!"

"I would expect not." Drathorn released the Hergapy and stepped back. "Go back to your seat and leave us well enough alone."

The Hergapy seemed to glare with anger and hatred but he joined the cloaked man in the corner. They seemed to begin muttering quietly and seemed to follow Drathorn with their eyes as he moved. Everyone was watching him but he gave the room a sweep with his eye and they all returned to their business. "Troy! Drathorn! And who'd be this pretty lady?" Felix said as he walked over to the trio, arms spread wide in greeting.

"This is Thira. Thira, this is Felix. He has long been a friend of the Blaygard family." Drathorn introduced. "Felix . . . we need to talk."

Felix nodded and led the trio to a back room. "What can I help ye with young master?"

"We are aware that you have hired a large half-giant and his Ali-Manicota friend to protect the woods from Bandits." Drathorn said. "I want to inform you that the raft is already destroyed. But we have replaced it with a permanent and indestructible bridge."

"Permanent an' indestructible?" Felix's eyes bulged. "How? An' how was the raft destroyed? I'll have them two fired for lettin' that happen!"

"We accidentally destroyed the raft when we were running from a Hell's Door Beetle that had been running loose in the woods." Drathorn informed. "But we managed to trap it in the river and it has made a permanent and safe crossing."

"Well thank ye fer that!" Felix said, a smile growing wide. "Now to what do I owe da pleasure of seeing da Blaygard family so many times this past month?"

"You have heard that I am in fact Drathorn Hellbound correct?" Drathorn asked. Felix nodded. "And I'm guessing that Ben, Hailey, Linda, Pat and Robby all came through here about this time yesterday?" He nodded again. "Well *we* are on our way to Signaroc. We believe that the Darklord intends to strike there next. We plan to warn Signaroc and brace their defences before the enemy arrives. No one will believe the others but they have business there anyways. *They* are going to take care of their business and return. *We* are going for a battle. I wouldn't let them come with us because they would be in more danger that way."

"I understand." Felix said, nodding again.

"My parents will be here about this time tomorrow." Troy said. "We want you to take care of them until we send word from Greengate. Is that acceptable?"

Felix nodded; "O' course! Anything to repay my debt to yer father!"

"Thank you." Drathorn said. "Now; we need a place to stay for this night. We will set out early tomorrow morning."

"I have a perfect three-bedroom family suite up stairs ye can share. Or would y'all each prefer yer own rooms?" He asked.

"Whatever is cheaper, we are short on coins." Thira replied.

"Cheapest would be to share. But ye can keep yer coins, no Blaygard will ever need to pay for my services! So again I ask, share or split?"

"We shall share." Drathorn said. "I trust your protection but I am weary and would like to have my companions near if disaster should strike."

"Ye need not to worry 'bout disaster here, Drathorn." Felix said. "But I will not argue with ye. Ye alone would know what'd be best. Now let me get y'all a late lunch so you don't have to wear out yer supplies!"

"We would greatly appreciate that." Drathorn said.

Troy, Thira and Drathorn sat down at a table and waited for Felix to return. The Hergapy and the cloaked man still seemed to stare at him and seemed to be discussing him quietly. Drathorn ignored them and waited patiently. Troy showed Thira his two sketches; one of them leaving, with

Mr. and Mrs. Blaygard waving from the porch of their home, and one of Thira landing in front of them on the path. Thira admired them greatly and insisted on seeing the others. She examined them with great admiration and paused on the one of her kissing Drathorn with a look of sadness or perhaps regret on her face. But she said nothing as she looked at them all. Troy began to work quietly on a picture of Drathorn jumping the Gaberdan River on Starcruser while the Hell's Door Beetle chased him. Thira and Troy were on their horses, examining the jump with mixtures of awe and fear on their faces.

Drathorn leaned back and waited in silence, listening to the scratching of Troy's drawing utensil on the paper and Thira's slow breathing as she sat with her eyes closed, her fingers following the delicate pencil marks of a drawing Drathorn could not see from this angle. He could only guess it was again the one of the two of them outside the orphanage.

Later that night the trio sat together in their suite. Thira had been given the largest room and Troy and Drathorn were in the other two but they stayed up late together, talking about the past, the future and their dreams.

"I want to travel the world and learn the recipes of the different cultures and races of Corrone. I also want to be a world renowned artist. But more than anything I want to find Emily." Troy said.

Drathorn already knew this and said nothing but Thira said; "You're well on your way then!" She smiled and surprisingly did not ask about Emily. "What about in the future? After you have achieved your dreams?"

"I want to settle down." Troy shrugged. "Find a nice quiet home with a wife and raise a kid or two. Just a simple, quiet life . . . how about you?"

"The first thing I want to do is see that the one who was responsible for the destruction of the orphanage is punished." She said with venom. "And then I want pretty much the same thing; settle down and raise a family . . . How about you, Drathorn?"

Drathorn was quiet for a long time before answering. "I have not thought about my future that much." He admitted. "I only want the Darklord to be stopped.

"What about after the Darklord is stopped?" Troy asked. "What do you want?"

"I'm not sure . . ." Drathorn said. "I don't want to get too attached to the idea of a future . . . not until this is over with, not until I know if I'll even *have* a future."

"I guess that's pretty smart." Thira agreed quietly, but there was a great sadness hidden in her voice as she spoke.

After a few moments of thought they started talking again. They were all really happy and sat, joking and laughing for three hours before Troy finally said "I want to go and talk to Felix; I want to make sure that he wakes us up on time tomorrow."

"Bring me a glass of water when you return please." Thira said.

Troy nodded, "You want one too, Drathorn?"

"No . . . I'm fine . . ." Drathorn said.

Troy left the room with a shrug and Thira and Drathorn sat still and silent for a moment. Soon Thira yawned and stood. "I think I'm going to get ready for bed." She said. "It's getting late and we have another long day tomorrow." Thira walked over to her room and closed the door behind her. Drathorn moved from his chair and stretched out on the couch, waiting for Troy to return.

He suddenly grew bored and decided to go out and get some air. He walked to Thira's door and knocked. "Don't come in." She called through the door. "I'm changing."

"I'm not." Drathorn said. "I just wanted to let you know I'm going out to get some air."

"Okay I'll let Troy know when he gets back." She called.

Drathorn equipped his sword and left the room.

Troy was walking back along the upper hallway with Thira's water when he heard talking from behind a closed door. Normally he would have continued without listening, but he heard Drathorn's name and had to stop.

". . . Drathorn . . . we musst do sssomething! He leavesss tomorrow!" The Hergapy's voice was complaining.

"I will deal with him." Said another voice. "He will be nothing to me."

"Fine . . . go through the window and be ssswift and sssilent while he isss alone. I am leaving."

Troy gasped and ran to their room. He barged into the room and called; "Drathorn? Drathorn where are you?"

"He's outside, getting fresh air." Thira said, coming out of her room in her night clothes. "Why do you seem so panicked?"

"It's that Hergapy and that man from the corner of the restaurant!" he said. "They've plotted to kill Drathorn tonight! The Hergapy is leaving but the man will be attacking Drathorn any minute!"

Thira tossed Troy his crossbow and grabbed her staff without another word. They left the water untouched as they ran from the room . . .

Drathorn walked slowly around the cottage's garden, thinking about the future and trying to decide what he *did* want . . . he really had never thought of it before. He suddenly heard footsteps behind him and turned to see who was there. It was the silver-cloaked man from the restaurant earlier that day. "May I help you?" Drathorn asked.

"Yes . . . Are you Drathorn Hellbound?" The man asked.

"Yes, and who might you be?" Drathorn asked.

"I am Strok Evoran, but that maters not." He said. "I need your help."

"If it is because that Hergapy stole from your pocket then I'm afraid I cannot help you." Drathorn said, turning to look into the trees. "I am here for rest and fresh air and I will leave early tomorrow. You should speak to the guards, they can help you."

"No, it is a much greater matter than that of a few missing coins." Strok said. "There is only a simple deed; a simple second of your time will help me very much."

"What is it you need then?" Drathorn asked, looking back to the man.

"All I need for you to do is to stand still." Strok said. "It is very simple on your part. These few seconds will make me rich and I will be able to afford what I rightfully need and deserve. All I ask is that you die! *Armondur Nasgoth!*"

A bolt of pure lightning shot from Strok's hands. Drathorn was surprised by the attack but was able to jump out of the way just in time. "I have done nothing to you! Why do you attack me?" Drathorn yelled.

"You have done nothing to anyone as far as I know." Strok said, advancing on Drathorn slightly. "But the Darklord pays me to kill you and I humbly accept! I am a bounty hunter and you arc the bounty! *Armondur Nasgoth!*" Drathorn jumped out of the way as more lightning flashed from Strok's hands. *"Armondur Nasgoth! Armondur Nasgoth! Armondur Nasgoth!"*

One bolt hit the bark of a tree above Drathorn's head just as he ducked. Drathorn ran right but was forced to spin in the other direction as the second bolt struck the ground in his path. But the third bolt was even closer than the last two.

"I *will* kill you!" Strok yelled, "I must!" Strok raised his hands above his head and yelled; *"Morfandazman!"* His hands glowed golden and then he acted like he was throwing something. A great bolder of stone flew from the night sky; it seemed to have been hovering above his hands. The bolder was enormous! There was no way the boulder could be avoided, it was too wide for him to flee so Drathorn stood and awaited his fate.

The boulder rushed ever closer and Drathorn noticed something odd about Strok. He seemed to still be concentrating on the boulder. Maybe if Drathorn could break his concentration the boulder would stop moving? But it was too late; the boulder was too close and Drathorn could not reach Strok. But then two guards suddenly rushed out of a side door of the cottage. They each fired their crossbows. Strok was forced to break his concentration to dodge the bolts and the boulder fell to the ground only a second short of Drathorn. Drathorn ran around the boulder to see the two guards dodging more lightning from Strok, swords at the ready. Drathorn ran forward, sword raised.

"*Molando!*" Strok called. A flaming arrow shot from his hands at Drathorn's face. But, as Drathorn knew it would, the fire sunk into Drathorn's skin and did not harm him. Felix soon joined the fray. The four swordsmen all attempted to reach the mage but were fended off by his spells. "*Armondur Nasgoth!*" He yelled again. He finally caught one guard hard in the chest. It went straight through the guard, guided by his armour. There was the smell of burning flesh and then the guard dropped to the ground; dead.

"*Isarmontrol!*" Strok said now. Suddenly great stone pillars sprouted from the ground. They grew close together and trapped the second guard between them. There was no escape for this guard; he was stuck between the stone pillars. Drathorn and Felix now fought this assassin alone but suddenly a crossbow bolt flew through the air and startled Strok out of a lightning spell. Thira was running toward them with her staff spinning wildly. Troy was limping behind her, reloading as he went.

"More to the party?" Strok laughed. "Then more shall die! *Armondur Nasgoth!*"

The bolt flew straight at Thira. But Felix reacted first. He threw his long sword in front of the bolt. The bolt hit the sword and no harm was done to Thira. Thira threw her staff like a javelin at the same time as Troy shot the crossbow again. Strok dodged the bolt but the staff hit him square in the chest, temporarily knocking him off his feet. Drathorn was inches away; his sword was ready, ready to kill Strok where he stood. "*Nymphorniac!*" Strok yelled. Vines shot from his wrist and tripped Drathorn. Drathorn lay on the ground, his ankles tied together by a thick vine and he watched as the vines struck Thira and Troy as well. Strok seemed to take pleasure in making sure Thira and Troy were completely immobile before turning to Felix and encasing him in the same type of stone tomb that the guard was stuck in. Drathorn took his sword and sliced the vines around his ankles. He got to his feet but Strok yelled; "*Isarmontrol!*" again and stone pillars began to grow around Drathorn.

They shot up too fast for Drathorn to avoid. He was suddenly trapped in the tomb of stones. But he would not stay that way. He ran at one stone and kicked off of it to the other side. He was met by another stone that he kicked off hard. He was propelled back toward the first stone and even higher. One more good kick off and he was propelled over the stone walls. Strok stopped and stared as Drathorn fell from the top of the stones, his sword ready. "*Isarmontrol!*" Strok yelled again. But this time Strok created the pillars around himself. Drathorn's sword struck the stone and was launched from his hands in a shower of sparks. The impact knocked Drathorn off of his feet as well. "*Lipesia!*" Yelled Strok's voice from behind the stone wall. The stone walls exploded in every direction as a force of pure energy pushed from the mage. Strok emerged from the arising dust and stepped over Drathorn, a dagger ready to slit his throat.

"I will enjoy this." Strok said, readying the dagger to kill Drathorn. But Drathorn was first; his hand found the long sword of the dead guard. He gripped it tight and swung it over his head. The long sword cut Strok's hand right off. The hand and dagger both fell to the ground. Strok screamed and released Drathorn. He scrambled blindly to escape from Drathorn but Drathorn got to his feet and threw the guard's sword. It spun through the air at a great pace, chasing down its target.

The blade stabbed right through Strok's chest; a perfect shot. Strok stopped dead in his tracks and fell to the ground with a grunt. Slowly the stone pillars sank back into the ground and the vines became dust on the night wind. Felix and the guard ran forward but found no quarry. Thira and Troy stood and looked at Strok's dead body with wide eyes. As the others tried to comprehend what had happened Drathorn again had a feeling that this quest was too dangerous for them. But he again pushed it from his mind.

XV

Road Worn Travelers

Troy explained his overhearing of the Hergapy and Strok talking and Felix was soon able to confirm that the Hergapy had indeed fled. The guard said that he and his partner had heard the commotion and rushed outside expecting bandits. Felix had followed the guards hoping to help scare off the bandits. The guard buried his partner and the assassin Strok in the gardens beside the cottage. The guard was then hired by Felix to assist Regal and Zorg in the forest and he departed quickly to join them.

Friday May 9th, 18291, the trio woke later than they had wanted. The night's events had taken much out of them. Troy, Thira and Drathorn all gathered outside that morning and mounted their horses.

It had been a long night but they wanted to leave no time wasted. They said a quick good-bye to Felix and were soon on their way but now traveled at a rushed pace. The horses grew tired as they ran at their dangerous speeds but Drathorn refused to slowdown; he wanted to make up for the time they had lost while they slept late. "We were supposed to leave at six this morning. We're leaving three hours late!" Drathorn had complained just before leaving.

They traveled quickly north, Drathorn in the lead, but after hours of traveling at such a pace the horses needed rest and the companions needed food. "Lunch time." Troy said as he began to collect firewood to begin cooking.

Drathorn and Thira sat down on the hard ground and waited. "It will be a few minutes." Troy informed them. "The fire may be started but I need to wait until it's hot enough to cook."

"Let's go for a walk while we wait." Thira suggested. "We can leave the horses here." They all gathered their weapons and anything that was invaluable. Then they tied the horses to a tree branch that was hidden from the path.

"How long until we reach Greengate?" Drathorn asked. "We should have arrived by now."

"We left three hours late." Thira said.

"We'll be there in about three more hours." Troy said. "Depending on how long we take to eat."

They wandered for a few minutes and then a high pitched squeaking sound filled the forest. They all looked up to see the trees were alive with movement. "They're moving!" Troy exclaimed.

"No!" Thira said. "They're enchanted wood monkeys! They are guardians of the forest!"

Sure enough one of the creatures jumped out of the trees at Drathorn. Drathorn swung his sword wildly and cut off its head with a dull thud. When he took a closer look at its body he realized that it was in fact made of wood; and it was a wooden carving of a monkey. Drathorn looked at it, confused. *How was this statue attacking them?*

But suddenly the trees stirred and more monkeys appeared in their branches. They threw rocks and twigs and even bird's eggs down at them. "Run!" Drathorn yelled.

Troy shot his crossbow and it stabbed into a monkey's forehead. The monkey yanked it out and threw it back at Troy. Drathorn and Thira ran for their lives and Troy limped as fast as he could behind them. Troy's steady limping was too slow and the monkeys quickly began to overtake him. Drathorn stopped and turned back for Troy. He ran at the monkeys, his sword raised. He chopped one in half with a dull thud then kicked another out of his way. "Go Troy!" Drathorn yelled. Troy limped as fast as he could. He shot another bolt at a nearby monkey and its squealing was interrupted by a dull thud. It grew angrier and attacked with greater ferocity.

Drathorn kept Troy's pace and forced the monkeys away from Troy. They rounded a large tree and suddenly Drathorn collided heavily with Troy as he in turn struck Thira and the trio fell forward.

They fell a short distance and then landed on what seemed to be a slimy underground slide, a moment later they were speeding downwards. They were forced deeper and deeper without any indication as to where they were going. Then the slide ended as abruptly as it had started. They hit a stone floor hard and fell forward. Drathorn stood and looked around.

They were now in a small tunnel lined with torches. Drathorn found his sword and grabbed a torch off of the wall. "Are you guys there?" he called, waving the torch around to find his friends.

"We're right here." Thira said in the dark. Drathorn waved his torch in her direction and saw her helping Troy to his feet.

"Are you guys okay?" Drathorn asked.

"We're fine." Troy said. "But where are we?"

"I don't know." Drathorn said. "Let's follow this to the end. Maybe there's a way out."

They moved slowly through the tunnel, keeping their weapons ready and their ears strained. They stayed close together but finally relaxed when they saw light ahead. They walked out into the open. Drathorn sighed as a strange but marvellous scent filled his nostrils. He looked over at Troy and Thira, a smile on his face, but they seemed not to notice him. Their eyes had glazed over with white and they were moving into the open with emotionless faces. Drathorn looked in the direction they were heading.

A great tree stood in the middle of what seemed to be a giant crater in the ground. Drathorn could see the forest above them and nothing but this single tree on their level. The great tree in the middle was an even stranger thing though; it was tall and menacing, it had no leaves and its few branches looked like arms. It seemed to have a giant mouth lined with thousands of pointed teeth. It even had eyes that seemed to glow like flames.

On either side of the tree were bushes. They held small red berries that gave off the amazing scent. Drathorn supposed that those berries' smell was what was hypnotizing Thira and Troy. Beside one bush was a giant green tentacle with violet spikes sharp enough to tear through the thickest armour. On the other side was what seemed to be a giant fly-trap that could swallow a small person whole.

"*Come to me . . .*" whispered the tree. Thira and Troy walked forward without answering. "*Taste the berries, the berries so many have journeyed to find . . .*"

Drathorn suddenly thought back to history class. This was an ancient monster called the Sentrate Tree, a beast illustrated in a story where one was defeated by the Garish hero named Jhur. Using the hypnotizing smells of its berries it lured its prey toward the berries and used its weapons; the tentacle and the fly trap, to immobilize its prey. Once the prey was killed the tree would use its arm-like branches to pick up and eat it's victim.

"No!" Drathorn yelled, throwing the torch at one of the berry bushes. The torch collided with its target and the bush caught fire almost immediately. The tree screamed in pain but Drathorn ignored it as Troy and Thira continued to walk mechanically toward the tree. Drathorn turned and ran back into the tunnel. He grabbed the closest torch and ran back out. Troy and Thira were dangerously close when he returned. He threw the torch and the second bush began to burn.

With the magic of the berries defeated Thira and Troy returned to their senses. It took them only seconds to realise the situation. They ran back to where Drathorn stood and waited for his orders. Drathorn stared at the tree and sized up his companions. "Thira, you take the Fly-trap. Troy you take the tree." He said. "I'll deal with that tentacle."

They all split up and prepared to attack.

Troy stood in front of the tree, his crossbow waiting in his hands. He took careful aim and fired. The crossbow bolt struck deep into its trunk with another dull thud and it roared angrily. The tree ignored the burning bushes and actually *leaned* toward Troy. Taken by surprise, Troy was forced to dive sideways to avoid the tree's flailing branches. He reloaded and fired again upon the tree. But one of its branches lurched forward to slap the bolt aside. Troy frowned as he suddenly realized that this would take some skill to defeat.

Thira twirled her staff and charged at the fly-trap. It lunged out and snapped its jaws at her. The staff got caught in the creature's mouth and it clamped on hard; making it impossible to remove the staff. Instead of pulling Thira pushed forward and jabbed the fly-trap in the back of the throat. As it screamed in pain it released the staff. The fly-trap looked angrily at Thira; it would not fall for that again.

Drathorn didn't stop to think or watch is friends; He ran right at the tentacle as soon as he had given his orders. It lurched toward him but missed badly. Drathorn cut the side of it with his sword and it writhed in pain. Drathorn tried to move closer but it swung wildly and knocked him to the ground. Drathorn felt a large cut on his upper back where a spike had hit him. He stood and grunted in pain but wasn't fast enough. The tentacle whipped around again and swept Drathorn's legs out from under him and another spike pierced his upper leg. Drathorn rolled away from the tentacle and threw his arm into the nearby burning bush. The pleasant flames tickled his hands and he felt the wounds heal extremely fast. He looked at his leg and smiled; there wasn't even a scar.

Troy reloaded but didn't shoot this time. There was no way he could hit this tree; its branches blocked his every shot; He needed a distraction. The branches came down at him and he dodged them. He seized his chance while the branches were down to shoot. The tree stood upright and roared angrily, it was then that Troy was struck by a sudden idea; he would shoot into the tree's mouth as it roared! But how could he possibly reload fast enough?

This time the fly-trap moved first. It lunged forward and forced Thira to jump side ways. Thira struck at its head as it went by. The wooden staff hit the back of the trap hard. "Take that!" Thira yelled at it. The fly-trap angrily righted itself and looked at Thira. Thira had not expected what came next. The trap lunged forward then unexpectedly curved like a snake. It wrapped around her tightly and began to squeeze.

Drathorn sliced again and again, fending off the tentacle's blows. Whenever he was hit he returned to the flames for healing. But on his next strike he swung too hard and didn't pull back hard or fast enough. The blade got stuck in the side of the tentacle. As the tentacle began its traditional writhing in pain Drathorn was launched, defenceless, backwards. After getting to his feet Drathorn drew the dagger, *Venomstrike,* from his belt and prepared to attack again but his eye was caught by Thira. She was trapped by the fly-trap; it was wrapped tightly around her and slowly squeezing the life out of her body. Drathorn looked at *Venomstrike* and then to the tentacle and then to back to Thira . . . And then back to the dagger. Without another thought he threw the dagger at the fly-trap. It cut right through the. fly-trap's vine. He saw Thira stand again and he quickly looked back at the tentacle. No longer armed, there was nothing he could do.

Thira was extremely close to suffocating but she was unable to escape or even move enough to attempt it. Out of the corner of her eye she saw Drathorn throw his dagger at her captor. The dagger seemed to do its job. The fly-trap released her immediately. She stood and saw that it had been severed from its root in the ground. She got down on her knees and used her staff to pin it to the ground. The poison of the dagger was affecting it greatly but it still writhed wildly and attempted to strike her. She sat and held it to the ground with the staff, waiting for the poison to finish the job and hoping Drathorn didn't do anything reckless while he was unarmed. Her wish, unfortunately, was not granted.

Troy saw the dagger fly by and was struck by an idea. He found his own dagger and readied for the tree's next attack. The tree lurched forward and Troy dodged. He threw the dagger at the tree and it stabbed into the trunk with another hollow thud. The tree roared with anger and Troy shot his crossbow. The bolt struck perfectly in the mouth. The tree seemed to choke and swing its branches at random. Troy reloaded as fast as he could and shot again. The branches did not block this bolt and it thudded again on the trunk. It hurt the tree even more but still wasn't enough to defeat it. He needed more firepower.

Drathorn ran recklessly at the tentacle, hoping to regain his sword. It struck out and missed. Drathorn curved right and kicked at the side of the tree. One hard kick off and he was propelled backwards, like when facing Strok, and over the tentacle to land lightly on his feet. He pulled out his sword and the tentacle lurched in pain as it was removed. He was knocked backwards by the sudden movement with the sword in hand. He had been hurt badly but he again had his sword.

Firepower! Troy realized. *Fire!* Troy rolled to his right and shot his bolt through the flaming bush Drathorn had been using for healing. The bolt caught fire and quickly emerged on the other side. Troy dodged another branch and looked up to see his flaming bolt strike the tree's trunk. It roared again and the flames slowly began to crawl up its unnaturally dry wooden trunk.

Thira watched her friends as she waited for the poison. She gasped when Drathorn was hit but she could do nothing until the fly-trap was dead. Her luck was finally pure; the trap suddenly stopped its pain filled writhing. She rolled and pulled her sling off of her belt. She loaded in a small stone and began spinning the sling rapidly. After a moment she noticed the trunk of the tree was ablaze. She ignored it and finally reached a high enough speed to launch the ball toward the tentacle.

Drathorn lay in pain with his sword on the ground. He watched Thira spinning her sling and the tree burning violently but could barely move. Thira released the ball and it struck the tentacle hard. The tentacle writhed in pain once more as blood exploded from the connecting point and Drathorn took his chance by summoning the last of his strength. He jumped forward with his sword and forced it through the tentacle. It went straight through. It struck with such force that the sword went hilt deep and forced the tentacle to bend toward the tree. He pushed harder. In the end the force of the blow caused the sword to sink not only through the tentacle but through part of the tree as well, keeping them stuck together as the fire blazed. The tentacle was now too weak from its wounds to pull itself free. Drathorn dragged himself to the burning bush and grabbed onto its flames as Thira and Troy ran to his side.

They watched with amazement as Drathorn's stomach healed itself in a matter of seconds. Drathorn stood and looked at their handiwork without saying anything. The tree burned with the tentacle stuck to its side, the bushes were now mostly ashes and the decapitated fly-trap was lying dead on the ground. "Are you guys okay?" He finally asked.

"We're fine, how are you?" Thira asked, handing him *Venomstrike*.

"I'm fine . . . but we should find a way back to the horses." Drathorn said. "We need to move on. We'll eat lunch while we travel. And we'll leave my sword and Troy's dagger here. If we remove them the tentacle might escape. And I don't want to go anywhere near that thing right now." They walked around the burning Sentrate Tree and found a small indentation they could use to walk back up to ground level.

They finally found their way back to the horses without incident. Troy cooked quickly, muttering apologies for tripping Thira into the hole, and they mounted the horses. They started at a slow trot while they ate but once they were done they returned to their wild sprint. As they ran Drathorn thought again that the dangers they were facing were indeed too much for his friends. *Third strike . . .* he finally thought.

They arrived in Greengate finally after their long day of traveling. They were allowed through the gates and left their horses at the public stables to rest and be cared for by the caretakers.

Troy was short of crossbow bolts and had no dagger and Drathorn was in need of a new blade. So they headed along the streets towards the armoury Drathorn had browsed when visiting with Thira. By putting all their coins together they were able to purchase Drathorn a new short sword and Troy some new bolts and a dagger. "We may still have enough for a cheap hotel room." Drathorn said as he examined the tiny bit of coin in the bag. "But there are a few matters I must discuss with Greengate's captain of the guard. So how about you guys go find us a hotel and we'll meet back here in two hours?"

"I want to return to the Orphanage . . ." Thira said. "I just want to visit the remains." Drathorn nodded and looked to Troy.

"I'll go look for a room . . . I heard the Wayside Inn was really cheap." He said. "We'll meet back at the stables in two hours and return to the hotel then." Drathorn handed him the money without another word and they all went their separate ways.

Thira walked to the burned orphanage and stepped out onto the rubble. The bodies had been removed and there was a sign telling everyone to stay away. Thira walked upon the ashes any ways. She examined the piles of ashes and kicked aside burnt wood. When she got to the middle of the wreckage she sank to her knees and began to cry for the loss of so many innocent lives and her home.

Drathorn entered the guard's office ten minutes later. He walked straight through and up to a reception desk. "I'm looking for Captain Xavier." Drathorn said.

The receptionist looked up at him through his thick spectacles. "The captain is busy doing paperwork and will have no visitors." He said. "No one will enter his office unless they are here on important business. And more importantly he will not be seeing *children* when he has so much work to do."

"I'm sure that I will be an exception." Drathorn said. Drathorn placed his right hand on the table so that his mark was clearly visible. "I *am* Drathorn Hellbound after all."

It was only moments before Drathorn was ushered into the office of Captain Xavier. "Drathorn!" the captain exclaimed, "To what do I owe the pleasure of seeing the hero of children and the only remaining Hellbound of Corrone?"

"Hello Captain." Drathorn said with a smile, surprised by his new authority. He sat down in front of the captain without an invitation. "I have a few things I would like to discuss . . . Such as the roads to the north and the problems concerning my companion's family."

Xavier sat down again and returned his hand, which had been waiting for a handshake, to the top of the desk. "Well the roads, as you have heard, are infested with bandits. Rumour has it that the Tribal village of Taldi has been taken by the bandits. The emperor does not see any reason to help or even investigate this matter so we've not bothered. As for stopping the bandits we *do* know of, our forces are slightly limited. The Emperor has ordered most of our Imperial Guard to the city of Herford. Herford is currently under siege by the Badlands. With so many of our guard removed from the city we don't have enough to patrol our borders. The crime level has risen and we believe the enemy may have spies hidden inside or near the city. As for your companion's problems . . . I haven't any idea what you speak of."

"I fear for their lives." Drathorn said. "I have reason to believe that the Darklord actually attacked the orphanage in search of me. I also think he now knows that I am in the custody of the Blaygard family. I wish for you to send a unit to protect the family. They should be at the resting cottage of Felix near the Gaberdan woods. I wish for your unit to go there and stay with them for three days. Then go to Gaberdan and continue to protect them for another month. Then they may return to Greengate. The family is to be able to continue all normal activity as if the guards were not there. I would entrust this to the Gaberdan guard but I have greater trust for you and your forces."

"I see . . ." The captain said. "But like I said . . . we have no forces to do that with."

"The darklord will use them to get to me." Drathorn said. "By protecting *them* you can say that you are protecting *me*."

"If you put it that way then we will set out early tomorrow morning." Xavier said.

Drathorn, Thira and Troy soon met up again and Troy took them to the room he had rented. Drathorn went to bed early; he went into a bedroom of the three bedded room and lay down in bed listening to Thira and Troy talking but not really hearing the words.

Troy got out of bed the next morning and began slowly getting a pot of coffee ready for the others. Suddenly he noticed a small piece of paper on the dining room table. He set down the coffee and read the first line of the note.

He dropped the paper and limped to Drathorn's room. It took only a moment for him to realize the truth behind his fears. He ran as fast as he could to Thira's room and threw the door open. "Thira! He's gone!"

Thira groaned. "Who?" She muttered as she hid her face under the sheets. "And don't you knock?"

"I'm very sorry Thira but its Drathorn." He said. "He's gone."

XVI

Departure

Drathorn and Xavier's conversation didn't end like it should have that day. Drathorn still had more to say. "But before the guard goes to pick them up from Felix's I need one more favour." Drathorn had said.

"And what is that?" Xavier asked.

"I am traveling with two companions." Drathorn said. "One is Troy Blaygard, as you have surely heard. The other is Thira Usonki, she escaped into the Gaberdan woods and we found her while we were cutting through."

"So she has been found!" Xavier said happily. "Thank Dimanious for her destiny!"

"You may thank the god of Destiny for her safety but I pray to Aleena that Thira isn't any more beautiful than she is or even Dimanious wouldn't have been able to protect her from the thugs of those woods." Drathorn said.

"Perhaps . . . but what is your point about these companions?" Xavier asked.

"The roads are far too dangerous for them . . ." Drathorn said. "As are the woods . . . Especially between here and Signaroc. I have already nearly lost them three times since leaving Gaberdan. Once to a Hell's Door Beetle, then to an assassin and the third time to a Sentrate Tree. I fear that if they continue at my side I will lose them both. I want your guards to stop in at the Wayside Inn before leaving tomorrow and pick them up. They are to be taken with the Blaygards to safety. But do not harm any of them."

"It sounds like you have met many dangers on the roads." Xavier noted. "The Hell's Door Beetles have been appearing a lot more often all over Tanroe, but assassins and Sentrate Trees? The age is truly darker than we believe. We shall do as you ask. I will *personally* go with two dozen of my guards to protect your family and friends. You have my greatest protection available to you whenever needed. I won't let anything happen to them."

With the protection of his friends insured Drathorn returned to meet Troy and Thira. He acted as if nothing were different but went to bed early. He listened to the soft sound of their voices but heard no words as he wrote his goodbyes upon a piece of paper.

After they were asleep Drathorn snuck out and placed the note on the table. He gathered his weapons and armour and prepared to depart. But then he saw a picture Troy had drawn. It was the three of them at Felix's. They were all laughing and having an amazing time. Drathorn picked it up and decided he would take it with him, to remind him of his reason for fighting . . . and for leaving.

Then he snuck out of the hotel room and out of the Wayside Inn. He walked to the stables and found the horses. He patted Troy's horse on the side of the face. He ran his fingers through Thira's horse's mane and then went to Starcruser. "We must go, my friend." Drathorn whispered to him. "The roads ahead are dangerous and we cannot take the others with us." Starcruser looked at him with an eye of understanding even though the great beast could not possibly understand. Drathorn placed a few food items in his saddle bag and then mounted. While on Starcruser's back Drathorn moved *Venomstrike* down his leg and tied it around his shin so it was hidden beneath his pants. "Just in case." He said. Then he kicked his heels and away they went; speeding out of the stables.

The night was still young and they had time to move forward. They would go north, stopping only for food. They would ride tonight . . . and in the morning but after that they would take the nights to rest. They *must* reach Signaroc.

Saturday May 10th, 18291; "What do you mean 'Drathorn's gone'?" Thira exclaimed as she leapt out of bed. She was wearing a thin night shirt and short-shorts and her hair was slightly a mess from sleeping but she was too worried about Drathorn to care about her appearance. She ran out of her room and into Drathorn's where she stopped and stared. The bed was made neatly and the nightstand no longer held his magical dagger. His new sword and his armour were no longer heaped in the corner, his saddle bags had disappeared as well. There was no evidence that anyone had ever been in this room.

Thira stared at the room; unseeing, unmoving, not knowing what to think. "He left this." Troy said as he handed over Drathorn's note. "Read it aloud . . . I only saw the first few lines."

Thira looked at the note and began to read.

"Dear Companions,

It is with deep regret that I must say this is the end. The roads are too dangerous for you to come with me. I want you to return to Gaberdan where it is safest."

"That's all I read." Troy interrupted. "And then I came and got you."

"I first realized the real dangers when we were ambushed by the Hell's Door Beetle. I ignored my fears and continued to allow your company. But after the encounter with Strok at Felix's cabin I wasn't too sure about this decision. Yet I ignored my fears again. But after seeing what nearly happened with that Sentrate Tree I have realized that you cannot *come with me.*

I know I promised Troy could come with me . . . and I promised Thira we would meet again . . . and I fulfilled both of those promises . . . we just didn't go all the way. Two dozen guards will be there shortly to pick you up. They will escort you to Felix's cabin and pick up the Blaygards. After that you will be taken back to Gaberdan and kept under their protection for one month. After that they will leave but I wish for you to stay in *Gaberdan.*

I do not believe that I am strong enough to protect you. Until I can become strong enough I must refuse your company. Perhaps when Signaroc has been saved I will rethink this matter and return for you. Either way; I will send a messenger from Signaroc after the battle to let you know how things are going. I hope everything goes well.

F.Y.S.
Drathorn Hellbound"

By the way Troy, I took that picture of the three of us at Felix's cabin . . . to remind me why I'm fighting.

"This is ridiculous!" Thira exclaimed. "He would be dead if I hadn't been able to save him from that tentacle with my sling! And what does 'F.Y.S.' mean?"

"I don't know . . . probably something Drathorn came up with. And not necessarily." Troy said thoughtfully. "If he hadn't had to throw you the dagger he would have been fine."

"So this is my fault is it?" Thira yelled.

"Of course not!" Troy said. "We could have found a way around that huge hole if I hadn't made Drathorn come back for me."

"So then it's both of our faults!" Thira screamed. "That makes such a big difference!"

"No, no, no!" Troy said, slowly raising his voice so she would listen. "You misunderstand me! I mean that we make tiny errors that can sometimes cause trouble and when one of us is hurt Drathorn blames himself for not being able to protect us from his enemy."

Thira looked at him with a confused look. "I knew that already. You think I'm an idiot?"

"I-" Troy stuttered. "Umm . . . it's not . . . it's not . . . Oh, Davearous, god of wisdom, what do we do?"

Before Thira could answer there was a knock at the door. "Do you think that's Drathorn coming back to say he changed his mind?" she whispered.

"Don't get your hopes up. It's probably the guards coming to pick us up." Troy whispered back.

There was another knock on the door. "What do we do if it is?" Thira asked. "I'm not letting Drathorn go alone."

"Well we can't just run away or they'll come after us." Troy threw a glance at the door. "We'll have to at least talk to them." Another knock hit the door, louder this time. "Just a moment!" he yelled at the door. "Get dressed. We'll explain the situation to the guards and go after Drathorn. If they try to stop us we'll fight our way out."

"Oh great and then we'll be running after Drathorn with the whole Imperial guard on top of us!" Thira rolled her eyes but ran to get her stuff. Troy could hear her muttering "He'll just love that won't he?"

There was another knock, this time followed by a voice; "Open up, this is Captain Xavier of the Greengate guard!"

"One moment please." Troy called. He ran to his room and pulled on a shirt to cover his bare torso. Then he returned and opened the door.

"About time!" Xavier groaned, walking into the room and looking around without an invitation. "Where's your friend? I'm sure Drathorn told you what was going on? Hurry up we must leave quickly we're already running late!"

Thira suddenly walked out of her room and said "Troy have you seen my sweater?"

"By Aleena! You *are* a beautiful one!" Xavier suddenly exclaimed. "It's much different to look upon you and not have you hiding your face in Drathorn's shoulder the whole time."

"It's on the chair you used to eat dinner last night. You took it off while we were eating." Troy said as Thira blushed crimson at Xavier's comment. "And you." Troy turned on the captain angrily. "Her name is Thira! Not 'your friend' and not Aleena! Get it right or don't say it at all."

"Of course." Xavier laughed. "I apologize. I guess it would be best if we introduced ourselves. We will all be together for quite a while after all. I am Captain Xavier of the Greengate guard. This is-"

"We care not for names or titles and we will *not* be traveling together." Thira said. "We're going after Drathorn."

"I'm guessing he didn't inform you on what was going on then?" Xavier asked.

"He didn't say a damn thing. Just left a note and disappeared." Troy said. "We're not letting him go alone! We're going after him and if you try and stop us we'll fight you." He picked up his crossbow from the couch and looked meaningfully at him.

Every guard drew their weapons. Suddenly everyone in the room was pointing weapons at each other . . . Everyone except Xavier.

Xavier remained quite calm. He looked around and thought about the situation. Then he sighed. "Drathorn left at three in the morning, he rode on his horse and moved at a breakneck speed. He is probably miles from here by now. If you wish to go after him then you may. We'll not stop you." At a wave of his hand his men lowered their weapons. "He will reach Taldi sometime tomorrow. I expect he will travel across the sea to Signaroc, as long as the boat house is safe. May Deheano grant you the time needed to catch up to him."

Troy wasn't sure what to believe but only a moment later the guards had left the hotel and were seen speeding away on horseback in a southern direction. "Get your armour on." Troy said to Thira. "We ride north."

She just smiled.

Drathorn had the advantage of speed and time on his hands but the friends who followed him without his knowledge still had a chance; especially when Drathorn had run into a problem of his own.

"ATTACK!" arrows flew at Drathorn from behind the bushes on one side of the road. It was nearly dawn and back in Greengate Troy and Thira were still sound asleep. "C'mon lads! Get 'im!"

More arrows and bolts flew past Drathorn. Bandits bearing swords, axes, spears and an assortment of other weapons charged from the bushes. Drathorn drew his new sword and leapt off of Starcruser. He swung his sword in an arc and ripped open an approaching bandit in a matter of seconds. A second bandit bearing a short sword ran at him. Drathorn stabbed him through and used him to shield himself from the enemy archers. Two arrows struck the dead bandit along with three crossbow bolts. The last bolt missed. It seemed that the archers were on the east side of the road and the others were rushing from their hiding spot on the west.

Drathorn pulled his sword out of his victim and smacked Starcruser's hind quarters. The horse suddenly bolted forward, quickly leaving Drathorn behind. Drathorn smacked aside a stray arrow and decapitated another bandit. After avoiding three more enemy shots and killing two enemy bandits Drathorn managed to get off the road and find cover in the trees. "Archers get a vantage point and aim at the trees." A large bandit with a shield and hand-axe called. "The rest of you get in there and find him!" The many heavily equipped bandits began to slowly and cautiously approach the forest. The leader and two others remained out in the open and the archers were nowhere to be found.

Drathorn quickly climbed a nearby tree and waited as the group of seven remaining bandits entered the woods all staying fairly close together. Drathorn used a nearby vine to make a lasso and threw it down on the forest floor and then he waited.

Murlok entered the woods with his companions; his spear held ready, two more tied to his back and a sword sheathed at each hip. Where was that man? Had he seen something fall from the trees? Was it really the trees rustling in the distance? They stepped further forward, cautious of the dark haired, sword bearing character they hunted. Suddenly the man he was following stopped and looked down. He followed his gaze. A vine had tightened around his companion's ankle. Within a second he was yanked upwards by the vine, screaming and kicking, all weapons abandoned.

"There!" the second in command called. Everyone launched spears into the trees, including Murlok. There were multiple sounds of spears striking wood but no sound of them hitting their enemy.

There was the sound of laughing from behind, mixed with the sound of "Please! Please don't kill me!" As everyone reached for more spears an object fell from the tree. No one moved. They all stared at the object lying in the grass; it was a head.

"Are you guys going to let me down or what?" a voice called. "Just let me down easy. Don't worry he's dead."

One of Murlok's companions cheered and ran forward. He grabbed an end of the vine and began slowly letting his companion down . . . But it wasn't his companion at all. Before anyone could yell to stop the bandit had lowered their enemy to the ground. Their enemy had hung himself by the ankle after killing the bandit to fool them. Before anyone could say anything the enemy had stabbed Murlok's companion with one of their own spears. In only a second the man had spun, while upside down and thrown a second spear at the bandit beside Murlok.

A sword fell from the man's belt right into his hand and he twirled with acrobatic skill and cut the rope. Before he could land on his head, however, he did a flip and twist in midair and landed flat on his feet, decapitating another of Murlok's companions in the process. Murlok threw his second spear at the man but he swatted it away with his blade. As Murlok readied another spear the man began battling with Murlok's companions. The man crouched down and cut off one of Murlok's companions' legs and he fell fast. Murlok threw his spear, hoping to stop the killer. But the man side stepped and caught the spear then twisted and drove it threw

Murlok's last standing companion. Murlok drew his blades and charged just as the man drove his sword into the one legged bandit.

Drathorn stood and watched as the young bandit charged at him. Drathorn could feel the bandits fear but his anger was much stronger as it continued to drive him towards Drathorn. Drathorn pulled his sword out of the chest of his enemy and waited patiently for the young bandit. The bandit attacked, Drathorn blocked and side stepped. As the bandit marvelled at his skill Drathorn slashed the bandit across the back. He screamed and fell to the ground, twisting and landing on his injured back. Drathorn smiled to himself, he was a much better fighter when he was not looking over his shoulder to make sure his friends were safe.

Unable to move, the bandit just looked up at him. "Get it over with then." He groaned. "I don't wanna suffer . . . just end it for me."

"What is your name?" Drathorn asked, sheathing his sword.

The bandit looked up at him. "Murlok . . . but why does it matter to you? Just kill me."

"Well, Murlok." Drathorn said after considering the young man, "One should not beg for death so readily. The wound you have sustained hurts greatly I believe but it will not kill you. I suggest you wait a little while and then go see a healer. I will leave you alive this time, but if you cross my path again I will not be so forgiving."

Drathorn turned and walked away from Murlok. He could not bring himself to kill this man; he was only a few years older than Drathorn himself, barely even into manhood. He looked out at the road from behind a tree. Murlok's commander was still standing in the open with his two men. Drathorn walked north for a few moments and then crossed the road to the side the archers were hidden on. He snuck slowly through the trees; two cross-bow bandits were standing together looking across the road at where Murlok was lying just out of their sight. Drathorn could feel their fear.

He snuck up behind one of them and tapped him on the shoulder. The bandit turned and looked at him. He gasped but it was too late. Drathorn stabbed right through him. His companion aimed at him but Drathorn pulled out his sword, cut the crossbow in half and killed him with a swipe across the chest.

As he snuck along looking for the others he found and disposed of two archers and then three more crossbowmen. On the back of his last victim Drathorn found a sturdy spear. He took it and began walking north again. He soon found Starcruser along the road. He greeted the steed again and was given a great amount of "kisses" from his wet tongue. Drathorn mounted Starcruser and turned back towards the remaining bandits. He dug in his heels and rode forward; the spear in his right hand, his sword in the other.

He rode fast up the path and then he could soon see the bandit leader and his two final bandits. The two bandits noticed him on his horse and one began to charge. The other stood his ground with a tall halberd. The leader looked and took a few clumsy steps back before readying his hand axe.

Drathorn stabbed out at the charging enemy with the spear, impaling him on the end and quickly pulling it out so as not to be thrown off Starcruser's back by the impact. At the last second they swivelled to one side of the second bandit and avoided being impaled on the bandit's halberd. Drathorn decapitated him as they rode by. The lead bandit threw his hand axe at Drathorn and he knocked it aside with his sword. The bandit turned and began to run in fear as Drathorn and Starcruser quickly gave chase. Seeing that Drathorn was catching up the leader threw away his wooden shield and ran faster. Drathorn threw the spear and it struck right through the bandit's calf.

Drathorn stopped and dismounted. He walked over to the bandit and looked at him. The bandit looked up at his face, breathing heavily but unable to move as Drathorn brought his face closer. "Who do you work for?" Drathorn demanded, grabbing the spear with one hand.

The bandit spat in his face. Drathorn wiped his face, disgusted. He pulled the spear out of the bandit and the man screamed loudly. "It's going to be a red dawn." He said as he looked at the sky.

By midday Thira and Troy stopped and looked down upon death. A large man was lying in the middle of the road, a spear through his chest and a hole in his calf. Two others were lying dead up ahead, one of them was headless. "Who could have done this?" Thira asked. "You don't think Drathorn-?"

"Let's look around." Troy said, trying not to picture Drathorn's dead body among the trees. They dismounted and followed footprints into the woods on the western side. A few moments into their search they found a group of dead bodies, one of them sat headless and in a tree.

"Oh my . . ." Thira said. "What happened here?"

"I don't know." Troy said. He walked into the middle of the bodies and looked around.

"H-help . . ."

"Who's there?" Troy called, raising his crossbow.

"Troy! Over there . . . a survivor!" Thira exclaimed.

They rushed to the side of a young man who was lying on the ground. "Are you okay? What happened here?" Troy asked.

"He . . . killed all of them . . ." the man said.

"Who did?" Thira asked.

"Dark hair . . . blue eyes . . . young . . . sword . . . we attacked . . ." groaned the man.

"Troy . . ." Thira said. "Troy that sounds like a description of Drathorn . . ."

"I know . . ." Troy said. "Thira . . . they're bandits . . . all of them . . . even this one."

"Please . . . don't kill me . . ." the man said. "He left me alive . . . said I wasn't worth killing . . . please . . ."

"Relax . . ." Thira said. "We understand . . . we won't kill you . . . we're going to take you to Taldi."

"Taldi? No . . ." But the man burst into a great coughing fit and Troy and Thira began picking him up and were loading him onto Troy's horse when he finally lost consciousness again.

"We must ride swiftly to Taldi . . . once this man is healed we will get the story from him." Troy said. "Until then . . . he rides with me . . ."

XVII

Bandixi

It was getting dark again when Drathorn finally stopped. He was tired and hungry and Starcruser was panting from the day of running. Drathorn dismounted and lead him off of the road. After making sure Starcruser was well fed and watered Drathorn had a small bite to eat and laid down to sleep.

But Thira and Troy traveled a little longer. It was well into the night when they stopped and they felt confident that they had gained ground. But Drathorn was still at least six hours ahead of them.

Sunday May 11th, 18291, Thira and Troy got up at sunrise and made breakfast. After feeding the horses and eating their own meal they began riding again.

Drathorn wasn't so lucky. His early morning the day before had caused him to sleep in. He began riding again nearly three hours after Troy and Thira. He rode fast, hoping to make up for the time he had lost as he slept. Drathorn soon reached the Taldi River. He sat upon the ground and cleansed his hands and face in the cool water while Starcruser drank gratefully.

"Hello young traveler." Drathorn stood fast and drew his sword. He was surprised to see an old man standing not too far away. His hair fell past his shoulders and his skin was as pale as his silver hair. His robes were white and somewhat dirty from travel. "I am Elforge, an elder of the Taldi twelve. I am looking for Drathorn Hellbound . . . I heard he was coming this way. Have you seen him?"

Drathorn lowered his sword but did not put it away. "Why would a man of your reputation be looking for him?" he asked.

"My town has been infiltrated by the bandits." Said Elforge, "I was sent by my fellows to find him and beg for his help."

Drathorn sheathed his sword. "I was just heading to Taldi, *I* am Drathorn Hellbound." Drathorn said. "My plan was to pass through on my way to Signaroc but if my assistance is required then I will not stand by. Tell me more."

"A pleasure to meet you, Mr. Hellbound. I'm afraid this is not the way I had pictured myself upon our meeting but at least we have met." Elforge said. "They came quite a while ago from across the sea. We heard that the Signaroc boat house was taken but we were surprised when bandits appeared on ships from there. They took our docks and then our city. No one has been let in or out. I escaped yesterday with much difficulty. Please, we need your help!"

"Of course." Drathorn said. "How far is it to Taldi?"

"A few hours' march I'm afraid." Elforge said.

"Can you ride?" Drathorn said, gesturing to Starcruser. "He is both strong and large enough to hold us both."

"Then ride we shall."

Taldi was a small town set into a giant crater in the middle of the forest. Much like the one the Sentrate Tree had been in. With a population of only five thousand and no proper protection the city was an easy target. But surprisingly this was the first time it had actually been attacked. Drathorn stopped at the top of the hill and looked down at the city. Thin walls made of sticks and small trees surrounded the town, the gate was open but a dozen armed guards were in front of it.

"Those are some of the bandits . . . There are far more inside." Elforge said.

"How did you get out?" Drathorn asked.

"I escaped from the place I was being held and ran to the wall. I single-handedly dug a small gap under it. It will be big enough for us, but not for your horse." Elforge said.

"That's fine . . . I'll keep him by the hole . . . direct me there." Drathorn replied.

They quietly followed the wall until they found a small gap. Drathorn left Starcruser on the outside of the gap and followed Elforge under. They were now in a little alleyway between two cabins. They snuck up and peeked out at the road before crossing. They snuck around bandit patrols and finally reached a large cabin. "This is where I was being held." Elforge whispered. "Me, the other Elders and a small group of citizens."

"We will free them first." Drathorn decided. He took another peek at the building and saw that there were two guards outside of the door. "What do we do?"

"Leave them to me . . ." Elforge said. He handed Drathorn his staff and began concentrating. "*Norfal Dorme Hielmore!*"

The guards both suddenly collapsed and remained motionless. "What did you do to them?" Drathorn asked as they walked to the door.

"They are asleep. And for now they must stay that way." Elforge replied. Elforge opened the door and they stepped inside."

"Elforge! About time you return!" a man stepped towards them as they entered. "What's this? We send you to get help and you come back with a boy? You fool!"

"Silence, Elder Garm." Elforge said calmly. "This *boy* is Drathorn Hellbound. He has promised to help us."

"Hellbound?" The elder named Garm laughed. "He doesn't look like his parents at all!"

"Silence!" Drathorn said, "I hear someone coming."

Sure enough everyone suddenly went quiet and listened. The sound of words could be heard.

"You fools better pray that none of them got away! Sleeping on the job!" said an angry voice.

"C'mon, let's check it out." said another.

"Drathorn hide!" Elforge said.

Drathorn hid behind the door just as it flew open. Four bandits walked in. Two were the spear-carrying guards that Elforge had just put to sleep. There was also another guard and a crossbow man.

"You're damn lucky you two!" said the crossbow man. "It looks like they're all still here. But I'll be reporting you to the boss."

The crossbow man walked out the open door. The spearman who had entered with him looked at the prisoners. "I've been told to inform you that your time as prisoners is almost up." He said. "In a few days time you will be transported across the sea to Signaroc. There you will meet a friend of our master's. He is going to decide the punishment you will receive for the crime of assaulting bandit camps in the region. The actions of the Taldi warriors have caused the destruction of many bandit camps and you will all be punished for it."

A man suddenly stepped out from among the prisoners. "Please! It's not our fault! Punish the damn warriors for all I care but leave our people and their families alone!"

The leader looked down at the small man. "You fool! How dare you speak back to me! You will suffer a punishment now!" The spearman struck the man with the bottom of his spear. The man fell to the ground and was hit again and again. The other two bandits laughed evilly.

"Stop!" Drathorn yelled. He slammed the door shut and drew his sword as he stepped out into the open.

"Aha! We have an intruder!" The spearman laughed. "I'll teach him a lesson when we're done with this man!"

The spearman struck the man on the ground again. "I said stop!" Drathorn leapt forward and slashed the bandit across the back, just as he had done to Murlok. The other two bandits tried to stop him. He twirled around and slashed one across the chest before stabbing the second through the heart. Drathorn then stabbed the lead bandit with his sword to finish him. He stood and looked at the man on the ground. "Are you alright?" Drathorn asked him.

He looked up at Drathorn, blood dripping from his face. "Thanks to you . . ." the man said.

"Do not thank me." Drathorn said. But suddenly he felt the bottom of a spear strike his head and he fell.

Elforge roared at the bandits who had just arrived, but the fallen man got there first. He took up one of the bandit's fallen spears and charged forward. The bandit smashed him aside with, not a spear, but a war-hammer. "Foolish man!" The bandit laughed. He looked to his companions. "Take the boy to my master along with the weapons of your fallen comrades!"

Four bandits entered the room with swords and began to drag Drathorn away from the cabin. "Leave him alone!" Elforge said.

The half-giant bandit laughed and flexed his enormous muscles. "What're you gunna do about it?"

Drathorn woke in a daze. He was being dragged away by two sword bearing bandits. Two others were leading the way up ahead. His legs hurt and he realized he was being dragged facedown by the shoulders, an odd way to carry but effective none the less. "The boss is gunna enjoy this." Said the bandit on his right. "The last Hellbound!"

"He will award us greatly!" said the one on his left.

Soon they entered a large doorway into a wooden hallway. There was a knock on wood and then, "Who is it?"

"It is a small group of your trusted servants." The bandit on his right said. "We have brought you an intruder."

"Put him with the other prisoners."

"But you will want to see this one sir!" said the bandit. "It is Drathorn Hellbound!"

" . . . Bring him in."

The door opened and the four bandits stepped inside. The two carrying Drathorn took the lead. "Sit up, fool!" Drathorn suddenly realised that the voice was *very* young. He used the strength of the bandits to pull himself to his knees and look around. He was in Taldi's church. All that remained was the alter at the head of the chamber. The rest was gone. Drathorn focused on the person in front of him. It was neither a man nor woman but was still human. It was a small boy.

He was around ten years old but walked with a two-handed sword taller than he was on his back. "I am Bandixi, leader of the bandits." The boy said. "My men tell me you are Drathorn Hellbound? Is this true?"

Drathorn laughed hysterically. "Yes I am Drathorn Hellbound, but you are no leader!" He watched Bandixi's face and realised one thing; if this was the bandit leader then he would have information. Drathorn *needed* information . . .

"I'm sorry to say you'll find that I am." Bandixi said calmly. "These bandits do everything I tell them to. And if they don't . . . they die. I am in the greatest position of power here . . . therefore I am leader. I am also one of the Darklord's famous Commandos."

So he works for the Darklord. Drathorn thought. *Now for information.* "I have no idea what you mean about Commandos but I continue to mock the idea of you as a leader of these men." Drathorn mocked him laughingly. *Who are these Commandos?*

"Question my authority if you will, but I am the leader. As for the Commandos we are the keepers of the keys, guardians of our master's life." Bandixi said. "Each of us holds a piece of the key attached to our hearts that can be removed only with death. Only by collecting the pieces of the key can the Onyx tower be opened and only by opening the Onyx tower can the Darklord be reached. It is a commando's duty to protect the key. I am one of the Darklord's most trusted warriors and therefore one of his protectors."

If this is true then I need that piece, I don't want to kill him but I will if I have to. "Then the Darklord is a fool. I would not trust a ten year old with my life." Drathorn laughed again, trying to provoke him. "Fearless leader indeed! Show me my punishment oh fearless leader!"

"Very well," Bandixi said. "Hold him to his knees so I may remove his head!"

The bandits grabbed Drathorn harder on the shoulders and attempted to hold him still but they weren't fast enough. He grabbed both of their swords and drew them out. In a quick move he slashed them both across the stomach and then killed the other two before turning back to Bandixi. "You are skilled, Drathorn. But you are a fool to attempt to fight me."

"I am a fool but you fell for the simple mocking trick." Drathorn said. "By mocking you I was able to find out what I needed to know to defeat your master. This will make my victory much easier."

"It is unfortunate that you will not live to attempt to hunt the other Commandos!" Bandixi said. "They would have much more glory over killing you than I will."

"But you will not kill me." Drathorn said simply. "Because you will not fight me. I will not do battle with a child. It would be a great sin to kill one of such innocence. How about I leave and we fight again some day when you're older?"

"Enough! We fight now!" Bandixi yelled, "Here in the church, under the view of your beloved gods!"

He drew the giant sword and wielded it with in-human skill. He ran at Drathorn and struck. Drathorn raised both swords above his head and blocked the giant sword. Drathorn kicked and sent the boy stumbling back somewhat. But he recovered fast and attacked again. Bandixi attacked with such speed that he might have been using a dagger, but his blows landed with strength like that of an explosion. Drathorn refused to attack and stuck to the defensive.

Bandixi struck hard and fast, keeping Drathorn moving. Wielding that blade would have made even the strongest men tired but Bandixi battled ferociously and without any sign of slowing down. Soon the splatter of rain on the roof of the church could be heard and seen through the windows.

"Why are we stopping?" Thira asked. Troy had slowed and stopped and was eyeing the sky sadly. He dismounted and led his horse underneath a large oak tree.

"A great storm approaches." Troy said. I can feel it. "We cannot make the horses run in this."

"Then we will slow to a walk!" Said Thira, determined to catch up to Drathorn. Even as they spoke the rain began to fall, slowly at first.

"No . . . the thunder and lightning will frighten the horses too much." We must find shelter." Troy said. "Don't worry, Drathorn isn't stupid. He won't try and brave this storm."

"Fine!" Thira said. They began slowly walking along, guiding the horses as the thunder began to frighten them. But after finding no place for shelter they were forced to take cover under a large tree. "This isn't safe! We shouldn't be under this thing!"

"Where do you propose we go then?" Troy asked.

"Where . . . are we?" The young man groaned.

"He's awake!" Thira exclaimed.

"It's no wonder with all the commotion." Troy frowned. He walked over to the man they'd tied to his horse. "We're in the woods between Taldi and Greengate. We're an hour from the Taldi River. We're heading to Taldi to find a friend of ours. What is your name?"

"I am Murlok . . ." the man said.

"You are a bandit, aren't you?" Troy asked.

"Yes . . . but please . . . hear me out." Murlok groaned.

"We're listening." Thira said. "But make it quick!"

"There's a giant tree about five minutes north of here." Murlok said. "It is strong and larger than even a house. It is also hollow enough for us and the horses to hide in. Take us there and we can talk."

After following Murlok's directions they found the tree he had spoken of. It was indeed much larger than a house and after a moment of searching they had found a large opening in its trunk. They squeezed through with the horses and found a large hollow opening. It was large enough for a large family to sleep comfortably in. It was actually quite empty with only the three adventurers and two horses inside.

"How did you know of this place?" Troy asked, limping to the side farthest from the entrance and sitting down to relax his tired leg.

Thira untied Murlok and did her best to help him to the ground. "We stopped here on our way through."

"You mean you and the bandits, correct?" Troy asked. "Thira . . . in my saddle bag there is an ointment for my leg . . . Can you grab it for me?"

Thira nodded and began searching his bag as Murlok answered. "Yes . . . I joined the bandits to get revenge . . . A month ago my family was slaughtered by a mage named Strok. I joined the bandits because I wanted their help to find and kill this mage. Also I had no money or home to keep myself safe and they provided. I have followed my captain who promised I would have my revenge.

"But when we were nearing Greengate, where we had been told he was headed, we put up camp. That's when a lone traveler was seen speeding along the road. The captain said he would be an easy kill and good practice for the battle against the mage that would soon come." Murlok groaned and sat down at Thira's feet as she continued to shuffle through the bag, listening intently. "I agreed to attack him so I would learn to fight so that I could have my revenge. But it wasn't an easy fight. He killed everyone . . . slaughtered . . . he was like a ghost . . . one minute he was there and the next everyone was separated and killed. When I attacked him he slashed my back and said I wasn't worth killing and that the wound wouldn't kill me. Then he left to kill the others."

Thira looked up and walked over to Troy with a small black bottle. "What did this man look like?" she asked as Troy opened the bottle and poured a little of the foul smelling liquid onto the flesh above his wooden leg.

"He wasn't even a man I don't think . . . he looked about your age . . ." Murlok said. Troy watched Murlok as he silently rubbed the liquid into the skin. "He had black hair and dark blue eyes . . . his horse was extremely fast and beautiful . . . with a star on its brow."

"That sounds like Drathorn . . ." Thira said as she looked at Troy. "How could he do that? Is he even strong enough to take out a full bandit camp on his own?"

"At this stage nothing would surprise me . . ." Troy said. "I had a feeling it was Drathorn from the beginning. He is supposed to be powerful . . . he is a Hellbound after all."

"Hellbound?" Murlok exclaimed. "That boy? If I had known I would never have attacked him! No wonder he was so strong and such a natural fighter at his age!"

For several moments the only sound was the whining of the horses and the thunder outside. Troy put the cap back on the ointment and finished rubbing it in before he said, "I know you cannot fight in your current condition but what was your specialty before taking this wound?"

Murlok looked at him. "I was a duel swordsman. I'd fight with a blade in each hand. Before fighting your friend I had never had a real fight . . . but I had practiced against my fellow bandits. I was quite good in my opinion. I bested some and was beaten by others."

Again Thira said nothing as she brought the ointment back to Troy's saddlebag; she worried for Drathorn. Murlok had no idea what had happened after he was injured. Apparently they weren't all killed before Murlok was hurt . . . Did Drathorn escape unharmed? He obviously wasn't dead . . . but maybe badly hurt? She worried even more as the picture of Drathorn with a cut like Murlok's on his back walking through the rain crossed her mind's eye.

"We are headed for Taldi." Troy said. "I want you to come with us."

"I'm sorry but I must politely decline." Murlok said. "I must find this mage, Strok and get my revenge.

"Then you'll be delighted to hear that Strok is dead." Troy said. "He was an assassin hired by the darklord to kill Drathorn. Drathorn cut him straight into two pieces at Felix's cabin between Greengate and Gaberdan."

"If that is so then there is no further way for me to get my revenge." Murlok said. "Although I am glad to hear of his passing I wish it had been I who had finished him . . ."

"That being said, will you come with us?" Troy asked, "We can help you find a healer for your back and then you can travel with us to Signaroc."

"I have nowhere else to go so I may as well go with you." Murlok said. "Maybe I'll meet Drathorn again . . . I'd like to thank him for defeating Strok . . . and for using his blade to show me the error of my ways."

"You have no wish for vengeance on him do you?" Troy asked.

"No . . . the bandits were hardly friends of mine . . . I had no care for them I only needed them to kill Strok. Since that is done I have no worry for them. As for my injury, I think it was his only choice; otherwise I'd have killed him. I have no grudge against him. I actually want to help his cause!"

"In that case you are welcome to come with us." Troy said. "When we reach Taldi we'll find you some weapons and healing and maybe a horse of your own. Then we'll secure passage on a boat to Signaroc."

"You forget that the boathouses are held by the bandits." Murlok said. "And I have heard rumours that Taldi is taken as well . . . though of that I am not sure."

"If Taldi is taken then Drathorn is walking into a trap!" Thira exclaimed. "I knew he would be in danger!"

"Calm down Thira . . . I already knew this . . ." Troy said.

"You knew? And you never said anything?" Thira yelled furiously.

"What good would panicking do us?" Troy said. "And after seeing the massacre back there I'm not too worried. As soon as he finds out that the bandits are there he'll disappear like smoke in the darkness. I just wanna catch up with him before he reaches Signaroc . . . that's all I care about."

"If I may ask . . . why is he going to Signaroc?" Murlok asked before Thira could continue the argument.

"Drathorn has heard the Darklord's plans . . . he is going to attack Signaroc to try and obtain the Journal of the Great Thirteen." Troy said . . ."Drathorn wants to warn them and help them . . . we were supposed to go with him but he ran away when he realized how much danger he was putting us in. He told us to go back to Gaberdan but we are going after him."

"That is very noble . . ." Murlok said. "But aren't you afraid he'll be angry with you for disobeying him?"

"He may be our friend and he can do what he wants but we don't have to do what he says. We have the right to make our own decisions." Thira said.

"Now . . . I need rest and so does Murlok . . . there's no reason to have anyone on watch tonight so how about we all get some rest?" Troy said.

Thira and Murlok nodded and were asleep within the hour. But Troy kept himself up and kept watch, not on the entryway, but on their new companion.

"You remind me of one of my newest recruits, Drathorn!" Bandixi laughed as Drathorn fought to keep the strong blows away from his body. "He too was a duel swordsman. His name was Murlok and joined so he could get revenge against someone who killed his family. I told him I would help him get his revenge by sending him after the man with a few others. I was hoping they would kill you along the way to their own death by my mage but I guess you got there first!"

Drathorn leapt back, away from Bandixi. "Your mage, Strok, is dead." Drathorn said. "Your minion, the Hergapy escaped but that fool Strok is buried in Felix's garden. And Murlok lives but his companions have been killed."

"Interesting . . . Well I'll have you know that Terry the Hergapy is not one of mine. He is another of the Commandos who work for my master." Bandixi laughed. "He came here looking for protection. He said he needed to find you but he didn't want to get caught up in a fight. So I gave him Strok. I told him to have Strok kill you instead. I guess he failed. But I'm happy the little thief escaped. My master is still as safe as ever!"

"Well he won't be as safe for long. Because once I take the shard from you I'll find the little thief and take his." Drathorn said. "You cannot defeat me. Just release the shard from your body!"

"Never!" Bandixi yelled, jumping forward with another attack that was blocked by Drathorn. Both of Drathorn's swords were being used to block Bandixi's single blow.

Drathorn slowly began to retract his left arm from the tangle of swords. "You're a fool if you think only one of your swords can stop mine!" Bandixi laughed. "One arm by itself is not enough to hold up against me!"

"*You* are a fool, I am a Hellbound and fight always with a single sword . . . my blade will equal yours without my other hand. And while you battle with my good arm this one is going to finish you. If you try and block it I will take your head with my good arm. I give you one more chance Bandixi . . . give me the shard!"

"I would rather die than betray my master!" He screamed, realising the problem in his situation.

Lightning flashed and Drathorn's weaker arm drove his sword forward. Bandixi's reflexes caused him to jerk his sword away and block it. But Drathorn's good arm used its sudden freedom to slice his head right off. Bandixi fell to the ground in what seemed to be slow motion.

He was dead.

XVIII

Rebellion in Taldi

Drathorn stared at the tiny body at his feet. He had killed before . . . many times . . . But this was not a grown man. It was a child. He had been tainted by darkness and forced to do the will of Icarus but he was still just a child.

Drathorn fell to his knees. The child's face seemed so peaceful now. Suddenly as Drathorn began to weep for the loss the body seemed to stir. He leapt to his feet and readied to defend himself from another attack. But it did not come. The body stirred and seemed to become dust. Then the dust slowly rose into the air, it swirled about the puddle of blood and then, in a small burst of light, became a crystal.

The crystal shard hovered in mid-air about the pool of blood waiting for him. Drathorn walked quietly towards it, dropping his swords as he went. He reached out for the crystal. It felt warm against his hands. He took it out of the air and brought it closer to his face. It had a colour of the greatest blue . . . it reminded him of Elgard . . .

An Angelic Symbol is a scaring in your flesh . . . a symbol carved into a selected part of your body . . . it's a sacrifice of blood to the gods, every time a person with an angelic symbol commits a sin they feel the pain of the cut again. The words pierced his mind in memory of Elgard's words. An Angelic Symbol . . . Suddenly Drathorn didn't know what he was doing anymore. He walked away from the puddle of blood that had once been the young bandit leader and took a dagger from the body of a fallen bandit.

Without thought he began to bring the blade to his arm. He cut his sleeve at the shoulder to reveal his bare skin. He wanted to stop, didn't want to scar his body with a mark of the gods . . . But he could not, a strange sensation of power flowed through him. He felt possessed, forced to do what he did not wish.

Drathorn finally looked up from his bleeding shoulder. The mark flooded blood over his arm. The symbol had no real meaning to him. He had invented it. He thought that it resembled a number five turned backwards with a letter 'V' for the top instead of a line.

Drathorn picked up the sleeve he had torn away and tied it around the mark to stop the dripping blood. The pain of the knife still brought tears to his eyes but he did not care. He took up a sword in his good arm and began to walk silently from the church.

Elforge stood at the head of the crowd, anger still coursing through him as he watched the large man in the doorway. No one had said anything since Drathorn had been knocked unconscious and dragged away. The large bandit stood in the door, watching them and making sure they didn't make another attempt at escape. "Whatchu lookin' at?" Elforge yelled suddenly at the bandit. "Stand aside and let us see the boy or you'll be hurt!"

"You're a fool." The large bandit laughed. "Even if all of you came and attacked me at once, right now, you could not best me."

"No but we can still try!" Elforge said.

"Try then!" The bandit laughed, "You'll not get far-." The tip of a sword suddenly burst through the Bandit's chest, piercing perfectly through his heart. He fell to his knees and then on his face. Drathorn Hellbound stood in the door way, arm wrapped in a torn sleeve, blood showing through, a bloody dagger was in his belt.

"Drathorn!" Elforge yelled. "You're alright! What happened? You're bleeding!"

"Bandixi is dead." Drathorn said. "I'm not hurt . . . that is an angelic symbol I carved after killing him . . ."

"You carved an angelic symbol?" Elforge said, amazed.

"Yes . . . but it doesn't seem to be working . . ." Drathorn said. "I thought they were supposed to burn every time I committed a sin? All it does is hurt . . ."

"Well yeah you just sliced yourself open!" Elforge exclaimed. "The symbol won't take effect until it's healed over and becomes nothing but a scar. Until then nothing will be different."

Drathorn was silent for a moment, looking at the body of the bandit. He pulled out the sword with his good arm and looked at the others. "It's time Taldi was free of the bandits . . ." He said. "It's time to fight . . . Who's with me?"

A muscular man stepped forward from the crowd of people and picked up the large bandit's war hammer. "I lost my wife to these guys!" He said angrily, "All I want is for them to be driven out of my town!"

The small man Drathorn had rescued before stepped forward. "I have a debt to pay to these bandits. If you have a spare blade I am yours to command."

Drathorn tossed him the bloody dagger. "This is all I have at the moment but it's better than nothing."

"I, of course will help you." Said Elforge, stepping forward and retrieving his staff.

"And the rest of you?" Drathorn asked.

"There are no weapons!" laughed a man. "How do we fight without weapons? We'll be killed!"

"Numbers alone can overpower any weapon." Drathorn said. "As long as you work together you will over power them and reclaim weapons to fight with. But if you do not fight then the bandits will select a new leader and you will never have a chance of escaping."

At first they all looked at each other, uncertain of what to do or say. Then one of the Elders stepped forward. "I believe I speak for all of us when I say that we have been trapped in our own city for far too long. All we want is our freedom back. We lost many lives when our freedom was taken and although we would rather not lose any more we realise that the only way for any of us to be free is if we lose a few more in battle." He stopped and looked at his people. Many of them stared at him angrily, others listened admiringly, and the other elders gave him nods of encouragement. "I think I speak for us all when I say we are willing to sacrifice a few more lives to save the city. We are not warriors but we will fight."

The people muttered words of agreement and others nodded slightly but most were still not impressed. Drathorn stepped forward and put his hand on the Elder's shoulder. "No one, no matter the reason, should be willing to make a sacrifice of someone else's life for the protection of their own." Drathorn said. "Even if the people agree fully with what you say, you have no right to tell them to give up their lives for this. They may fight if they wish. I would gladly ride alone to my death to protect this city but I cannot speak for others. The decision is to be made by the people, not he who is dubbed leader because of blood or skill or even respect. The choice is that of the people. No matter their choice I will march against these bandits."

There was now silence. At first Drathorn thought that his speech may have crushed any hope of the people joining the fight. But then a man stepped from the crowd. "This isn't right . . ." he said. "We adults are supposed to set the examples and stay strong when our children are afraid. Not the other way around. This boy is willing to charge into an army of heavily armed bandits, alone and without any hope and we, the adults, are afraid to even *consider* fighting? A child will fight but we dare not? Ridiculous! I say we fight!"

"I agree!"

"Me too!"

"To battle I say!"

"Let's drive these peace disturbers from our home!"

The people were suddenly angry and ready for anything. Before Drathorn or the elders could begin forming a plan of attack the entire mass of people in the building were lunging forward. "Drathorn!" Elforge yelled over the crowd. "Lead the revolt! The Elders and I must retrieve our magic supplies if we are to be of any help. Make your way to free the other prisoners. You can secure weaponry and armour in the barracks if needed." That was all Drathorn heard before Elforge and the elders joined the crowd. Drathorn stood still for a moment, watching the people charging forward, yelling, and roaring in anger, fists held high. Mothers with young children stayed behind and seniors who could not fight covered their ears to block out the sound of the stampede. Then he turned, sword held at the ready and joined the charging group.

The scene outside was confusing. Small groups of bandits emerged from nearby buildings, angry at the disturbance but were defeated quickly by the crowd and had their weapons taken away by those without. People were tripping and harming each other in the process of trying to find an enemy to strike.

Drathorn stood high atop the stump of a cut down tree and yelled into the crowd. "Everyone! Everyone calm down for just a moment! We must decide on a plan of action!" It was many minutes before Bandits stopped appearing and the group calmed enough to pay attention to him. "I suggest we split into groups and then meet in the town square. Any suggestions on leaders?"

There was an argument on who two of the leaders would be but it was soon decided that the war-hammer bearing man and the man Drathorn had rescued before would lead two groups while Drathorn lead the third. The war-hammer bearing man took the smallest group and headed toward the barracks to gain armour and weapons and free the largest amount of prisoners that was being held near the market district.

The man Drathorn had rescued had given away his dagger and was now wielding one of the bandit's swords. He was going to lead the largest group to free the prisoners close to the entrance to the town. Drathorn took the last group and planned to free the prisoners being held in the old windmill and the stables. The plan was to meet back up in the town center to gather and await the return of the elders.

It only took a few minutes to get the people moving again but once they had started they were an unstoppable force. Within moments Drathorn and his group were charging towards the old windmill which was located fairly near to the hole under the wall that Drathorn had left Starcruser by. Drathorn lead the rebels onward and they were met by many bandits who attempted to stop them. Drathorn was matched by none, but a few rebels fell at the hands of the bandits. These deaths only filled the people with greater anger and they drove forward harder and faster. When they reached the windmill Drathorn didn't even have time to speak to the captives before they had broken out of the building and joined the assault. While the two groups were joining and battling nearby bandits Drathorn and a few others destroyed the wall near the hole and Drathorn was able to mount Starcruser and continue to lead the rebels from horseback.

The bigger group of rebels finished the little fighting they could find and then began to trample towards the stables. Some of these bandits were smarter. They mounted horses and charged at the small army. They did a great amount of damage but the people of Taldi were unstoppable in their rage and forced them off the horses. Once the bandits in the stable area had retreated, the people of Taldi took the time to find weapons on the bodies of the dead and to mount on horses from the stables. Now with the group larger and even more dangerous they moved forward, the mounted units in the lead, those on foot making as much noise as they could to draw out the hidden bandits.

As they approached the town square they saw the team with the large leader battling for their lives against a large group of bandits. The battle seemed fairly even but Drathorn's team charged forward, joining the battle and turning the odds in Taldi's favour. Drathorn did not join the battle. He looked out over the city in search of the other group. "Continue the battle!" Drathorn called. "I'm going to find the others!"

He turned and spurred Starcruser forward, towards the entrance of the town. He forced speed into the run, he worried for the others. But after rounding a corner he saw the group and stopped his horse. But they no longer shouted the battle cry. They were running as fast as they could back to the town square. Of the original team very few people remained. The leader continued to call the people in retreat but few of them remained. The others were all people rescued from the nearby buildings. But they had no weapons and most were wounded.

Giving chase to the people was an immense group of Bandits. The enraged bandits were gaining on the tired people of Taldi. Drathorn turned and hurried to the town square. The people were standing around, gathering weapons from the defeated bandits and fallen friends. "Aim south!" Drathorn called. "The others are coming with a great foe on their tails. We need to be ready to intercept the enemy so those in retreat can gather weaponry. Aim all bows south!"

Everyone with long range weapons suddenly got in a large line, facing the entrance Drathorn had come from. Those bearing melee weapons stood behind them, waiting for their turn. "After the first shot I want all the archers to retreat and shoot from inside the buildings and the swordsmen to brace themselves!" The retreating refugees rounded the corner and were running as fast as they could toward Drathorn's army. "Branch right! Branch right!" Drathorn yelled. The leader and the fleeing people all curved right, giving the archers a clear shot at the pursuing bandits. The retreating people got behind the second and third lines of people and began collecting weapons to make a fourth line of attack.

The archers waited for the right moment before letting the arrows and bolts fly. The volley hit the enemy and put a large dent in their numbers. The archers scattered and began dividing into buildings while the second, third, and now fourth lines of attack prepared for battle. The lines then charged right at the unorganized forces of the bandits. The battle was fast and confusing. The archers shot from the buildings, the swordsmen battled as hard as they could and the riders waited for the right time. When the time had come Drathorn and the other horseback riders charged forward.

Starcruser galloped without fear, Drathorn on his back, into the confusion. He trampled over the bandits while Drathorn lunged out with his sword, striking all the bandits he could reach. But even with the help of the horses and the archers in the buildings they were badly out numbered and losing fighters fast. *We need time.* Drathorn thought. He turned and went around to the back of an out-of-the-way building and left Starcruser tied there. Then he entered and found the body of a slain archer. Drathorn took his crossbow and climbed the staircase. Once upstairs he climbed out the nearest window and onto the roof. He loaded the crossbow and fired down on an enemy that had cornered two unarmed fighters. The bandit died and the fighters went back to the battle.

As he reloaded Drathorn looked at the space the bandits were flooding through. It was a narrow street passage with thick buildings on either side. Drathorn suspected that only about six bandits could flood through at a time. *Time,* he thought again. He climbed to a higher point of the roof and shot again. *We need time . . . I must give us time . . .* He reloaded and then ran forward. He jumped off of the roof and across to another nearby building. After taking a shot he jumped to another. He continued to jump until he had crossed the square and was above the passage that was flooding with bandits. He loaded the crossbow one last time and threw the remaining ammo into the battle where the confusion hid it from sight.

With the crossbow ready in one hand and his sword wielded in the other he jumped down into the crowd of bandits who were trying to get into the square. His aim was true. He landed lightly in front of the charging bandits. They were surprised at his sudden appearance but didn't hesitate. They charged as one at Drathorn.

But the alleyway was so crowded that the bandits couldn't fight very well without harming one another. Drathorn swung his blade randomly, just trying to ward a few of them off so he could look around and plan his next move. What was meant to be a harmless strike ended up killing two bandits and injuring a third. *If my luck stays like that this will be easy.* Drathorn thought as he swung clumsily again and beheaded a reckless bandit. But the swing caused him to lose his balance and he was almost caught off guard by another bandit. Drathorn only managed to keep himself alive by shooting his attacker with the crossbow. The bandit fell with his comrades.

That was close. He thought as he blocked another attacker and knocked him unconscious with the wood of the crossbow. *If I keep fighting so clumsily I'll get myself killed before I can help these people.* The people were still battling in the square but they fought with greater power and courage seeing Drathorn risking his life. And since Drathorn was blocking the bandits from entering the square they soon gained the advantage of numbers. Another large, war-hammer bearing bandit suddenly appeared in the mass of bandits. Reflexively Drathorn threw his crossbow at him. The strike caused the man to stumble and Drathorn managed to stab him.

Without the large man in the way the other bandits suddenly seemed to be moving faster. Drathorn was suddenly forced to fight faster as the wave of bandits came with increased speed. *Please Elforge . . . hurry . . .* Drathorn was actually forced to take a few steps back because of the crushing numbers of bandits.

It was then, when Drathorn had taken that step back that at least one hundred arrows flew past him and began striking the bandits. He looked back to see the people of Taldi, united, and their archers shooting non-stop at the charging bandits. The threat that had remained inside the square was gone; their bodies were strewn across the streets like ants on an ant hill.

Drathorn ducked and jumped out of the way of the falling arrows. The bandits still tried their best to get through but they were hit by the arrows mercilessly. "We got your back Drathorn!" yelled the lead archer.

"Yes but who's got yours?" Drathorn yelled. A bandit-sorcerer was suddenly on the roof of a nearby building, casting devastating spells on the archers and the helpless fighters. The archers turned their aim on him and released their arrows. But one spell turned the arrows into a harmless flock of butterflies that fluttered away with no effect.

"You call that an attack?" yelled the wizard. "This is an attack! *Nervahn Est Mondor!*"

The poring rain was already enough to make the battle difficult but suddenly a controlled blast of lightning shot from the skies. It struck the ground with a bang that rattled the buildings and killed everything near it. The bodies of the electrocuted men fell, burned thoroughly, to the ground. The mage laughed evilly and took his gaze off of the skies. Drathorn expected that the spell had been broken with the removal of his gaze. But he was wrong. Another blast suddenly broke through and seemed to slice a building in half. Flames were suddenly everywhere, just adding to the chaos. The mage didn't bother casting any other spells and instead just watched his spreading devastation with glee.

Drathorn ran at the building the mage was on top of, his sword fending off any new bandits he met. Seeing this threat, the mage seemed to begin directing all of the sky's lightning at Drathorn. The next blast was so close to hitting him that the metal of his sword seemed to heat up. The heat didn't bother Drathorn and he just kept running. The lightning fell at impossible speeds but somehow Drathorn avoided them. The mage seemed irritated with Drathorn's illusive abilities and began shooting lightning even faster, but with worse aim.

Finally Drathorn was through the door to the building. He climbed the stairs and went out the nearest window. On the roof he found the mage waiting for him. The lightning had stopped and the mage was waiting patiently for his challenger while the fighting below raged once more. "Young Hellbound . . ." the mage said. "I have heard your name whispered among the bandits . . . but I didn't expect to meet you myself. This will be fun."

"If all of your spells are as well aimed as those lightning bolts then I have nothing to worry about do I?" Drathorn mocked.

"*Gortha!*" the mage yelled angrily. The spell erupted from the mage before Drathorn had time to think about his next move. Acid flew at him and the only thing he could do to save himself was to place his sword between the spell and his body. The substance hit the blade of his sword and at first nothing happened. But then the sword seemed to evaporate before his eyes. What was once a seemingly flawless blade was suddenly turned into nothing but a simple hilt. Drathorn held the small piece of metal in his hands, examining it with awe. *"Gortha!"* The acidic blast was suddenly flying at him again.

Drathorn had no sword this time. He couldn't move. The spell was moving toward him in slow motion, unstoppable. He tried to turn but the sight of the coming blast kept him amazed and motionless. Eight feet away, Drathorn could already feel the magic from the blast welling up around him. Six feet, a strange heat seemed to radiate. Four feet, something moved in the corner of his eye. Two feet, this was it, this was the end. One foot, wham! The bolt of acid struck a magical barrier that had been created around Drathorn.

Drathorn and the mage both looked down into the crowd; the twelve elders had arrived. The elders were slowly spreading through the square, casting spells on nearby bandits that devastated the enemy numbers and even turned the bodies of the dead to walk and attack again as puppets of the casters. Elforge was standing behind a group of archers and seemed to have been the one who had cast the shielding spell. Drathorn looked up at the mage.

He didn't seem to have noticed what was going on yet and was paying no attention to Drathorn as he searched for his new foe. Lightning flashed but this time it was no where near the city. The pouring rain and terrible weather seemed to be affecting the fighters below now. Drathorn made use of the mage's search to make his move. He threw the hilt of his destroyed sword and yelled, "Hey, over here!"

The foolish mage turned towards him and the hilt collided with his stomach. The strike knocked the breath out of the mage and he fell right off the roof. Drathorn looked over the edge just in time to witness the mage landing on his head. Over the pounding rain and screaming fighters the snap of his neck could not be heard. The mage was lying dead on the ground, his neck broken. He would never again cast a spell of murder.

Drathorn turned and examined the battle below. The rain and increasing wind caused the fighters to slip and slide on the cobblestone. Archers began to stop using bows and crossbows as their arrows and bolts were veering too much off course. Despite this, the arrival of the twelve elders and their magic abilities seemed to be turning the fight in their favour. The fighters of Taldi united to protect the elders while they cast their spells of devastation on the enemy rather then fighting their enemies separately.

Drathorn again jumped from the roof of the building and took up one of the bandit's fallen swords. It was a long sword just like the one he had slain the Sentrate Tree's tentacle with. He examined it and suddenly felt a small pang of guilt that Mr. Blaygard would never get that sword back. But Drathorn put aside that feeling and charged a nearby bandit.

Victory was near.

A lone bandit archer had followed Drathorn's progress throughout the battle. He had watched him fight valiantly with the help of his gathered fighters, he watched him jump from the building and kill hundreds of bandits on his own so that his fighters could regroup. He had watched the boy slay the master mage with nothing but a small hilt of a sword. He had seen the boy run with a new sword into the battle, alone while his fighters protected the mages.

The archer knew this boy was a great threat. Knew that they would not win the battle because of the might of the Elders. But Bandixi's master had been quite clear to Bandixi. The archer had heard him speaking to Bandixi many days ago. "Should the boy venture this way, I want him slain." The voice of the other had said. "Naturally my lord!" said the voice of young Bandixi.

But Bandixi was dead. That was also at the hand of this boy. *I will slay him.* He thought, *I will slay the boy and I will find the master's lord and give him the news and claim the reward. This boy shall not live.* The bandit raised his bow and aimed it at Drathorn. He readied an arrow and recalculated based on the might of the wind. His shot would not miss.

Elforge finished the casting of his spell and looked at the battle before him. The fighters of Taldi stood around him, slaying all who attempted to reach him. Elforge smiled when he realized that the numbers of Taldians was greater than that of the bandits. But as he did he saw something on the roof top: A lone bandit aiming down into the battle where the mass of bandits were. Elforge followed the archer's gaze and saw Drathorn, battling against many bandit foes on his own.

Elforge suspected that this was an extremely smart bandit and he was even now calculating the might of the soaring winds. *"Balasta Nige!"* A single arrow flew from Elforge's hands, unaffected by the winds. But it was too late. The bandit released the arrow just before Elforge's could collide. The bandit fell but his arrow flew still toward Drathorn.

But there was something weird about that arrow. As it spun it flashed red and green. *A magic arrow*, Elforge realized. "*Mort Narven!*" the shield spell was cast again. But too late: The arrow slipped through the shield as it was being formed and struck Drathorn in the back.

The arrow flashed green again, twice as bright as Drathorn fell, and then caught fire. "No!" Elforge yelled. Drathorn was lying on the ground, the arrow in his upper back. The hero had fallen . . .

XIX

Weretigers and Reptiles

Sunday May 11ᵗʰ, 18291, "How long?" the voice of Elforge asked.

"He'll pretty much be fine as soon as he wakes." Said another, calmer, womanly voice.

"How is that possible? The magic in that arrow . . ." Elforge said in surprise.

"You haven't been studying your Hellbound, master Elforge." The woman laughed. "The Hellbound cannot be harmed by flame. Heat feels like nothing but a breeze to them. And fire can heal them."

"What about the poison?" Elforge asked, a little on edge.

"The fire from the arrow's second function healed over the wound instantly but did not affect the poison in the bloodstream." The woman said. "I gave him one of the antidotes from my cellar."

"So he'll be back to one-hundred percent?" Elforge laughed happily.

"Yes . . ." The woman hesitated. "But he will forever bare a scar from this. And even worse, the antidote was not complete."

"What does that mean?" Elforge exclaimed.

"Not much." The woman reassured him. "But there will be some side-effects. A certain ingredient, though we do not know which, reacted with the magic that created the poison. The reaction formed an abnormal connection between his mind and his right hand."

"What will this connection mean?"

"Well the connection was only the first part to be honest." The woman said sadly. "But the effect is more of a *gift*. If my calculations are correct, he should be able to create a bioluminescent light with the palm of his right hand and control it's intensity with his mind."

"That's amazing!" Elforge exclaimed. "To create light without words or magic, like an animal from the ocean's depths, that is truly a gift!"

"Yes . . ." The woman sighed. "But I cannot tell what ingredients reacted with the magic in the arrow and even if we tried to run tests, the arrow would kill anyone else who was hit by it."

"It wasn't the arrow that did it." Elforge informed. "The bow changed the power of the arrow. It was *Firefang*, one of the two bows of magic, one of the mystic dozen. I doubt the bandit had any idea the power he was holding."

"I found a dagger on the boy." The woman replied. "It is also of the mystic dozen. It is *Venomstrike*."

"Is *Flamestrike* one of them?" Drathorn's voice was strained and scratchy but it surprised the pair, who had not known he was awake. He was lying in the Taldi hospital. The room was great and polished white with nothing but the bed he was laying on and two chairs on either side. He felt none of the pain from the arrow. It had healed completely. But he was extremely thirsty.

The woman jumped and ran to get him some water. Elforge moved his chair closer to Drathorn. "It's good to see you awake." Elforge said. "We thought we'd lost you. How do you feel?"

"Just thirsty sir." Drathorn replied.

"The doctor will be back shortly with something to drink." Elforge said. "How much of the conversation did you hear?"

"You woke me when you closed the door after coming in. I heard everything from the moment you sat in the chair beside me." Drathorn said. "*Flamestrike* . . . is it one of those mystic dozen?"

Elforge nodded. "The mystic dozen are twelve weapons that were enchanted so strongly that they never lose their abilities. They are; two daggers, two maces, two staves, two swords, a bow, a flail, an axe and a crossbow. They have existed longer than anyone can imagine. They also have the power to disappear completely and can be summoned from out of nowhere just by saying their names. But only the owner of the weapon can do it. In this way, you will always have your dagger with you; no matter how unarmed you appear. And now I have also made you the owner of the bow, *Firefang*. But where did you learn the name of *Flamestrike*?"

"I encountered a thief in the employment of the darklord that tried to use it against me while I was in Greengate." Drathorn said. "I defeated him but I couldn't find his body."

"Cherry Weldum . . ." Elforge muttered and Drathorn nodded in recognition. "He is one of the Darklord's most trusted. If I am correct he also has the blade *Lightningcast* and the crossbow *Ghostshadow.*"

"Well he's dead now." Drathorn said.

"No . . ." Elforge muttered. "Cherry is an Ali Manicota by magic. The darklord gave him an amulet that allows him to transform. You probably never saw the body because there wasn't one. Also, Cherry is one of the Ten Commandos, the Darklord's guardians."

"I know of them." Drathorn said. "I tricked Bandixi into telling me about them . . . he was one of them. I have his piece in my pocket."

Elforge was silent for a few minutes. He did nothing but look at the dagger, the bow, and the other objects on Drathorn's bedside table. "Is that an Ali-Manicota orb?" he finally asked.

Drathorn remembered the small blue sphere he had obtained when Elgard had died. He briefly told the story and explained that he was saving its power for a time of need.

For a short amount of time Elforge was silent. Drathorn decided to ask another question. "What is an angelic symbol?" he asked. "I know they are scars upon the flesh of those who have sinned . . . a mark that gives its wearer the forgiveness of the gods . . . But I didn't *want* to make one . . . it just happened." Drathorn touched his shoulder where he had carved the symbol without meaning to and was again surprised to find it was nothing but a pale scar.

"When a person conducts a great sin and fears the results they can sometimes be forgiven by the gods . . . but with this forgiveness comes a small punishment." Elforge said. "The gods' raw power is said to posses the body and force it to leave a scar upon its body that will never heal as a mark of that person's sin. Once the work is done the power disappears and the person is left in pain. Once the wound seals itself and becomes nothing but a simple scar like yours the effect of the mark begins to take place. From now on you will feel your sins through that mark but by feeling them physically you will be forgiven spiritually. As long as you do not give in to the physical pain of your sins you will always have a place in heaven no matter what sins you commit."

"Murder is a great sin . . ." Drathorn said, "I will feel the pain of such a sin very often if I continue this path as a warrior. But if it means

I will be forgiven for all my wrongs then I think it is worth it. What do the symbols mean?"

"No one really knows for sure . . ." Elforge said. "They are believed to be a sample of the ancient angelic language, symbols that only the gods understand . . . but there is no proof . . . People say that the symbol the gods force you to create is the mark symbolizing your greatest power."

"I see . . ." Drathorn said, not knowing what to say, he wondered what the mark on his shoulder meant, he wondered what his 'great power' was.

"Well, Drathorn." Elforge said after many minutes in silence; "The doctor will be back any minute and I have to oversee the cleaning of the city. The bodies must be removed. Your horse has been brought to the stables. Come and find me when you are released from the hospital." Drathorn nodded and Elforge left the room.

Drathorn waited a moment and then climbed out of bed. He put his clothes, ruined and stained with blood, back on and put on the Gorganite amulet again. It surprised him that Elforge had not asked him any questions about it. He sheathed *Venomstrike* by his ankle and put the Ali-Manicota orb in his pocket. Then, as he reached for the bow dubbed *Firefang*, the doctor re-entered the room.

Drathorn had been examining the bow. It was made of a wood that Drathorn could not name. It was carved to look very menacing and dangerous. Apparently shooting a regular arrow from this bow would give it the ability to poison its target and then catch fire after the poison was released. Drathorn quietly accepted the glass of water as he rubbed his fingers along the runes that formed its name. "Do you know how to summon the weapons?" the doctor asked him as he set down the glass on the bedside table.

Drathorn shook his head, "I have no idea ma'am."

"May I?" she asked, holding her hand out for the bow.

Drathorn handed the heavy weapon to her. She concentrated on the weapon and then held it with one hand above her head. "*Thi Sein Whor.*" The bow suddenly flashed brightly and disappeared. Drathorn was utterly shocked that the large weapon had just disappeared.

"Where'd it go?" Drathorn asked, surprised.

"I sent it away to the place of keeping." The doctor replied. "Anyone can send it away but only the owner can reclaim it. Elforge killed the old owner and became the owner but he gave it to you so now you are the only one who can summon it."

"How do I do that?" Drathorn asked.

"Just call upon it the same way I summoned it away." The doctor stated.

Drathorn raised his hand above his head the way she had done. He felt ridiculous, sure this would not work. "*Firefang!*" Drathorn called. At first Drathorn saw no difference in anything. But there was suddenly a flash of light and the bow was sitting heavily in his hand. Drathorn stared at the bow, surprised with what he had done.

He looked at the doctor. "I suggest that you keep your magic weapons hidden so they are not stolen." She said.

Drathorn nodded and repeated the incantation she had used before. In another flash the bow was gone. He did the same thing with *Venomstrike*. Then a question struck him. "Where do they go when you say the incantation?" Drathorn asked her.

"No one knows." She said. "But it is believed that they go to the heavens for safe keeping, for that is where they are said to have originated."

Drathorn didn't answer. There was so much about his powers, and about the rest of the world, that he did not understand. He absentmindedly picked up the shard he had taken from Bandixi and put it in his pocket as well. "Elforge is in the church." The doctor said. "He wants to see you."

Drathorn nodded and finished his drink before leaving the building. Just outside the hospital was the town square. Bodies were everywhere. Those of the bandits were piled and burned unceremoniously while the bodies of the Taldians were identified and taken to their proper homes where they could be mourned and buried.

He had no idea what was being done anywhere else. He walked slowly, watching the mourners and looking at the horrifically slaughtered men and women. He found his way to the church and entered. As he did his left shoulder began to tingle. Drathorn glanced at it and saw the white scar. It was a fascinating symbol. The Angelic Symbol seemed to be reacting to the church.

"Elforge?" Drathorn called. The elder stepped, alone, to where Drathorn stood in the entry hall.

"It's nice to see you up and moving again." Elforge smiled. "I want you to come with me into the basement of the church. The acts of Bandixi's men have made this place into an unholy place of evil. Although the power of the thirteen still flows here it is no longer a place of worship. We will use it to give you the gift of our people."

"A gift?" Drathorn asked, already convinced that the magic bow was a great enough gift from the people of Taldi.

"You saved our people." Elforge said. "It has been a tradition that the saviours of Tribal towns such as ours give a gift to those who save us. Our traditions all vary but every tribe has two of the same. The first is that they never relate with the people of the Empire. The second is that they lay upon their saviours the power of the Weretiger."

"Weretiger?" Drathorn asked, confused.

"The Weretiger is an ancient beast. Your grandfather was one." Elforge informed him. "Your grandfather saved one of our elders from a Vampire that had terrorized us for many years. So we made him a Weretiger."

"What does it mean to be a Weretiger?" Drathorn asked as they began to descend the stairs beneath the church. "Is it like a Werewolf?"

"In a way." Elforge nodded. "Being a Weretiger allows the human to transform into a tiger. This transformation also only takes place during the night. But unlike the Werewolf, a Weretiger can change every night and at its own will. They have complete control over their counterparts except under the full moon."

"So in a way they are the opposite of Werewolves?" Drathorn concluded.

"Yes." Elforge nodded. "Unlike Werewolves, who infect humans with a scratch or bite to create their brethren, the Weretigers are born by drinking a special potion. That's all they need to do is drink the potion."

"And this potion is down here?" Drathorn asked.

"Yes." Elforge replied yet again. "It is an unholy ritual but even some of the most holy and pure hearted have become Weretigers at some point. In fact, Elder Narcon is a Weretiger."

This is very confusing to me . . ." Drathorn said. "Especially after learning all about the ten Commandos and the Mystic Dozen. Actually . . . are the Mystic Dozen of any importance to my quest?"

This time Elforge shook his head, still descending the stairs of the church. "They have nothing to do with anything. They are just twelve weapons enchanted to last forever. They are indestructible, yes, but they mean nothing to you."

Finally Elforge and Drathorn reached the bottom of the stairs and walked through an open door. The room was a cellar. Along the far side was a cage made of thick bamboo. The bars were extremely flexible and probably nearly indestructible by human hands. In front of this cage sat a single table and two chairs. On the table was a large goblet that steamed with a red aura.

"You'll need to go in the cage before drinking the potion." Elforge stated. "The first twenty four hours of being a Weretiger are uncontrollable . . . the rest are fine."

"So what do I do?" Drathorn asked.

"Remove anything from your pockets and then remove your clothing." Elforge said. "I'll lock you in the cage and pass you the goblet. As soon as you drink the potion you'll feel its effects and when you wake up twenty-four hours later you will not remember any of the time as a Weretiger." Drathorn did as he was told, changing in the dark gloom of the basement. He climbed into the cage, testing the strength of the bars as he did. It seemed that they would hold against the might of the tiger. Elforge stuck the potion in between the bars and locked the cage tightly. "Drink up my boy."

Drathorn eyed the potion in his hands. The liquid was a disgusting red colour, bubbling around and he could see visible chunks of some disgusting substance in it. "What . . . what exactly is this made of?" Drathorn asked.

"If I told you, you would not drink it. It might be best that you ask when your twenty four hours are done." Drathorn nodded and began to drink the foul potion.

It was hot. It coursed down his throat quickly, burning his insides but Drathorn, of course, did not notice it. It tasted of blood but that did not surprise him, for he had guessed that it contained some. He immediately agreed that this was *not* a holy ritual. The Angelic symbol seared on his shoulder, causing him to scream in pain and drop the goblet. The symbol was doing its job; punishing him for his sin with pain. Drathorn suddenly realised that whatever he had drank was filled with sin and evil. Had he been tricked? Was this really Elforge?

His insides churned and his head ached and he fell to his knees. He put his face into his hands only to feel that they were suddenly furry. In the dim of the basement he could see orange and black fur growing rapidly from every part of his body. Something on his lower back should have burned like on fire but he could not feel it. He twisted and looked at his lower back. There was a small black spot there. It looked like a burn mark but he knew it could not be.

But soon that mark was gone to and Drathorn was no longer human. Elforge watched as the enraged tiger smashed around the bamboo cage. Its wood groaned as if ready to break but it held. The face still held many human features but that was the only thing to show that this creature had once been human. The rest was nothing but an overgrown tiger. The only other difference is that it did not have a tail. Where the tail should have been there was nothing but a bald spot in the fur, revealing pink skin that seemed to have been burned to a hideous black. Drathorn Hellbound was now, a Weretiger.

Troy, Thira and Murlok woke that morning, still tired. Despite that fact, Thira insisted that they had slept far too long and that Drathorn was going to get away from them if they slept any longer. They climbed out of the hole in the tree and mounted up, with Murlok on the back of Troy's steed. Troy still did not trust Murlok to be alone with Thira. He could easily betray them and kill the young acrobat. So Troy openly insisted that Murlok stay with him. They could not ride as fast as they had before because the extra rider weighed them down. But they kept a good pace and ran into no one.

Murlok insisted that they did not have far to go. But the storm had messed with their sense of direction and they traveled for almost an hour before they realised they were going wrong way. After righting their path they rode off again, this time in the right direction, hoping that this detour would not make them lose the precious time they had gained on Drathorn.

They stopped a lot later for lunch than they had planned. Troy wasn't happy. They should have been two hours farther ahead of where they were now. He muttered angrily to himself as he cooked a small meal and put a special meal together for Thira to eat so it wouldn't go against her vegetarian condition. After eating Murlok told them that they still had about six hours of riding ahead of them at this pace. If he was right then they would only make it as far as the Taldi River. They planned to camp there for the night and ride into Taldi in the morning.

By the time they *did* reach the river it was pitch black because of the many detours and stops to rest. It was hard to find a spot along the river where they could tie the horses but leave them close enough to drink. The trio finally walked slightly upstream from the animals and began to set up camp.

They rested on the banks, tired from the long day of riding. Thira and Troy were both full of excitement at being so near the town. If they were quick they might make it to the town before Drathorn left. And if not then they would find another way to catch up with him; they were determined.

Troy stretched out by the water, resting his leg and trying to avoid rubbing the cream on his skin to stop the irritation. He was not yet used to the constant traveling and his leg irritated him constantly when it was over worked. He massaged the skin but did not put on any of the ointment.

Murlok had fallen asleep by the fire and Thira was curled up, examining some of the newest pieces of art Troy had done. She paused over the one of Drathorn jumping Starcruser to the raft with the Hell's Door Beetle chasing him. Then she moved onto others that she had not seen. One was of the scene of devastation they had come across when finding Murlok. Another was nothing but a portrait of Murlok himself. The third was one that Thira blushed at.

It was not a new one. But she blushed at it greatly. Troy suddenly noticed she was looking at the picture he had drawn of Drathorn and Thira interlocked outside of the orphanage. Her face was so red that Troy could see it very clearly despite the darkness around them. She was obviously re-living the moment . . . re-feeling the emotions . . .

She noticed Troy was looking and then moved to the picture of Troy waving goodbye to his parents. "Drathorn's face was almost as red as yours when he saw that picture." Troy recalled with a laugh.

This made her blush even deeper. "I . . . I wasn't thinking . . . I was upset . . . I had no idea . . ." she denied it strongly and turned even redder as a single tear formed in her eye. The memory obviously pained her.

"That's what he said . . ." Troy said. "Apparently you guys were really good friends at the orphanage." But Troy didn't have time to say anything else. A sound of panic suddenly came from the nearby horses. There was a splashing sound and it seemed like one of them had fallen in the water somehow.

Thira jumped to her feet and Troy struggled to do the same. They left Murlok where he was and grabbed their weapons before racing off to find the horses.

Even in the darkness they could make out the scene in front of them. Troy's horse was in the river, two strange creatures jumping on it. Thira's mount was struggling greatly to untie itself from a nearby branch to escape a third creature.

The creatures were fairly small. They had tails as long as Troy was tall but that was easily the biggest part of their bodies. They had tiny heads with razor-like teeth. Two powerful legs allowed them to walk easily on land but on either side of both ankles there were little fins that could easily propel them through water. The legs were long and powerful and tipped with razor-like claws. The arms were tiny and had only two fingers that were also tipped with claws. The skin was of reptilian scales and their yellow eyes were pointed ever forward like a reptile. They were of a muddy colour to help them blend into the bottom of the Taldi River.

The two creatures jumped on Troy's horse and dug their small clawed forearms into the skin of the animal. Troy turned his aim onto one of those two creatures, who were now attempting to take a bite out of their prey. But as he was just about to pull the trigger and hopefully kill one of them he heard Thira scream. He hesitated long enough to see that Thira was doing her best to kill the nearest reptilian animal with her staff.

He had to admit she had great skill. She was easily keeping the horse safe. But in the process she was putting herself in danger. *It's too bad her tiny body renders her too weak to use any real weapons.* Troy thought. He instead opened fire on the creature cornering his companion, for her life was far more important than that of his ageing steed. The bolt caught the reptile in the side and it screeched in pain. It turned its evil eyes on Troy, giving Thira a chance to untie her horse and mount it. She rode past quickly, getting the steed back to camp. The monster, seeing that his original prey had escaped, turned away from Troy and toward the other two, who had managed to both grab the horse and were trying to wrestle it into the water.

Troy barely managed to reload and shoot again before the reptile could join his comrades. In the dark Troy saw the reptile change course and charge instead for him. He tried desperately to reload his slow crossbow but the reptile was too close. Troy abandoned his attempt to reload and braced himself with the crossbow raised.

The reptile opened its mouth and tried to bite Troy. He swung at the perfect time. The heavy crossbow collided with the reptile's temple, and it fell sideways. But the inhuman beast recovered fast and jumped at Troy. The archer attempted to step back but lost his balance on his wooden leg and fell. The reptile landed on top of him, knocking the crossbow out of his reach. Each of the creature's legs were on either side of him, the claws planted firmly in the ground. Its two forearms came down like pickaxes at Troy. He put his hands up and caught them both safely by the wrists.

Human and beast lay entwined on the ground. Troy could not move with the beast's crushing force moving in on top of him. The reptile's face, and teeth, inched closer. In only a moment they would close around Troy's face, killing him instantly. Troy closed his eyes and prayed to Borjil for strength as he pushed back with all his might. Suddenly a small pebble, launched with break-neck speed hit the creature in the shoulder, forcing it to lean back and cease its assault on Troy for only a moment as the collision spot exploded in a shower of blood. Troy seized this opportunity to kick upwards with his wooden leg. The genderless reptile was not affected as a human would have been, but the force with which the kick had landed caused it to fly off of him completely. Troy rolled out of the way and another pebble struck the creature. Seizing his crossbow Troy saw that the new attacker was Thira. She had returned and was using her sling and make-shift ammo to fight off the creature. He finally succeeded to re-load the cross bow and fired at the same time as Thira took another shot.

The bolt and the pebble struck at the same time, the bolt in the eye, the pebble in the throat. They would never know which attack had finished the creature but they didn't care. They turned their aim to the two creatures in the river. They had finally managed to drag the horse under the water and it had now drowned. They were viciously tearing apart its flesh, not paying any notice to the two fighters on the side of the river.

Thira prepared to attack the creatures but Troy held up a hand to stop her. "The horse is already dead." Troy said to her. "Attacking them would only increase the chances of one of us dying as well. Leave them alone and let's get out of here."

Thira seemed about to disagree but instead followed him slowly back to camp. He reloaded the crossbow and left it lying beside his sleeping bag. He was lucky today. All of the important possessions had been removed from the horse. The drawings, spare pair of clothing and cooking accessories had been moved into the camp a while ago. Troy looked through the saddlebags that were sitting around. He finally found the ointment and began to rub it in. Tonight was just not his night. By the time he was done rubbing in the ointment Thira had fallen into a restless sleep. Troy could not sleep so he stayed on watch again. Would he *ever* get his sleep?

XX

Travelers in Taldi

Monday May 12th, 18291, Troy and Thira filled Murlok in on the night's events that morning. Murlok's wounds and Troy's leg forced the two of them to ride Thira's horse and meant that they had to move much slower while Thira was stuck walking. Despite this they finally crossed the river and after a much longer walk then they had hopped they finally looked down a hill at the city of Taldi. Little did they know that if they had been only a little bit faster they might have met up with their evasive friend. But Drathorn had left nearly an hour ago.

Drathorn Hellbound woke in the cage, cold and tired. There was a black mark on his lower back that resembled a burn that was the only symbol of what he now was. Elforge was not there. He walked over to the bars and reached through them. As he fiddled with the lock on the cage he realized that there was still a bitter aftertaste in his mouth. He walked over to the table; his body was cold from the dampness of the basement. He found a set of clean clothes sitting on the table, along with a new long sword and dagger so that he would not have to carry one of his magic weapons. He put on the new clothing and almost immediately felt warmer. Being naked so far beneath the ground had chilled him so much that it was obviously the reason for his early awakening.

He collected Elgard's Ali-Manicota orb, Bandixi's shard, Troy's drawing, and the new weapons and then began to slowly climb the stairs. The light coming through the church windows was blinding to him at first. Again being in such a holy building made his arm tingle but he ignored it and continued on.

He walked out into the city. His first realization was that the people had made much progress in the cleansing of the city. The bodies of the dead had been removed and the streets were now fairly clean again. He walked along; examining the destroyed buildings and the blood stains that still lingered. He felt no different than he had before taking the potion, except perhaps a little more tired.

He didn't even notice all the people watching him walk. After a moment he asked where he could find Elforge and was pointed in the right direction. When he finally found Elforge he was over seeing a small group of fighters who were being equipped for battle.

"What is this all about, Elforge?" Drathorn asked the elder as he approached.

"These men are going to accompany you to the boat houses." Elforge replied. "I sent the rest of the army yesterday to clear out the bandits that were holding it. These men will guard you up till the boathouse and then you can sail with them to Signaroc. Your path from here remains clear my friend."

Drathorn nodded gratefully. "I see you got all of your possessions okay." Elforge acknowledged. "Well then it's time for you to go my friend. I wish you luck, the people of Taldi are forever in your debt and will always be loyal to you."

Drathorn mounted Starcruser and the surrounding fighters gathered around their mounts and saddled up. Drathorn trotted over to Elforge and bent low to the man. "What was in that potion?" he asked him.

"It is a horrific ritual." Elforge said. "It involves blood and guts . . . do you really want to know?" Drathorn nodded, dreading the answer. "This is the easiest yet most gruesome way. By stealing the guts of a man and boiling them while reciting an ancient ritual you create the potion."

Drathorn almost fell off of Starcruser. His face turned pale and then slightly green. He nearly threw up but he had had nothing to eat and therefore had nothing to remove from his stomach. Still he felt extremely sick, knowing what he had drunk.

"I said you wouldn't drink it if I told you." Elforge said, also disgusted.

"I suddenly feel like I don't very much like this gift." Drathorn said.

"By drinking the potion again you can undo the effect you know." Elforge replied.

Elforge managed to laugh at the look on Drathorn's face. Drathorn decided he did not want to talk anymore about the potion. "Good day, Elforge." Drathorn said, still struggling with his stomach. "I hope we will meet again soon."

Drathorn had taken the lead of the small group of fighters and they traveled at great speed for about thirty minutes out of the town before finally reaching the boathouses. Here too there were signs of recent battle. But to Drathorn's surprise the people were not preparing to sail to Signaroc. Actually they didn't seem to be doing much of anything. A captain suddenly approached Drathorn and his group.

"Sorry sir, but we cannot depart." He said. "The bandits also seem to have taken the ships of Signaroc and have created a blockade on the ocean around Hellfire Bay. We cannot hope to slip past them and safely disembark."

Drathorn swore under his breath. "I must reach Signaroc and warn them!" he said. "What are you doing about this predicament?"

"We're doing everything we can to gather troops and repair the ships. We plan to go to Nargak, one of the neighbouring tribal towns and request assistance from their armada." The captain smiled, hoping this would satisfy Drathorn. But instead Drathorn spoke again.

"How long will it take for their armada to prepare for battle?" Drathorn asked.

"For the amount of ships we're going to need . . . about a month sir." The captain's smile faded.

"I cannot wait that long." Drathorn said.

"The only other choice, sir, is to take the paper pass around Mt. Tanisay. But the pass is held by bandits." The captain informed him.

"Mt. Tanisay . . ." Drathorn muttered, thinking of the great mountain sitting perfectly on the edge of the ocean. He suddenly spotted it far in the distance. "That is where I must go."

The captain looked at him. "Sir! The small group you have here is not large enough to get you through the pass alive! And the rest of us have strict orders not to leave unless we're going to Nargak!"

"I won't be taking these men . . . and I won't be taking the pass either." Drathorn said, more to himself than those around him. "I'll be going over it."

It was nearly another half hour before the argument was resolved. Drathorn finally won them over. He dismounted Starcruser and commanded that they take good care of him and bring him to Signaroc as soon as possible. Then he began his march alone. The walk to the mountain would take a fortnight at least. But that did not concern him. Once he had gotten past the mountain it was only about a week's walk to Signaroc from there.

Three weeks was a lot less time than a month to him. And so he began his journey, alone, silently, and with no regrets.

The trio marched into Taldi quietly. They had not expected to find the town like this. Blood stained the once clean cobblestone streets, planks of wood and other debris lay randomly in a jumble. Some areas had been badly scorched by flames that were now gone. As they got closer to the city square they noticed that many of the buildings appeared shattered and broken. But of all this the trio did not show any signs of notice. They concentrated on the city square and that's where they soon arrived.

In the center of the square was the most gruesome sight they had ever seen, it was worse even than the scene in which Murlok had been discovered. In the very center of the square was a bonfire larger than any they had ever seen. But no wood fuelled those fires. The smell of burning flesh wafted to them from the burning mound. They forced themselves to look away from the gruesome sight and noticed that similar, but smaller, fires seemed to be spread throughout the city, all burning the bodies of dead men.

The homes and buildings of the square were even more devastated by flames and other unknown devastation. The street was still covered with blood and water that had yet to dry or evaporate in the heat of the afternoon sun. Only three of the buildings in the square could be considered close to intact; the hospital, one of the nearest houses, and the meeting hall. The latter seemed to have had minor repairs done to it and it was also the one toward which they headed.

However, someone walked out of the hospital toward them before they even had a chance to approach it. There was actually *two* someone's. One was an older man, carrying a large staff; the other was a short woman with long brown hair. "Hello travelers!" the old man with staff said. "I'm sorry for the horrible scenery. As you might have heard, we were under siege from the bandits of this region until quite recently. I am the Elder, Elforge, leader of the council of elders. This is Madam Teline, doctor and healer of Taldi. I'm afraid I have matters concerning the cleansing of the town to take me away from our conversation . . . I will leave you in the care of Madam Teline until I have the time to speak to you myself. Good day travelers." With that the elderly man walked off and out of their sight.

"Is there anything I can do to help you dears?" the doctor asked. Troy dismounted and the doctor eyed his leg with curiosity.

"Our friend is badly injured." Troy said, gesturing to Murlok. "We came here in hope that you could help him."

"Well let me take a look at him." She said.

Thira and Troy helped Murlok dismount and then Troy led the injured fighter into the hospital while Thira tied her horse to a support on the porch of the building. They all went inside and Troy had Murlok lay on a bed, stomach down so that the healer could see his back. Troy and Thira sat down in chairs while the doctor examined his back. "I've seen things like this before. It didn't hit any of the major organs or muscles. With proper healing he'll be fine. Excuse me for just a moment." The doctor left the room and the trio was again left alone.

Troy looked around the room. It was empty and clean. The only thing in it other than the two chairs and the bed was a bedside table on which Troy had laid his crossbow. There was a scream of pain from one of the other rooms followed by the doctor's voice, "Relax! It will only sting for a moment!" The screaming continued and there was a thud as something heavy hit the ground. "Ridiculous!" the doctor said. "Get him back up on the bed while I go see to the newcomers."

After a moment the doctor re-entered the room with a small bottle of a strange green coloured liquid. "This will clean that wound right up." She said to Murlok. "We need to clean out all the dirt and such so that it doesn't spread any infection once the cut seals."

"Is that what you gave the other man?" Murlok asked; a slight tinge of fear and regret in his voice.

"Yep." The doctor laughed, "But don't worry, he's a big baby and it only hurts if the cut is really dirty. Yours isn't that bad. It will hurt . . . but not as much as it hurt that particular patient I'm sure."

She poured a small amount of liquid on a cloth and examined it. Then she added a large quantity more to the cloth. She touched the liquid drenched cloth to the wound and there was an immediate and sharp intake of breath from Murlok. All his muscles tensed and his eyes slammed shut, grimacing in pain. The cut bubbled as the liquid touched the dirt and other things deep inside. Murlok groaned and breathed sharply again as the doctor moved the wet cloth down to another spot of the cut.

The doctor went on for another minute before another woman ran into the room. "Madam, the patient in room forty two-" said the woman breathlessly.

"Right of course." The doctor looked over to Thira. "Here dear, take these and do just what I was doing until the wound is clean or until I return."

Thira was suddenly left standing with the wet cloth and the bottle of liquid over Murlok's back. She looked at Troy, who shrugged with a smile. Thira gently touched the wound with the wet cloth. Murlok yelped and his body twitched quite suddenly. "I'm sorry, I'm sorry!" Thira cried, "I didn't mean to hurt you!"

Murlok sighed, "Its fine Thira." He almost seemed slightly amused at her reaction. "It was just so sudden; you didn't give me much time to brace myself. Go ahead it won't happen again."

Thira slowly brought the cloth down to the wound. Murlok breathed in sharply again and his body stiffened. She hesitated for a moment and then did it again. When Murlok winced she just shook her head. "I can't do it. Troy you do it; I can't do it when I know it's hurting him."

Troy limped over to her and took the cloth. She sat down in the chair, holding the bottle and took to watching instead. Troy brought the cloth to the wound and felt the muscles stiffen again. But he, unlike Thira, did not stop. He continued to use the cloth on the wounds and even replenished the cloth's liquid once.

The doctor finally returned and took the cloth from Troy. She examined the wound and pressed in on a few spots that they had missed. Then she threw the cloth onto the bedside table beside the crossbow. She held her hands only inches above the wound, palms down and fingers wide, she closed her eyes and bowed her head. She began to mutter words beneath her breath. From her hands came a small blue light. The wound began to heal, closing in on itself.

After a moment there was nothing left of the wound except a long scar across his back. Murlok rolled over suddenly, a smile on his face. He sat up on the bed. For a second he winced in slight pain.

"You'll still feel a little bit of pain now and then." The doctor said. "But the inside will heal just as the outside did. Until then I want you to take it easy. And you can keep that bottle of cleanser as a gift. You can use it next time one of you is hurt." Then the doctor left the room.

Murlok got to his feet with a smile. "I was worried she wouldn't be able to do anything." He said. "It feels so good to be able to move again. Now I can actually be of help to you!"

Thira looked to Troy, uncertain still of the ex-bandit's intentions. Troy watched Murlok for a moment and then he said; "Murlok . . . we would be glad to have your help." He held out his hand. "The more fighters we have getting us through our enemies the faster we can catch up to Drathorn."

Murlok smiled and shook Troy's hand. For the first time Thira realized how old he was. Probably about eighteen she thought. "Speaking of Drathorn," She said suddenly, "We should find that elder again and ask him if Drathorn's been through here lately."

Troy nodded and grabbed his crossbow as Murlok spoke. "He said he had things to deal with . . . maybe we should go next door and talk to one of the other elders?"

Thira and Troy agreed and the group left the hospital. They turned and entered the meeting hall. There were only two elders inside now. One was large and balding; the other was a thin elderly woman. "Welcome young ones." The woman said. "I am Elder Mikiera."

"And I be Elder Uri." The large man said. "Be there anything we may assist you with?"

Troy and Murlok bowed respectfully to the elders and Thira said; "Yes kind ones, we are looking for a friend of ours. We believe he may have come by here?"

"Taldi has been under siege from the bandits for many a month." Elder Mikiera said, "None have come through here but our dear saviour, young Drathorn Hellbound. If he be the one for whom you search then I'm afraid he has already left."

"What?" Troy asked, surprised and somewhat annoyed that they had failed to catch him yet again. "Where has he gone?"

"He travels west, to the boathouse." said Uri. "He plans to cross to Signaroc by the ocean."

"We would like to meet up with him and join his cause." Murlok said to the elder. "Could you possibly supply us with two proper steeds to assist us?"

"Indeed we can." Uri smiled. "And also, we would have you know that we are loyal to the friends of the Hellbound. He freed us from the wrath of the bandits. The destruction and death you see here is the result of our revolution."

"You mean he did all of this?" Thira exclaimed.

"Yes." Mikiera said, "He rebelled against the bandits the moment he arrived. He killed their leader and then gathered the people and started a riot. Once the riot reached its peak it turned into a full battle. He saved thousands and even single-handedly killed a mage."

"But that is in the past." Uri continued. "You must reach him and help him in his quest. Mikiera, please go get steeds for them." Mikiera bowed and walked out of the room. "If you go to the armoury we have a large supply of weapons that you may choose from. We took them from those who had fallen. There is barely any room left there . . . please help yourselves while Mikiera sees to the horses."

The trio bowed their thanks and left the elder alone in the meeting hall. They walked together through the town, now and then asking directions from passers by. They finally arrived at the large armoury and entered. There was no one inside but the whole building was filled with bloody weapons and armour. Together the trio began going through the whole area, pulling out weapons and armour that they were interested in.

Troy found a bow that was quite light. He immediately favoured it over his crossbow. Bows were much faster to reload and were even more deadly than a crossbow when in the hands of an expert. He also took a large quiver of arrows. He threw both of these over his back and then found a nice short sword that he sheathed around his belt. His leather armour was still good so he did not need to trade it in. But he did take a new dagger which he hid in his boot as an extra precaution.

Thira traded in her simple staff for one made of a strong and well polished maple wood. She found a set of leather armour that fit her fairly well and she put it on, all but the cap which she left behind because it was soaked with blood. Troy found that the leather seemed to emphasize every muscle and curve in her body, somehow making her appear even more attractive. She also took a small dagger and sheathed it in her belt.

Murlok found some of the best equipment. He found a good set of chain-mail leggings and vest. He managed to also find a pair of heavy plate boots and a simple iron helmet. Troy nearly traded his leather for a second set of chain mail but found that its weight slowed him down too much for his archery. As Murlok searched, he found two menacing blades that were slightly different from each other but were roughly the same size and would be good for the duel-swordsman's skills. He, like the others, found a nice dagger which he strapped around his shin with some leather material. He also put on a pair of leather-backed chain gloves.

The trio finally left the armoury well armed and feeling strong. They walked back to the meeting hall, heads held high and imaging the look on Drathorn's face when he saw them marching into the boat house. But when they rounded the last corner and gazed into the square it was to see the head elder Elforge talking gravely with a messenger. They jogged noisily to the elder and he looked up at them.

"Hello friends of Drathorn." Elforge said. "I'm afraid I have grave news for you." When no one said anything he went on. "It seems that the bandits have indeed taken the ports of Signaroc. My forces managed to get the bandits out of our ports but the bandits are using a few of our ships and the entire Signaroc armada to create a blockade that keeps us from reaching the Hellfire bay and assisting Signaroc."

"That's horrible!" Thira exclaimed. "What is being done about this?"

"We have sent all of our troops to the boathouse so that we could assist Signaroc. But since we cannot get there we will be instead going to Nargak." Elforge informed them. "Once there we will ask our brothers to join our cause and send their armada to the bay. Together we should be able to break through the Signaroc blockade and land in the bay to assist Signaroc. This whole ordeal will take about a month to put into action."

"What of Drathorn?" Troy asked, already fearing the answer.

"He has gone north." Elforge said. "He cannot wait the month and will therefore be going *over* Mt. Tanisay. My captain did the best he could to talk Drathorn out of it but had little success. Drathorn has already been traveling north for about an hour. He left his horse in our care; the mountains are no place for such an animal."

"That means he is moving on foot." Murlok said. "If we take our mounts we can catch up to him and stop him!"

Thira and Murlok both looked to Troy. They now saw Drathorn's brother as their leader and he was easily wiser than either of them. "No . . ." he finally said. "We will not give chase." Murlok's jaw dropped and Thira tried to argue but he went on. "We will go to Nargak and take charge of Taldi's forces in Drathorn's name. Even with Drathorn's help Signaroc will not be able to resist the power of the Darklord. He needs us."

"But we won't make it in time!" Thira protested. "We'll be too late!"

"Maybe so . . ." Troy said. "But we'll get there *during* the battle, not after it, if Drathorn is correct about when the battle will take place. If we're lucky *we* will be the saviours this time."

This time it was Elforge who spoke. "That is a wise idea." He said. "And I would gladly put my warriors in the command of Drathorn's friends. We elders cannot go to war; we are needed here to see to the reconstruction of our city. I bestow upon you the power to make all negotiations concerning the people of Taldi, seconded only to the orders of Drathorn Hellbound, should you ever meet up with him." Elforge handed Troy a small scroll. "Show this to the captain and he will leave you in charge."

With that he bowed and led the messenger inside. Before any of them could say another word Mikiera came from out of nowhere with two strong horses each laden with supplies including food, sleeping bags and spare clothes for their riders. Troy and Murlok took the animals gratefully. "Thank you, elder Mikiera." Troy said, bowing once again. "We must be going now, the boat houses await us."

The trio mounted their horses and looked down at the elder. She smiled and stepped aside so they could ride forward without harming her. "We ride west, to the boat houses. We ride to war!" Troy spurred his horse forward and behind him heard Thira and Murlok follow his lead.

An hour later the trio arrived at the boat house. They were greeted by the captain. Troy handed the captain the scroll. He read it quickly and then looked to Troy. "You are Troy Blaygard?" he asked.

"Yes sir." Troy said nodding. "And these are my companions."

"You needn't call me sir." The captain said. "You are in charge here. This note from the master says that the archer named Troy is to lead our troops. You are apparently in charge of all our negotiations and any choices we have are yours to make." The armoured captain bowed to Troy and his companions in respect.

"Don't bow, this is only temporary." Troy said. He dismounted and spoke quickly. "Where is Drathorn's steed?"

"We've moved him onto a cargo ship." The captain said. "That ship will carry a large group of our troops and all our supplies while the rest of us defend it with our battle ships. I'm sorry to say that the ship isn't meant to carry people and it will be very dirty and cramped."

"That is not a problem captain." Troy said. "As long as we reach Nargak in one piece I don't care. When can you be ready to depart?"

"We are leaving tomorrow morning at the first sight of the sun, as long as that is alright with you?" The captain added the last phrase unexpectedly.

"That is quite fine captain." Troy said. "Take our steeds and put them with Drathorn's to be brought along."

The captain had his men lead the steeds away without a word and then went on, "Sir Troy, your rooms are this way."

The trio followed the captain to the main building of the boathouses and opened the door. "This building contains four bed rooms, two bathrooms, a kitchen and a meeting room." The captain informed them. "You may occupy it as you wish; I will sleep in the barracks with the soldiers. If you wish for anyone to join you just ask the two guards who will be positioned at the front door."

The captain bowed himself away, leaving the trio alone in the cabin. Murlok walked noisily to the meeting room, which more resembled a living room, and sat down. Following his example, Troy and Thira began to make themselves at home.

XXI

Samgarnok, Chief Nargak

Tuesday May 13th, 18291, the trio was awoken by the captain. "I'm sorry sir but you must wake." He said. "You commanded that we leave at first light. We are ready to leave."

The sun was indeed beginning to rise in the sky and the sleepy group put their armour on and readied their weapons in the near dark. "Why are we going so early?" Thira groaned to Troy.

"I want to leave early so that the bandits can't see us too well." He replied, wide awake. "If we leave while it's still early we'll be halfway there before they notice us. And by the time we arrive the fighters of Nargak will be awake and will send ships to intercept us and assist us in landing in their ports."

Neither Murlok nor Thira could argue with that. They dressed and walked out where the captain was issuing last minute orders to the scurrying warriors. "Sir! We are ready to depart! Please board the cargo ship!"

The trio climbed on board the large carrier and realized just how full it was. There were at least a thousand fighters on board and a few had brought their families and steeds as well. Crates of supplies lined the walls. Troy led the others through the fighters to find their four steeds, where Murlok admired Starcruser with a trained eye.

"We should get a little more sleep." Troy said. "If something goes wrong we'll need our strength."

Murlok and Thira agreed and laid out their sleeping bags but Troy waited a minute. He climbed up to the top of the ship where the captain was barking orders but he soon realised that he was just in the way and returned to the others where he too, fell asleep.

Drathorn walked. Hours went by but still he walked. He had always ridden; he had never felt the strenuous pull of his muscles before but after five hours of continuous walking, he could feel it now. He had never felt the sun so hot on his back. He wished he had brought Starcruser. The horse's powerful legs and body would have carried them both forward at more than three times the speed. But Drathorn knew that Starcruser could not climb the mountain with him. Therefore if he had brought the horse he would have had only one other choice; to attempt to smash through the bandit toll area.

That was not an option. Going through that area would waste precious time. He was aware that it would take a fortnight to reach the mountain's feet. He estimated almost a day of climbing to cross the mountain and about another week to the city itself. He sighed aloud. *I hope I won't be too late.* He thought. *They need me . . . they have no warning . . . I must reach them . . .*

With those final thoughts in mind he strode forward at a slightly greater speed. The five hours of walking had already made his legs ache and he wondered what the near month of it would do to him. *I'll get used to it in a few days.* He decided. But as if the pull of his leg muscles was not enough Drathorn could suddenly hear barbaric screams from the woods on either side of the dirt road on which he traveled.

Drathorn's timing was perfect. He pulled his sword from his side and whirled to the right. He blocked just in time to save himself from an assaulting bandit. The bandit was holding a small hand axe but the force of his attack colliding with the sword caused it to break cleanly in half. Drathorn prepared to slay his attacker but was stopped when an arrow flew past his cheek, missing by only inches.

More bandits bearing crude weapons came from the forest on either side. Drathorn blocked one oncoming attacker but was again stopped by an arrow that barely missed him. Drathorn examined the bandits surrounding him; there were seven in total. The two he had managed to disarm had pulled out new weapons now. Before he or any of the attackers could move, arrows flew from the trees. Two arrows, one from each side of the road, flew at him; one aimed high, the other aimed low.

Drathorn jumped, avoiding the shot aimed at his legs, and did a small summersault in mid-air to avoid the one aimed at his head. The arrows struck the ground harmlessly and Drathorn rolled gracefully forward and cut off a bandit's leg with his long sword. Pain exploded in his shoulder as the sin of causing injury to another was committed. Drathorn ignored the pain and raised his sword. But before Drathorn could finish the bandit he was again stopped. Two other bandits with curved swords stepped toward him.

The first bandit swung forward and Drathorn blocked the clumsy attack easily. But the second bandit nearly caught him off guard. Drathorn managed to force them both back but was nearly slain by a third bandit carrying a large pitchfork. Drathorn breathed deeply as the bandits slowly moved toward him again, the pitchfork bearer in the lead. There was a twang of a bowstring and an arrow was suddenly flying toward Drathorn. He wouldn't be able to avoid it this time. This time it would hit him; he knew it.

Then there was the sound of a second bow releasing an arrow only a second later. Drathorn watched, eyes wide, as a second arrow flew from the direction he had originally been heading for and knocked his attacker's arrow right out of the air. And as if that wasn't amazing enough, it continued to travel forward and struck the pitchfork bearing bandit in the neck. The bandit made a gurgling sound and fell, dead, to the ground. Drathorn looked behind him at his rescuer.

The archer had long blonde hair that fell to his shoulders, but he was obviously a man. He ran fast while pulling a second arrow from his quiver. Drathorn supposed he was a hunter, his boots seemed padded as if to hide any noise he might make and even as he sprinted there seemed to be a feline grace to his movement. But Drathorn was most surprised that the man had managed such an amazing shot from such a long distance away.

Drathorn was forced to look away from the archer when he heard bandits approaching behind him. He turned back to see that they were almost right on top of him. Driven by a new determination Drathorn leapt at his attackers before they could get within range. He thrust his blade forward, driving it deep into the chest of a nearby bandit. Pain exploded again in his arm as the bandit died. There was the twanging of another bow string and Drathorn ducked reflexively. But from his ducked position he caught a glimpse of another arrow flying into the bushes. There was a grunt and a bandit fell from his hiding spot, dead, onto the road.

Drathorn managed to slice off another bandit's leg while he was crouched and then sprang sideways to avoid another sword strike, his arm burning with an agonizing pain. But he rolled right in front of another bandit. The bandit raised an axe, ready to kill Drathorn with a single blow, but Drathorn's saviour came through again.

The mystery archer jumped right over him, landing a kick in the bandit's face. The bandit fell back and the archer spun and hit another in the side of the face with his bow. Then, with surprising speed and accuracy he shot another arrow into the bushes and another enemy archer fell out a second later, an arrow in his forehead.

Determined to assist the hunter, Drathorn got back to his feet quickly and struck a bandit who had been trying to sneak up on the hunter. Drathorn suddenly realised that the bandits were now ignoring him completely and were teaming up on the powerful hunter. The hunter however, did not notice this. Another swift kick to the nearest bandit caused him to collapse and allowed the hunter to shoot again at an approaching bandit.

Realising that the pair before them was too powerful for their skills, the bandits called a retreat to the woods. Those who could still move scurried away helplessly, leaving the dead and wounded behind. The hunter did not move, he watched the bandits flee and stood without a word. Drathorn sheathed his long sword and took a cautious step toward the man. "Uh . . . Thank you . . ." Drathorn said.

The archer turned to him, his expression was a happy, welcoming smile that made him seem young and innocent compared to the murderous man Drathorn had believed him to be. "If anything, I should thank you." He said.

He definitely sounds young. Drathorn thought. But instead he allowed a different form of surprise to show. "But I did nothing to help you, you saved me!"

The man laughed. "I have been chasing that group of bandits for many days." He said. "I am Lindik Nolad. My father runs the rest house near Mt. Tanisay. I have taken to hunting bandits in the region for a little extra money. I thank you for slowing them down for me."

Drathorn realised that his thanks was truly not needed. They had obviously not known he would be coming. But he accepted the words of thanks anyway and said instead, "But the bandits got away!"

Lindik laughed. "They'll not get far." He said. "But I suppose I should give chase before they get a chance to regroup. Thank you for your help, I will leave you to deal with the wounded."

Before Drathorn could say anything else the man was off following the retreating bandits. *What a strange man.* He thought. With those words Drathorn killed the bleeding, legless bandits and made sure the others were dead. For a minute Drathorn thought of following Lindik after the bandits, but he realized that the hunter had the speed advantage and that Drathorn had his own business to attend to. With that he rushed off, along the way he had originally been heading. But this time he was sure to be much more aware of his surroundings; the pain in his arm still flaming.

The trio did not wake until midday and by that time they had already been set upon by the Nargakian Armada. The three warriors climbed to the upper deck of the ship and looked out. Their vast ship was no longer surrounded by just a few small ships from Taldi's port but also a large group of ships from the city of Nargak. Far ahead they could make out the Neeshara Desert and the city of Nargak. The heat was already unbearable even this far from the sands.

Only an hour later they had landed in the port of Nargak and the first thing they noticed was the heat. It was remarkably warmer on this side of the ocean, and also much drier. Outside the town's walls they could see the starting of the Million Mile River that stretched the whole length of the desert allowing small establishments to be built, a thick stone bridge had been made over the river.

The trio was joined by the captain and they were escorted by armed fighters from Nargak to the chief's home. "Who be you, travelers from Taldi?" the leader of Nargak asked. Troy looked at the man. He was brutishly large and extremely fit. Scars of battle crossed every inch of skin and his voice spoke with brute anger. Yet Troy recognised it as a fairly friendly greeting.

"I am Troy Blaygard, assigned negotiator of Taldi's naval units." Troy said. "With me are Thira Usonki and Murlok Niopski. They are my trusted advisors. The few ships we have brought are all that remain of Taldi's once proud army."

"I can see that much has befallen the city of our brothers in the past months since our last negotiation." The leader said. "I am Samgarnok, chief Nargak. What can we do for the negotiator of our brother?"

"I come bearing a message from the head Elder of Taldi, Elforge." Troy answered. "He says that I am to inform you that his homeland was invaded by bandits and the town was under siege. He understands that the people of the tribes usually remain neutral in the battles of the Empire's people but requests that you assist us in rescuing the city if Signaroc from the wrath of the darklord."

Samgarnok stared at Troy and his companions. He was silent at first but then spoke, without emotion. "And why should we consider helping such a city?"

"Elforge wishes that I inform you that his town was saved by none other than the hero, Drathorn Hellbound." Troy said, without missing a beat. "The citizens of Taldi remain in the debt of Mr. Hellbound and he says that any debt of one tribe affects the debts of the others. Therefore if Taldi chooses to help Signaroc then Nargak must do so as well."

"And why does our debt to young Hellbound have anything to do with the fate of Signaroc?" Samgarnok asked.

"Master Drathorn believes that the Darklord is about to attempt to seize the Journal of the Great Thirteen, a holy manuscript of the gods that may lead to the Darklord's complete rule of our world." Troy went on. "Drathorn has rushed to Signaroc to warn them and prepare them for battle. But Signaroc cannot stand alone against the might of the Darklord. Taldi has answered Drathorn's plea for help and requests that its brother do the same."

Samgarnok examined Troy and again asked a question. "How do you suppose we reach Signaroc before it falls?"

Troy hesitated and then replied slowly; "We are aware that it will take nearly a month to prepare for a full naval assault but we believe it is the only way." Troy said, "We request the aid of your naval units to assault and land in the Hellfire bay. From there we shall march on Signaroc."

Samgarnok was silent for a moment before he spoke, again without expression. "Am I to understand that the rumours befalling the capture of Signaroc's port are true?"

Troy nodded. "If the port had not been taken then your assistance would not be required and the whole of Taldi would have been transported there today. But that is not the case, oh humble chief."

Samgarnok was silent even longer this time. He examined Troy and the others quietly. He eyed Thira with particular interest and then moved his gaze to Murlok where it again rested for a moment. Finally, after Troy had begun to grow impatient, Samgarnok answered. "We accept the request of our brother. We will prepare for a month and a day and then we shall set sail for the city of Signaroc. It will mean deaths of many but we will finally play our role in protecting the great Hellbound."

XXII

Hunter in the woods, Rider at the gates

Thursday May 28th, 18291, the trio had been in Nargak for just over a fortnight. The ships were prepped for war and they trained with the fighters from both cities. Not a day passed where they did not look out across the ocean at the dreaded Mt. Tanisay as though expecting to see Drathorn from across the ocean.

One day the leader, Samgarnok, summoned them again to his throne room. "We need to discuss our battle technique." He said as the trio arrived.

Nargak's captain stood in front of a large table where a detailed map of the Hellfire Bay was drawn along with sketches of three different ships. "First we need to discuss the tree different ships that will make up our main armada." The Nargak captain said.

Troy nodded and Murlok said "Start the lecture then."

"The major ship is the battleship." He said. "It's a sturdy ship made for holding weaker artillery. From the ship our fighters can fire flaming arrows at enemy ships to damage and hopefully destroy them. They can also be used to get close to, and even allow infantry units to board, enemy ships." The captain pointed at the first drawing where a battleship was labelled crudely with the names of parts and the type of wood it was made of.

"The second is the destroyer." The captain went on. "Destroyers are meant for long range assaults and are equipped with two heavy catapults on the top deck and four fair sized ballistae in case an enemy gets too close. Because of how large these weapons are the ship is fairly slow and hard to defend."

"The third ship is an average transport that isn't equipped for battle. You can easily transport fighters on a battle ship but transport ships can hold many more fighters and are much faster than either the destroyer or the battle ship." The captain finalized. "We only have three destroyers and about forty battleships. The rest of our armada is made up of Transports. We need to come up with a way of taking over the enemy destroyers and using them against the enemy otherwise we'll never be able to pull this off."

Samgarnok spoke next. "I have no ideas as to how we could manage this." He said. "So as you are negotiators from Taldi we ask if you can think of any possibilities."

Thira frowned and after a moment Troy shook his head. But after a second Murlok walked over to the map of Hellfire bay and began muttering to himself. "Do you have an idea?" Troy asked.

"I think so . . ." he said.

"Do share." Thira said, moving closer to the swordsman.

Murlok circled the area of Hellfire bay closest to Nargak where a small amount of dots represented the enemy destroyers they would need to get through. "If we could somehow get our battleships close enough to these ships to render their catapults useless we might be able to board them and commandeer them for use against our enemies . . . but it will be very difficult and it may cost us the loss of many ships."

"If that were to succeed then what?" the captain asked.

"We could use all the destroyers to decimate the bandit ships and keep our transport and battle ships protected while we infiltrate their defences." Murlok said. "Then we could use the destroyers to lay waste to the bandit boathouse and safely land our transports on the docks of the bay."

"That could work . . . but how would we get the ships close enough to the enemy destroyers?" Troy asked.

"How about we disguise our ships as bandit ships?" Thira suggested.

"The Nargak ships and the Taldi ships are much too different in design to send some of each; we'd be discovered right away. And we only have five Taldi ships . . . and we have no bandit flags to put up to disguise us." Said the captain.

"We could send a ship or two back to Taldi and check if there are any flags left from the bandits that we could use." Samgarnok said suddenly.

"Good idea . . . we can send a few ships back to gather flags and such . . . then the three of us will lead the Taldi ships forward, pretending to be bandits and get past their greatest line of defence. Once we're in we will board the enemy ships and take them over. Then we'll send a signal for you to send in the Nargak ships." Troy was getting some of his old excitement back now and began talking faster. "Then we will destroy the bandits and save Signaroc!"

Samgarnok turned to the captain, obviously confident in the plan. "Collect two battleships and one transport and head for Taldi immediately!" The captain nodded and ran from the room.

It would happen soon. In about another fortnight they would be setting sail for Signaroc. Troy kept himself in a strong, leader like, form but inside he was filled with joy at the fact that he was finally going to be able to help Drathorn.

Drathorn was a changed man. The fortnight of solid marching had strengthened him. He was dirty and had met no one since his encounter with the strange hunter. The roads were oddly silent. He had not used his voice in a long time. He suspected that when the time came it would be very weak from lack of use. But his body had hardened from the non-stop marching. With his sword sharp at his side he walked on. He knew he was getting close to the mountain; it loomed ever large and nearer than before.

To Drathorn that meant nothing but the fact that there was a resting home nearby where he could cleanse himself and restock his food supply. Drathorn began to notice a change in the weather now. The farther north he progressed the colder it seemed to get, especially at night. The two weeks had taken far too long to pass in Drathorn's mind. *Signaroc could have already fallen,* Drathorn thought. *I may already be too late.*

But the warrior drowned that thought the moment he saw the smoke rising farther north. *It comes from near the paper pass.* He acknowledged. *The bandits must indeed have hold there. I hope the resting home still stands.*

Drathorn suddenly quickened his pace to a slow jog. *I must make sure all is well . . . I must reach the resting home before morning's light . . .* With that last thought he broke into a run.

It was burning. The rest house was a burning wreck, flames sprouting across it from every direction. Bandits were everywhere, throwing burning torches at the building and laughing evilly. Drathorn knew what had to be done. Elforge had told him how before he left but Drathorn wanted to avoid it as much as possible. Apparently there was an unbearable pain during the transformation.

Drathorn was absolutely still. He stared deep into the flames and continued to stare until it hurt his eyes. He didn't want to do it . . . but he had to. *Weretiger.* He thought. The very word pulsed through him. A strange energy flowed into him. The pain was unbearable. But as quickly as it had started, the pain stopped.

There was no trace of the human; the clothes had not torn apart during his growth to tiger form. Actually the clothes were nowhere in sight, nor was the sword. The great tiger had no tail, a small burn mark where it should have been made it look as though it was burned off. The only human features were in the creature's face. But instead of making the tiger appear civilized and friendly it made it even more frightening.

Unlike his first transformation, which Drathorn could not remember, he found himself in complete control of his new brute strength. With his feline eyes Drathorn saw clearly in the night. He saw two bandits bearing pitchforks and blazing torches nearby, the first threw his torch at the already blazing building. In one enormous leap Drathorn covered the distance between him and the bandits. In fact, he landed *in front* of them.

The bandits stopped laughing and examined the beast fearfully. Drathorn meant to speak, to yell and demand that they stop this attack, but it came out as a loud roar. The roar seemed to stir the bandits to life. The one who had thrown the torch lunged forward with his pitchfork. Angry, Drathorn slashed out with his enormous paw and broke the pitchfork cleanly in two pieces. The assault not only disarmed the bandit but it also sent him flying backwards. The second bandit ran at him with his own pitchfork but Drathorn clamped his mouth around it and wrenched it free of the attacker's hands.

By flexing his powerful jaw muscles he again snapped the weapon in two. He ignored the torch bearing bandit, aware that his Hellbound abilities made him invincible to the flames and turned to the first bandit who had pulled out a dagger. Drathorn made to kill the bandit with a single swipe but there was a strange sensation of pain on one of his hind legs. He roared again and turned his head. As he turned the pain stopped and he saw flames of a torch fly at his face. He was too slow to stop them reflexively and they collided with his face.

But instead of the pain from a simple collision he felt the burn of the flames . . . The flames burned his face, sending him shrieking uncharacteristically in pain. *As a tiger I am not resistant to fire!* Drathorn suddenly realised. *I was careless.* Drathorn roared again. He jumped this time for the bandit bearing the torch. The bandit put the torch between them but it was swatted away and Drathorn landed on top of the man. With a single swipe of his paw he decapitated the man and turned to the first bandit.

The bandit stepped back and tripped over his own feet. He fell hard, looking up at the powerful figure of the Weretiger. Drathorn hesitated; perhaps he would spare this man? But the bandit took his hesitation as the perfect moment to attack. The tiny dagger was stabbed into his front leg and he roared in pain. The bandit attempted to scurry away but Drathorn pushed down on his back and drove him into the ground, breaking the bones of his back and leaving him permanently paralyzed. It was then he realised that in his Tiger form he also could not feel the pain of his Angelic Symbol.

With one paw Drathorn easily turned him over. The bandit looked, unmoving and fearful, into Drathorn's eyes. Drathorn considered him and then killed the man with a single bite to the neck. The taste of the potion came back to him. In his human form he had not originally recognized the horrid taste of blood and guts, stolen from the bodies of the dead. But the taste had sickened him. Yet now, as a Weretiger, the taste filled his mouth as he bit. He did not care. For some strange reason this taste contented him. He knew he should be disgusted but as the liquid found his stomach he could barely find it in himself to release the dead man. Drathorn finally managed to remove his murderous bite. He looked, ashamed, at his handiwork. The blood tasted so good to him in this form even though he was mentally disgusted.

In his mind, Drathorn was revolted. He instead turned his head back to the burning building. There were still many bandits attacking the resting home. The next set of bandits didn't know what hit them. Three of them were bearing torches and laughing loudly as they lit the sides of the house. The giant Weretiger fell on top of the first bandit as if born from the sky; the weight of the beast landing on him in such a surprising manor had killed him instantly. The other two looked at Drathorn and charged forward. A single swipe knocked the first of the two far to the side. The second bandit didn't hesitate; he ran right at Drathorn, now wielding an axe, and swung it wildly. The blade cut deep into Drathorn's fur and he roared and swiped out again. The bandit fell to the ground, many bones broken from Drathorn's attack. He would die in a matter of moments.

Drathorn turned his head to look at the first bandit he had knocked aside and found him not alone and wounded, but standing tall with a spear and joined by nearly two dozen others all wielding torches along with spears, bows, small axes or swords. Drathorn attempted again to speak to them. "Leave this place alone, go now!" he tried to yell. But it came out as a low growl that a few of the bandits took as a warning causing them to hesitate for a minute. But with a nod from their leader the bandits began to spread out around him, leaving no way of escape.

Drathorn would not let them make the first move; he struck out at a nearby bandit and felt the pain of a large arrow digging into his side. He turned his head to his attacker and saw him reaching for another arrow but before Drathorn could consider his next move two other bow wielding bandits shot at him. One arrow flew along his side and left nothing but a single scratch along his skin. Drathorn managed to avoid the second arrow but then found him-self even closer to the knot of angry bandits.

A spear wielder in front of him lashed out and Drathorn swatted his weapon away. This defence allowed another bandit to stick an axe in his lower back and he roared in pain again. No matter what he did he could not escape. He slashed out, fighting blindly and smashing bandits away two or even three at a time. But he could not see through the blood that somehow poured into his eyes. More and more pain came from everywhere.

Drathorn stood up on his hind legs and roared angrily. Through the blood he saw the small figures of the bandits moving in for the kill. He swept his forearms forward, knocking them all back hard. He took this time to attempt to wipe his blood filled eyes on his fur. As soon as he did he felt the shaft of an arrow break from the top of his head and he realised that was where the blood had come from. Another wipe and he could see again. The bandits were advancing again now. Drathorn was weak, the falling blood forming puddles around him. He could see that he had managed to kill two of his attackers in his blind rage. But there were still too many bandits for him to take care of alone in his weakened state.

One bandit broke from the group and ran forward with his axe, Drathorn made to swipe at him but the warrior ducked and raised his axe to strike Drathorn. But he stopped suddenly, and the shaft of an arrow was sticking out of his neck. Drathorn and the bandits looked at the new addition to the battle. Drathorn recognized him quickly in the darkness, his feline eyes showing even the finest features of his saviour. Lindik Nolad, Drathorn's saviour from the woods nearly a fortnight ago, was running forward; bow in hand. Lindik fired another shot and another bandit fell. As Drathorn's feline eyes watched his saviour he realised that the hunter was being followed. "Look out!" he tried to yell. But the words were just a strangled growl.

Somehow Lindik seemed to understand and turned around. He turned just in time to duck as a spear was launched over his head. The other bandits were too close to Lindik for his bow to be as powerful of a threat as it should have been in his hands. Drathorn suddenly realised that the only way they would escape is if they worked together against this force and to do that he would have to save Lindik as he had already done twice for him.

Drathorn turned from his own attackers and began to charge toward Lindik. Lindik seemed to panic, suddenly fearing Drathorn had turned on him. Lindik pulled out an arrow and aimed it at Drathorn's frightening figure but Drathorn jumped high over him before the hunter could fire. He landed on one attacker and swiped another across the stomach. Both died instantly and Drathorn was now the only thing standing between Lindik and his attackers. All was suddenly quiet. Drathorn and Lindik were now surrounded, both groups of bandits bearing weapons and nearing them, forming a tight and unbreakable circle.

Drathorn didn't know what to do, his only choice would be to jump at the nearest bandits and hope for the best. He growled, this time purposely a warning. The bandits didn't even hesitate this time, they moved in closer. That was their first mistake of the night. The ground exploded beneath a group of them, sending them flying in random directions. A small boomerang type item flew from the darkness and struck another bandit. "Mother . . . father . . . thank you." Drathorn heard Lindik say quietly to himself before returning to the attack. Drathorn was confused.

It was only a moment before Drathorn saw a large man in powerful iron armour run into the battle with a large battle axe in his hands and a few more of the boomerangs at his belt. A second later he noticed a robed woman in the trees near the house; a lightning strike flew from her hand and struck another bandit. Drathorn realised that these two must be the owners of the rest house; Lindik's parents. He suddenly realised that he was not just protecting an inn; he was protecting a family and a home. He roared again and leapt at a group of four bandits, striking fiercely and giving them no moment to retreat; they would all fall.

"I am Jorindan Nolad; I run the rest house between Taldi and Signaroc." said the man. Once the family had assisted Drathorn in saving the rest house he had transformed to find that none of his Weretiger wounds seemed to affect his human form. After a few moments of awkward silence and thanks Lindik's mother had put out the flames using magic and invited him inside for a meal. Drathorn reluctantly accepted and followed the family in. As the mother began to work in the kitchen Drathorn sat down with Lindik and his father at the table. "My boy here is Lindik."

"We've already met, father." Lindik said, smiling. "He is the young boy who helped me two weeks ago . . . Drathorn Hellbound."

"A Hellbound? Here?" Jorindan questioned. "Are you here about the bandit crisis at the pass?"

"Actually . . . No." Drathorn said. Both Lindik and Jorindan frowned with disappointment. "I have already removed the bandit leader from Taldi . . . it shouldn't be long before the bandits realize how weak they are and go into hiding."

"Then why do you come this way?" Jorindan asked in confusion.

"I'm traveling to Signaroc . . . I believe that the Darklord plans to strike there next and I plan to stop him." Drathorn said. Jorindan and Lindik exchanged strange glances. "What's wrong?" Drathorn asked, "Am I too late? Has the city fallen?"

"No . . ." Lindik said, shaking his head. "But the Darklord's army invaded the city of Narvahan Shé a little more than a week ago. A small party of riders escaped and headed west. As far as I can tell the Darklord's armies are using the city as a base and will attack Signaroc within the month. Their numbers are too great, even for the city."

"I *will* stop them." Drathorn said, slamming his fist on the table. "They are after the Journal of the Great Thirteen. The Darklord believes that he can use its power to destroy what remains of the Hellbound's power and crush any hope of victory for the free peoples. I will *not* allow it!"

"Calm yourself, Hellbound." Jorindan said. "Tell us, how do you plan to reach the city? The paper pass is held by over three hundred of those damn bandits."

"I plan to scale the mountain." Drathorn said. "If I can reach the top alive then I'll be able to reach the other side with ease."

"The mountain path is dangerous . . . filled with Drooling Azadons." Lindik said, "I've been there many times . . . but I dare not scale it to the peak. I mainly only go up to the lower levels to find special spices for my mother's cooking. And I still prefer not to go up at all. Bandits are nothing compared to the Azadons . . ."

"But if you are strong of heart and might you may survive to reach the peak." Jorindan interrupted. "I'll have my son take you to the foot of the mountain in the morning. Until then eat a well prepared meal from my wife and you may bathe and have clean clothes."

"Thank you for your kindness, Jorindan . . ." Drathorn said, nodding his head.

The trio rose that morning to the sound of trumpets. They were not the horns of war that they were expecting so they gathered their equipment and rushed from their cabins, fully armed. Troy was the first one out but he fell behind as the others hurried to the gates. They waited for him at the foot of the tower beside the main gate and then rushed up with him tagging along slowly behind. He finally reached the top and opened the door to find Thira and Murlok looking down, stunned at the seen below them.

Troy limped over, his new bow at his side, prepared for the worst. But it was not an army at the gate. Two dozen men on horseback waited at the gates, their spears bloody and all of them covered in wounds. At the head of the small group was a single rider. He too was wounded, the shaft of an arrow sticking out of his shoulder and his right arm wrapped tightly to stop the bleeding of a very deep cut. His spear was more blood stained and battle worn than any of the others.

They all wore the leather riding armour of the tribal city of Narvahan Shé, the leader also wearing the chief's family crest on his chest. A flag of Narvahan Shé was hanging from the spear of one of the riders.

The leader sat high and proud, despite his injuries. His skin was the brown of chocolate and his bald head shone bright in the desert sun. His eyes were filled with many emotions, including anger and pain. He wore the chief's family crest but he was not old enough to have been the chief himself. By the crest on his front and the fact that he led, Troy supposed he was in fact the son, or perhaps grandson, of the city's chief. *The son of Narvahan Shé's leader at our door step,* Troy thought; *its riders wounded and weak . . . it is as Drathorn feared, Narvahan Shé has fallen . . . the forces of the darklord will soon march on Signaroc . . .*

"Open the gates! Someone fetch the healers!" Troy ordered. It was a long day and the trio fell asleep quickly that night from exhaustion. Helping the healers tend to all the injured from Narvahan Shé seamed like an endless task but they kept at it till all were resting comfortably in the town hospital.

Friday May 29th, 18291, the dawn was cruel that day. It had come far too early in Drathorn's opinion. He dressed quickly in new clothes provided by the Nolad family and strong leather armour, provided by Lindik himself. He left the room with his sword sheathed in its scabbard on his new belt. Lindik was outside already, his bow held at his side and his eyes set on the rising sun. "My father shall not come with us . . . he will be staying with my mother to repair our home." Lindik said before Drathorn could say anything, "I plan to take you to the foot of the mountain as fast as possible and then return to assist them."

Drathorn nodded, "Let us be off then, I'd like to reach the mountain peak before dark." Lindik nodded in agreement and headed out in the direction of the monstrous mountain.

After breakfast the trio headed for town hall. There they met with Samgarnok and the leader of the Narvahan Shé survivors.

"I am Feronis, son of the chief." said the leader. "My riders and I are the last of the people of Narvahan Shé . . . we were attacked from our own port by an enormous fleet of Badlands' ships. While we struggled to resist the enemy ship's boarding party the Orange Riders of the Badlands struck us from the west. We could not stop them. As we escaped we saw the riders head south-west, slightly away from the city of Signaroc. We believe they are returning to the Bad-lands."

Feronis was the leader. He had bright green eyes that clashed drastically with his dark skin. Troy supposed that he would be recognized for that feature in the future by all. On the palm of his right hand was a yellow mark shaped like the sun and he was much taller then anyone in the trio. He also appeared to be about nineteen years old.

"What of the army from the ocean?" Samgarnok asked.

"They have fortified the city and are using it to base their men." Feronis said.

"Then it is as we feared, they will soon strike Signaroc . . . they may have already done so for it has been more than a week since your escape." Samgarnok said.

"I doubt that." Troy said, "The army would need at least a week to prepare for another attack . . . treat the wounded, burn the dead, salvage resources from the city's remains . . . I believe we have time enough yet."

Neither Samgarnok nor the dark skinned captain spoke. "How goes the preparation of the ships for the attack on the bay?" Murlok interrupted.

"The Taldi ships have been equipped with the bandit sails as a disguise and all ships are being loaded with large supplies of medical and assault equipment as we speak." Samgarnok said.

"Attack on the bay?" Feronis inquired. "You mean the Hellfire bay?"

"Yes rider, we are planning to attack the bandits holding the bay." Thira said. "We have reason to believe that the army that took your city has actually set a goal to strike the Empire controlled city of Signaroc and is using your homeland as its base of operations in the process."

"Reason to believe?" Feronis quoted, "Now what on mother's rock is such a pretty little lady doing here, talking of war and politics? And why do you have a 'reason to believe' such a thing?"

Troy looked angrily at Feronis, his hand slowly inching toward the short sword at his belt; did this man mock Thira's ability? Was he truly a noble from Narvahan Shé? If he was would he really speak to Thira in such a crude manor?

Thira spoke first; "Do not speak to me like that, rider of the eastern shores." she said, a hint of annoyance in her musical voice. "We believe that the darklord wants to get his hands on the Journal of the Great Thirteen and use it to destroy Drathorn Hellbound and the last of the resistance and take over Corrone. We believe this because our friend, Drathorn Hellbound himself, has seen it."

"You are in acquaintance with the last of the Hellbound? Where is he? I would dearly like to speak to him!" Feronis said.

"Drathorn is not here, he has taken to the mountain pass over the great Tanisay to reach the city on foot. He plans to warn the city against the attack." Troy said. "We are going to aid the city by joining forces with Signaroc's army."

Feronis' look of surprise turned suddenly to outrage. "Samgarnok, you know better than to assist the cities of the Empire!" he roared. "They are liars, cheaters and barbarous murderers who would kill our people and steal our crops because we fail to believe in their government system!"

"I am not helping the city, rider, I am helping Drathorn Hellbound, the last hope of the free people!" Samgarnok said calmly.

"And for what reason do we have any need to help him?" Feronis asked.

"Drathorn Hellbound saved the village of Taldi from the wrath of the bandits." Samgarnok said. "We, as a tribal group, owe him our gratitude. It is to repay our debt that we now assist him in the battle for the journal."

"Damnit Sam! Where are the Elders of Taldi? I have seen their people but I do not see them!" Feronis said, his voice still bearing anger.

"The elders have remained in the city of Taldi." Troy said. " My two companions and I have been sent by them as negotiators and combat generals in their place."

Feronis looked at Troy, then to Thira and Murlok, and back again. He eyed Troy's hand, resting on the hilt of his sword as though he was waiting for Feronis to make an aggressive move.

"Who are you?" he asked.

"I am Troy Blaygard, foster brother of the great Drathorn Hellbound." Troy said. "This is Thira Usonki, Drathorn's best friend and greatest companion whom he met in the orphanage. And this is Murlok Niopski, a friend we made as we searched to meet up with my brother after he ran off, fearing to endanger us should he have stayed in our company."

"Blaygard?" Feronis noted, "You are of one of the Imperial cities, why should the tribes of Tanroe trust you?"

"Did you not listen? I am the brother of Drathorn Hellbound; Taldi is as much in my debt as they are his!" Troy said.

"And any debt one of us pays is a debt we all must pay." Samgarnok said, "Nargak and Taldi will join forces against the foes of Signaroc, and if you honour the code of the tribes you will do the same."

"Then we shall help young Drathorn." Feronis growled. "As long as there is still hope in his name I will assist the Hellbound and his friends."

"Your riders will ride in one of the Transports." Samgarnok said. "Once our disguised ships do their job we will escort you to the boat house at the bay and your riders will assist my troops and what remains of Taldi's warriors. When the final battle for Signaroc arrives we will separate into three battalions; Nargak (lead by me), Narvahan Shé (lead by Feronis), and Taldi (lead by Troy). Thira and Murlok can join the Taldi battalion. The three of you will ride your steeds with your battalion while Feronis and his riders strike. My warriors should arrive at a fair time."

"It will not be long now . . ." Troy said. "The disguised ships are ready to sail and the troops are training hard . . . soon we shall sail."

Lindik and Drathorn stood, side by side at the foot of the mountain. It was an hour to noon. They had arrived quickly and without trouble. "It will take you nearly six hours of non-stop climbing to reach the peak." Lindik said. "I'm sorry but I'll not be coming with you."

Drathorn looked away from the mountain as he adjusted the coil of rope on his shoulder. He smiled at Lindik; "If it weren't for you I would not be alive today." Drathorn said. "Somewhere on the other side of this mountain is my friend, Bronc Silvermask. Together he and I will travel to Signaroc and he will teach me to be a *true* hero. But until that day I will continue to thank brave warriors such as yourself for your assistance."

"And I will thank you, for being a beacon of hope for the free people of Corrone." Lindik said. "May your travels undo the evil of the Darklord and save us all."

The two clasped hands and then Drathorn watched as Lindik began to slowly work his way home. Drathorn finally turned to the high peak. "Here I come . . ." he muttered. And then he was climbing the steep, rocky slope of the mountain.

XXIII

Battle on the Mountaintop

It wasn't long before Drathorn could no longer walk up the side of the mountain. Soon Drathorn was forced to use the rope with a strong hook to pull himself up steep sides and even swing from one spot to another. The farther he went the slower he was forced to move, even more so when he was high enough for the never melting snow of the mountain to begin.

Drathorn estimated that he had climbed for at least seven hours and was annoyed by that idea because that put him way behind schedule. Angrily he threw the hook high above him and felt it catch between two large chunks of ice. He tested the rope and then began to scale the cliff edge he had been resting by.

As he worked, with every muscle in his aching body straining, his mind strayed once more to his friends. Troy; the loyal, trusting, one legged, joke loving archer . . . *He must be home with his family by now.* Drathorn thought. *And the guards must be caring for them greatly. I miss his company so much . . . If only my brother could see me now . . . I can already picture his drawing of me climbing this wall of ice and stone, Thira waiting patiently to see the unexplainably amazing new drawing.*

Thira . . . Drathorn's thoughts suddenly turned to her. *How she must miss me so . . . I remember our last parting so clearly, she was so upset . . . I can only imagine her now, crying into Troy's arms as she mourns my absence.* Drathorn frowned as he finally pulled himself over the sheer edge. *It pains me to think that I may never see her again. I hope Troy and his family take good care of her . . . She means so much to me.*

He looked around the small ledge he was on and then looked up. About twenty feet above him he could see the peak of the cliff. But from his recollections he supposed it was a long flat expanse of ice; for the name Tanisay meant flat in the Dwarven language.

He looked out at the nearby ocean. He could see straight across it. It was past dinner and fires could be seen lit for light far off in the town of Nargak. He couldn't see Signaroc from this side of the mountain but he supposed that both Signaroc and Narvahan Shé were visible as well. As for the town of Taldi, he supposed it was hidden by the trees. Greengate and Gaberdan were too far away for him to see.

It was beautiful; the trees, the ocean, the gentle breeze, the slowly setting sun. *If only Thira could see this. If only Troy could draw this . . . If I should survive this quest I would like to return here with them.* Drathorn tossed the grappling rope upwards as hard as he could and felt it catch something. He tugged and found it quite tight. He began to scale the wall again as a new thought occurred to him.

But what if I don't survive this quest? He asked himself. *What if I die? What if I never see Thira or Troy again? What if I never get to personally say goodbye to them?*

He was nearly at the top of the slope now. Another step on the ice, another, another . . . He peeked over the edge of the ice and found exactly what he had expected; a wide expanse of ice and snow and rock and even spots where it had melted away to form dirt. In one of these patches of dirt was a large tree, growing tall and strong, it was on this tree's bark that Drathorn's rope had caught. A little over from the tree was an enormous boulder, sticking out awkwardly from the cliff side, right above the area of the paper pass.

Drathorn groaned as he began to lift himself over the edge, when suddenly there was movement on the peak. From behind the tree there stepped a man wearing heavy fur clothing to protect him from the cold of the mountain. Drathorn didn't really notice the cold, his leather armour protected him against most of it but his fingers were numb and rope burnt and his face was chilled. The man in the furry leather armour also seemed to be wearing a heavy helmet with a visor shut to hide his face. A long sword hung at his waist and his hands were heavily gloved with thick leather, in one hand was a lethal dagger, in the other was a thick wooden shield.

Drathorn was prepared to yell to the man, to ask for assistance in pulling himself over the icy cliff edge, when he suddenly held his dagger up to the rope. "Hello, Drathorn Hellbound." Laughed the man, it was a voice he recognized. "You really made it too easy. The Darklord will pay a pretty piece of gold to know that you're dead."

Drathorn tried to yell at him to stop but it was too late, the dagger cut the rope and Drathorn felt himself falling in only a second. As he fell he felt the wind rushing by as if in slow motion. He whipped what was left of the rope in his hands out at a thick tree branch and was astounded when it actually caught on. He stopped falling with a jolt and began to scurry up the rope again as fast as he could. When he could see over the edge again it was to see the warrior moving to cut the rope a second time.

Drathorn quickly released the rope with one hand and yelled; "*Venomstrike!*" the dagger was suddenly in his hand and the warrior had stopped in his tracks to look back at Drathorn. Drathorn threw the dagger and it twirled toward the warrior. The warrior easily put up his shield and the dagger stabbed into it without causing him any harm. But the distraction was enough for Drathorn to make it over the edge and climb to his feet. The armoured man roared and ran at Drathorn.

Drathorn wasn't fast enough to reach his sword and was forced instead to dive to the side, slipping on the ice. The assassin slipped too and nearly fell over the edge of the cliff. Both men straightened themselves; Drathorn drew his sword and readied himself. The assassin charged at him, sword held high.

Drathorn blocked the attack and the clash of metal rang like a bell. The force of the collision knocked both warriors back. "Why are you doing this?" Drathorn asked, his voice a croak from thirst. "I only wish to free our people from the darklord!"

"No one can free us from his power!" said the assassin. "It is pointless to fight him, so instead I join him. In this way my family and I will remain unharmed by his armies. You must die!" Suddenly Drathorn remembered where he recognize the voice from; it was the Garish man who had been at the armoury the day he and Thira were in Greengate together! The Gar had probably been trying to gain equipment that would allow him to easily kill Drathorn that day.

The assassin jumped forward again and swung at Drathorn. Drathorn ducked under his arm and rolled away from the attacker. Angrily, the warrior turned to face Drathorn again. Drathorn caught him off guard and punched him hard in the stomach. But the warrior laughed. "My armour is too thick for your fist to harm me! Now die!"

The assassin lunged this time and Drathorn was hit hard by his blade. The tip of his sword had pierced Drathorn's armour at the shoulder and Drathorn had to twist just right to avoid loosing his arm. But this twist tore through the armour and the clothes beneath it. The sleeve fell from Drathorn's arm, leaving it bare and exposed to the cold. The white lines of the Angelic Symbol showed against his slightly tanned skin but the blade had not pierced his flesh.

Drathorn backed away from his attacker, his bare arm already beginning to sting from the cold, but the warrior followed him. Again he lunged at Drathorn and Drathorn batted it aside with his own sword. Drathorn followed up his block by reaching out to *Venomstrike* and pulling it from the wooden shield. He attempted to kill the attacker with his sword but he slipped suddenly on the ice and fell to the ground.

The angry assassin prepared for his final blow, ready to pierce Drathorn through the heart. But Drathorn blocked the attack and then, with a flick of his wrist, turned the block into a swipe and sliced the assassin across the chest. The blade barely made it through the armour but the long scratch across the assassin's chest caused him to stumble slightly and Drathorn kicked out with both legs at his injured chest.

The force of Drathorn's kick caused the assassin to stumble backwards into the large boulder and with a deafening crack the stone broke free of the ice. Before Drathorn could even pick himself up off the ground the Assassin and the boulder tumbled over the cliff side. Drathorn stood and rubbed his side. *Who was he?* Drathorn wondered, reliving his short memories of the man. *Oh well, he was an enemy. He's gone now.* "*Thi Sein Whor.*" He said aloud. Then *Venomstrike* was gone.

Drathorn sheathed his sword and turned around to face Signaroc. It was then he noticed someone else standing there, beside the tree. His hand went again to his sword but he did not draw the weapon. The man who stood there was unarmed and supported a bare torso with nothing but clean white pants to cover his body. But the man did not shiver from the cold. He was red headed and looked very calm and showed no emotion. Great white wings stuck from his shoulders; the wings of an angel.

"You should not be here, Drathorn." The angel said in a musical voice. "You should not be *anywhere* on Corrone."

"Corrone is my home." Drathorn croaked. "I cannot leave, people need me here."

"You must not reach Signaroc, you must not unlock your true power, and you must not become a true Hellbound." He replied, still without emotion yet in a slow, musical voice.

"I don't understand what you mean . . ." Drathorn said. Tthe effort of speaking when he was so cold and thirsty ached his throat. "But I must help Signaroc, you will not stop me!"

"Then I am sorry, but this is the will of the gods . . . you must die." Drathorn drew his sword, preparing to defend himself but he was not prepared for what happened next.

The angel's hands suddenly glowed with white light, his eyes held no pupils nor colour . . . they were completely white. He said no words of magic; he did no actions other than move his hand forward and *push* the light. A beam of pure magical energy flew at Drathorn and hit him square in the chest. Suddenly time seemed to freeze. Drathorn saw, in slow motion, his armour disintegrate as soon as the beam touched it. His shirt ripped open in a perfect line down the middle making a vest-like article of clothing without the left sleeve. But after this the beam seemed to stop. The amulet that shone around Drathorn's neck shone like the sun.

The beam didn't move and suddenly the man's eyes were wide with fear. The necklace seemed to come to life. It lifted itself away from Drathorn's chest and touched the tip of the frozen beam. In a single second the bean seemed to get sucked into the necklace. Then, an explosion of the very same energy erupted from Drathorn. He heard the angel scream and then he was gone.

Yes, for now Drathorn *knew* who this man was; he was an angel from heaven, a messenger from the gods. Drathorn knew that the gods did not want Drathorn to reach Signaroc and had sent this angel to stop him. But the gods' power had not allowed them to see the amulet, nor to realise that its power would destroy his attacker.

But the explosion knocked Drathorn down as well. He flew back and slammed hard against the tree. He was unconscious, the angel was vanquished and the amulet glowed with magical power around his neck.

At the foot of the mountain, upon the paper pass, a single bandit looked up from his fellows at the mountain peak. It was then that he saw the stone falling towards them. "Look out!" he yelled. The boulder knocked thousands of ice ledges and other rock outcroppings aside and within seconds an avalanche was streaming down the mountain side. The bandits scrambled, trying to escape the path of the mountain's furry. But they could not. After only a moment snow, ice and stone had crashed into the bandit toll camp on the paper pass.

Troy never knew why he looked up that night, never knew why he gazed suddenly toward the peak-less mountain. He had felt something, a strange presence. He knew something was wrong there. *Something* was out of place.

Seeing Troy was disturbed Thira and Murlok followed his gaze. It was at that moment the mountain's peak seemed to explode. Light flooded the area from its peak, surprising everyone within sight of the mountain. There was a scream from within the light that all could hear . . . and then, as quickly as it had begun, the light stopped. Confused, the trio looked up at the mountain. But it appeared completely unchanged. The trio was concerned, what had happened? Was that Drathorn's doing? Was he dead? None of them slept well that night; they all feared for the life of the young Hellbound.

XXIV

Reunion

Saturday May 30th, 18291, the wind blew softly . . . but it was cold. There was the sound of it rustling through a tree, a tree without leaves . . . Drathorn opened his eyes. It was bright now, the sun beating down but doing little to warm him. His sword was lying on the snow a few feet away, his armour was nowhere in sight. His left arm was bare from the shoulder down, leaving his Angelic Symbol visible to the public. His chest was bare too; the strange attack had torn open his shirt. Drathorn was utterly confused. Why had the angel attacked? Why must he not arrive in Signaroc?

He sheathed his sword and wrapped himself as best he could in his torn shirt. He was freezing and his throat hurt horribly. In an attempt to quench his thirst he began eating the snow and sucking on any icicles he could manage to pick off the branches of the tree.

His thirst finally quenched but his fingers had become numb and he was sure he would get frostbite. He peered out over the landscape to the north and saw only the very tops of the high towers of Signaroc in the distance. *It's still so far away . . .* he thought. *I will surely die of the cold and join that accursed angel in the heavens if I try and walk down this mountain.*

He studied the slope of the mountain and quickly realised that its north side was not covered in cliffs but actually had a good slope. It would be hard to climb in an upward direction but it was slippery and steep enough to slide down if it had been all ice. Drathorn looked at the tree he had crashed into. After a moment of thought he reached up and grabbed a piece of bark and pulled. A fine, thick sheet of bark tore from the tree. With the remains of his rope Drathorn tied the piece of bark to his two feet and in only a moment he was standing upon it and surfing down the side of the mountain. This was much faster than walking; he would reach the bottom in no time. But he forced himself not to allow his mind to wander, he needed to concentrate on his balance in order not to crash.

The wind sped by, making his vest-like shirt flutter behind him making him feel even colder. But he fought the cold, he would reach the bottom. He would battle angels, bandits and monsters to reach Signaroc and he would not fail the free people. It wasn't long before the freezing air turned pleasantly warm and the slope was free of all snow and ice becoming dangerously rocky. Drathorn was forced off his board by the rough stones and had to walk down the rest of the mountain on sharp rocks. He soon realised that his boots had been worn away by his endless marching and were uncomfortably wet. He regretfully removed them when the sharp rocks began cutting into his feet.

By the time he reached the foot of the mountain he was too sore to continue and he lay beneath a tree in the shade and slept, bare chest and feet.

Tuesday June 2nd, 18291, it had been three days since Drathorn had woken; cold, sore and confused atop the mountain. Now he walked, along the winding road that lead from the devastated paper pass to the city of Signaroc. His shirt was still ripped but he had grown used to the soft breeze striking his chest. He had grown used to seeing the scar upon his bare shoulder while still feeling the soft fabric on his other one. His feet no longer pained him as he walked bare-foot on the rough ground; he was used to it. *I like this form of dress.* Drathorn thought. *It suits me . . . I think when I arrive in Signaroc I will buy a new pair of shoes . . . but that is all. I like this fashion.*

Drathorn laughed aloud at this thought. He had never been one to care about what he wore, but this was extremely comfortable to him. The wind blew softly upon his skin, cooling it in the heat of the day. He knew it would be getting colder and he even noticed the nights were holding slightly more chill the farther north he travelled, but he did not worry about snow. The Himegard region eventually curved west into the Neeshara Desert which was populated mainly by humans and Dragonians with a few Gar in some areas . . . From the desert you could go in four other directions; slightly south and then east was the sacred forests of the Elves, still farther south were the dreaded Badlands ruled by the

Darklord and his armies, in the far western areas were the Swamplands of the Gar and in the north were the mountain rages populated mostly by the Dragonians and Dwarves. It was only in these northern mountain regions that snow was seen on days outside the winter months. The only exceptions were the sky-high peaks of mountains like Tanisay.

He walked along the road for some time and it was about two hours past noon when he heard a loud cracking noise followed by a yelp of pain and the evil laughter of many men. Drathorn drew his sword without thinking and slipped off the road and into the trees. Another crack followed by more laughter came from nearby and Drathorn followed the sound as it happened again and again.

It wasn't long before Drathorn was hidden behind a large tree and looking into a large clearing. A dozen small tents had been erected in the clearing near two wagons. The larger he recognized, but he didn't know from where. The other wagon was topped with bars and a roof; a slave cage. In the center of the clearing was a large wooden table. Three men sat at it with drinks as they laughed evilly at another group of men. The second group, of eight men, were all gathered around two men. One of the men had his back to the others and was bleeding from several long thick cuts that ran the length of his back at many angles. The other man was holding a long coiled whip.

The bleeding man was bound to a tree with rope and was being whipped by the other man. The eleven armed men laughing at the whipping were all bandits, as was the man with the whip; the other man was probably the owner of the wagon Drathorn recognized. The whip cracked again on the man's skin and the bandits laughed loudly. Drathorn grew angry. *What vile human could cause such pain to another like this?* It was evil of the purest nature and it drove Drathorn to even greater anger to realize that he probably knew the man being whipped.

Drathorn forced himself to think rationally and began to sneak into the camp. He rolled from behind one tent to behind another, trying desperately to get to the slave cage without being seen. It took longer than he had thought it would and by the time he was near the cage he was swelling with anger again at the bandits' cruelty. He finally managed to look inside of the cage, gasped and nearly fell when he saw who was in it.

"Hailey? Pat? Linda? Robby?" Drathorn whispered. Now Drathorn knew where he recognized the wagon from.

"Drathorn?" Linda asked, "What are you doing here?"

"Same question I had for you." Drathorn replied; he turned his head to the man being whipped. "Is that-?"

"It's Ben." Pat whimpered. "He talked back to the bandits earlier so they took him and began to whip him." She was hiding Hailey's face in her shoulder, and both of them were crying.

"Don't worry, I'm gunna get you outta here." Drathorn said. He turned back towards the bandits, "*Venomstrike*" he said. The dagger was suddenly in his hand.

"Drathorn be careful." Robby said.

But Robby's rough voice was slightly too loud. "Somebody shut up those other prisoners!" the whipmaster of the bandits roared as he whipped Ben again. Anger roared even greater within Drathorn as the whipmaster laughed again. One of the bandits sitting at the table stood up and began to walk toward the cage. As he drew nearer Drathorn threw venom strike and it struck the bandit in the throat. The bandit fell instantly, even without the effect of the poison.

"Hey! There's someone here!" yelled a bandit.

"Search the camp!" called the whipmaster. He turned and whipped Ben yet again as the bandits began to spread out slightly, looking for the intruder.

Drathorn's anger suddenly reached an impossible pitch. Unable to control himself any longer he stepped out into the open. Three bandits armed with swords were only feet away from him. The second he saw them his anger seemed to fade away and their evil smiles turned to faces of fear. Drathorn noticed suddenly that his left hand was tingling. He looked down at his left hand (the one not holding his sword) and was shocked to see that it was on fire.

He suddenly remembered his aunt Helen, standing in the darkness of the alleyway with her hand blazing as she stood between Drathorn and their attackers. His mother had told him about this when he was very young. *"When we grow angry we can channel our anger into the flames of Sylvaston and throw them at our enemies without using the words of magic."* That was what she had said.

Drathorn looked away from his hand and up at the bandits with a mischievous smile. He threw the fireball in his hand and it struck the center bandit in the chest. The ball exploded and nothing remained of the bandit but a pile of ashes. The explosion also reached the bandits on either side of the first and they were soon running around the camp, their bodies ablaze.

Drathorn ran at the burning enemies and used his sword to slice them both down. Then he quickly took up one of his enemy's swords and turned to face two more angry bandits. He blocked one enemy's attack with his own sword and then spun and plunged the bandit blade into the stomach of the other. He left the bandit blade in his enemy as he fell and turned to block the first bandit again. After the attack was blocked Drathorn side stepped and kicked his attacker in the stomach.

The man had his breath knocked out of him from the force of the blow. "Drathorn!" Robby called. "Release Ben so he can help you!"

"Alright!" Drathorn yelled. Drathorn ran forward, blocked an attack from an enemy bandit, and sliced the ropes binding Ben to the tree. Ben came free of the tree as Drathorn blocked another attack aimed at the disoriented man. He kneed the attacker in the stomach and tossed the bandit's sword to Ben.

Ben caught it clumsily and sidestepped another bandit attack just in time. But the bandit wasn't as lucky and Ben's sword soon sliced cleanly through his neck. The two bandits Drathorn had kicked stood now to face the two warriors, along with the others. Six bandits still remained alive and Drathorn had now lost the element of surprise.

One bandit leapt at Drathorn. Drathorn blocked high and then low and then leapt into the air and kicked the bandit in the chin with all his might. The kick pushed Drathorn back to the ground and lifted the bandit up into the air. Drathorn twirled the blade and swiped at the perfect time. His blade cut cleanly through the air-born bandit's stomach, spilling guts and the remains of the bandit's lunch all over the ground.

Sensing movement behind him Drathorn dropped to one knee and stabbed backwards almost like he was sheathing his sword. He felt the sword dig into someone's flesh and turned his head to see the whipmaster standing behind him, howling in pain. Drathorn elbowed the whipmaster south of the stomach and pulled his sword from the man's leg. He stood quickly, blocked an attack from another bandit and stabbed him in the chest. Then in only a second he spun and cleanly cut off the Whipmaster's head.

Drathorn turned his gaze to Ben. He was standing over the body of one bandit he had just recently killed and was in the middle of a heated sword fight with another. Drathorn quickly glanced around the camp and saw the final bandit standing nearby, a crossbow aimed at Ben.

Without thinking Drathorn bent low and picked up the whip. He lashed out at the crossbow, hoping to stop the attack. But he did better than that. It was pure luck that the whip had struck the side of the crossbow and jolted it only inches to the left at the exact same moment that the bandit had pulled the trigger. The bolt flew from the crossbow and collided with its target. But the target was not Ben anymore; the new target had been none other than Ben's current opponent. The bolt struck the bandit in the back and caused it to stop in mid strike, allowing Ben to stab it through the chest.

The crossbow wielding bandit tried desperately to reload but Drathorn was faster. A moment later the bandit was lying dead on the ground and Ben was rushing toward the cage to free his family. Drathorn wordlessly sheathed his sword and watched as the family was released.

"Thank you so much for your help back there Drathorn." Ben said yet again.

They were in the wagon now. They had gathered what weapons they could find from the bandits as well as many other provisions, *Venomstrike* was returned to Drathorn. Drathorn had been living off of road-side berries for days now and the small meal they managed to make from the bandits' bags tasted great to him.

According to Ben they had been captured by the bandits over a week ago and were kept there in the clearing inside the cage for no reason. All of them had been beat several times but Ben's whipping had been the worst. They all now rode together in the wagon, heading for the city of Signaroc. Drathorn's hand rested on the hilt of his sword, his eyes on the road behind them. Hailey and Pat were rubbing the hilts of small daggers, both fearful and uncertain of how much help they would be in a fight. Ben sat with Drathorn, a sword at his side. Linda was leaning with her head on his shoulder, a loaded crossbow lying on the bench next to her. Robby was up front, driving the wagon, he too supported a sword.

Before Drathorn answered he looked down at his side. The Whipmaster's whip was coiled around his belt, ready for Drathorn to use it in a time of need. A spare dagger was tied to Drathorn's left forearm so that it would be within easy reach if it was needed. He found it very uncomfortable but he no longer had a boot to strap it to so this would have to do. As the wagon rumbled along more weapons clanged in their sheaths on the ground. Drathorn had insisted on brining them so that they could sell them to a trader in town or give them to a needy warrior when the battle to save Signaroc had begun.

Drathorn didn't say anything to Ben to acknowledge he had heard him. Instead he looked up as the wagon stopped. "Drathorn, you might want to come see this." Robby's voice echoed into the back.

Drathorn climbed up front beside Robby and looked at the forest around them. It was lush and green, and normal; nothing out of the ordinary. But up ahead the forest abruptly ended. The lush green trees were now dead, their leaves eaten away by some unknown creature. The grass no longer existed and the soil had become hard and rough from the heat of the sun. It was a wasteland.

XXV

Hidden Treasures

There was no sign of life. Every plant in sight was gone. No animals scurried here . . . they had all been long gone. There was nothing. Only the distant figure of the city kept them moving. Was this the work of the darklord? An act meant to sabotage the city's hope of survival even if they *did* survive the battle? Drathorn was sure it was but he did not say that to anyone. They rode on in silence; no one felt the slightest bit of happiness here. The sun was not merciful and soon they found themselves thirsty and tired. They stopped early that night . . . just a few hours after dinner. They pulled off the barely visible road and fed the horses and then they pulled out their bed roles and set up a small camp out on the hard ground.

Hailey fell asleep almost instantly. Pat wasn't awake long after her. After making sure the fire would last a few more good hours Robby soon slept alongside his wife. Ben had agreed to take first watch and he was sitting with his back to a dying tree, Linda asleep with her head in his lap. Drathorn stood and walked over to him. "I can't sleep." He told Ben. "It is still too early for me; I'm going for a walk . . . I'll be back shortly."

Ben nodded quietly and Drathorn began to walk away, his hand on the hilt of his sword. He made sure to stay where he could still see the fire of the camp. But he soon began to forget the camp as his mind wandered again. Where were Bronc and his Gar companion, Eldrath? Had they been captured or slain by bandits? Were they already in Signaroc, waiting for him? Why had the angel attacked him? Drathorn looked back behind him as he walked. He could still barely see the flickering flame. He began to turn his head to look forward again when the ground disappeared from under him.

He gasped as he fell and groaned as he hit the ground hard. He shook his head as he lifted himself up. He was lying in front of the opening of a small cave. The hole in the stone wall was large enough for their wagon to fit in easily and he could tell that it had often been used by something of that size in the past. Drathorn looked up and saw that he had only fallen a little over ten feet. He saw that the cave was etched into the side of the small cliff but there was an obvious path leading up and around to the top again.

He shrugged and decided to take a look inside. The entrance was as large as he had thought but it quickly got thinner and shorter. It seemed to be a small tunnel. Drathorn followed it easily for a short distance before it opened into a large cavern. Right at his feet was the body of a man long dead. But that was not the reason for the gasp that echoed from his lips.

Treasure beyond his wildest dreams glistened everywhere. Gold coins glinted in the flickering light of torches lit upon the walls. Against a far wall was a powerful looking spear made of finely polished wood and a tip made of pure diamond. At Drathorn's feet was an elegant long sword with a blade made of silver, the handle part of the hilt was fixed with expensive black leather for grip and a ruby was set in the pommel. The widening part of the hilt curved upwards like waves at sea. Drathorn thought that it must surely be of ancient Elvin make. Hanging on the wall between two torches was a giant blade with a hilt made of gold and a diamond shaped blade that was so immense that no normal man could carry it but so dull and fragile looking that it was surely just a decoration . . . an *expensive* decoration. A large stone shield was propped against a chest full of coins, a golden star embedded in the front; obviously a decoration as well. Then there was a spiked crown laden with jewels, a golden goblet with handles shaped like dancing women, and even a heavy helmet imbedded with a giant sapphire. In the hands of a decorative suit of armour was an immense battle axe with a handle covered in thick black leather and its steel blade was imbedded with an emerald shaped like an arrow pointing to the sharpened point. On the opposite side of the deadly yet beautiful axe blade were three different sized steel spikes that were just as lethal as the blade itself. And yet this was only the beginning of the treasure. Many chests full of coins and gems littered the cave, coins spilled onto the floor in great amounts, piles of plain weapons and other fancy ones covered everything, a large box of scrolls containing knowledge on things Drathorn could only imagine sat at the foot of a statue of Alexandria, goddess of fear, made of pure Amethyst. There was even a wooden barrel of arrows bearing the feathers of an extinct eagle.

And yet among the treasure there could be found the bones of many people who had died among the riches. He wondered what had killed them and suddenly feared that some evil guardian hid somewhere in the cave. He slowly began to walk among the piles of treasure, examining it all. As he walked among the treasures he began to realise that there wasn't quite as much as he had thought, but it was still a large amount. *There was enough for the Blaygards to move away from Gaberdan . . . to Greengate or Veedion or some other large city. They could buy a mansion like the one my family had and live happily . . . I don't know anyone who deserves it more than they do. I will gather Ben and Robby and we will spend the night loading the wagon with as much as it can carry. Then we will travel to Signaroc and put it in the bank all in one big deposit . . . But not Icarus' bank . . . a smaller, less renowned bank.* Suddenly Drathorn's thoughts were interrupted by the sound of pounding feet.

Drathorn dived behind the Amethyst statue of Alexandria and waited; a large shadow appeared in the entrance, soon followed by a stench that turned Drathorn's stomach. Drathorn was just wondering what monster could possibly smell this horrible, house this much treasure, and kill this many adventures when he saw it. It was about eight or nine feet high and at least twice as wide and thick as Cherry Weldum had been. It had a large stomach that forced it to lean back to stay balanced. Its beefy arms were empty but Drathorn knew they had once carried the treasure here. His skin was grey and fell in folds, its large eyes bulged like dinner plates and its bald head made it look like a design moulded from clay by an extremely poor artist mocking human expressions. One word escaped his lips in a slight hiss so quiet that the creature could not possibly hear it with its over-sized bat-like ears. "Ogre . . ."

The beast did not hear his voice, did not see his shadow, and Drathorn didn't know how it could have smelled him over its own stench . . . but it did. "Intruder . . ." the ogre growled in its low, stupid voice. It sniffed loudly, trying to find Drathorn.

Drathorn held his breath. The ogre took a step forward, searching with its large eyes. It disappeared for a moment behind a pile of chests and a stone statue of ex-Emperor Tal-krin-fel, the first Garish emperor of Corrone but reappeared a moment later. Drathorn watched as the monster slowly began to move in his direction. "I . . . Smell . . . You . . ." it growled, "I . . . will . . . find . . ."

The ogre was now walking toward the statue; it now knew where Drathorn was. Drathorn waited, biding his time; then, at the last moment, Drathorn kicked the wall and pushed the statue forward. With the strength of the wall added to his own he was able to force the heavy stature over. The ogre roared first in triumph, and then in pain as the statue landed with an earth shaking thud on its foot. Drathorn drew his sword and leapt off the fallen statue. The ogre bent forward and grabbed the statue around the neck and lifted it up, in only a second he launched it at Drathorn and it missed only by inches, striking the wall behind him with such force that it shattered. Shards of Amethyst flew in every direction. Alexandria's head bounced off of a coat of armour, a piece of the leg off the heavy stone shield with the golden star imbedded in it. "Where . . . you?" roared the ogre as Drathorn disappeared again.

How do I kill an ogre? Drathorn thought. *I know trolls hate fire and are extremely weak against poison . . . but what about ogres? How did Mr. Blaygard defeat the one in Gaberdan? He only used a two handed sword and armour . . . He used strength and speed to out match it . . . but I have no time for this, Ben will be waiting for me . . . I need to remember more! Troy told me the whole story. I just need to remember!*

Suddenly a chest of gold shattered against the wall, sending coins flying in every direction. Drathorn shielded his face from the falling coins as another chest exploded in the same spot. The ogre was throwing the gold, trying to scare him out of his hiding place. *Smarter than I thought . . . that's just what I need; a* smart *ogre!* The very idea of an ogre who could think in a human way sent a chill up his spine. He shivered and then jolted, not because another chest exploded only a few feet from him, but because he now knew the ogre's weakness.

It had been mid-winter when Mr. Blaygard defeated the ogre. It had been weakened by the cold! Suddenly things from Drathorn's history classes stirred in his mind and he remember stories of a hero who hunted ogres with a bow enchanted to shoot arrows of ice. Drathorn suddenly realised that the bow was probably one of the mystic dozen but shook the thought from his mind. That was not important now. How was he supposed to use the power of the cold to defeat this beast?

Another chest exploded right above his head, scaring him out of his thoughts and giving away his position. In only a minute the ogre broke through the pile of chests carrying the beautiful battle axe Drathorn had been examining earlier in one hand and roaring in triumph. Drathorn swung his sword in a wide ark from his seated position on the ground. The sword barely cut into the ogre's leg. It sunk in about an inch and then was stuck. The ogre roared in anger and Drathorn scurried away.

Out of the corner of his eye Drathorn saw the ogre bend and pull the sword out of his leg and then threw it across the cavern. The hilt connected with the back of Drathorn's leg and he fell. He rolled over, ready to face his death. But the ogre was no longer facing him. It was facing the entrance. Someone spoke words Drathorn couldn't hear, there was a flash of light, and then the ogre fell; a thick spear of ice through his chest.

"Hello Drathorn, it's good to see you again." Bronc Silvermask was standing in the entrance to the cave, a wide smile on his face.

"Bronc!" Drathorn exclaimed, getting to his feet. "Headmaster, sir! I knew we would meet again! Have you come to travel with us to Signaroc?"

"I'm afraid not, young Drathorn." Bronc said. "I was in Signaroc but a few days ago . . . my companion died not long ago of a disease he did not know he had. I have come to inform you that I cannot join you in the fight for Signaroc. I have been called to the imperial city of Veedion by the Emperor himself. I don't know what he wants but I have little choice but to answer his summons. I'm sorry."

"But you are so powerful!" Drathorn said, pointing at the dead ogre. "Your help may be the difference between victory and defeat in Signaroc! We need you!"

"I am truly sorry Drathorn . . . but I cannot come." Bronc said.

"Ignore the calls of the emperor!" Drathorn exclaimed. "The saving of Signaroc is more important!"

"But is it more important than the summons of my only child?" Bronc asked. Drathorn stared at him.

"You have a child?" Drathorn stammered.

"Calverton Silvermask is my son." Bronc said, nodding. "And his summoning suggests that he needs my help. I must go to him. And remember; the fate of Signaroc matters not! It is the book that you must protect! If the Darklord discovers the secrets in that book we're all doomed!"

Drathorn was stunned. "When are you leaving?" he asked, still trying to absorb this new bit of information.

"I am going right away . . . I have little choice in the matter. I hope we will meet again soon." Bronc looked away from Drathorn to examine the dead body of the horrible ogre and then he muttered a few words and in a flash of light Bronc Silvermask had disappeared as quickly as he had appeared.

Will I ever *know all of his secrets?* Drathorn wondered.

XXVI

Feelings Confessed, Arrival of the Hellbound

Wednesday June 3rd, 18291, it was in the early afternoon when they finally neared the first gates of the city of Signaroc. The thin walls were made of nothing but wood and were more to keep children in and animals out than to stop an army. There were no guards at the wooden gate and the wagon passed through without interruption. Small farms dotted the land; children ran and laughed while the men worked hard in the fields. The women tried desperately to do house chores and assist with farming the land but with little success. The agricultural lands of Signaroc were just as barren and sun-dried as the surrounding wilderness. In the distance they could see the stone walls of the city.

Drathorn feared for the farmers who lived here; their homes were definitely going to burn and fall when the dark lord struck. *I will do what I can for them, only while I do what I must.* Drathorn thought sadly as the wagon rolled noisily. The fortune of the family seemed to be great on this day, for they had not met any bandits along the road. He found this odd because the wagon was so much slower than usual as it was weighed down by the immense supply of treasure.

Drathorn had swapped his regular long-sword with the ancient ruby incrusted Elvin long-sword from the ogre's cave. It was much lighter than his original blade and the new sheath he supported with it was carved with elegantly twirling lines across its length. Other than that single blade Drathorn had only claimed one other piece of treasure; a small ring.

It too seemed to be of Elvin make and that was much more obvious in the fact that it was so light and well crafted. The light weighted gold that was used in its creation shined bright in the sun. The band was carved to look like intertwining leaves and vines. The detail was so fine and so beautiful that the leaves actually looked real. He didn't know why he had favoured the small, delicate appearing (though definitely not) ring.

It now wrapped nicely around the index finger on his right hand as he gently rubbed the hilt of the elegant sword. His whip still remained at his belt, and his dagger on his sleeveless forearm.

All of the other treasures had been loaded almost carelessly into the wagon. It had taken most of the night to do it, especially since Robby and Ben seemed so interested in the endless supply of gold. The gems, gold and other treasures littered the wagon and left very little room for the family to sit. He had decided to give the treasure to the Blaygard family so they could move ahead in life instead of staying in such a broken down place as Gaberdan. He imagined that Troy and Thira would be surprised to see his find and he hoped Thira would be accepted as part of the family and be given a fair share of the money.

It was Pat that finally broke Drathorn's train of thought. "What are we going to do with it all?" she asked. "I understand that you wish for us to have it, but how will we ever get it back to Gaberdan un-harmed?"

"You won't." Drathorn said simply. "You guys are going to open a family bank account and store it in there so it can be accessed from any bank."

"Icarus banking corporation is going to love us." Pat laughed.

Drathorn's simple manner disappeared, his face filled with worry and disappointment. "No." he said. "Not the Icarus Company."

Pat's happiness disappeared at his tone. "Why?"

"I don't trust Icarus." Drathorn said, hoping she wouldn't think his thoughts foolish. "I don't want the family anywhere near anything to do with him. I'd much rather you went with one of the smaller, less renowned banks in Signaroc."

Pat frowned, contemplating him for a moment before she finally said, "That's fine, technically it's all your money so whatever you want to do with it is fine. But the smaller banks won't take these antique swords and statues . . . money, gems, jewellery and magic related books and scrolls only."

"That's fine," Drathorn said. "When we reach the city I will go to see the king. While I'm away you can change and get settled in. When that's all done you can take the big stuff to a pawn shop and sell it for any price you want . . . don't even bother looking for the best price . . . we could probably just give it all away to the homeless and still have enough money to support the family for a dozen generations. Once you've made all the money you can, open an account with one of the smaller banks and store it all. Then all you need to do is get ready for the battle while I prepare the king and the army."

"Do you not plan to wash yourself and make yourself presentable for the king before you go?" Pat asked.

"If he doesn't like me the way I am then that's too bad. These clothes are becoming comfortable." Drathorn said. Pat rolled her eyes but didn't argue. The ride went on in silence through the small farming areas. Hailey was quietly going through the treasure, looking at rings, crowns and goblets that caught her attention. Linda and Ben watched her from the bench, both still supporting their original sword and crossbow from the day before. Robby was driving again, his original sword also at his waist. Even in the confines of the wooden walls of the city they did not let down their guard; Thieves and Muggers were still common.

It took more than an hour to cross the small farming lands but soon they were at the great iron gates of Signaroc. The iron gates were set into the great stone walls that surrounded the city. Towers grew from the stone, defending the gate on both sides and surrounding the city defensively. This gate was open too but there was a single guard on either side of it. The guards watched quietly as the wagon approached and remained quiet until Robby stopped the carriage at the entrance.

"Good evening Robby!" said a guard., "It's been a long time since I've seen you here!"

"Good evening to you too." Robby said politely. "But I'm afraid I'll not be staying long. The family needs to make a social call and then Pat and I are moving to Gaberdan to be with the family."

"To Gaberdan?" the guard asked, surprised. "Normally I'd try to talk you out of going to that stink hole but I guess anywhere's better than here right now . . . considering our current crisis."

"Ah, yes," Robby said, sorrow in his voice. "The forests . . . What has happened here?"

"Locusts . . ." the guard grimaced. "A giant swarm of them crossed the Hellfire Bay about a month ago. They've been eating everything . . . crops that we manage to grow disappear quickly and none of the farmers can manage to pay their taxes to the king. Many people out in the farms have died of starvation and murder in these harsh times. But there is nothing we can do. The damn Locusts have eaten everything in the area . . . even

Narvahan Shé's forests have disappeared . . . and so have its people actually. They're all dead . . . killed by an army that struck from the sea. The people are scarred but the king insists that no army has passed the great capitol and that we are safe."

"This truly is a time of crisis then . . ." Robby frowned. "What do the high-arches say?"

"Orfac and his fellow mages have kept watch on Narvahan Shé from the wizard's tower . . . but if they've seen anything they have yet to share their news." The guard turned his head and Robby followed his gaze. Drathorn finally noticed the single giant tower in the center of the city. It, too, was surrounded by its own set of stone walls. It was the wizard tower of Signaroc . . . the place where the Journal of the Great Thirteen was kept safe by the many mages controlled by Signaroc's High-arch; Orfac O-Bryant. If Drathorn's knowledge was genuine then the manor belonging to Signaroc's king was located at its foot just inside the stone walls. That's where he had to go . . . to see the king and warn him of this threat.

"Well my friend, I must depart for now." Robby said, returning to the conversation. "Have a good day." The guard nodded, still apparently watching the tower in silence.

"So an army from the sea has struck Narvahan Shé, slaying its people." Robby muttered.

"We have very little time." Drathorn said. "I must warn the king of the coming threat!"

"Odds are that he already knows." Linda said. "But I agree; you should go straight there."

With heavy hearts the family was silent as the wagon moved through the city. Finally they stopped at one of the shabbier houses on the far end of town. Robby climbed out of the driver's seat and walked to Drathorn through the treasure. "We're gunna get cleaned up and try and sell some of this." He said. "Follow the road straight ahead and you'll find a set of closed gates to the king's courtyard. The king's manor is on the other side."

"Thanks," Drathorn said with a nod. "I'll be come back later tonight . . . it's possible I wont be here until really late, don't wait up for me." Without waiting for an answer he climbed out the back of the wagon and out onto the street.

He immediately attracted many stares. The people of Signaroc eyed his dirty figure; his bare feet, his torn shirt (torn both at the left shoulder and down the chest line), his worn leather greaves and his filthy black hair were very uncommon in this place. But the few people who stared at him long enough to get past the clothes and dirt soon became shocked. His body was hardened by muscle, his chest showing pure power, not a scrap of fat anywhere in sight. The white scar of the Angelic Symbol on his shoulder shone in the sunlight and even the most hardened warriors glanced at him in awe. But after the repulsiveness of his clothing and the awe of his strength came a slight fear.

Drathorn was a mystery to these people. No one here knew who he was; not yet. The sight of this dirty, powerful, attractive young man walking down the streets frightened the people. For at his waist was a magnificent jewelled sword unlike any they had ever seen. Strapped to his forearm was a bloodstained dagger. Hanging at his belt, within easy reach of his hand was the menacing whip. His dark eyes did not examine the curious people; they looked determined and menacingly ahead. And yet after the fear was something else; hope.

This mysterious warrior from the south wore an Angelic Symbol. His body was marked by the harshness of battle. He was obviously a hardened warrior. And by the way his eyes were trained on the wizard's tower it seemed obvious that he had a matter to discuss with the king and/or the high-arch. Very few people were allowed to see the king these days. But this young man walked with such confidence and defiance with his weapons and his torn clothes that few people doubted he would make it through the gates. They were fed hope by the eyes that had seen so much killing. They felt, somehow, that this warrior had come to help them. And they were right.

Unfortunately it would not appear so when he reached the gates. All along the way he stared at the tower and the thick stone walls around the king's courtyard. He knew exactly what he would say, exactly what he would demand of the king. There would be no flaw in this plan. "Halt! No one sees the king! Get back citizen!" no flaw except that.

Drathorn stopped in front of the four armed guards standing at the closed wooden gates. They each bore a menacing spear and had daggers at their waists. Drathorn looked slowly at each guard, his eyes locking on each in turn and then up to the tower. "Get back citizen!" the lead guard repeated.

Slowly, and very quietly Drathorn said; "I must see the king. This is a matter of great importance." His voice was barely above a whisper and the guards had to lean in to hear it. But even then all of them knew what had been said.

"No one sees the king." The lead guard said. "If you'll not leave the area willingly then we'll have no choice but to use force!" The guards all nodded, gripping their spears tighter.

Drathorn sighed; the lead guard settled, mistaking the sigh for surrender. None of them had time to move. Drathorn leaped forward and punched the lead guard roughly in the stomach, ripping the spear from his hand and then striking him down with the hard wood. He twirled and struck one of the other guards across the chin and then disarmed a third with the same move, all the while being careful not to leave so much as a scratch on any of the guards. The fourth guard stumbled back, dropping his spear in fear and bumped into the gate. Drathorn smiled and pointed the tip of the menacing spear at his throat. "Now . . . May I *please* see the king?"

With fear in his eyes, and to murmurs of disapproval from the watching people the guard turned to open the gate. Drathorn smiled; some soldiers they were.

Since the night they saw the explosion of light Troy never stopped glancing out at the mountain. He didn't know what he expected to see from this distance but he just couldn't stop himself. It was all he could think about. And he only stopped staring out at it when he was busy staring at a map of Tanroe in his room. He had been going over the plan again this morning, running his finger over the ocean area between Nargak and Hellfire bay, absentmindedly thinking of Drathorn and the strange light atop mount Tanisay, when he realised his finger was tracing itself farther and farther from Nargak . . . in the opposite direction from Signaroc. He stopped moving his hand and looked down at the map; he had stopped on the one place he wanted to be more than anywhere else right now.

He was stressed, as far as he knew Drathorn could be dead and he was about to lead an army across the sea to strike a foe that might not be there if that was the case. He missed his home, his brother, his family, his school, his team, even his job. He needed comfort, comfort that neither Thira, nor Murlok, nor their new friend Feronis, could give him. He knew he had come too far to go home now and that the comfort he searched for would not be there anyway. It was in a place not quite two days south west of Nargak that he would find his comfort.

His finger had landed on the spot carelessly but he now wished he was there more than anything, to be comforted by *her* . . . They had moved to Veedion so long ago, it felt. He had never received any letters, no post cards, and no word that they had survived their journey but still he felt somewhere in his heart that they had. But if they had, why was there no word? He thought to himself; *two days to get there* . . . he could stay for a day, maybe two, and still be back in time to lead the army to Signaroc. It would be easy and seeing her would calm his worries and fears and bring him the comfort he so desired . . . .

"*Emily* . . ." he whispered to himself. Thira looked up. Had she heard him? That wasn't possible; he had been far too quiet for her ears to possibly hear . . . hadn't he? No, for a minute later she had stood quietly and gracefully, not waking Murlok from his deep sleep on the uncomfortable couch, and walked with barely a sound to where he sat.

She looked down at his finger still resting, pointed at the place where his best friend was. His best friend and yet she meant so much more to him. No, not a friend . . . she was far more . . . despite his pretences she was more to him than a friend. Even she did not know just how much he thought of her, how much he missed her . . . how much he loved her. "Are you okay Troy?" Thira asked gently, sitting quietly in a chair across from him. She eyed the tiny dot that was Veedion with understanding eyes. "Your friend . . . Emily . . . you miss her?" she guessed.

Troy didn't answer except to nod. Feronis watched quietly from the other side of the room where he had been reading a book based on naval travel, he could not hear the conversation but for a low wordless mummer but he still knew it had a great emotional purpose to the archer and decided to stay out of it. Troy hadn't looked up. He spoke no words. But soon a gentle, warm, caring hand rested upon his. He looked up.

Thira was the one holding his hand, as he had thought. She smiled with care at him; a heart moving, beautiful smile. He supposed that to a normal person she would appear extremely beautiful, more beautiful even than Emily. But with the tears now glistening in his eyes he could not picture it. The tears shouldn't have been there, he was over reacting . . . the stress was making his emotions run wild. Although he was looking right at her he could not see the beauty, he saw only Emily, reflected in his eyes as she had been the day she had said goodbye; a goodbye very much like the one Thira had given Drathorn at the orphanage so long ago. "Are you okay Troy?" Thira asked.

What would he say? Could he master her perfect whisper and stay quiet enough not to attract Feronis' attention when the tears shook him violently? Yet how could he answer without speaking? If he did nothing she would suppose the worst and move to embrace him or something . . . although that would be comforting it would be awkward . . . especially when he believed Thira and Drathorn felt as much for each other as he did for Emily. He settled with a shrug and then breathed deep, trying desperately to calm himself. It was loud and the action broke off with a soft, uncontrollable sob. It was still fairly quiet but Feronis heard it and understood the pain behind it. He didn't seem to move but his ears pricked up and his eyes no longer followed the words on the page . . . he was listening.

"Troy, talk to me . . . I can help . . ." she said soothingly.

Again he was silent before answering, trying to get his voice under control. Thira didn't rush him as the shaking slowly stopped beneath her hand. He breathed deep again to test his composure and then answered in a low, slightly shaky voice. "I need to see her Thira . . ."

Thira's mysterious eyes flashed down to the page where Troy's hand was and examined the name of the city again. "Emily?" she asked. Troy nodded quietly. She frowned and looked back to him. "You have feelings for her." She said. She was stating a point, not asking a question. "You never said anything . . . did Drathorn know?"

She had done it again. Ever since the explosion of light she had been talking of Drathorn as though he were a thing of the past, as though he no longer existed and she knew it. "Why do you talk about him like that? Like he's already dead?"

"We don't know he isn't." she said.

"We don't know he is."

It was her turn to be silent. ". . . It's easier not to worry if I think of him as already gone . . ." she finally said. "If I pretend he's gone it hurts less than worrying weather or not he is, worrying if he's suffering."

"You have feelings for him." Troy said; mimicking the no-questions-asked accusation she had given him. She said nothing but released his hand and looked out the window again at the mountain across the ocean. It was so hard to believe there was snow on its peak; snow didn't seem to exist here on the eastern edge of the Neeshara Desert. It was far too hot; he wondered why the ocean didn't evaporate. He pushed those questions aside and asked; "Does he know?"

Her thoughtful stare out the window ended as she looked back at Troy with a devilish grin. "I asked you that first."

Troy frowned, it was true. He sighed in defeat; "I guess he did . . . we didn't talk about her much. He promised me he would take me to see her if we ever went near Veedion. And he asked about the picture of her . . . he may have supposed something but I never told him anything."

"But you do?" she said, confused for reasons Troy could not understand. Troy just nodded again. "And you miss her, very much?" she pressed. He nodded again, looking away. "And you wish to see her . . . now?" Again, a nod. "All this time you've been glancing at the mountain and worrying over Drathorn, fearing for his life, saying his name in your sleep . . . and you've really been thinking of *her*?" she asked, now making the reason for her confusion much more obvious.

Troy had no idea he had been speaking as he had nightmares about Drathorn's possible demise atop Mt. Tanisay. But now he knew the reason behind Thira's confusion. "No . . . I only just thought of her now actually." He admitted, his voice began shaking again and he noticed his whisper getting out of control and slightly high pitched as the tears welled again. The look of confusion on her face grew as she watched his tears. He struggled to control his tears again and looked away from her out the window to the mountain again. Out of the corner of his eye he saw Thira's confused expression turn suddenly into understanding and care.

"I think I understand now . . ." she said, placing her hand on his again. "You worry so much about Drathorn and you're so scared about what will happen once we cross the ocean that you feel the need to have comfort, you want her to comfort you . . . you want to be with her again so you can be happy and forget your worries."

Troy sighed and looked back to her and, eyes filled with tears now, he nodded. "Oh, Troy . . . I'm so sorry!" she said, a little louder than her perfect whisper as she jumped up and ran around the table.

Before he could brace himself she had embraced him, he felt slightly comforted and, like he had thought he would be, slightly awkward. But as she hugged him warmly he found himself hugging back, resting his tear stained face upon her shoulder. They stayed like that for a moment, and ignored Feronis' confused stare as he was no longer pretending to read. Try as he might he barely had any idea what the conversation was about; he only watched, confused and slightly annoyed.

It was a moment before Troy could collect himself well enough to stop the embrace. Gently he pulled away from her hug to look into her face. She allowed him to move away slightly and looked at him again. "I understand I can't be there to help you the way she can. Murlok can go with you for protection . . . so that you can . . . go see her." She said.

That was the last thing he had expected to hear from her. She was always so rough and strong and waiting for the fighting to start, so hopeful that she would soon slay her enemies and see Drathorn again. She usually got annoyed whenever he neglected his training for even a moment to look up at the mountain. But now here she was, sitting near him, her shirt stained with his tears, telling him to run away from the training to see the girl he wanted to see more than anything right now. And she was trying to get Murlok to go with him and miss out on his training as well? He had to admit he liked Thira's compassionate side better than the hardened warrior she always tried to be while here in the desert.

But he couldn't leave, as much as he wanted to, at the moment. "No," he said, shaking his head. "As amazing as that sounds, I can't leave right now. The battle for Signaroc, for Drathorn, is more important than being comforted by a childhood crush." He was trying to sound strong, trying to make her stop being so understanding and force her back to being the warrior she had been ever since Drathorn's disappearance. Emily was more than a crush and they both knew that. But the mention of Drathorn brought Thira back to her own reality and her own worry; her own feelings.

While Thira's thoughts of Drathorn reflected again, Troy took the moment to stand. "He's not gone Thira." He said to her, no longer whispering. "As much as you talk about him as if he is, he's not. Not yet. And I'm not the only one who says his name in my sleep."

He turned, still welled up with tears and left the cabin. Feronis' eyes widened at the last phrases but before he could ask a single question

Troy was gone and Thira was sobbing in her room; her thoughts filled with Troy's pain, worry for Drathorn, and fear of the upcoming battle. She didn't bother to be quiet. She had rushed by the couch and slammed her bedroom door in her haste to be alone. The slam woke Murlok and by the time he had gathered his senses all he heard was the click of the lock of Thira's door and her loud, uncontrollable sobs between the names Drathorn and Troy. Murlok watched the door for a moment in confusion and then looked over to Feronis. He was still sitting uncomfortably in his chair, staring in shock at Thira's door.

Murlok was just as confused and shocked as Feronis was but he couldn't help glowering at the strange rider from the east. Murlok had no idea what he had missed but he glared angrily at Feronis with accusing eyes; somehow he felt that Thira's pain was his fault.

Drathorn's bare foot smashed down the wooden door of the king's manor with ease. As two guards rushed at him he tossed aside his prisoner form the gate and uncoiled his whip. The guards, believing their king was in danger, did not hesitate. They rushed at him with their spears raised. Drathorn's whip lashed out loudly at one guard's spear and coiled around it. With a single pull he ripped the weapon from the guard's hand and it soared toward him as if it had been thrown. Drathorn caught it and used the non-lethal end to sweep both guards off their feet. As they both sat up, preparing to jump to their feet, Drathorn jumped into the air and, with a single split kick, knocked them unconscious. He re-coiled his whip and stepped over their bodies. He didn't like making himself look like the bad guy but this was the only way he would get in to see the king; he had no choice.

He walked to the door of the study and stepped in. The king was sitting at his polished wooden desk, calmly watching Drathorn walk in. He was in fancy red clothing with his crown perched upon his head. Beside yet slightly behind him was a thick Dwarf in the same type of red garments; just without the crown. He was holding a large battle axe and eyeing Drathorn with anger and hate. A single mage in long red billowing robes stood in front of the desk, slightly to the side. There was no hood on these robes and his head was covered in long grey hair and a beard that made Bronc Silvermask's look like a toddler beside a giant. Two other mages stood on either side of the first, each in long blue robes and much, much younger than the lead mage but still older than Drathorn. They seemed to be twins. There were also two more armed guards standing nearby. Drathorn nodded at the man sitting in the chair with his crown upon his head. "Servite Salamoray, king of Signaroc." Drathorn stated nodding towards him.

"What brings you here?" demanded the king.

"Your arrogance." Drathorn shrugged. "The bandits are everywhere, and you do nothing! They spread in great numbers and you did not try and stop them." Drathorn's voice rose slightly in anger as he spoke, until he was nearly yelling at the king. "They captured the paper pass, they invaded the city of Taldi, slaying many innocent people, they captured my family and attacked rest houses and you did nothing! An Ogre took up root in the forest and preyed on passing travelers, your own port was taken and you have yet to try and reclaim it! The fortress of Narvahan Shé has fallen and you made no attempt to assist it in its time of need! Your city is plagued by Locusts and you ignore the suffering of your people! You'll not hear the complaints of your people, nor reduce the taxes to save the dying farmers outside your heavy stone walls! You are a sorry, irresponsible excuse for a king!"

The room rang with his accusations, the Dwarf growled in annoyance, the mages scowled and the guards glanced uneasily at their king. The king frowned slowly before saying three words. "Who are you?"

Drathorn walked deliberately to the desk, one of the guards leapt forward to stand in his path but fell back instantly as Drathorn's fist broke his nose. He set his right hand on the desk, palm down to reveal the mark on the back of it; the three dragon's tears. "I am Drathorn Hellbound, and I'm here to repair your horrible reputation as the king of these people."

XXVII

Preparing for Power

Drathorn had expected the king to be angered by his insult. He expected the king to order them to arrest him. He expected him to be surprised at his arrival. But he wasn't prepared for this. There was anger, at first. But after seeing the mark it changed to the surprise he had also expected. But then, after his surprise he smiled, startling Drathorn. "We've been waiting for you, young Hellbound." He said.

The mage in the red robes stepped forward, closer to Drathorn. "This is Orfac O-Bryant, the High-arch of Signaroc and the head of the mage's school here in the city." The king said. The two mages in blue stepped up behind their master.

"These are my most powerful students; Torbille and Zander." Orfac said. His voice radiated with power even in his old age. It was full of mystery and knowledge. "They assist me in educating our younger mages."

"And this is Argoss, my assistant from the north." The king said, gesturing to his Dwarven companion. "You can put your weapon away now, Argoss." The Dwarf grumbled under his breath and then lifted the heavy axe above his head and strapped it to his back where it was in easy reach. "We have been waiting for you for many days . . . ever since it was announced in the news scrolls that you had been found and were on the move. We heard a rumour that Taldi's siege was broken and it was soon in the scrolls that you had been the one to save them. As soon as we discovered you were headed in this direction we prepared for your arrival."

Drathorn said nothing. Did they know of the threat? Were they going to beg for his help? "I need you to come with me young sir." Orfac said. "Your destiny waits."

"I need to speak to the king." He objected.

"I insist!" Orfac said. "You must learn of everything! But first you must obtain the treasure of the Hellbound and unlock your true power!"

"True power?" Drathorn asked.

"The power of the Hellbound." The king nodded. "When Gradorn Lebasta Hellbound died he died on our plains, battling his foe. He and his treasures were buried deep within the Lone Mountain. No Hellbound or indeed, no creature, has touched them since their burial. Only by regaining the power of the first Hellbound can you hope to stop the darklord."

The power of the first Hellbound . . . The stories rushed into Drathorn's mind. He remembered the stories of the dragons. There had once been thirteen, one for each god. When Gradorn had miraculously survived the curse of the Dragon's tear he and the dragon who had cried upon him became great friends. When the war against the badlands started he and the dragon had set out to find the other dragons and unite them to defeat the foe that threatened Corrone. They had planned to get all the dragons together to help but some refused. The first refusal was the dragon that followed Colaspis, god of pain. Gradorn and his dragon had barely survived the dragon's attack and it ended up killed by the pair. They had decided to forge a mystic blade that could slay dragons with ease in case it happened again. Once they had forged the blade they had returned to their quest of uniting the dragons. In the end only four other dragons had joined them. The others were all killed by Gradorn and the mystical sword. After Gradorn's death the dragons disappeared from the world and so did the sword.

Drathorn shook his head. "The treasures of the Hellbound, the sword you mean?" he asked.

Orfac nodded. "The sword, *Dragontongue*, which is said to deflect all magic spells, and kill dragons with rarely more than a single strike. And the band of heroes, the bracelet embedded with the five sacred stones said to contain the remaining dragons. Also, there lies Gradorn's journal, the secret to how he survived the Dragon's tear and his whole life is within it. They are all immense treasures."

"And all yours." The king added with a nod. "Only by retrieving the bracelet will you be able to call upon the dragons to help save our world. And only by wielding the sword will you posses the ability to command them. He who bears the bracelet and the sword controls the dragons."

"What if the enemy got his hands on the sword?" Drathorn asked. "He would surely be unstoppable then?"

"Yes, perhaps he would if he could wield it . . . but they say only a true Hellbound can wield it." Orfac said. "It is said that the blade is far too heavy for a normal man to lift but is light as a feather in the hands of the Hellbound. Once you grasp the blade it will recognize you as the owner and only when that is done will you obtain its power and control over the dragons."

"Then I must retrieve the sword and the bracelet!" Drathorn exclaimed. With the long lost blade and the sacred dragons in his command he would be able to stop Icarus, he would be strong enough to protect Thira and Troy again, he could return to them. It was all he needed. "Where is it, when can I go to retrieve it?"

"The tomb is hidden in the center of the Lone Mountain. It is guarded by many ancient curses and many creatures of the deep as well as some prehistoric traps." Orfac said. "As a Hellbound it should be no trouble to you."

"The sword and bracelet are in a magic case that can only be opened with a key in Orfac's tower. The case is inside the tomb. Inside the tomb is also Gradorn's coffin, inside the coffin Gradorn lays with the journal. Bring back the case and the journal and Orfac will open the case so you may claim your heritage and save us all." The king said.

"You will need to be informed of what lies ahead though." The high-arch said. "If you'll come with me to my tower I will explain everything."

Drathorn nodded at the mage and followed him and his apprentices out of the manor, all of his original plans completely forgotten.

They climbed three flights of stairs in Orfac's enormous tower before the high-arch ordered the twins away and they slipped silently into their room. Up ten more flights of stairs they stopped and entered the highest room. If Drathorn had been expecting a room full of books he would have been strongly disappointed. This was a mage's tower, but there were no more than three thick volumes sitting on a small rickety table in the middle of the room. A heavy cauldron sat on the floor beside the table, a wooden stool between them. Long, open windows were set into the thick walls, allowing the room to see for miles in every direction. In the far distance he could see Narvahan Shé and in another direction he could barely see smoke rising from the village of Nargak across the ocean. But he could also see Hellfire Bay clearly from here. There was smoke rising there as well and many bandits moving throughout the port.

Orfac went directly to a little cupboard set into a corner of the limited wall space and threw it open. He moved things around noisily before pulling out two pieces of paper and a small box.

He walked over to the small table and sat down in the stool. Drathorn walked over to the tiny table to examine the objects. The first was a map, on it were several passage ways twisting and turning in a confusing way but yet somehow there seemed to be a pattern to them. The map was labelled "The Home of the Lone" along the many passage ways were multiple open caverns and small rooms. Only one, near the top of the map, was labelled. It was labelled as 'The Hellbound's Tomb'. "This is a map of the inner architecture of the Lone Mountain. It was dug by the Dwarves thousands of years ago in honour of Gradorn. The Dwarves who dug it have long since died but they left with us this map. Gradorn and his followers hid here during the war and used it as a base of operations. It has been sealed ever since Gradorn was buried within it."

Drathorn gazed at the map Orfac gave him before the high-arch went on. "This is a list of clues to the special enchantments in the place." He said. "Before entering the Home of the Lone you'll have to follow a long passageway covered in ancient traps, and curses and guarded by creatures of the deep and of the dark."

Drathorn took the short list without question; very few words seemed to mean anything to him. He saw things as simple as 'look up' and soon gave up on trying to figure them out. He finally looked back at Orfac, paying strict attention.

The high-arch had taken the small box and was playing with it aimlessly. Beneath his hands he could twist the box many ways and after a while Drathorn noticed that on each of its six sides was a design that had to be completed by turning and twisting the pieces. After about two minutes the old man had cleverly completed the puzzle and each side was covered with beautiful designs. But now that it was complete Drathorn noticed something else; in its completed form it was literally a box. Orfac opened it without a key to reveal the inside. The outside had been cleverly carved of wood, most likely of Dwarven or Elvin design as only they could have invented such a puzzle-box, but the inside was gently lined with a soft green silk. On the silk was a single silver key.

"This is the key that will open the magic case that contains the sword and the bracelet." Orfac said. "The box seems to be made of delicate wood but it's enchanted to be indestructible and can only be opened by those wise enough to complete the puzzle. The more powerful the object inside is, the trickier the puzzle. The key will remain here until you return with the case and the journal." With a strange finality in his ancient and wise tone he closed the box and the cube began to shift into an unrecognizable puzzle again all on its own.

"I won't take long," Drathorn promised.

"Of course you won't." Orfac said. "Now, the entrance to the tunnel is not very well hidden. Climb up the south side of the mountain about fifty feet and walk along the ridge until you find an ancient door of stone. Say the Dwarven word of peace and the door will open. On the other side is a set of stairs. After that, all the necessary information is on those pages I gave you."

"What's the Dwarven word of peace?" Drathorn asked, very weak when it came to Dwarven runes.

"It is *Drishinek.* Say that once and the door should open of its own accord." Orfac said. "Also, for the last enchantment you will need this." Orfac said, turning and taking a small paper-wrapped package from the closet. He unwrapped the object quietly and then held it out to Drathorn. "It is the mirror of Ghlen." He said. "The door to the Home of the Lone is blocked by the door of Ghlen. It is carved to look like her face and is said to speak. Only by reflecting light onto the stone of the door can you force it open. Once the door is open there should be no problems." Drathorn nodded. The mirror seemed quite original; small and with a handle trimmed in gold. Nothing special, but he knew better than to trust appearances. He pushed the mirror deep into his pocket along with the map and the list to join the other objects within. His hand brushed Elgard's Ali-Manicota orb and the crystal shard Bandixi had once protected but he said nothing about either. "When should I leave?" Drathorn asked.

"In the morning, that should give you enough time to rest before your journey." Orfac said. "Until then, return to wherever you'll be staying tonight . . . and come back as soon as you have the case, the journal we can spare but the case is a necessity." Drathorn nodded before leaving the room. He walked down the stairs and out the gate, walking slowly back the way he had come. His mind was too full of the idea of commanding Dragons and saving the world to notice the people staring at him.

The wagon was gone when he arrived but Pat and Hailey were still home. Robby, Ben and Linda had all gone to try selling the items they new the banks would not take. He explained that he had to leave in the morning and they were very unwilling to let him go. Drathorn had to be very convincing to get Pat to be rational. In the end he finally convinced her to take Linda and Hailey and go away from the city. They were also to try and convince Ben and Robby to go with them; he didn't want to have to worry about any family while he fought. In the end she agreed to try and get them to leave. They would go back north, and take the paper pass for it was now certainly clear of danger. The well loosened bandit hold should give them very little problems there and they should be able to reach Taldi safely and gain an escort to Gaberdan.

After writing a note for them to give Elforge, Drathorn ate silently and went to bed early. He planned to leave while they all still slept, and if things went as planned he would not see them again unless he returned to Gaberdan when the book was saved.

And that was the plan, for he *had* to see Troy and Thira again. He couldn't stand being so far away from them. *It won't be long now . . .* he told himself. *A few more days and you can take a ship to Taldi and then a wagon to Gaberdan and see them again . . .* and he fell asleep with thoughts of Dragons and killing the darklord on his mind.

Twirled, blocked, slashed at the first attacker, parried, slashed at the second, blocked an attack from both sides, took out the third attacker with a pincer like move to the neck using both swords, jumped and split kicked the two attackers on the sides. And then dived forward and stabbed the final attacker in the gut. His opponents fell for the fifth time that day. Murlok beamed as Troy watched wordlessly.

Thursday June 4th, 18291; Murlok frowned at Troy's absent minded expression. He dropped the two wooden swords on the ground as his fake opponents began to recover, all groaning and moaning from abuse. "What's wrong Troy?" Murlok asked.

Troy had not been the same since yesterday. Murlok had angrily glared at Feronis every chance he got since waking yesterday, believing that Thira's crying and Troy's sudden silences were his fault. But it wasn't long before he found himself wrong. Feronis was just as confused as he was and even very silently told him the small bits he had heard. It sounded like they had been arguing about Drathorn and Thira had told him to leave. It made no sense and neither Thira nor Troy said anything to either them or each other on the matter. Actually Thira barely said anything to anyone. She spent every hour that was not devoted to training in her room. The crying seemed to have stopped but she seemed oddly depressed.

Last night had been worse than ever for Thira, she had screamed Drathorn's name in fear multiple times in the night, along with many verses of "No! No! Let him go! Don't hurt him!" Murlok could only imagine the horrible nightmares about Drathorn's supposed demise that she seemed to be having. The endless wait and wonder about Drathorn's condition bothered Murlok but since he did not know the Hellbound in any particular way he did not find it hard to cope with. Nowhere near as hard as Thira and Troy had found it.

Troy and Thira had finished their separate training sessions and Thira was now back in her room. Troy had come to the skirmish hole to watch Murlok's progress. This was the first time Troy had ever seen him fight and Murlok was annoyed that Troy would have any criticism on his fighting skill so early. "Troy, what'd I do wrong? I thought I nailed it!"

"You did . . ." he said. "I was just thinking about Drathorn."

Murlok groaned like the battered trainers and walked over to the one legged archer. "When are you gunna tell me what you and Thira were fighting about yesterday?" he asked.

"We weren't fighting!" Troy said defensively "And maybe you should keep your nose in its own business. I was actually wondering how Drathorn managed to defeat you in that forest so long ago . . . when there were so many others there as well."

Murlok had not expected that. "He's a legend, an incomparable fighter. Of course he can beat me. And I'm a lot better now than I was then." He said.

Troy shook his head. "I've seen Drathorn fight before . . . he was no where near strong enough to kill all those bandits by himself."

"You said he left because he was worried he couldn't keep you guys safe, right?" Murlok asked.

Troy nodded, "He said he wouldn't be able to do his job properly if he had to worry about people other than himself getting hurt."

"Well that's it then." Murlok said. "He was holding out on you guys. He was always so worried about keeping you guys safe he kept getting hurt and weakened in the battles and couldn't do his job. So without you there he was able to concentrate more and grasp his full potential." Murlok smiled as if he'd settled the matter.

"He must have cared a lot . . ." Troy said, his eyes looking somewhere very far away even as they sat here; gazing, un-seeing, at the warm sand of the training hut. "If he could hold out on his fighting that much to worry about us he must of cared a *lot*."

Murlok frowned, annoyed that this topic was not yet over. "You seem surprised."

Troy frowned. "Drathorn and I haven't known each other very long." He said. "It doesn't make sense that he would endanger himself so much to protect me and a mere friend from the orphanage."

Murlok frowned now. *What was his point?*

Troy looked up and noticed Murlok's annoyed expression and smiled apologetically. "You're coming along very well Murlok, sorry for getting side tracked. Let's go get something to eat."

Thankful for the end of the subject Murlok lead the way out into the scorching heat.

Troy stood around for only a minute longer as he gazed out across the sea at the mountain's peak, more of a habit now than out of worry. *A mere friend from the orphanage . . .* he repeated to himself in his mind. *Perhaps she had been more than a friend to Drathorn, as Emily is to me? If so, he too must be hurting, just like her.*

Someone cleared their throat loudly and Troy looked up again to see Murlok peeking disapprovingly at him from outside. Troy smiled apologetically again and rushed to find breakfast with his friend.

Just as Troy had thought, Drathorn *was* in pain.

That night had started with dreams of Dragons and killing the darklord and restoring peace and happiness. But soon Troy and Thira's faces interrupted the dream. Thira was crying, and not the silent steadily streaming tears she had cried before; no these were tears of pain and sadness. She shook violently as she sobbed loudly and cried his name. But somehow she was asleep in the middle of these sobs.

And then Troy's face floated in his unconsciousness. His face was stained with dried tears but his eyes no longer cried. His face showed pain, pain beyond tears. In his hands he held a drawing. Before Drathorn could try and take a closer look at the figure on the page the dream had changed again.

He saw from afar the white explosion of light atop Mt. Tanisay. Then he saw the blood stained streets of Taldi and the room full of weapons. And then ships, many great ships on the horizon, all bearing the bandit flag. And then an alleyway, long and dark and at the end of the alleyway was a figure in a dark black cloak. A boney hand reached out from the cloak and held a towering scythe. In the other boney, mangled, hand, stained yellow and crawling with small insects feasting upon rotting flesh that did not disappear, was a string that reached down to a small hourglass.

Words appeared in Drathorn's mind but before he could make sense of them all went black, all but Thira with her beautiful skin and her shining brown eyes. She stood sideways, holding out her hand to him. He took a step forward to take it but suddenly she seemed that whole step farther away. He took another and she was even farther away. He tried to look at his feet to make sure they were really moving forward but he couldn't look away from her face. He took another step forward and yet was somehow farther from her. She frowned in confusion. Drathorn frowned too and began to run, trying desperately to reach her. But with every step she grew further and further away. He knew he should stop running, that surely if he stopped running she would not get any farther away, but he could not stop no matter how obvious the logic. She began to fade into the blackness. "Thira!" he yelled. And then the dream was gone.

He woke with a start, covered in sweat and panting like he had really been running that whole way. He knew what all of them meant; Thira was in pain, Troy was in pain, they had seen the flash atop Tanisay and feared for his life, the people of Taldi were gone from the mess of their city, the bandit ships were gathering, and the second last image meant death, it was coming and he felt it inside. But for who?

And then another question; why had he dreamed of Taldi and the ships? He had been dreaming of happiness before and it had turned to Troy and Thira and pain. Unless they were not in Gaberdan he should not have been dreaming of those places, he should have been dreaming of Gaberdan. But as he thought harder on the details of Thira's room where she cried he had to admit he did *not* recognize the place Thira and Troy seemed to be in. He frowned at the idea that Troy and Thira were not yet in Gaberdan.

But then his thoughts turned abruptly after thinking Thira's name. What did that final part of the dream mean? Was he running farther and farther from Thira each day? If so then that was certainly what he had wanted; to be far enough away not to cause them harm. But if not seeing them could cause them and himself so much pain how could it truly be right? What did these dreams mean? He shook his head as if doing so would clear his mind. Then he stood and put on his filthy, ragged clothes. He searched his pockets and pulled their contents out.

He put the map, list, and mirror in one pocket and then looked at the objects in the other. The shard from Bandixi and Elgard's Ali-Manicota orb sat in the palm of his hand. He would much rather have nightmares of the nights he won those two objects then witness the pain he caused his friends. He considered for a moment, using the orb and becoming an Ali-Manicota or becoming the shard's guardian, just so he could live forever and have two lives and a greater chance of seeing his friends again. But to live forever was a curse as well as a gift. For what happened when all that you loved died out? When you were alone in the world and unable to die? And when Troy and Thira did die and he was alone would there even be a reason to keep on living?

He stuffed the objects in his other pocket, annoyed with himself. He snuck quietly from the house and found the wagon sitting empty in the driveway. No treasure, no people, just emptiness. He walked past it, through the quiet city. No one stirred this early in the morning, the sun was just beginning to rise. In the west the sun was surely high in the sky, enveloping the desert in its heat. He reached the city's stone gate and found it closed and guarded by two men. "Good morn, sir." One guard said. "The king told us to let you through. We don't normally open the gates before the rooster's crow but the king told us to make an exception for you."

Drathorn thanked them and they opened the gate noisily. He walked along the stone wall, eyes from the guard towers watching him suspiciously, until he reached the north side of the city. He cut straight across the barren farmlands; toward the nearby mountain where his ancestor lay buried. By the time he reached the open northern gate of wood the roosters had crowed and the farmers had begun their daily routine. He walked through the gates and marched off without speaking. By noon the sun was high in the sky and by dinner he was sitting at the foot of the Lone Mountain on a large boulder, eating a sandwich made from vegetables and fruits he had packed and munching on berries from the forest's bushes.

The path wound high up the mountain, quite steep but still fair for walking. Fifty feet above he could see where the path would lead. A great door of stone embedded in the side of the mountain.

He thought back to the night before, when Robby had come into his room around midnight and woken him. He had told Drathorn they had agreed to leave Signaroc before the fighting. He was a little disappointed not to be fighting alongside Drathorn but agreed that his family was more important. He had given Drathorn a gift; a book called "*The Traveler's Aid*". It was a thick book considering the fact that it had only three chapters but the index alone managed to be nearly forty pages long, not including the well labelled map of Tanroe at the very front.

The first chapter was called "*Items of the Beginning Traveler*" it contained detailed advice on items new travelers should carry with them in the different areas of the world and explained in detail their effects and how to use them. The second chapter was labelled "*Spells for the Apprentice*" It was mostly unreadable because it was all in the language of magic. Drathorn only recognized a few of the runes when he had taken the time to examine it but otherwise ignored the two hundred pages of magic.

The third was called "*Monsters of the Wild*" and each page told about a different creature in great detail as well as showed a detailed drawing of the beast. It was nowhere near as detailed as Troy's drawings but it was still much better than anything Drathorn had ever done. He had the book opened to page four hundred and fifty two, a page dedicated entirely to Wyverns. According to this article the Wyverns were a much more modern and less fearsome form of dragon. The Wyverns were much smaller and could not breathe fire. Wild Wyverns apparently had large blades on the tips of their tails that made Argoss' axe look like a child's toy. They were also said to be extremely poisonous. The Wyverns bred in captivity were without this blade and had clipped claws and had been put in heavy muzzles. They were now used in airports, along with the cheaper griffons, to fly business men and small families between the largest cities of the Empire.

There was only one reason he read this passage, a page that had no relation at all to the mythic dragons he would soon command. He had looked closer at the map Orfac had given him and (though he had once thought it unlabelled) he found one enormous room on the western side that was labelled with minuscule writing. *"Wyvern Pit (opened to a cliff unreachable on foot to allow Wyverns' access to the sky)"* As Drathorn remembered the old stories of Gradorn and his army he remembered a single detail that most people never paid much attention to; Gradorn's ancient army had once rode Wyverns into battle, using their venomous teeth and tail and armour piercing claws to win many battles. If Orfac was correct and the Home of the Lone was indeed Gradorn's old base then the Wyvern Pit was surely still there. If the Wyvern pit was still there then surely the Wyverns had not stopped using this place that remained so safe from the reach of the free people.

There were certainly still Wyverns in that pit, and possibly spread throughout the entire maze. Drathorn frowned as he looked between the map and the fearsome picture of the Wyverns. The fastest, most direct route to the tomb was right through the middle of that pit. The only other route to the tomb cut across its edge. Either way he would have to go through that pit, either way he would have to face the Wyverns.

XXVIII

Booby Trap

Ready. They were all ready. All the ships, all the men. The training was done, ended so the men could keep up their strength for the coming battle. Troy wanted to leave now, bring down the bandits and reach Signaroc to join their friends in their hour of need. Thira and Murlok agreed with him. But Chief Samgarnok and Feronis refused to move ahead of schedule. They would leave only when planned. Troy honestly considered leaving without them but the small group of boats he rightfully commanded from Taldi didn't stand a chance against the enemy. He surrendered in defeat as he and Thira angrily returned to the small table with the map in their cabin. They no longer spoke of pain, except what they would cause their enemy. They no longer spoke of fear, except what they would fill their foe with. They no longer spoke of Drathorn, and that was the end of it. Their friendship had returned mostly to its former state and Thira didn't cry anymore. But they both complained continuously to each other that they had to wait until noon the next day before they could set out.

"*Drishinek*" Drathorn said, loudly and clearly, as Orfac had instructed. After his dinner he had put aside his fear of facing the Wyverns and hiked up the path to the flat door that bore no marks upon its surface nor budged beneath his push. It was remarkable how fast it worked. He had pushed and kicked and hammered upon the flawless stone surface with no success. When he finally remembered the word Orfac had told him the door swung open toward him as if by a soft wind. He stared in shock at the opening in front of him.

He stepped into the darkness and immediately sunk onto a step. He was already at the staircase Orfac had told him about. He took another step down the stairs and then another. He had taken eight steps and could see no more. He should have brought a torch, for without light he could not read the map or the list of traps. He wondered if he would be able to light his hand on fire again to make light but try as he might he could not summon it. He sat alone in the darkness upon the step. He huffed a huge sigh of annoyance when he realised he would have to walk all the way back to Signaroc to find some force of light. *If only I were a viperfish and I could create my own light.* He though to himself. And then a conversation from long ago came back to him. A conversation he had not been part of, but overheard while laying in a bed at the hospital in Taldi.

"But there will be some side effects. A certain ingredient, though we do not know which, reacted with the magic that created the poison. The reaction formed an abnormal connection between his mind and his right hand."

"What will this connection mean?"

"Well the connection was only the first part to be honest." The woman said sadly. *"But the effect is more of a gift. If my calculations are correct, he should be able to create a bioluminescent light with the palm of his right hand and control it's intensity with his mind."*

"That's amazing!" Elforge exclaimed. *"That is truly a gift! To create light without words or magic like an animal from the ocean's depths!"*

"Yes . . ." The woman sighed. *"But I cannot tell what ingredients reacted with the magic in the arrow and even if we tried to run tests, the arrow would kill anyone else who was hit by it."*

Drathorn gasped as he remembered the conversation Elforge had had with the nurse in Taldi. Elforge had never taught him how to use it . . . he probably didn't know. But if it was a reaction of chemicals it should be as easy as mixing two things together right? He remembered a chemistry class at Troy's school in Gaberdan and how he had created a small explosion by mixing three chemicals. Would that possibly make light too, if he mixed the right chemicals? But he had no chemicals . . . none except what the nurse claimed was in his body. The arrow had injected a poison into him and the antidote had reacted wrongly, creating a supply of chemicals that should create light. But why did his hand not shine now? Were the chemicals not mixed? Were they used up like in the explosion Troy had caused?

There was only one way to find out. Drathorn shook his left hand roughly in the darkness he slapped his knuckles off the wall and began to bleed. *Oh great yah, let the chemicals leak out then you idiot!* He said to himself in his mind. Then he realised the nurse had said his *right* hand. He stepped away from the wall and shook his right hand, a little more carefully this time. There seemed to be a small glow . . . was he imagining it? Was it really there? "Ow!" he gasped. He had smacked the stone wall again. No blood came this time but it hurt painfully. He rolled his eyes and held his hand out in front of him before shaking it this time. If he could see himself he probably would have laughed at how dumb he looked standing there.

But soon he *could* see himself. A glowing white light was gently radiating from his hand, soon he could count his fingers and then he could measure his arm. After only a moment he could see ten feet ahead of himself. The light seemed to radiate directly from his palm; no other part of his hand glowed. Strange considering the arrow had not struck there . . . perhaps that was where they had administered the antidote. He shrugged away his questions and looked to the side, pointing his palm where he wanted to see. The wall was a lot closer than he'd thought. If he stood in the middle of the staircase he had less than half a foot of space on either side. Ahead of him was emptiness. He held his hand higher, letting the light flow farther and saw no end to the staircase. *I wish this light was a little brighter* he thought to himself.

As if answering his thoughts the light intensified. He could see farther ahead but still no end to the stair case. *Brighter?* He thought. Again the light intensified slightly. Again no end to the stairs. He frowned, not out of confusion for having his wishes granted, but out of confusion for the length of the staircase. He shrugged and pulled out the list, planning to check for any traps along the staircase.

The words were simple, but unexplained. *Never ending staircase.* Drathorn frowned, how could it be never ending? Surely there was an end? He began to walk down the steps, glancing now and then at the list as if he was expecting the words to change; they didn't. He looked ahead for the ninth time and still saw no change.

He looked behind him and sure enough he was still only ten steps from the exit, he could see the light of the sun growing dimmer outside. He had been walking downwards for nearly ten minutes but there was no change in the distance between him and the entrance. He frowned and looked again at the walls on either side of him. The wall on his left was stained slightly by the blood of his knuckles. The wall on the right appeared solid and normal. Or so it *appeared.*

As he looked closer at the wall he noticed that in one spot, three steps back the way he had come, the wall seemed lighter and less solid. He stepped toward it. He reached out to touch it but found suddenly that he was grabbing air. He smiled at himself and stepped through the fake wall.

Then he fell.

But it wasn't a pit fall, it wasn't death. He didn't miss a step on a hidden set of stairs. He slipped onto a slippery slide much like the one near the crater containing the Sentrate Tree. Suddenly he was on his back, hurtling forward at full speed. He yelled in surprise when his feet suddenly connected with solid ground a minute later and he stumbled forward and face planted in sand. After spitting out a mouthful of dirt he stood and looked around with the light from his palm.

The room was moving. The walls were anyways. The floor seemed completely normal. There was a door every few feet; seven of them in total, each a different colour of the rainbow. The walls sped up and became a whirl of color that made him dizzy he closed his eyes and there was nothing, no sound, no movement, just nothing. He opened his eyes again and the spinning was still there, even faster. He closed his eyes again, fighting the dizziness and pulled the list from his pocket. It only said two words. *Look up.* Drathorn did as he was told.

While the room spun out of control the ceiling seemed to be moving closer . . . it *was* moving closer. Thousands of tiny lethal looking spikes covered the roof in all but one spot. In the very center of the roof was an empty spot that seemed to open to another dimension. Drathorn stepped toward the middle of the room but the moving walls made him feel so strange that he stumbled and fell.

He could not move without losing his mind here, he could barely stand. He looked up again and the dizziness lessened when he could no longer see the walls. He smiled. He used the roof to guide himself to the middle of the room and it took only a minute for the roof to miss him as he stood in the one safe spot. The needles dug deep into the sand and didn't move. He looked around and noticed that the doors had stopped moving. Each was one of the colours of the rainbow and each had a dark black number on it going from one to seven. Somewhere nearby was a loud dripping noise. He looked at the list again.

Don't look up. He read. He was suddenly struck by the urge to look upwards again but he resisted. Instead he contented himself by looking down. He suddenly realised he was standing on a heavy trap door. He reached down and pulled on the ring. It was *really* heavy. He strained against the trap door's weight and had to put down the small leather bag his book was in to lift it. When it was open he could hear the screeching of chains and a strange heavy blowing sound coming in a pattern.

He looked at the list, hesitating. *What are you waiting for?* Was the fourth step on the list. Drathorn laughed and picked up his leather bag before dropping down. He floated down and landed gracefully on the ground in a well lit passage.

Finally not needing the light from his palm anymore he thought *"be gone"* and the light in his palm went out. He through a glance at the list. *Swinging axes, Walls shooting fire.*

Drathorn laughed at the part about the fire. This was going to be easy. He walked forward and turned around the corner to see a long corridor. Giant axe heads swung back and forth from one side of the passage to the other in widths, blocking his way. A giant battering ram swung along the length of the passage with perfect timing so it didn't hit any of the swinging axes or the flames coming from holes in the wall at regular intervals. Every second there was an axe, battering ram or flame spurt striking the empty air. The flames wouldn't be hard . . . the rest would. He waited for a minute, calculating before he leapt past the first swinging axe that had cut a deep yet fairly thin scar through the hard stone. He waited a second and jumped past another axe, right into a burst of flame.

He brushed the flames out as quickly as he could; trying to salvage his ruined clothes and the objects they carried. He looked up just in time to see the giant battering ram coming at him. He rolled forward, without thinking and barely felt the giant wooden battering ram scrape the top of his spine. He nearly lost his head after the roll from another axe. Before he could recover the battering ram was back. He dropped to the dirt as it swung past and then the fire blasted from the wall a minute later, narrowly missing him lying on the ground. Two axes swung at either end of his body, one missing his head by just over an inch as it cut deep into the ground, the other missing his legs by only half a foot.

He frowned in concentration. Trying to avoid the fire in order to save his book and clothes was hard enough without other objects threatening his life. As soon as the axe by his head passed he crawled forward quickly. The battering ram missed him again by inches and the fires came nowhere close to him on the ground. If he stayed low he could avoid both of them and if he timed his movements right he could also avoid the axes quite easily.

During one of his many pauses he looked again at the list and saw the word battering ram written underneath the last step in miniscule writing. He smacked his forehead for his stupidity and nearly lost his hand to the battering ram in the process. Swearing loudly in annoyance he continued to the end of the passage. It felt great to stand up at the end of the corridor.

With a more careful look at the list this time he read that the next enchantment was a classic leap of faith. He went through the wooden door ahead of him and walked onto a small platform. The platform was dimly lit by torches and across the room he could see the other platform lighting up the door on the other side of a twenty foot gap.

Using the newly discovered light in his hand Drathorn illuminated the gap below. Ten feet below was the floor. It was covered with thousands of needle-like spikes sticking out of the floor. Just like the roof had been in the spinning room except there was no gap anywhere and it wasn't moving. The spikes were littered with bodies of men and woman who had tried to make the leap of faith. Drathorn thought back to the other traps and only vaguely remembered the decaying bodies littered nearby. He had never paid them much attention but he had very slightly noticed that the body count decreased the further he went. Fewer and fewer people made it this far. Drathorn expected there would be even less bodies on the other side. He remembered the dripping sound in the spinning room and was grateful he had not looked up. *Someone must have tried to break in very recently.*

It was a leap of faith, of course he had only to throw caution to the winds and jump. Why wouldn't he survive? It was simple! He took a single step closer to the edge and his foot sunk. He looked down at the pressure plate he had stepped on. *Damn.* The wall behind him groaned and began moving forward somehow. So this is how the others had died. It was a *leap* of faith and the illusion was so real that they became scared to jump. They would never have seen the wall pushing them onto the needles and they would not have survived because they would have fallen off, not leapt.

Drathorn didn't hesitate; he backed as far as he could to the wall that was slowly pushing forward. He ran and then jumped as far out as he could. At the peak of his jump; the point where he would have begun to fall down towards the earth, the jump seemed to end and Drathorn became weightless. He moved forward, frozen in mid jump as the wall finished pushing along the platform. He moved along slowly as if propelled by the wind but unable to move even his eyes. He watched as the other side slowly grew closer. And then, once he was over the platform in front of the door he dropped out of the air and landed flat on his feet, unharmed.

After Drathorn got over his shock at having survived the jump he looked again at the list, slightly burnt on one corner. The next line simply said; *Hope you speak goblin.* Drathorn didn't know how to speak goblin. He had never seen goblins, but he had read about them. They were in the book but he didn't need to read about them to know they were bloodthirsty and highly protective of treasure. They would gang up and kill anyone who trespassed near their home. Drathorn read the next line, hoping it would give him an idea of what to say. It didn't.

Now reflect the mirror of Ghlen at the hour of twelve to open the way to the Home of the Lone. So Ghlen's door was on the other side of these goblins, and so was the tomb. Drathorn stuffed the list into his pocket and drew his elegant long sword. Then he opened the door and walked into the next room.

In the very center of the room was a giant rotating pillar made of wood. It was so thick Drathorn thought it could hold the Blaygard family and wagon with room to spare if it had been hollow. It rotated with a great speed, but not quite as fast as the spinning room from before. Sticking out at random spots starting just above shoulder level of the average human and going up several feet higher were many thick wooden posts that stuck out at odd angles reaching every wall of the room accept the small indent where the door was. Some posts were spiked, others had large axe blades sticking out of them and even others were bare but for the wood itself. No matter what was on the limb it spun with enough force to knock someone unconscious, or indeed drive spikes through someone or cut them in half.

Even worse was the fact that the immense rotating support wasn't all one piece. It was divided into many parts that spun in different directions. The one at Drathorn's shoulder spun clockwise while the two above it spun counter clockwise at different speeds and then the next one spun clockwise again at a slower speed and so on.

Worse still was the large group of goblins that ran around, too short to be harmed by the giant mechanism. Some had daggers; others had small swords or even crossbows. All were a sick green colour and had yellow teeth and blood covered lips. All of them had sharp toe and finger nails that pierced the wood of the mechanism and let them climb up and down it.

The blood thirsty goblins turned his way, their greedy eyes dark with hunger. Drathorn ran straight into the room and the goblins swarmed. He swung his sword at one and cut through its boney frame easily. Another leapt at him and impaled itself on the blade's point. With his long sword in one hand and his old bloodstained dagger in the other Drathorn dodged the spinning mechanism and fought off the beasts. *Perhaps it is hollow?* There was no door here so Drathorn decided to try and work his way up to the top and look for a way inside the mechanism. As four goblins surrounded him he jumped up and grabbed onto a passing bare limb of the mechanism. It carried him around the room swiftly and his feet connected with many tiny goblin heads. He struggled to get on top of the log and succeeded. But a goblin leapt at him and he had to kick with both legs randomly to keep it away. He kicked with such force that the goblin flew back into an approaching spike covered limb and imbedded itself deeply on the spikes. The limb broke off from the force of the impact.

The above portion of the mechanism was moving much faster than the one he was on now and was much deadlier. As the broken limb passed another followed behind it, this one was bare like the one Drathorn was on now. He leaped at it as it passed over his head and used his dagger as a handle to pull himself up. He looked down and saw two goblins using their sharp claws to climb the spinning mechanism and chase him. A large group of goblins were fighting each other over the scraps of their dead brothers.

Drathorn ripped his dagger out of the wood and threw it at one of the approaching goblins. Unlucky today, the blade did not stab the creature. But the hilt did collide painfully with his skull, knocking him unconscious and sending him back to earth with his bloodthirsty brothers. Drathorn turned to look for an escape from the other goblin, unwilling to throw his sword at the foe. The spinning limbs above him held no safety; all were either spiked or tipped with axe blades. But he couldn't stay there; he decided to try his luck with the axes.

The goblin leapt at the same time as Drathorn. The goblin had seen what he planned to do and leapt at him with much more force. Drathorn landed on the flat of the axe blade at the last second. From two levels down the goblin had jumped powerfully, been unlucky in his timing, and was cut cleanly in half by the blade. Blood splattered Drathorn and the blade as the two parts of the creature fell back to the ground. One of the goblins had stopped fighting over scraps and had loaded a bow and arrow.

Drathorn ducked and the arrow collided with the wood above his head. "*Firefang!*" Drathorn called. The bow of the mystic dozen was suddenly in his hand and he pulled the arrow from the wood, glad he had some ammunition. He aimed, pulled back and shot. The arrow struck one of the fighting goblins and killed it instantly. The poison did nothing to the already dead creature but a minute later he burst into flames from the inside, lighting many of the nearby goblins on fire and sending the whole place further into chaos.

"*Thi Sein Whor!*" The bow suddenly flashed brightly and disappeared. "*Venomstrike!*" the dagger replaced it in his hand. As the goblins fought and fled from the fire. Drathorn sheathed the elegant long sword and stabbed the dagger into the wood above his head. The rotating wood immediately yanked the dagger from his grip and he was left standing alone. "*Firefang!*" he yelled again, re-summoning the bow. Another arrow collided with the arm he was sitting on as it spun past the archer. Drathorn yanked it out of the wood and held it securely in his teeth as he waited for *Venomstrike* to come back around. It didn't take long.

With his free hand he grabbed the dagger and it wrenched him off the wooden limb. Hanging from the dagger with one hand he tried desperately to pull himself up and only barely succeeded. After a minute of struggling he was balancing on the unbreakable dagger. He aimed and fired at the archer goblin with his bow and the enemy fell and burst into flames. A normal person would have been dying of the heat in the blazing room now, but to Drathorn it was like a warm breeze as he swept over the flames on his metal, axe-blade, perch. *"Thi Sein Whor!"* he said over the flames, and then the bow was gone again.

Drathorn braced himself and leapt to a bare limb above his head that was moving slightly slower than he was. Once safely on the end of the limb he shifted along the limb until he reached the center piece of the mechanism. He climbed up on the giant part and looked around. To his horror he found he had climbed here for nothing. He had expected a ladder leading up to the world above or a hole in the wood to lead him to the door but there was nothing. Here he was standing, out of breath on top of a giant support that supported nothing.

As the support spun Drathorn caught sight of something that made his spirits rise. In the wall, directly above the entrance to this room was a hole; the exit. The only way to reach it was by walking along one of the thick limbs and literally diving through. Drathorn began doing just that. He crawled along the bare limb again, afraid to lose his balance walking. It was a few moments before he reached the end. While he waited for the limb to swing back around to the hole he called *"Venomstrike!"* and the dagger disappeared from the wood below and reappeared in his hand. *"Thi Sein Whor!"* he added as soon as it was in his hand again. The dagger disappeared. A second later Drathorn stood and dove through the hole.

XXIX

Mirror, Pit, Dead Guy?

The corridor was short and carved roughly out of stone. And it was empty. There were no bodies here, no blood, no evil creatures; just a short corridor ending with the face of the most beautiful girl Drathorn had ever seen.

Ghlen's hair flowed like a river but was solid as stone for she *was* stone. It was a carving of such detail that even Troy's drawings could not compare. The eyes were shut, hiding the beauty that surely hid beneath the smooth lids. Her lips were full and perfect; her expression was of pain and sadness but still held so much beauty. From the closed eyes stone tears seemed to fall silently but were stuck in the stone upon the face. He was immediately overwhelmed with sadness at seeing the pain in this woman's face. He wished he could help her, and knew that he couldn't.

He pulled the mirror out of his pocket. To the left of the great carving a square was cut from the rock and it formed a tiny window out to the sky. No beam of sunlight struck the mirror, nothing reflected. He looked again at the list. *Now reflect the mirror of Ghlen at the hour of twelve to open the way to the home of the lone.* At the hour of twelve. Of course, the hole was positioned strategically so that light would only filter through at noon when the sun was in exactly the right place. But he didn't have time to wait until noon; surely the goblins would reach him before then.

Good thing he had his own light source. His hand shook and again the light glowed from his palm. He forced it to intensify greatly and shone it on the sad face.

Nothing happened. Drathorn frowned and put the mirror in front of the light. The light struck the mirror like all light should, but its reflection was something different. The light bounced off the mirror and changed colour. Or perhaps *colors.* For the color that bounced off the mirror was not one, but seven; the colours of the rainbow. The colours spread out the further they got from the mirror. Drathorn shifted so that the light from his palm shone perfectly on the face. But still there was nothing.

He examined the face of Ghlen; he traced the hair with his eyes down to her forehead. On the forehead was a carved tiara. Seven stones were set into the tiara, set evenly apart. He adjusted the angle of the mirror and took a step back. That was when he hit a rock. He looked at the rock and noticed a hole in it . . . a hole that would hold the mirror. Drathorn put the mirror's handle into the hole and stepped back, careful not to get in the way of the rainbow's path. Each colour struck a different colourless gem of the beautiful tiara upon Ghlen's head. As the rainbow struck, the colorless tiara's gems filled with colour and the great face split down the middle and swung forward. Drathorn reached to remove the mirror but found it encased in stone now that it was where it belonged. It would not move. So he left it there and walked alone into the Home of the Lone.

The rooms where empty. There was nothing here but stone walls and floors. Somehow the torches on the walls never burned out, even as he wandered trough the tunnels, holding the map where he could see it. It must have been a spell, for no torch could burn so long. But after nearly half an hour of following the map and peering into all the empty rooms he passed he came to the intersection where he would have to make a decision.

Would he take the fastest route and cross the greatest expanse of the Wyvern Pit? Or would he take the longer path and cross only a small corner? He felt he was running out of time and should take the shortest path, but he was scared of crossing through the Wyvern nest. He again read the passage in the book that told about the Wyverns but could find no new information. *Better safe than sorry.* He decided. He went for the longer path.

He continued along the path, checking the doors as he passed but still finding nothing. It took him nearly half an hour at the rate he was moving but he finally reached the heavy wooden door to the Wyvern Pit. A small barred window sat in the door for surveying the creatures. Drathorn looked through the bars.

It really *was* a pit. The room was carved to look much like a bowl and was filled with sand. The Wyverns were quite large and there were at least fifty of them there. A pile of Wyvern eggs sat in a small hole dug by one of the females. The wall directly ahead of the door was gone, opening out into the sky where many more Wyverns flew with the wind. Drathorn stared at the nearest Wyvern.

It was indeed large enough for several people to ride between two places. Its dark armour was green and it had spikes coming from its reptilian eyebrows and stretching back over its head. Its serpentine tongue flickered out from between its lips and its scales shone in the sunset. Its great tail was indeed tipped with a great poisonous weapon. Its claws and teeth made the goblins' downstairs look like butter knives. Somehow black hair grew along its neck, adding somehow to the fierce creature's appearance. Its eyes were blood red.

Then there was the smell. The smell of rotting flesh and the creatures' nauseating breath. Drathorn nearly gagged. He had no other choice; he opened the door as quietly as he could and unsheathed his sword. He walked forward, his sword ready. He was cautious and fearful as every Wyvern in the vast room looked up at him. They could smell the fear. Drathorn forced himself to remain calm as one of the creatures walked toward him. It sniffed at his throat in a way that would have tickled if Drathorn was not petrified that he was about to be torn to shreds. The smell of the creature's breath was nearly toxic itself.

But instead of destroying Drathorn the creature seemed to smile and nod in approval. Drathorn was no longer tense as he remembered that these Wyverns were children of Sylvaston, just as he was. They were his brothers in more ways than Troy was. Drathorn relaxed completely with this new knowledge; they would not harm him. He turned his back on the creatures and walked to the only door that lead to Gradorn's tomb.

It wasn't locked. There was no trap or enchantment on it. It opened with just a push. The tomb was large, in the middle was the stone coffin; decorated with ancient runes. Along the four walls were over fifty plain wooden coffins leaning against them. In between each coffin was a torch that was aflame with eerie blue fire. The flames put the room into a strange unnatural glow.

Drathorn walked slowly toward the stone coffin. He ran his hand along the stone, feeling the carved runes beneath his hand spelling out his ancestor's name. Then he slid his hands to the side of it and pushed open the top. It was heavy but it slid in utter silence until it fell off the coffin and landed loudly on the ground. He stopped dead.

The noise echoed so abnormally in this room. It was too loud and the echo lasted far too long to be normal. But after a moment he shrugged and looked down at the body. It had been completely stripped of flesh and organs in the past four hundred years. There was nothing inside but the skeletal remains and the corpses of long dead insects. Nothing except the case and the journal held tightly in the dead man's skeletal grip.

"Good evening Gradorn . . ." Drathorn muttered. He reached in and took the large case that contained the sword and the bracelet. Then he reached for the journal. His hand touched the cold bone of his ancestor and suddenly there seemed to be a movement behind his dead eyes. Drathorn stared cautiously before pulling the journal slowly from beneath his forefather's hand. Once the book was free Gradorn's hand fell to hit his empty chest. The hand broke through the bone that was far too fragile. It shattered as it hit the stone bottom.

But unlike the falling of the stone lid, the falling of the arm made no sound. Drathorn's fearful stumble backwards was silent. There was no sound. But Drathorn knew there should have been a strange creaking as it moved. For it did move. The movement behind its eye sockets was much more pronounced as the broken skeleton sat up and looked at him with pure hate. The body stood in its coffin, its broken ribs somehow supporting the upper half of its fragile body, the fallen arm still lying silently beneath the shadow of the slim form. "*Who . . . disturbs . . . my rest . . . ?*" the whisper chilled Drathorn to the bone, just like the image of the skeleton.

"D-d-d-Drathorn H-Hellbound sir." Drathorn stammered.

More hate glistened behind the empty sockets. "*Die . . .*" it whispered but it was not him who moved. The other coffins in the tomb, the ones of Gradorn's fallen soldiers opened all in one creaking sound. The half decayed bodies stepped out, some still with fleshy remains or bits of clothes and organs. It was a horrifying thing to witness. Drathorn stumbled back and nearly fell on the stone but there was no sound. The only sound was the steady creaking of the dead stiff limbs as they moved slowly toward him. He stumbled backwards again as they moved closer, an unwelcome cold flooding from them into his body.

He stumbled back, one step for every three of theirs; all the while Gradorn's corpse stood watching. Drathorn finally stepped back out of the tomb and the door closed with a horrible cracking noise as though it had been kicked by a giant. The door was closed and suddenly the cool northern air that flowed in through the opening of the cave seemed so warm to him. The fear was gone, it was all gone. But soon he went into shock. It was over an hour before Drathorn could take his eyes off the tomb door to look at the journal and case in his hands.

XXX

The Journal

It was her, she did it to me, and it was her fault. My mother. Her beauty, her voice, everything about her drew him in. What more could he have done? An Elf in love was an unstoppable thing. She immediately attracted him. He fell in love without even meaning to. It was her fault I was born. The Elves knew it. They destroyed her for it. The one human they had let past the great tree had been a human by the name of Hellbound. She had begged for him to live and her wish was granted and so he stayed in the Elvin forests and they secretly had me. When the Elves found out they burned her at the stake. They tried to kill my father, they tried to kill me. But my father escaped and raised me outside of the woods in the human world where we would be safe.

By the time I was twelve I knew I was different from the other boys. I was so much more attractive to the young girls than any other boy. I was much nicer and I could see farther, had better aim and was much smarter than anyone else. In a way I was a freak, in another I was everyone's best friend. They all loved me. I had my father's hair and my mother's eyes. Brown eyes, black hair . . . I was much stronger than I appeared too, and light as a feather. When I was thirteen I was the tallest, fastest, strongest boy in my high school and I only weighed a remarkable seventy pounds. I began to wonder why I was so different.

I demanded the answer from my father. He gave it to me, he gave me everything he could afford to give me and this knowledge came with a price. I was the only one of my kind, the only one ever to exist and the only one who ever would. I was a Half-Elf. Unlike an Elf I could grow facial hair, and I aged normally and had a human voice. But I was strong, slender, smart and quick like an Elf. My sight was a cross between Elvin and human . . . somewhere in between. As soon as I found out what I was I felt lonelier. I was the only one in my world who had to live with the fact that he was more alone than anyone else.

I hated my Elvin heritage and my Elvin mother. I hated all the stories of the Elves, hated the very name. I ignored my natural skill with a bow and took up the sword. I was soon a strong swordsman, even with my Elvin blood. When I was seventeen, my father died of the Plague. I turned to living alone and thought nothing of friends. Actually I didn't even have any friends anymore. As by the time I was fifteen my loneliness had affected everyone around me. They avoided my misery and my penetrating glares. The people I once called friends shunned away from me, girls stopped asking me out everyday, and then every week and then it was never. The occasional new girl in the school would eye me with an interested glance but she soon learned to ignore my existence. After my father passed away it got worse. He had remarried after my mother's death and had a child with a woman whom I had happily called mother. But she had died only days before my father.

I was now stuck raising my young half sister alone. She became my life. I watched as she grew healthy and strong under my teachings. I had dropped out of school to care for her while she was a baby and by the time she was old enough to spend the day at school I was too old to go back to school and too poor to go to college. So we stayed in the small town of Signaroc together. She grew to be much like me. Very distant from the people around her. I wouldn't allow her to drop out of school; I was like any other parent. But she never made any friends; she never brought any boys home . . . nothing. She was like me . . . lifeless outside of our little house.

But when we were both home together I was the best big brother any child could have asked for. I played with her every day; no matter how childish the games were. We talked about things that neither of us would ever talk to others about. We were everything to each other. There was nothing without the two of us. But it all changed when I was twenty-nine and she was fifteen. We had known all about the war with the leaderless badlands. How the empire struggled every day to destroy the forces of evil and complete its hold on the island. But we were too far from the badlands for it to affect us.

Now and then we had talked about the war and how great it would be to end it and for the empire to hold everything. It was on a normal summer's day when we were skipping together, despite our age, down the streets of Signaroc, singing a happy song. I still remember the words of the songs she sang for me in her beautiful voice. The dragon came without warning. It destroyed half the city. It killed her. I sat in the middle of the street over the body of my dead sister. Everyone had lost someone that day but none had shared the unquestionable bond I had had with my sister. They watched my tears in pain. They looked at me with pity; they eyed her charred body with sadness.

It scared everyone when I roared, as fierce as the dragon, in pain and anger. It was irrational what I did next but I wanted revenge. The great red Dragon; Pyros, had gone to rest in a cave of the Lone Mountain less than a day's walk from town. I took up a sword and roared again before charging from the town with the sword above my head. I have no idea how I found the great dragon in my blind rage. All I know for sure is that in my will it will state that I'm to be buried in that cave where I found him . . . I hope that my wish is granted.

I found Pyros and through anger and pain I stabbed the creature. It roared and its flame melted the stone roof. He shook his head and tears fell, spreading around the room, also melting the rock. Three of the tiniest tears reached my hand. It seared the skin. Burned it away and left a scar. "You KILLED her!" I yelled at him, knowing the tears would kill me. But I repeated the words, brandishing my blade at the dragon. The only other hit I landed before I dropped into unconsciousness was a deep cut across his eye.

I awoke many days later; a changed man, a product of the gods' research. Zathius played with the creations of his fellow gods as he always did and created me; a failed experiment. I was not what he had hoped for and he abandoned me, the lone half-elf. And so Sylvaston had decided to try an experiment of his own on me. And unlike Zathius' it had worked. I became the first again of my race; the Hellbound. Straight jet black hair, tall and strong, eyes of an evil reptilian yellow with vertical slits for pupils. I was stronger now than I had been as a half-elf. I no longer felt the pain of losing my sister. Like the dragons I had no emotion but anger within me, like the dragons I could spew fire, like the dragons I no longer aged. For my heart was affected as well as my body by the tears. I had the heart of a dragon. I discovered *many new abilities when I woke and Pyros actually* spoke *to me through my mind.*

Despite his murder of my sister we formed a brotherly bond; we were both sons of Sylvaston now. I told him of a dream, a dream to end the war in the name of my sister. I could not love her without emotion in my heart, but I still felt the need to fulfil her dream of salvation. Pyros agreed that since his deeds had torn away my humanity he owed it to me to help me with this. So together we sought Colaspis' dragon Marginous. We believed that he would join our cause because his father was our father's brother. He was family. But Colaspis' dragon was not loyal to Sylvaston, even though Sylvaston had created him. Sylvaston had created the twelve dragons as gifts to each of the Gods and made them loyal only to their owners. Then he had created Pyros for himself. Pyros was angry with Marginous, Colaspis' dragon, and a fight between the two dragons began. With my assistance Pyros killed the black dragon of pain.

We decided afterwards to find all the other dragons and attempt to rally them to our cause. But Pyros was worried for me and insisted that I create a mystical weapon that could defeat any other Dragons who turned against us. And so we created Dragontongue, *the next of Sylvaston's great inventions. The creation of* Dragontongue *forced me to go to the Elvin lands to find a magic to bind the parts of the sword. There I found the amulet of Drathorn Sky. The Elves gave it to me as an apology for killing my mother. They saw that I was not evil and that I was a good person using my gifts to save everyone. With the sword complete and the new amulet I continued my campaign against the Dragons. Together we destroyed Milakree, the dragon of Alexandria, and Marginous' mate. With the two dark dragons defeated we sought the others. Five others joined us and the rest we were forced to kill. As more dragons rallied beneath me and others were slain I became famous and respected. When the threat of the Dragons was gone we turned our thoughts to the war and began the battle to save the empire.*

As the battling continued I began to forget where I spent some of my time, even now I don't really know. There were great blank periods where I had no memory of the events and the dragons had no idea what to think of it. I ignored my disappearing mind and continued with the war; the closer we got to winning the more the blank periods came. Soon I was insane. One of the dragons betrayed us. It was Zathius' dragon.

He saw me losing my mind and tried to stop the alliance between man and dragon. I killed him without any help from the others.

It was Pyros' idea to create the Bracelet of Dragons, a piece of jewellery that would tie each of the dragons to me and my descendants. And so we did and each of the remaining dragons poured their will into the bracelet. Each was represented by a single gem. And the creation of the bracelet actually created an entire new realm. The Dragon Realm was an ancient place that the Dragons could live in. By pouring themselves into the stones of the bracelet they entered the Dragon Realm and could not be seen or heard by the people of Corrone. Only I had the power to summon them from the depths of the spirit world and the confines of the bracelet.

With the dragons loyal to me I continued my campaign against the badlands. The blank periods of my memory grew even more pronounced. I began to lose my mind completely so I decided I must be too old to continue the war. I settled down for a little while and had a young son with a woman I could not love. While my son began to grow I took the dragons back to the Lone Mountain and carved the Home of the Lone with the help of some loyal Dwarves. I said goodbye to the dragons and placed the bracelet and the sword in a case. I gave the amulet to my wife. Then I wrote this journal. It's the eve before the final battle. I don't plan to live, but I plan to turn the battle in the favour of the empire before I go. I will die and my spirit will go to rest with my sister finally. Who knows what waits for me in this final battle? All I can hope is that by the time someone reads this; the war will be over and the island will be controlled by the empire, as my sister wished . . . I did it all for you, Ghlen.

Gradorn Lebasta Hellbound,
My final day

And so that was my ancestor's story. Drathorn thought in wonder. He had survived the tears because his father had fallen in love with an Elf and had him. The mysteriously beautiful Ghlen was actually Gradorn's dead sister, killed by the dragon he befriended while seeking revenge. Drathorn had never heard anything about Gradorn being insane and according to this story the Home of the Lone was only used as a base of operations before the final battle. And so Gradorn had allowed himself to die in what should have been the final battle. He didn't use the sword or the bracelet and he had removed the amulet. He had died just like everyone else in that fight. He had allowed an archer to shoot him in the chest.

According to the most recent stories the darklord had come from almost nowhere shortly after Gradorn fell and used a combination of swordsmanship and magic to destroy the army of the good people nearly single-handedly. Ghlen's wish had never been fulfilled. The story made much sense to Drathorn. He was surprised that his great ancestor was a Half-Elf, therefore making Drathorn himself part Elf.

But after the surprise was another; Gradorn had had all of the same powers as Drathorn. They were very much alike. Was it also true that Gradorn had no human emotion, just like the dragons? If so then why did Drathorn have those emotions? Was it because he had no yet morphed into a true Hellbound by touching the sword? Or was the gift slowly wearing away with age? Drathorn shook his head. If becoming a true Hellbound meant giving up his humanity then he wanted no part of it.

And then a slight fear. Gradorn had not aged. His heart had refused to let him age just like the dragons. Would Drathorn become trapped at a certain age when he touched the sword? Would he be damned to live forever when the ones he loved died? No, if becoming a Hellbound meant giving up his humanity he would not do it. But he needed answers. With the case and the journal added to the book's leather bag he climbed upon the back of one of his reptilian brothers. "To Signaroc., My brother. Go!" and the Wyvern took off into what was now sunrise.

XXXI

Under the Sea

Friday June 5th, 18291; the boats had finally left the port. The Taldi ships were disguised with the bandit sails and they glided across the water silently. Troy, Thira, and Murlok were in the lead ship. It was getting late when they finally saw the other bandit sails. The other ships were far behind the disguised Taldi boats. *Hopefully this won't take long.* Troy thought as they neared the bandit blockade. "Unidentified vessels, name yourselves!" a voice yelled from one of the nearby ships.

"We are friends, fellow followers of the fallen Bandixi!" Troy yelled through his rough megaphone. "We were held captive by the Taldians and escaped in these vessels not long ago. Their brothers from Nargak give chase on us."

There was silence over the still waters before the voice answered. "Drop anchor so we may board and examine your state!"

Troy turned to the ship's captain. "Release the anchor." Troy commanded. The captain did as he was told and the nearby ships moved closer. Troy recognized the lead ship of the blockade as a simple battleship. Not far behind the ship were the eight well armed destroyers; the targets. "Get ready Murlok." He added to the warrior.

Murlok nodded and rushed below deck to prepare the troops for boarding, as the enemy ship slid their planks into place and a group of men crossed over the ocean to board them. Troy could barely see Murlok secretly leading the warriors from below into the enemy ship using his own plank. "State your name." the captain of the enemy ship said.

"I am Troy Blaygard." Troy said. "I took charge of these men when Bandixi was killed by Hellbound. We fled as soon as we could get the chance and they've been acting under my orders since our master's demise."

"And her?" the captain asked, gesturing to Thira standing behind him, pretending to be frightened. "Don't try and tell me she's a bandit. Bandixi doesn't allow women."

"She helped us in our escape." Troy said simply. "She was an old childhood friend of mine. She helped us escape and in return I promised her protection."

"Childhood friend huh?" the captain said. "You both look like kids to me."

"And Bandixi was different?" Troy said raising an eyebrow.

The captain huffed before saying; "We'll escort you to the bay."

He turned and walked across the plank back to his ship, his guards staying with him.

The anchors lifted and the ships began moving together toward the nearby destroyers. "Get ready." Troy said.

As if all the Taldi ships had heard him there was a scuffling sound from each of them. Soon the battleships of Taldi were squeezing between the destroyers, too close for the catapults but in danger of the ballistae. That was when Troy gave the order. They didn't spare the destroyer next to them. A hundred arrows of fire shot from the side of each Taldi battleship and struck the nearest Destroyers.

Just ahead Troy could see the signs of Murlok and his team striking at the enemy on the lead battleship. "Brothers from Nargak, we call for your aid!" Troy yelled into the great megaphone. He had no idea if they had heard his shout but he could only hope. Then he turned to the unharmed enemy ship on the left side of their ship. A great ballista shot smashed through the side of their ship and Thira was knocked off balance. "Board them!" Troy yelled. Grappling hooks were thrown to the enemy ship and many warriors quickly boarded its deck, trying desperately to stop the ballista from firing again at the weaker Taldi battle ship.

Troy and Thira remained unmoving in the center of the deck, barking orders into the chaos around them. The ship Murlok had commandeered was turning back toward them, Murlok and his men having already taken control, to aid them. The fleet of Nargak battle ships and its four destroyers glided swiftly toward them from the rear. The enemy ship to Troy's right began to sink below the sea, the men trying desperately to swim away from the undertow it caused. Blood spread through the water, they could hear the screams and thrashings of the warriors, as sharks feasted on them.

Troy turned away from the water to look at the approaching ally ships. They were so near that the destroyers were already launching catapult shots over the current battle toward the fleet of enemies ahead. By the time the Nargak ships arrived the worst of the confusion was done. The Taldi ships had secured three new destroyers and the lead battleship, the rest were destroyed. The ships sailed forward with Nargak's help. The fleet of bandit ships struggling to avoid the firing catapults from the allied ships. Troy smiled as he saw Murlok leap to a slower moving destroyer. This was going to be easier than he thought. A ballista shot missed Troy's head by just over a foot and he realised with a jolt that the enemy fleet was protecting one final destroyer. "Get below." He said to Thira. "We're sitting ducks up here." They ran under the deck and Troy readied his bow, prepared to light the arrow when an enemy ship passed by. Thira stood beside him, following his lead with a large crossbow.

From the porthole Troy saw Murlok shoot himself from a ballista and disappear. How did that man fire himself like an arrow so easily? It was ten minutes of yelling and screaming before Troy and Thira had a clear shot at and enemy ship. They opened fire rapidly on the ship's wooden side, or on the bandits inside that were struggling to do the same to them. Troy frowned as he saw Murlok above; battling six enemies at once while a group of Taldi soldiers jumped from the Taldi ship onto the bandit ship. High in the sky was a single catapult shot, falling straight toward the ship Murlok and the men were fighting on. "Murlok, get off that ship!" he yelled at the same time as Thira.

Murlok laughed as he blocked three simultaneous attacks. "Why? We're winning!" he killed two enemies and blocked three more attacks before the explosion, before Troy could make his command final. The already weak ship shattered when the catapult shot collided. Murlok and over fifty men, allies and enemies, disappeared in a flurry of fire and wood. When everything had settled the waters below seemed still. Murlok was gone.

"NO!!!" Thira screamed.

Troy was speechless. Murlok, joking, laughing, playing, strong, young Murlok was gone; dragged to the depths of the sea by the current and probably being chewed to bits by sharks.

Troy spun around and ran up to the deck again. There were flames everywhere—the ship would not hold out long. He prepared to dive. "No!" Thira yelled again. "Don't Troy! You'll just end up dead too! We need you!"

Troy looked into the churning waters and knew she was right . . . with his leg he could not swim strong enough to pull Murlok to the surface even if there was no current. The hunk of wood probably would have made him float anyways. He looked to Thira, a new tear in his eye for vengeance. "Let's kill these bandits!" he growled.

Within the next hour the bay was empty of bandit ships and the remaining destroyers were firing upon Signaroc's port. The port was far from the city so it was likely they didn't know they had arrived. Troy and Thira were standing together on the deck while the transports arrived, preparing to unleash the army of Nargak upon the port. It had been almost too easy. If Murlok had not drowned he would have called it child's play. But Murlok was gone, dragged to the depths of the ocean by his heavy armour and mauled to bits by frenzied sharks. He was gone. Would more die? How much of Signaroc remained? Had the battle for the journal begun? Was Drathorn alive? It was only two hours' march to Signaroc from the port. It would only take another hour to fully claim the docks. Three hours and they would be standing with the armies of Signaroc, waiting for the enemy. If it wasn't already over.

XXXII

Meanwhile

The Wyvern landed in the king's courtyard and was immediately surrounded by anxious guards. But as soon as Drathorn stepped off its back and onto the distant ground they backed away. Drathorn turned away from the guards to look at the Wyvern. "Thank-you, my brother." He whispered. "Your haste is appreciated." The Wyvern seemed to nod. "Now my friend, return to your family in the Home of the Lone and live on in peace."

The Wyvern snorted and lunged into the sky. Drathorn was already turning toward the wizard's tower before its shape was gone from the sky. It was still early . . . perhaps an hour or two until noon. He walked into the tower and through the entrance hall. He began to take the stairs up to the High-arch's room. He passed many mages in training on his way but spoke to none of them. In his pocket the Ali-Manicota orb and Bandixi's shard seemed heavy. The list of traps and the map of the Home of the Lone remained in that same pocket as the other now held the journal of Gradorn Hellbound. In the leather bag hanging from Drathorn's belt was *The Traveler's Aid,* the book he had read about the Wyverns in. In the same bag was also the long narrow case that held the sword and bracelet.

It seemed to take hours to reach the top of the tower, but it had only taken fifteen minutes. He walked to Orfac's door and knocked loudly. "Sire, you must be patient. The young man was well armed and is a direct descendant of Gradorn Hellbound. He'll return when time permits!" Orfac grumbled from the other side of the door.

"Or he may return now." Drathorn suggested through the door. There was a yelp of surprise and then a shuffling sound before footsteps walked toward the door. Orfac quickly opened the door, his face full of surprise. Drathorn couldn't help but smile. "Wasn't expecting me to return so fast?" he asked.

"No not really, how did you get back so fast? Did you forget something?" Orfac asked.

"Actually yes I did." Drathorn answered, remembering his mishap with the torch, and Orfac's face fell in disappointment. But Drathorn smiled and pulled the case from his bag. "But I worked without it." He added.

Orfac's disappointment disappeared momentarily. "You got it?" his excitement was not contained in the slightest. "And the journal? That too?"

Drathorn pulled the small pocket book from his pocket. Orfac reached for it but Drathorn shook his head and put it back in his pocket. "The secrets within should not be leaked to the public."

Orfac's face fell. "In the name of science . . . if we knew how Gradorn survived we might be able to create an entire race of people, of warriors, from the secret!"

"I know how he survived." Drathorn said. Pain echoed in his voice as he remembered the pain Gradorn had illustrated in his writing. He had been the only one . . . alone in more ways than one both before and after the tears. "His secret is a family secret . . . therefore my secret. Knowing will do you no good . . . the ability for such a creature's creation was lost forever with the abandonment of the Elves."

Orfac's face showed even deeper disappointment now but he worked to conceal it with a new desire. "The case? Let us open it!"

Drathorn smiled and walked into the room with Orfac. Several books were on the table now but the mage shoved them aside to make room for the thin case. As Drathorn set the light box down on the table Orfac fetched the strange cube and began to unlock the puzzle and obtain the key.

When the key was free from its prison Orfac turned and put it into the small key hole on the case. He turned the key and the box clicked open. Without so much as a breeze the lid lifted back on its hinges slowly; revealing the priceless treasures within.

Dragontongue was as magnificent as the legends foretold. The great blade curved very slightly and was sharper then anything Drathorn had ever seen. It seemed to be made completely of Strominite, the same metal the Gorgan Billy's blade had been made of. The hilt was unique. The grip was made of pure gold with a gently twirling design and a smooth yet easy-to-grip design. The pommel was a small sphere of gold with four decorative but dangerous looking teeth sticking out at odd angles. They were sharp enough to be called a weapon themselves. On the top of the handle the golden hilt glowed in the morning light. It made a thick, awkward looking cone that got larger as it reached the blade and suddenly stopped as the deadly Strominite exploded from it. It was nearly impossible to tell where the decorative hilt and the grip-able handle ended and begun for they were so perfectly co-ordinated next to each other. On one side of the gold cone a deadly spike stuck up randomly, making a third weapon as dangerous as the blade itself. It too was made of pure gold but filed to a deadly point. Based on the curve of the blade this spike was to be co-ordinated alongside the arm. Lying beside the sword, looking completely insignificant, was the heavy wooden sheath with the sword's name carved into it in small runes.

Between the blade and the sheath was the bracelet. It actually seemed very plain next to the sword. It was made of delicate looking silver entwining wires that came closer and more complicated together as they reached the five beautiful spheres they guarded. In the middle was the largest; a bright red stone that could only be the resting place of the great Pyros. On his right was a slightly smaller blue gem and on his left was a brown. On the brown's other side was a white gem and on the blue's other side was a yellow. Each released a steady power flow that Drathorn could easily feel.

Orfac reached out to the blade and it glowed menacingly as his fingers approached. Orfac's eyes glazed over in fear and he took a step backward. The glowing stopped instantly. "It's true then . . . only a true heir can wield the blade." He said. "As soon as my hands got near it I saw death . . . and fire and fear . . . torture . . . the images were too much I stumbled back, unable to move closer."

Drathorn nodded, "Do you wish for me to try?"

Orfac nodded.

Drathorn reached out, half expecting fear and hate to engulf him. But he felt nothing. He saw nothing. He picked up the sword, it felt awfully heavy and off balance in his hand . . . it was the absolute opposite of comfortable too. He grimaced at the blade. But as he was about to put it back it started to glow again, this time in unison with the mark on the back of his hand.

Drathorn's vision went hazy for just a moment. The room seemed to shrink, so did Orfac. The blade suddenly felt so light and perfect in his hand. Something suddenly flew down his upper back; his eyes suddenly went into deeper focus on everything. He felt suddenly stronger. His hearing picked up a conversation one floor down and then he heard Orfac's gasp as his breathing accelerated. Drathorn turned to him and Orfac gasped in fear this time as he looked into Drathorn's eyes. But Drathorn could *feel* the fear now, he could taste it on his tongue, feel it reverberating through his body. "What?" he asked. His voice seemed different; louder, more commanding. Orfac seemed much shorter now and Drathorn was able to count his wrinkles, with his suddenly amazing eyesight, even despite his distance from him.

"L-look in the mirror." Orfac stammered.

Drathorn frowned and turned to the mirror on the inside of the cupboard door. He gasped and so did the figure in the mirror. It wore the same look of shock and confusion as Drathorn but it *couldn't* be Drathorn. It wasn't Drathorn.

The Drathorn in the mirror had grown nearly a foot taller. His already muscular body had enhanced greatly, the clothes had grown with him somehow to fit his need. His hair was longer. It had always been a shaggy mess of black . . . but now it was long and straight and it fell in curtains just to his shoulders and could easily hide his face. From where he stood though the eyes were the biggest change. They had once been dark blue, an attractive blue. That was gone now.

The eyes were now yellow. But an un-earthly yellow. An evil-creature-of-the-deep yellow. These eyes alone were enough to drive fear into the most hardened of warriors. There were no proper pupils anymore. They were now vertical slits that were so deep and mysterious that you could get lost in darkness by looking in them. The evil look in his eyes was full of surprise and fear though.

How could this be him? Surely it wasn't possible? But there was evidence of the real Drathorn in there. The Angelic Symbol glowed white against his sun-tanned skin. The mark of the Hellbound did as well. His nose was still the nose of his mother, the chin of his father. He arched his back to see the burn mark that marked him as a Weretiger and found it still there, unharmed by the impossible transformation. So different . . .

so much more mysterious and powerful he looked. This transformation was impossible . . . but he liked it.

He smiled . . . and then he started to be afraid. "The journal . . ." he mumbled. "It said Gradorn didn't age . . . will I?" he asked.

He turned back to Orfac, unintentionally forcing fear on the old man with his eyes. "N-no." he stammered. "Once you reach a certain age you will stop . . . just like the Elves."

Drathorn frowned. Eternal damnation. Forever doomed to pain as he watched everyone die of old age. Forever different. Forever inhuman. *I suppose that I could kill myself once my job is over . . . join Gradorn and the Gods in heaven with the rest of my family. I might as well use it to my advantage while I still can.* He thought. *No reason to worry about that now.*

"Teach me." He said. "Teach me to be a Hellbound, Orfac. Help me unlock my power so I can defeat the army and stop them from stealing the Journal of the Great Thirteen."

Drathorn expected Orfac to be filled with excitement when he said this. But Orfac was filled with shock. "WHAT?" he exclaimed.

At first Drathorn was confused. And then it struck him. "Oh by the Gods I forgot to tell you!" Drathorn exclaimed. "I got side-tracked about the whole *Dragontongue* thing and the bracelet. The enemy that destroyed Narvahan Shé is coming here; for the Journal of the Great Thirteen! They plan to steal it and use it to eliminate me and conquer Tanroe and then the seas. I came all the way here to warn you and help. I almost forgot!"

Orfac was silent for only a moment. "We must see the king, now!"

Drathorn nodded and placed *Dragontongue* back in the case, closed it and took the key. They ran down the stairs together, Drathorn's longer, stronger form moving much faster then Orfac's frail, old one.

They finally reached the manor and found the king in his study. The guards didn't even try to stop them from busting in. "Sire! The enemy that struck Narvahan Shé is coming here!" Orfac exclaimed.

The king looked slowly at Orfac. His Dwarven companion's face fell and the guards in the study looked to the king in fear. But Salamoray was quite calm. "When?"

Orfac looked to Drathorn and all eyes followed. There was a short look of shock from everyone as they saw Drathorn's changed appearance. Drathorn looked into the king's face and only barely saw the fear his eyes caused, but he did *feel* it. "They'll be here shortly." He said, now as calm as the king. "Tomorrow night they will be at the gates." Drathorn closed his eyes and concentrated for a moment before continuing. "One thousand Gar from the swamps will be striking the outer gate to remove any defences we post there first. Then the survivors will retrieve the rest of the army to move the assault onto the main city. The main army is going to consist of an extra three thousand Gar, one hundred ogres, two hundred and fifty trolls, and ten thousand of the darklord's Vikorgan."

He opened his eyes again to see Orfac and the king exchanging nervous glances. "Who will lead them?" Orfac asked.

"If what I have been told me is correct and Cherry still lives then I suppose he will still be leading the attack as the Darklord planned." Drathorn said. "He also said something about supplying a few of his own."

"That isn't a big matter." Salamoray said. "Cherry's men consist of muggers and thieves, he has no real power but for what the darklord gives him. But if what you say is true then I believe we can guess where his men are going to come from."

"How so?" Drathorn asked.

"I suppose you learned this in the Greengate area?" Orfac asked. Drathorn only nodded and Orfac went on. "The Greengate prison was broken into the other day. Fifty prisoners escaped. We believe this was Cherry's doing."

Drathorn's thoughts went to Mardy and the other boys from the orphanage whom he new to be in the prison. Had they been in there during the escape? Drathorn ignored the thought and went on; "The army will be here tomorrow night, they'll be marching straight to the front gate, no surprises; they do not come for conquest, they come for the journal."

Salamoray nodded as if he had suspected this. "He will attempt to use the cleric Carzak to remove the anti-evil enchantment on the journal and use its secrets to destroy you and take over Corrone. We are all that stands in his way." He said. "We must prepare."

"Your highness, I've already devised a plan, if I may be so bold?" Orfac asked. The king nodded and the wizard continued. "I and my fellow mages will defend the tower as best we can. We'll evacuate the women and children and fortify the city. Station the archers in the towers, footmen on the ground with the Calvary. While the city spends its next hours in preparation I will train Drathorn to the best of his abilities. That will mean that we will be finishing my planned fortifications last minute; we'll need a distraction."

"We'll send a small unit to defend the wooden gate." Salamoray said. "Drathorn and two of your mages can go to help with that distraction while the final fortifications are prepared."

"I will send the twins and the captain can select his best men . . . but it will mean sacrificing all the men." Orfac said.

"Not your best; they will be needed here." Drathorn stated. "Find me two dozen men that have nothing to lose, and only glory to gain. Train them with swords and then find me another dozen of the same and train them with bows. Those will be the men I stand with. I, the twins and those men will be a good enough distraction for you to finish the last minute fortifications."

Orfac and Salamoray nodded. As an after thought Drathorn said, "The king, Argoss and a few body guards should remain here in the manor for protection. If I'm right we won't have to worry about the enemy attacking them . . . they probably won't need to enter the courtyard. I expect that a group will probably just teleport into the tower in mid-battle to secure the book."

Again there was agreement, this time from Argoss the Dwarf and the body guards as well. There were a few more moments in which everyone in the room sorted their thoughts and ideas and then Orfac spoke. "Drathorn, run to your family's home and prepare, meet me behind my tower in an hour to begin a hurried training . . . I must speak to my mages."

As Drathorn turned to leave he heard Salamoray begin barking orders to his body guards, demanding to see the captain of the guard and begin the search for the men who would cause the distraction.

Chaos began before Drathorn was even half way home. Guards separated men from families; women cried or rushed the children to safety as the word was spread. Drathorn ran all the way to Ben's home. "Drathorn, is it true? Is it starting?" Ben asked.

"Not till tomorrow night, but you and the others must leave immediately. The time for action has come." Drathorn answered.

306

"As you wish, the wagon is already prepared." Robby said, cutting off Ben's argument. "We'll get out of here as soon as we can and head back to Gaberdan." Drathorn nodded and ran to his room. He removed his Elvin long sword from his side and set it in a trunk at the foot of the bed. With it he placed Elgard's Ali-Manicota orb and the Bandixi's shard; he wouldn't need any of them in the upcoming battle. Then on top of those items he through the book '*The Traveler's Aid*' and Gradorn's journal for safe keeping. Then he placed the strange empty puzzle box on top with the list of traps and the map of the Home of the Lone. He then closed and locked the trunk and left the room. He turned and locked his bedroom door and then hid the two keys in a drawer in the kitchen.

He finally went outside to see his departing family. He hugged Hailey gently as she cried, afraid she would never see him again. Then he turned and hugged Linda. "Don't worry Drathorn, we'll be safe and we'll see each other again when this is over." She said it strongly as if she really believed it and was determined not to let this be the end. Drathorn just nodded and turned to Pat, who was crying just like Hailey.

Drathorn smiled reassuringly to her and hugged her. Then he shook Ben's hand and Robby approached him last. "Watch your back out there Drathorn." He said; sticking out his hand as well.

"Stay safe." Drathorn said, grasping it and shaking it firmly.

"We'll do our best; apparently the bandits have been running with their tails between their legs lately." Robby winked.

"Stop at both rest houses. Give my name at the nearest one and you'll be welcomed greatly; they are friends of mine." Drathorn said.

"We will." Robby released his hand and walked to the wagon. "All aboard guys!" he called. Drathorn finally noticed that they all bore weapons, even if just a dagger, at their waists; they were ready for trouble this time.

Drathorn grabbed his own hand as though trying to hold the warmth from Robby's on it and remembered the strange Elvin ring that was around his middle finger. He examined it for a moment and considered placing it in the chest with his other belongings. But he changed his mind and decided he'd like to hold onto it. He traced his finger over the impossibly complicated design for a moment as the wagon pulled away, and then he headed back to the manor.

XXXIII

The Dragons

Drathorn stood beside Orfac now, *Dragontongue* at his side and the bracelet of the Dragons around his right wrist. He stood, straining his mind to use the power to summon the dragons. "Push it, push to your limits!" Orfac commanded. Drathorn pushed, he thrust his hand forward—releasing the power.

The five gems jumped out of the bracelet at his thrust. They flew forward like beams of light and separated, apart by fifty feet. The light exploded, blinding both the young and the old. When the light finally disappeared they saw them; the Dragons.

The one directly in front of him was the largest. It was red as blood and shone like the gem from the bracelet. Its wingspan was nearly fifty feet and its tail was nearly as long; full of muscle and sheer power. The beast's great head was the size of Drathorn's torso and the scar along its face was as long as his forearm. Its claws were long enough to go right through Drathorn and its teeth were the same size as the deadly spikes on the bottom of *Dragontongue*. Its red body seemed enhanced by the deadly yellow eyes that were the exact same as Drathorn's. Deadly spikes lined the beast's immense back with just enough room between them for a human being to sit. Drathorn could tell from his position that even the sharpest weapons would have trouble piercing its armoured hide. Drathorn recognized the dragon as Pyros, the first of Gradorn's allies.

On Pyros' left was another dragon, almost as tall as the great red. It had the same yellow eyes as Pyros. It was brown and its hide was not made of regular dragon scales like the others; each scale was made of heavy stone. The giant legs were as thick as tree trunks and its head was greater than Drathorn's entire body. Its powerful claws and teeth were larger than Pyros' and it had no spikes along its back. Its wings were very obviously too weak to allow the dragon to fly but Drathorn suspected they at least allowed him to glide. Even the great wings seemed to be made partly of stone. This was very obviously the dragon of stone and strength; the dragon of the God Borjil.

On the dragon of Borjil's other side was the smallest dragon. She was snowy white and had thin but powerful wings. She was obviously a dragon built for sheer speed and was very weak. She had the same eyes but seemed to Drathorn to only be about the size of the Wyverns. She was obviously the Dragon of Seleen, Goddess of Hope and light.

On Pyros' right was an odd blue dragon. She was a beautiful sapphire coloured creature with the same yellow eyes. But somehow her yellow eyes seemed softer than the others. She was odd because she did not have legs. Instead of legs or wings this strange blue dragon had fins, four powerful fins and a rudder-like tail. Even as he watched she seemed to smile softly at him. Drathorn supposed she was the dragon of Deandra, Goddess of Dreams and the patron of water.

The last dragon was yellow, or perhaps gold. It could barely be called a dragon however. Instead of being on four legs (or fins) like the others this dragon somehow walked on two legs and had no arms. Its wings folded back behind its body like a bird and its giant hip bones stuck out oddly like a safe place to stand. Its eyes were the harshest of all but still somehow the same. It was sleek and had a small, aerodynamic face that made it look even faster and stronger than the small white dragon. Drathorn had no doubt that this was the fastest of the dragons, with powerful wings larger than all the others it was without a doubt the dragon of lightning. It was without a doubt the dragon of Dimanious, the God of Destiny.

Even the smallest dragon was taller than Drathorn. He was so small and powerless before them. But he watched helplessly as the dragons took in his appearance and noted the bracelet, sword and mark on his hand. It was silent for a moment and then the dragons all knelt forward to the best of their abilities. "*Welcome, Hellbound.*" A voice uttered in his head. It was a voice full of power and anger; the voice of a dragon. Drathorn's eyes widened in shock. "*I am Pyros, and you are my brother, and master.*"

Orfac smiled beside Drathorn. "I cannot hear what they say to you, but you are their commander, get to know them . . . then we will discuss how to proceed." Orfac backed away and Drathorn didn't answer as Pyros' voice spoke again in his head.

"Your mind is much different than that of Gradorn." He said. *"You are filled with emotions that are not anger, emotions that I, having the heart of a dragon, cannot understand. I feel only anger and hate."*

"You can see my mind?" Drathorn asked allowed.

"Yes, and that means you need not speak aloud to us." Pyros answered. *"We can hear your every thought, and we follow your every order. We are all children of Salamoray in our own way, we will all follow you without question, but I am the leader of them as you are of me. I am the most loyal of us remaining five. I see you have read my master's journal."*

"Yes, I have." Drathorn said with his mind. He vaguely remembered the last times he had spoken with his mind. *"I learned much of our secrets and took it upon myself to keep them as secrets."*

"We will follow your example; none will know of Gradorn's past, none shall know of Ghlen." Pyros said. *"But now, be in acquaintance with my brothers and sisters."*

Drathorn looked at the menacing brown dragon of stone. *"I am Ragnarok."* The great dragon said in a deep menacing voice to match his size. *"I am the son of Sylvaston but I am loyal only to Borjil, my father, and you; the bearer of the bracelet."*

"I am Drathorn." Drathorn said politely.

"You need not introduce yourself. We know already your every thought, both recent and old . . . and we see in your mind the memories you have had." Ragnarok said.

Drathorn nodded and turned his head to the tiny dragon. *"I am Willow, daughter of Seleen."* She said. But then her body was shook by what seemed to be a horrible cough and a blast of smoke and a few white sparks flew from her mouth. *"My apologies, Master, I have recently taken ill. I wish I could be of service in the upcoming battle but there is little I can do in this state."*

Drathorn was shocked that it was possible for a dragon to be sick but was then filled with sorrow at seeing her weak form and her miserable cough. *"I'm so sorry to hear that Willow."* Drathorn said sincerely. *"You don't need to worry about the battle, I won't hold anything against you; it's not your fault you're sick."* Willow seemed shocked by his sincere care and he had a feeling that all the Dragons were searching his mind for some sign of a lie or pretence. But they found none so the tiny white dragon bowed lowly before coughing violently again. *"Return to the*

Dragon realm, Willow, you need rest. I don't wish for you to be sick and strain yourself to be here."

Again the dragon bowed obediently. *"As you wish master."* Then Willow morphed into a ball of pure white light and shot at the bracelet. Drathorn looked at the bracelet and saw the white gem had returned to its place on the far left. He looked up at the other dragons and forced his gaze on the gentler blue dragon.

"Just because I'm good looking doesn't mean I'm gentle." The blue dragon's beautiful voice laughed.

"You look gentle." Drathorn commented.

The dragon growled menacingly and Drathorn took a step back. Despite being unable to feel emotion Pyros and Ragnarok both suddenly burst into laughter. *"I am Aurora, daughter of Deandra. I am a water dragon. I'm not much use up on land but I am the fastest creature in the sea."* She said.

She didn't look fast, nor did she look menacing anymore and her voice had returned to the musically gentle sound it had been at first. Despite not looking fast he took her word for it. *"It's a pleasure to meet you."* He said.

Aurora smiled and did not answer. Drathorn turned his eyes on the menacing yellow dragon. The other dragons followed his gaze and looked at him critically. The great yellow looked the angriest and scariest and had remained silent even while the others laughed; he had barely even bowed upon meeting. *"Are you the son of Dimanious?"* Drathorn asked.

The dragon nodded and spoke in a vicious monotone. *"I am Zapix."* The Dragon offered no more conversation.

Drathorn waited for him to say more but it was Pyros' sigh that interrupted. *"He is a dragon of few words; he speaks little and cares what happens to this world even less. Probably a side effect of having his father able to alter the destinies of everyone in this world . . . aside from yours it seems. That amulet, the crystal of the Gorgans, is a fancy piece of jewellery. Our master once wore it long ago; he rid himself of it when he grew suspicious that it had cursed him."*

"That's why he got rid of it?" Drathorn asked. *"I suppose he didn't know what its powers really were?"*

"He knew very little about it. Even we know only now that we have read its abilities in your mind . . . quite fascinating." Ragnarok said.

"Zapix is the fastest of us all." Pyros continued, ignoring the Gorganite Amulet again. *"He was often used by the master as a scout and messenger. I believe I have an idea for his use that may assist you."*

Drathorn was surprised. They had already begun plotting to help him! They were indeed very loyal to him. *"We believe, as well as many others here, that the city's locust problem is very possibly the doing of the darklord . . . Icarus, as you know him . . . One of his Commandos has the uncanny ability to control insects. If you are planning to gather the shards you should start by hunting and killing this bug-man. Zapix would be more than happy to search the area while we crush your foes beneath our feet."*

Drathorn threw a glance at the menacing yellow dragon again and doubted that Zapix was farther away from feeling happy about anything then the rest of the dragons were. As the thought crossed his mind Zapix's lips twitched in a mock smile and the other attending dragons frowned. *"Is there no part of my mind that is safe from yours?"* complained Drathorn.

"All you need to do is command that we do not read your thoughts and the deed will be done." Pyros answered.

"But then I cannot converse with you." Drathorn pointed out.

"Word your command just right and we'll not be able to read your thoughts but for to communicate." Zapix said; sounding slightly annoyed that he had to explain this.

Drathorn thought for a moment and the dragons waited silently. *"I wish for the five of you to stay out of my thoughts except when you need to speak to me."* Drathorn said. Immediately all the surrounding dragons nodded. *"Can you still hear me?"* he asked.

No one said anything for a moment and then Pyros finally spoke. *"Yes."* There was a moment and then he said, *"The old one grows impatient."*

Drathorn turned his head and saw Orfac standing not too far away, watching with a look of disappointment, probably angry that he was missing the conversation that was obviously taking place without him able to listen. *"He can wait a few more moments."* Drathorn said. Aurora, Pyros and Ragnarok laughed emotionlessly again and then Zapix spoke again.

"Am I to scout again or not?"

Drathorn frowned and looked over at Orfac. "Orfac, the dragons and I have had an idea." He called. The wizard smiled and took a few steps closer so that neither of them had to yell. "We believe that the locust problem around Signaroc is caused by an agent of the darklord. Pyros believes we should have Zapix scout the area while the fight continues here. That way when the fight is done we can eliminate the enemy that endangers you."

"That is a good idea, but won't the dragon be needed in the battle?" Orfac asked. "Surely for a force as large as the one on our doorstep all five will be needed? And where is the small one gone to?"

"Willow is sick; she had to return to the Dragon realm to rest, she will not be able to join us . . . nor will Aurora." He gestured to the beautiful blue dragon. "Her fins will not allow her to fight on the ground or in the air."

"Even more reason for your Zapix to remain here." Orfac said.

Drathorn frowned and turned back to the dragons. "*It's fine Drathorn.*" Pyros said. "*Ragnarok and I will be more than enough to help defeat your foe. Signaroc will be safe.*" Drathorn nodded and turned back to Orfac.

"Pyros and Ragnarok will be enough to protect us." Drathorn agreed aloud. "They are powerful. I need Zapix to scout the area for the darklord's agent."

Orfac nodded and then looked to the three dragons that actually had legs. "Which is Zapix?" he asked.

Drathorn nodded to the menacing yellow dragon.

"The first cloud of locusts to harm our fields came from the west." Orfac said to the dragon. "I suggest you begin your search there."

Zapix's menacing eyes turned on Drathorn. "*You heard him, go find out where the little buggers are coming from.*" A smile played on Pyros' lips as Zapix sighed in a bored manner and took off. The gust of wind nearly knocked down the aging Orfac and Drathorn was also surprised by the strength of the gust.

Now only three dragons remained.

"Now what?" Orfac asked Drathorn.

"I suppose I'll have the dragons return to the dragon realm for now . . . so we can move on with my training." Drathorn said.

"Very good." Orfac answered.

"*Can we still communicate while you are in the dragon realm?*" Drathorn asked Pyros.

"*Yes, but it is a little less convenient . . . it only works while you wear the bracelet . . . even while we are summoned we can only stay attached to your mind while you wear it.*" He answered.

"*Then return to the dragon realm with Aurora and Ragnarok for now.*" Drathorn said.

Pyros nodded. The three dragons that remained in the courtyard suddenly morphed into beautiful balls of light and sped into the bracelet. Their three gems suddenly back within its complicated frame. "*We'll keep in touch.*" Aurora's gentle voice flooded through his head but it was much fainter and slightly harder to understand. He now knew what Pyros had meant by saying it was less convenient.

Drathorn stood there for a moment, gazing absentmindedly at the bracelet and was finally aroused from his thoughts when Orfac spoke. "Are you ready to begin your training?"

Drathorn sighed and turned to Orfac. "Let's do it."

XXXIV

Training

"The Hellbound are one hundred percent fire proof." Orfac said. "They feel normal heat, like that of a person's body just like a normal person . . . but when flame or a burning piece of metal or even magma touches their flesh they feel not but a pleasant breeze. This is because body heat is a natural part of life, which is Zathius' power, not your father Sylvaston's. You are completely resistant to fire and even the heat of the sun somehow and smoke from the flames is pretty much invisible to you.

"As if this isn't enough to make you odd, contact with such flames that you are resistant to actually *heals* you. The Hellbound naturally heal faster than any other race, about three times faster. But when in contact with flame they can heal approximately one hundred times faster than any other race. You can actually *watch* wounds heal over. Multiple times in history a Hellbound recovered from the brink of death by lighting themselves on fire. It is completely natural to the Hellbound race. And yes, you heard correctly; the Hellbound has been considered an official, and nearly extinct, race of people on Corrone."

Drathorn sighed as Orfac spoke. "Are you going to teach me anything I don't know?" Drathorn asked.

Orfac frowned and opened his mouth to speak but then closed it again. He sighed and said; "What *do* you know?"

"I know about being fireproof and absorbent, I know we're stronger and faster than most other races and I know that I now have senses as good as those of a Dragon, except I can see in full color as well." Drathorn laughed. "I also know I can command Dragons, wield *Dragontongue*, and make people fear me, I can also feel the fear within others, I'm resistant to hypnotic traces (he remembered the battle against the Sentrate Tree so long ago) and I can throw fireballs."

"You know you can throw fireballs?" Orfac asked. "I never thought you would discover that for yourself!"

"It was an accident really . . . and I don't remember how I did it . . . I can't seem to trigger it into happening again." Drathorn admitted.

"Then we will definitely work on that together . . ." Orfac asked. "Is there anything else you can do?"

"As far as I know that's the extent of my Hellbound related powers." Drathorn said. "But I'm also a Weretiger, and I posses two of the mystic dozen and can make a bioluminescent light with my right hand."

"Really?" Orfac asked, curious. "That is truly astounding . . . to create light so simply, it is truly a great gift."

"It was a side effect of an incomplete antidote and poison from a magically poisoned arrow." Drathorn said.

"Intriguing . . ." Orfac muttered. "And a Weretiger too . . . how is that?"

"I haven't been in my Tiger state since the sword changed me but before the change transforming made my senses a lot better." He said. "It had a nasty side effect . . . I'm not fireproof when I transform . . . learned that the hard way . . ."

"Truly intriguing . . ." he muttered. "Well, back to the initial subject of your Hellbound powers; throwing fireballs is a very basic power that every Hellbound has had. It was triggered quite simply too. But before we go on with fire-throwing lessons I'll list a few other powers.

"When you become older and more powerful as a Hellbound you'll unlock many more advanced abilities." Orfac went on. "You'll be able to speak to all creatures created by your father Sylvaston; all your brothers will become close friends and fight on your side. This includes all reptiles and fire-related monsters. Even before you learn to communicate with them they will not attempt to harm you. Once you learn to converse with them you will be able to command them. Since you are the most powerful and high ranking of Sylvaston's creations thus far you are recognized as the mortal master of all of them.

"Also as your powers progress you'll be able to call upon the spirits of the dead for guidance." Orfac said.

"I can revive the dead?" Drathorn exclaimed.

"No." Orfac said simply, Drathorn's face fell. "You can summon the spirits of those in the heavens and speak to them. They can give you guidance but they will never take a physical form and can therefore not assist you in battle or anything of the sort . . . and only *you* will be able to see them, no one else."

Drathorn fell silent again so Orfac continued his list. "When falling from great distances you can land gracefully on your feet without being harmed in the slightest, but that's not the half of it." He said. "While falling you will fall at normal speed, but when you reach roughly fifteen feet away from the ground you will supposedly begin to slow rapidly. The closer you get to the ground the slower you'll get. The second you touch something solid a ring of pure power will blast from your body, seeking through the minds of everyone within ten feet of you. If the power detects anyone who plans to do you harm the spell will push them away with a great force. Anyone who means you no harm at all will be completely unharmed by it. The farther you fall from, the more powerful the push will be. That particular power grows stronger as you age and reaches its maximum capacity when you reach about the age of twenty five. That's also when you stop aging permanently. As far as I know the farthest any Hellbound has ever fallen is about four hundred feet, he survived to tell the tale without so much as a scratch.

"Another ability you posses is a powerful magic shield." Orfac went on. "Each Hellbound obtains this power at a different time. Your mother learned it when she was only two . . . her father didn't learn it until he was forty-eight in human years. The shield is completely impenetrable by magic but living creatures can still move through it. It's a very handy ability just the same.

"The last ability of the Hellbound isn't one that can be learned . . . and it comes with each Hellbound the moment they are born, just like your powers over fire. It was actually a gift of the God Zathius, who took a personal interest in the Hellbound project." Orfac smiled at Drathorn. "Although the Hellbound could not love another human being they still married. Did you ever wonder how both your mother and your father were Hellbound?"

Drathorn thought about it. He knew his father's original name had indeed not been Hellbound but he knew for sure that he had had the powers. He had never thought about why that was. "I never really thought about it." Drathorn said.

Orfac nodded. "Zathius could not force the power of love on the Hellbound as he intended, but in return he managed a different side effect. Whenever a Hellbound is engaged in holy matrimony with another mortal that mortal gains all the exact abilities of his or her partner. The moment the marriage is complete the mortal becomes as much a Hellbound as the original. This allows the Hellbound to spread and reproduce."

Drathorn was shocked. "Do you mean that if I turned around and married someone they would become a Hellbound? Exactly like me?"

"Your non-Hellbound-related powers would remain unique to you, such as being a Weretiger and summoning light, but yes that is the concept." Orfac said. "If you really wanted to you could marry every woman in the city and they would all become Hellbound the moment you said 'I do'."

"That's . . . incredible." Drathorn muttered. *The idea is ridiculous of course but if I did that there would be no way for the Darklord to stop the Hellbound . . . we would be unstoppable! But of course I could never curse these innocent people like I am cursed . . . I would never consider that.* "So that's how my father became a Hellbound?"

"Yes." Orfac said. "One side effect of course is that the person the Hellbound marries must agree to take the Hellbound name . . . otherwise the ability is reversed and the Hellbound becomes mortal."

"I can become a normal human if I wanted to?" Drathorn exclaimed.

"Yes, you're great uncle did it." Orfac said. "But the Darklord hunted him down and killed him and his wife anyways."

So I can undo this curse . . . Drathorn thought. *When this war is over all I have to do is take the name of another mortal through marriage and I'll be normal again . . .* Drathorn smiled to himself. "Is there anything else I can do?"

"Each Hellbound also had its own unique powers . . . sometimes those were transferred to their children and other times they weren't." Orfac said. "You may have many other abilities but the only ones that the others possessed as well are the ones I just told you about."

"So will you teach me how to use them all?" Drathorn asked.

"I can teach you how to throw fire, and we can practice the soft falling technique . . . but the shield will come naturally when you are ready. The ritual to summon spirits can easily be taught but I know for a fact that you are *not* ready to use that ability and any attempt to do so this early in your abilities may lead to your own death. And your command over the children of Sylvaston will come gradually over time. It is not necessary for me to teach it."

Drathorn was disappointed that he would have to wait for some of those powers but easily brought back his enthusiasm. "Teach me how to summon fire." Drathorn said.

"Ah," Orfac smiled. "Summoning fire is quite simple according to the other members of your family. The trigger, like most inner abilities of the supernatural races, is through emotion. Each Hellbound had the same trigger; can you guess what that was?"

Drathorn didn't need to guess. "The only emotions the Hellbound could feel were Hate and Anger."

Orfac nodded. "Hate does not actually qualify as an emotion, not in the way the Hellbound classified it. To them it was just that; a classification of a group of people . . . the ones you 'hate' and the ones you don't. The only *true* emotion the Hellbound felt was Anger, and that was the trigger. I see no reason why you shouldn't have the same trigger, even if you *can* feel the emotions they couldn't."

"Why do you think I can feel the emotions they couldn't? Is the power of the Hellbound wearing away?" Drathorn asked.

"I doubt it; there has never been even the slightest alteration of the Hellbound's power." Orfac said. "But I do have a hunch. I believe that you have had an emotional breakthrough of the Dragon's heart you possessed. Losing so many loved ones and being put through so much pain while you were young may have had a permanent effect on both your mind and heart before they could harden. It's possible that those losses may have disrupted your Hellbound development and made you very slightly different from your ancestors."

"That makes a little sense . . ." Drathorn said. He frowned as he considered it and then shook his head, "Anyways . . . so anger should be the key?"

"It should be." Orfac said, thankful for returning to the original subject. "But just to be sure, try and remember back to the time you threw your first fireball and remember how you were feeling at the time."

Drathorn thought back to the scene. It didn't take him long. He nodded. "I was definitely furious, a group of bandits had captured a few members of my foster family and one of them was being whipped, and they were laughing." Even as he spoke he started to feel the anger rising again. "All of them were bruised . . . they had been beat violently . . . and the bandits didn't care."

Orfac nodded. "Anger is the key, summon your anger, think of everything that makes you angry, and call upon the fire!"

It was Icarus, the Darklord! Drathorn thought. *His bandits struck my family, his men killed Elgard. His bandits took over Taldi and killed hundreds of people. His assassin killed my parents, his mage forced me to see my weakness and abandon my best friends!*

The fire roared to life in his hand as the anger flowed freely into it. "Keep it up Drathorn!" Orfac yelled. "The more anger, the more power behind your fireball!"

Drathorn barely heard him as the fire within his head roared louder. *His bandits took the good soul of a young man named Murlok and turned him into a cold hearted bandit, his evil forced my hand to slay a young ten year old, his evil burned down the home of the Nolad family and the orphanage!* The fire grew steadily larger and pure power radiated from it. The fire within Drathorn's head was louder than ever and he could not hear what Orfac was yelling now.

His locusts weaken the dwindled supplies in Signaroc, starving its people! His evil destroyed Gradorn and caused the dragons to go into a rage and kill Ghlen! It's because of him I can't be there to comfort Thira while she cries, his fault I'm here, preparing for a battle we might not win!

The fire was greater than ever, stopping all sound outside his mind. But it didn't stop what was within his mind. The words were sudden and inhuman. *"Calm yourself Drathorn or you will burn down Orfac's tower."*

Drathorn was surprised to hear the words in his head above the roaring of the flames that seemed to be taking over his mind. "Pyros?" he said with both his mind and mouth. His shock distracted him from his anger and he suddenly was able to hear Orfac again.

"Stop it Drathorn! You're going to destroy everything! Calm down!" he was yelling.

Drathorn sighed and took the old man's and the dragon's advice. He took a few calming breaths and the fire began to disappear back into his hand. As it shrunk to a fair size Drathorn changed his mind and made a throwing motion at the sky. The blast of pure fire exploded from his hand, a ball of pure heat, into the sky. Orfac and Drathorn watched it soar out of sight, and then they stood in silence.

Drathorn looked down at himself and saw that his clothes and body were completely unharmed by the fire that had so recently blazed, but the grass around him has burned away completely. "Thank-you . . . for stopping me." Drathorn said to both Orfac and Pyros.

Orfac nodded and there was no answer from Pyros. "You have more potential with the fire than I thought." Orfac said. "That was quite amazing. If we could train you to control that anger and use it as a weapon you would be a very formidable opponent. It's highly possible that if you lose control like that again you can become lost in your anger and destroy many things you wish to save. Try to summon another one . . . but smaller and more controlled this time."

Drathorn frowned and closed his eyes. He thought hard about the Darklord and his men and how they were responsible for taking away Elgard's life. He concentrated a lot longer this time but finally the snowball-sized flame was sitting in the open palm of his hand, a very soft roaring in his head.

"Very good, Drathorn." Orfac said. "A fireball about that size is enough to turn a human being to ashes."

Drathorn smiled; here was his greatest weapon.

They spent the rest of the day working with Drathorn's fire throwing ability. After he seemed to be getting better at choosing which size of fire he wanted and summoning it, he called Pyros back and used his heavy fireproof hide as a target. Drathorn soon found that if he did not want to throw his summoned fireballs he could simple shrink it to a suitable size and close his fist around it to completely extinguish it. By seven that night they had called Ragnarok out as well and Drathorn was running around the courtyard dodging fireballs summoned by mages to simulate arrows while throwing other fireballs at targets that covered the fleeing dragons' backs. This particular training exercise was very energy consuming and by the time he left the courtyard to go home to sleep he was absolutely exhausted.

Saturday June 6th, 18291; Drathorn was back in the courtyard early, this time sparring with wooden sticks against a group of twenty volunteering guards. They started with simply taking turns fighting one at a time against Drathorn and being easily beat. But after the first two hours of endless defeats Drathorn started fighting groups of five at a time and soon the guards were not the only ones suffering small bruises.

The painful training didn't end until around four that night and the guards had to keep switching shifts with others throughout the day. By mid day Drathorn had won over a hundred matches against nearly two hundred different volunteers. But finally Orfac called the session to a stop for an extra hour of fireball practice. After that they sat together in Orfac's study for an early dinner.

"When tonight are they coming Drathorn?" Orfac asked.

Drathorn frowned and tried to remember the scene in his dream so long ago. "It will be dark, pitch black." Drathorn finally answered. "I believe it will likely be around nine or ten o'clock."

"Then we have very little time." Orfac said. "We are definitely going to need that distraction, the fortifications have only begun now that all the citizens are evacuated."

"Are the citizens armed?" Drathorn asked. "They may be attacked out there all alone, where have they gone?"

"We sent them with two hundred guards and the captain's second in command for protection." Orfac said. "I also sent two of my best mages with them. They're going to travel south until they reach the forests and will wait there until we send someone to retrieve them. If no one arrives for them within three days they are to flee across the paper pass and head straight to Greengate, it is the nearest city controlled by the empire."

Drathorn nodded, even these harsh times would not undo the hate the empire had for the tribes. "Speaking of the empire, is there no way we can get help from one of the other cities?"

Orfac shook his head. "Veedion is too far to send help. The only other option is for Greengate or Gaberdan to send help from across the sea. They would have had to leave early this morning to make it on time but the Signaroc port is controlled by bandits so even if they did that they wouldn't make it. We stand alone here."

Drathorn nodded in understanding. The fight to save the world was to be fought by the city of Signaroc alone. *"Not alone."* Pyros reminded him; Drathorn had changed his mind and given the dragons permission to read his mind only while they were within the dragon realms. *"The dragons of the dragon realm will assist, as will the great Hellbound."*

Drathorn did not relay that message to Orfac, instead he asked, "So, where do we come in?"

Orfac smiled. "In about an hour the captain will gather your warriors and meet us out front of the courtyard. Then you and the twins will lead them to the wooden gate to cause the distraction. You will leave Pyros here with me and when the fortifications are complete I will send him to pick up you and the twins and bring you back here."

"What about the warriors?" Drathorn asked.

"They have been told that they can either stay and fight or retreat once you're in the clear. But they must fight until you and Pyros have disappeared from view."

Drathorn frowned. "Either way there's no way they'll escape." He said. "Three dozen men will die at that gate." Before Orfac could speak he said, "If I should fall I want you all to keep fighting. This city is all that stands between the darklord and his control of the world. Even if I am killed you must not give up hope."

Orfac nodded. "If you fall the dragons will no longer be loyal to the Hellbound and they will be free of will again. Without their help Signaroc stands no chance, especially if the Dragons switch sides after your death. But either way we will continue to fight."

There was silence for a moment as Orfac finished his meal and then Drathorn walked over to one of the giant windows. "If I jump, will I survive?" he asked.

Orfac frowned and got up to stand beside him. "A normal person would not, but if your power of free fall is active you will survive without harm. If you don't I'll have everyone light you on fire as soon as possible."

Drathorn laughed. "Well, here goes nothing!"

He didn't even wait for Orfac to say something in return. He climbed up into the open window and dived out. He cut through the wind like a knife before opening his arms wide and adjusting his fall. The feel of the wind rushing past his face was incredible. He was falling, closer and closer to the ground. It wasn't going to work, he was falling to his death, and he wasn't slowing. He closed his eyes as he got closer to the ground. And then the wind stopped. He opened his eyes just in time to see himself hovering inches above the ground, and then the power erupted. A ring of silver smoke exploded out from him with more force than Drathorn had thought possible. His feet touched the ground lightly and he whirled around, fearing the tower had been damaged.

But the tower was completely unharmed. He smiled; it had worked. It had been slightly more sudden than Orfac had described but it had definitely been effective. He stood there for a moment, looking around, and was soon joined by a beaming Orfac. "Great show Drathorn!" he said.

Drathorn laughed. "Is that what it feels like to ride a dragon?" Drathorn asked.

"I wouldn't know I've never done it before." Orfac admitted.

"*It is very much the same young Hellbound, except we'll be moving forward, not down, and you'll have to hold on tight to my neck to stay on.*" Pyros' emotionless voice echoed in his head with slight laughter.

"*Why wouldn't you let me ride you before hand so I could experience it?*" Drathorn asked.

"*Your first time should be in the midst of battle, it's only proper.*" Ragnarok answered.

"*By the way, when are you planning to summon me?*" Pyros asked. "*I believe Orfac said that my strength would be useful to carry equipment for the fortifications?*"

Drathorn nodded. "Should I call upon Pyros now?" he asked Orfac.

Orfac nodded, "We'll need him to carry thousands of pounds of arrows to the towers and wood for making barriers around the city." He replied.

Drathorn reached down to the bracelet and touched the red gem. "*Come on out Pyros.*" He said using both his mind and his mouth.

The gem erupted from the bracelet in a beam of light and it was only a blinding moment later that Pyros stood in front of them. "*Just help Orfac with whatever he needs while I'm gone. I won't be far and if I need help Ragnarok is only a realm away.*" Drathorn said.

Pyros was silent as he nodded. So Drathorn turned back to Orfac. "He'll help in what ever way he can." He said. "Now, I believe I should go to meet my warriors?"

Orfac nodded. "Wait here just a moment, oh mighty dragon."

Orfac lead Drathorn out of the courtyard and to a long street where a great number of people were gathered. Two dozen dirty looking men,

Gar and Dragonians bore swords, axes and spears with makeshift wooden shields and old mismatching armour. Another dozen warriors wore the same odd assortments of armour but bore bows and crossbows with quivers of arrows and bolts on their backs. The twin mages; Torbille and Zander stood in the lead. They seemed identical in every way down to the strange orange robes they were dressed in today. Their belts held pouches of herbs and magical components for their more powerful spells and each held an open book to their eyes, memorizing spells. And standing in front of them was the captain of the guard in full shining plate mail and supporting a helmet bearing horse hair dyed red for Signaroc under his arm. His broadsword was at his side and a heavy kite shield was slung across his back.

"Ah captain, are the men ready?" Orfac asked.

"As ready as they'll ever be High-arch." The captain said. "They're not very well trained but they're disciplined enough to follow the boy's every command as well as your twins'."

"And Torbille and Zander will follow as your seconds in command, Drathorn." Orfac added.

Drathorn nodded. "Make haste to the farm gate and defend it until we send Pyros." The captain said, "These men should be able to help well enough."

"You should reach the gate only half an hour before we're expecting the Gar if I'm correct." Orfac said.

Drathorn nodded yet again and the captain and Orfac turned and ran off to help with the fortifications. Drathorn turned to the small battalion that had assembled; everyone there followed his every move. *If they're expecting a speech, they're about to be disappointed.* Drathorn thought. Ragnarok and Aurora laughed in his mind and even poor Willow gave a weak chuckle. "Alright then, we should get going too." He finally said. He turned away from the warrior's piercing stares and began to walk through the city.

The warriors did not assemble in a formation like seasoned soldiers would have but they still followed without a word. Despite the fact that none of them talked, their mismatched armour rattled noisily behind him. He sighed and then noticed that Zander and Torbille were on either side of him. He distinctly remembered that Orfac had told him Torbille was often rude and had a scar across his cheek. Drathorn silently figured out which one Torbille was. Both wizards walked in silence, their footfalls making very little noise compared to the large company behind them. Neither one seemed to be looking where they were going, they were both holding their books only inches from their faces as they murmured words and phrases Drathorn didn't understand.

They walked through the city and passed many of the well armoured soldiers bearing both swords and bows. Most were busy helping fortify the city but almost all stopped as they passed to bow in respect for the homeless warriors who had nothing to lose and were going to die to give them just a little more time.

None of the warriors spoke, the only sound was that of falling feet.

It had taken longer than he thought, all night and more than half the day, to defeat the bandits in Hellfire Bay. Troy and Thira stood on a small hill, Samgarnok on one side of them and Feronis on the other. The bandits had only recently been completely removed from the port and only now, at dusk, had the army managed to gather outside of the small encampment that remained of the port in Hellfire bay.

Troy was annoyed; the bandits had been joined by a second group that reinforced them suddenly after the transports had emptied onto the shore. The battle had taken a long time and many wounded warriors had been sent back on transports. They were leaving fifty warriors of Nargak to stay behind and defend the ships and gather the bodies of their comrades.

Still the remaining riders of Narvahan Shé had lost only one member. The warriors of Taldi were only slightly dwindled and there were still a good three thousand Nargak fighters ready for battle. Troy had given his and Murlok's horses to two Nargak warriors and they were replacing the fallen Narvahan Shé rider. Troy now rode Starcruser, Drathorn's long abandoned steed. Thira and Feronis still rode their own horses and Samgarnok stood on his feet, a large and menacing looking warrior with his giant axe in his hands.

After all that had taken place here Troy had finally resumed leadership and gathered the armies again. He now turned to face the far away city of Signaroc. Darkness was slowly falling and he doubted they would be on time. He could only pray that they arrived at a reasonable hour.

XXXV

First Defence

There Drathorn stood, directly in front of the gate. On either side of him there stood a dozen warriors. Up above the gate stood Torbille and Zander, no longer reading but searching the darkness with their now magically enchanted eyes. On either side of the twins there stood half a dozen archers ready to take cover behind low wooden walls on top of the main one.

Every one of the warriors had their weapons drawn and were eyeing the area they could see carefully. The area round the warriors was lit by a light summoned above Drathorn's head by Torbille. In Drathorn's left hand blazed a ready fireball, *Dragontongue* was drawn in his right. Tied to the forearm of his fire-wielding arm was a new dagger, another was tied to his shin. Within easy reach of his left hand was a small hand axe, and within easy reach of his right was the whip he had kept ever since rescuing the Blaygards from the bandits not long ago. The Angelic Symbol and mark of the Hellbound shone, on the same arm, in the firelight reflected off *Dragontongue*. Even with the enchantment Zander and Torbille had placed upon themselves to see in the night Drathorn had better eyesight than them. It was he who first saw the shadow of the lone Gar walking forward from the barren field.

The warriors tensed and the archers took aim. The Gar stepped alone into the circle of light above their heads created by Torbille. His reptilian head was cursed with empty black eyes and his scaled face was menacing. His eyes examined the small group, eyeing the mages and then Drathorn the longest. He waited for a moment as if expecting the fire in Drathorn's hand to disappear, but it only grew larger. "Step aside, my brother, and your fates will remain undecided." The Gar hissed at Drathorn. "Fail to do so and you'll be meeting your lost grandparents at the gate to hell."

"What a bold statement for a lone fool." Drathorn said clearly. "We'll not stand aside, we stand with Signaroc."

"Hellbound." The Gar mumbled, rolling his eyes. "Always in the way." The Gar turned his head slightly to look into the darkness behind him. "A pity they sent the king . . . I very much wanted to deal with the mages personally. But the master believes it wiser for them to meet their own blood. That is fine; I and my brothers will have the head of the Hellbound." The Gar continued to grumble to himself about cutting off heads and gutting bodies until one archer got tired of his ramblings and the Gar fell where he stood.

There was a mutter of approval from the warriors as they relaxed. "Don't let down your guard!" Drathorn warned. It was only a second too late for one of them. A single crossbow bolt fired from the low darkness and killed one man. "They crawled, he was a decoy!" Drathorn yelled.

That, too, was too late. The gar infantry had indeed been lying just out of sight, crawling slowly forward while the decoy did his job. They had succeeded in the surprise and before Drathorn could impale his first foe two more warriors had fallen to the blades of the suddenly vicious Gar.

From every which direction the Gar sprang up into sight and charged the small party. If it had not been for the volley of arrows from the wall and for the Twins' perfect timing with their quick spells the battle would have been lost in merely a matter of moments. Before the odds were settled again the Signaroc group had lost a total of four warriors and one archer had been wounded on the wall.

Removing *Dragontongue* from his first victim Drathorn threw the fireball at two charging Gar who were about to attack another warrior. The ball collided with one and exploded, leaving nothing but a pile of dust remaining of both of them and even viciously scorching the side of another's face.

Drathorn felt the fear of his warriors. Felt them ready to flee for their lives even though they had nothing to lose. Another Gar was about to charge past him and strike a warrior but Drathorn slashed out at the perfect moment, slicing him nearly in half. "Fear not warriors of Signaroc!" Drathorn yelled. There was a pause as he blocked and disarmed an enemy before kicking him and turning on another. "Today we fight not for our city, not for our people!" he slapped the foe across the face with the flat of his blade and stabbed viciously to finish him. "Today we fight for all of Corrone!"

Everyone in the city knew why the enemy was here; it was the reason so many had joined to stop the army of foes. As Drathorn reminded them that they were protecting, not only their lives and their homes, but the entire world their fear completely evaporated. With renewed courage at his simple words they fought hard and for the first time it seemed like they might stand a chance.

When the Gar and the warriors became too closely knitted for heavy devastating spells to be cast the Twins jumped gracefully from the wall and used magic to land safely on the forefront of the battle where they began to quickly even the odds of the battle by striking as many enemies as they could with simple fireballs and lightning strikes.

But the twins were only two, and Drathorn was only one. There was nothing special about any of the others and Drathorn was forced to helplessly defend himself, as another warrior fell hopelessly, from three Gar. Enraged by the sight of seeing a comrade fall to such uneven odds a new fireball erupted in Drathorn's left hand. With great strength he threw the ball at his own attackers first. One was hit and the other was caught in the explosion, both disappeared all but for a pile of ashes on the ground. He slashed his third attacker across the chest and threw a new fireball at his comrade's attackers who were likewise reduced to ash.

Slashing through another foe, Drathorn surveyed the battle. He was surprised at how even the battle seemed. They were few but between him and the twins the battle seemed to almost lean in the favour of the defenders; until Drathorn watched two warriors fall beneath one simple lightning strike. He turned, planning to yell at a twin for this atrocity but found neither Torbille nor Zander. The new mage wore long violet robes and a cruel expression. The cuffs of his sleeves were green and his reptilian face was a brownish colour. All in all this man was colourful. Even his eyes shone with a strange orange tint. On the man's neck was a similar orange coloured tattoo in the shape of an arrow head pointing at his collar bone.

He was an Ali-Manicota, a mage by legal standards. But yet he served the darklord and was therefore *not* pure of heart. *Perhaps he was once pure . . . before he was corrupted by power.* Drathorn thought. Drathorn knelt quickly and grabbed the dagger tied to his shin. He pulled it from its bound leather sheath and threw it at the mage. Seeing the weapon coming, the mage held up his hand and said *"Mort Narven."* An invisible shield appeared and blocked the dagger.

Drathorn snarled in annoyance as the Gar laughed. He stepped toward Drathorn with a sly movement. Somehow he managed to speak in a calm voice that Drathorn could hear even over the sounds of battle. "No dagger shall slay me." He said. "I am Eldragor, the invincible king of worms! And for my master I will slay you now! *Armondur Nasgoth!*"

A bolt of lightning flew from the mage's hand and straight at Drathorn. Drathorn readied *Dragontongue*, planning to use it's indestructibility to reflect the magical attack. But the bolt collided with another invisible barrier that had been created around Drathorn. Confused, both Eldragor and Drathorn looked around.

Zander and Torbille were now only feet behind Drathorn and rushing closer. "Run Hellbound!" Torbille yelled.

"Die fellow wizard!" Zander continued, sounding exactly like his brother.

"*Armondur Nasgoth!*" yelled Eldragor.

"*Mort Narven!*" countered Torbille.

Drathorn ducked and rolled as Zander yelled *"Locorman Zang!"*

Drathorn barely escaped as Eldragor's lightning strike flew past. It collided with Torbille's shield. Then suddenly a light flowed from Zander and three dead bodies suddenly stood with expressionless faces. The three newly animated bodies began to move closer to Eldragor.

"*Molando!*" Torbille continued. A single shot of flame in the shape of an arrow flew from his palm at Eldragor. Eldragor immediately repeated the words and sent an identical fire strike. They collided in mid-air.

Zander followed up his brother's attack with a complicated hand movement and the words *"Mozar Notic!"* A dome of ice grew from the ground and surrounded Eldragor and the three slowly moving animated bodies. It was thin enough to see through but thick enough that mortal weapons would do no harm to it.

"*Molando! Molando! Molando! Lipesia!*" Eldragor yelled without taking a breath. Three fire strikes erupted from him, killing the animated bodies for a second time. And then Eldragor's fourth spell sent pure force from his body, the icy dome exploded from the force of the spell but before any shards could strike the ground he followed it up with a simple call of *"Lorzore!"* The falling shards stopped abruptly and went flying at Drathorn, Torbille and Zander.

Zander echoed Eldragor's spell. The two mages were soon locked in a battle of push and shove with the sharp icy shards; if one were to fail they would be slain by the sharp pieces. It soon looked as though Zander *would* fail. But before Zander's strength could fail Torbille repeated the spell and added his strength to Zander's.

With the twins pushing on one side and the powerful Eldragor on the other the ice halted in mid air and floated, neither side allowing it to move an inch. But two Gar were now sneaking up on the twins and Drathorn forced his eyes off the fighting mages to kill them. Pulling his hand-axe from his side he ran at them. He spun and slashed both the axe and *Dragontongue* through the first Gar simultaneously. Without waiting for the Gar to fall he followed this spin up with a kick.

The Gar flew into another Gar that had been attacking a Signaroc warrior, saving the man's life. Drathorn then ran at Torbille's attacker and drove *Dragontongue* through him with ease. Noticing a crossbow armed Gar nearby he threw the hand-axe and it spun twice before imbedding itself in the archer, saving the life of one of the Signaroc archers on the wall. Drathorn pulled *Dragontongue* out of the Gar and summoned a fireball to his left hand.

Focusing again on Eldragor, still locked in the battle of force with Zander and Torbille, Drathorn threw the fireball. Eldragor saw this new threat and ended his push spell to say *"Mort Narven!"* the shield stopped the fireball but was too weak to stop the thousands of ice shards flying at him. The shards broke through the shield and were only inches away before Eldragor managed to cry *"Tela Zrome Larn Sime!"*

The ice wouldn't have melted faster if it had been dropped into a volcano. One instant there were thousands of deadly shards of ice traveling at the Gar and the next they were each a harmless drop of water drenching the mage's robes but causing no harm.

Not having heard this spell, or expecting Eldragor's survival the twins were not ready for the lightning strike Eldragor sent afterwards. It was barely feet away from Zander when suddenly it was stopped by a gigantic hulking red figure. Pyros had arrived. The lightning was absorbed harmlessly by the great Dragon's powerful hide.

Pyros sent a blast of flame at Eldragor and he disappeared in the stream of fire. "*Get on!*" Pyros roared in Drathorn's head.

"Let's go!" Drathorn called to the twins. A moment later Drathorn was sitting on a brand new saddle strapped to Pyros' back and the twins were hanging tensely off of his back spikes. The great dragon kicked off the ground, gouging holes in its crusted surface. The wind whipped their faces with immense strength and Torbille nearly fell back to the battle below. Using his powerful wings to carry them, Pyros flew swiftly back to Signaroc.

Drathorn looked back just in time to see over a hundred bodies charred on the black ground, some from Signaroc, most were enemies. In the center of the burned area stood Eldragor, watching Pyros fly away with hatred in his coloured eyes; he still lived and he was angry. Far in the distance Drathorn could barely make out the enemy's main force moving swiftly to the first gate to join the nearly victorious Gar.

Drathorn frowned, upset that he must leave so many men behind and looked ahead of him at the stone walls of Signaroc that were already only fifteen minutes away . . .

XXXVI

The King of Wyrms, an Old Friend

They landed in the king's courtyard where the King, Orfac, Argoss the Dwarf and a dozen guards stood. Drathorn and the twins climbed off Pyros and Drathorn marched toward the group, but Zander spoke first. "Master, he's here."

"Who?" Orfac asked, looking puzzled at his student.

"The king." Torbille answered to him.

Orfac looked at lord Salamoray. "Of course he is." Orfac said, sounding confused.

"The King of Wyrms." Zander and Torbille said together.

Most of the guards appeared puzzled by the fear in the twins' voices and were even more so at the sight of the others' reactions. Argoss dropped the heavy axe in his hands and nearly cut off his foot, the king and two of his guards gasped in shock, Orfac's face paled in fear and his jaw dropped. "A-are you sure?" Salamoray asked.

Torbille nodded. "He attacked Drathorn during the battle." He said. "It was through sheer luck that we managed to save Drathorn and combine our powers to keep everyone safe from him until Pyros arrived."

Orfac asked no further questions. "Your highness, you must hide with your guards and stay hidden. Twins, you shall come with me to my tower and assist me and the other mages in the safe keeping of the journal." Orfac then turned to Drathorn.

"Who is this king of worms and why do you fear him?" Drathorn asked. "He's just a powerful mage, surely you can defeat him?"

Orfac shook his head. "Eldragor is an old friend of mine . . . he hates and despises my very name. He has become much stronger than me and most mages I know with the hopes of some day killing me. It seems he has joined our enemy to gain that power. He is not to be trifled with, both in animal form and in human . . . *especially* not in animal form."

With that Orfac led his mages away. Drathorn turned to Pyros. *"What's so fearsome about Eldragor's animal form? He calls himself the king of worms so i'm guessing that's all he transforms into."*

Pyros frowned at him. *"Not worms Drathorn . . . Wyrms . . ."*

"What's the difference?" Drathorn asked.

Pyros sighed in his mind. *"You shall soon see I'm afraid."*

Drathorn was annoyed that Pyros would say no more but he ignored his annoyance and turned to Salamoray. "Now what?"

At that moment a man on horse back rode up to them, the horse's eyes filled with fear at the sight of Pyros but the warrior held him steady. "The wooden gate has been burned; the enemy's main force is on its way! The gates are closed and the army is ready, but the enemy is huge!"

The king nodded. "Drathorn, you are in charge of my army. Lead them to victory young one. Rider, return to the army and prepare for battle." With that the rider rode away again and Salamoray lead his guards and Argoss into the manor.

Drathorn frowned; now it would begin.

Drathorn sat in the saddle of Pyros, looking down from the highest of the archer's towers by the city's stone gate. A seemingly endless army of enemies pounded upon the fortified gate with all their might as the archer towers sent endless volleys of arrows down upon them. A single line of archers stood, aiming at the gate, ready to release their arrows upon their enemies when it opened. Behind them nearly a thousand riders were ready to charge forward. Behind the riders stood the captain and an uncertain number of soldiers and mercenaries all ready to fight for the defence of their city. The men were divided into two groups, one that would charge behind the riders with the captain and a larger one that would remain inside the city to defend the interior, to stop the enemy from reaching the courtyard, and protect their homes.

Another line of archers stood behind the warriors crouched behind wooden barriers with bows and crossbows ready to block enemies from entering the major city. Drathorn thought it was well planned out for his first attempt but as he examined the enemy's force he wondered if it was enough.

Among the black mass of the army stood the hulking figures of Ogres, much like the one Bronc had saved him from, and Trolls. The Trolls were tall, long armed, hairy beasts with yellow teeth. They carried no weapons but their clawed hands touched the ground even as they stood straight. The manes of tangled hair around their head hid their ears but Drathorn knew they were bat-like with excellent hearing range. They were extremely weak against fire and poison.

A fair number of Gar were scattered around the group of enemies. Neither Eldragor nor Cherry were visible from this height. But the main force of the army was all too visible; the Vikorgan. Their skin was a sickly green colour with warts and wrinkles commonly spread over it. Their powerful bodies were hardened by muscle that showed through the small bits of mismatching leather armour they wore. Most bore swords or axes, and a few also had maces, and round wooden shields. A large number of the enemies also had longbows and arrows. Their fingers ended in short sharp claws and their yellow teeth were filled to deadly points. They had forked tongues like snakes and disgusting breath. They were all Cyclops'; all had a single giant red eye in the center of their foreheads.

Drathorn was patient as he waited for the gate to break. One, two, three minutes passed. Then there was a cracking noise and the fortifications broke despite the archers' efforts to keep them away from the gate. There was another moment and the gate blew open. The first line released their arrows and the attackers were halted for only a second. It was in that second that Pyros leapt off the tower.

They glided straight down toward the ground, the rush of air exhilarated Drathorn. Pyros pulled up at the last second and glided through the open gate. Fire roared from his mouth, burning the invaders and then the power of his body sent them flying, clearing the gate. The dragon pulled up back into the sky for a moment once free of the stone wall and the Vikorgan army surged forward. They were again held at bay by the archers and Drathorn took the time to force Pyros to make a pass with his fiery breath.

It went like that for about five minutes. Drathorn threw fireballs at the enemies below while Pyros made passes with his breath. The few enemies that reached the gates stood no chance against the archers. Finally the enemy pointed toward the skies and volleys of arrows were released. Pyros dodged most but a few clattered off his armoured hide. Laughing at the pitiful attempt Pyros and Drathorn assaulted a group of archers. They lasted only seconds but Pyros was caught off guard by a second group of archers from behind. Two arrows managed to pierce the thin flesh of his wings and he roared in pain. He flew upwards, hot blood dripping upon the enemies below.

Another pass of his flames and then another volley of arrows struck. This time many arrows pierced him. *"Pyros, are you alright?"* Drathorn exclaimed.

"Fourteen through the right wing, eleven through the left." Pyros groaned.

"You've done well my friend; it's time to continue the scene from the dream so long ago." Drathorn stood in the saddle and looked down at his foes below. They were far below them, just out of arrow range. Drawing *Dragontongue* and summoning a new fireball he concentrated and then leapt gracefully off Pyros and into the night.

He angled himself like a falling arrow and through the fireball. It killed a nearby foe and injured two others. As he neared the ground he quickly righted himself. He stopped abruptly when his toe touched the ground and the great force from within him pushed outward. Vikorgan smashed into each other, two trolls stumbled and crushed a group of Gar, a single Ogre was knocked over and destroyed a heavy wooden battering ram and one human was propelled with such force into two other Gar that all three of them were killed.

For a moment all fighting seemed to have ceased as both sides watched to see Drathorn's next move. He took in a great gulp of air and roared, "TAKE NO PRISONERS!"

A moment later the cavalry was charging out of Signaroc, ploughing through the Vikorgan invaders. A second later the first group of footmen were flooding through the gates. Drathorn could barely see the first line of archers disappear into the buildings and towers inside the city. A moment later the enemy was upon him. But Pyros streamed out of the sky and scorched the surrounding land before Drathorn demanded that he return to the dragon realm. Drathorn charged with *Dragontongue* in hand and fought his way back to the gates with the help of the swordsmen.

After a moment the foot soldiers were surrounding the gate, trying desperately to keep all foes out of the city, but it was already being flooded. Vikorgan, Gar, a few Humans and even an Ogre had slipped past the footmen and were engaging the second group of defenders. Soon the once well organized city was a confusing mass of fighting between the two armies. As Drathorn stabbed through a stronger Vikorgan he saw Eldragor. Somehow the mage had slipped past all the fighting and was now positioned on the rooftop of one of the archery towers. Ten archers were dead around him but the others were still firing arrows from within, oblivious to their danger.

Drathorn charged for the tower as bolt after bolt of lightning flew from Eldragor's hand and into the fighting crowd. Drathorn killed three Vikorgan at the tower's door and rushed in, stabbing a fourth on the stairs. As he climbed the tower he passed many levels on which the archers of Signaroc were either battling enemies who had arrived on that floor or firing arrows into the battle below. Drathorn rushed past all but the highest level where he peeked in the door and yelled "Follow me up!" before turning and swiftly ascending to the roof.

He was soon on the roof; Eldragor was still firing into the crowd. Drathorn summoned a fireball and threw it, hoping to end the fight here and now before it could really become a fight. The fireball struck Eldragor's shoulder and exploded. Eldragor stumbled but then turned to face him, in pain but not destroyed like all Drathorn's other victims were.

"Welcome back Hellbound." Eldragor said politely. "For that you will feel the power of the king of Wyrms! *Armondur Nasgoth*!"

Drathorn dived to the side and the lightning strike exploded off the wall right where his head had been a moment before. Drathorn charged at the mage and he too dived gracefully out of the way. "*Armondur Nasgoth*!" Eldragor yelled.

Drathorn slapped the bolt aside with *Dragontongue* and it disappeared into the night sky. "*Locorman Zang!*" now the surrounding ten dead archers stood, re-animated. They could not wield their bows, but they marched forward trying to force him away from the spell caster.

Drathorn slashed though one and stabbed another but was forced back again as two more came near, flailing their arms as though electrified. It was then that the archers arrived. They fired upon the dead men, slaying them again. Eldragor turned upon the archers; one spell could have killed them all while they were in that doorway. But Drathorn took advantage of the distraction. Drathorn charged and twirled *Dragontongue* through the air and sliced off Eldragor's hand.

The mage screamed in pain, his reptilian face contorted in pain. His human hand landed on the tower roof. "*Armondur Nasgoth!*" He yelled, his voice strained in pain.

The lightning bolt was reflected with deadly accuracy off *Dragontongue* back at Eldragor and the wounded mage barely managed to dodge. "*Nymphorniac!*" he yelled. The vines shot without warning and knocked *Dragontongue* out of Drathorn's hand. The sword clattered to the floor as the vines wrapped around Drathorn, binding him.

But Eldragor forgot the Archers and he was soon assaulted by another volley of them. One pierced his shoulder, the other his leg. The others missed only barely. Eldragor screamed in pain and the vines released Drathorn. Drathorn jumped forward and tackled Eldragor. Still screaming, the mage fell off the tower and into the battle below. Between his screams of pain and fear of falling Eldragor could not find the time to cast a spell that would save him. The slap of flesh on cobblestone was not heard over the fighting.

The Archers rushed to Drathorn's side as he picked up *Dragontongue*. They looked at Drathorn with happy smiles; the mage was defeated! Drathorn shook his head and sheathed *Dragontongue*. "This isn't over."

Just as he spoke there was a strange glow of orange light from the body of Eldragor hidden in the darkness below. With the human form of the Ali-Manicota destroyed the animal form was activated. Drathorn gazed at the light knowingly; he now remembered what a Wyrm was from '*A Traveler's Guide*'. A moment later his fears were confirmed.

The beast was nearly as tall as the tower. It was a worm in almost all ways. It had giant black beady eyes and two slits for nostrils. Its mouth was a giant circular hole beneath the nose that was lined all the way around with arm length sharp yellow teeth. The creature seemed to grow out of the ground until it was as high as the tower and continued past. Drathorn watched the ground and saw the other end of the creature appear a moment later. It was three times longer than the tower was tall. It bent in mid air with its mouth wide and dived into the ground, swallowing members of both armies and causing an earthquake that shook the foundations of the city and knocked many fighters off their feet. As quickly as it had appeared it had disappeared into the new hole that it had dug.

Drathorn waited patiently and then the creature exploded out of the ground, sending men from both armies flying in many directions, in a new spot. When the creature was almost as high as the tower it stopped growing and bent low over the battling warriors. It breathed a sudden blast of pure fire, scorching the fighters to death much like the Dragons . . . only much larger.

The archers on the ground and in the towers opened fire on the creature, including the ones who stood with Drathorn. Drathorn ignored the creature for a moment and then picked up a quiver of arrows from one of the fallen archers. "*Flamestrike!*" He called and the magnificent bow was suddenly in his hand once again.

He took aim quickly and followed the archer's lead. Unlike when he was struck by the archers' arrows the creature roared in pain when the magically enchanted arrow struck him. It grew again and jumped into the air before bending and disappearing again beneath the ground, taking many men with him and knocking even more off their feet.

Drathorn and the other archers waited and then it appeared again. They opened fire immediately, over two hundred arrows striking it at once. At the same time five swordsmen had braved the creature below and were desperately stabbing their swords into the creature's sides.

Drathorn growled when it appeared that the arrows were doing little. "We must strike his Ali-Manicota symbol." He said.

"We don't know where it is." said the archer nearest him. "But we're trying!"

Drathorn remembered suddenly that Eldragor's mark had been on his neck. He smiled as he realised what would have to be done to get close enough to find the tiny symbol. He turned to the leader of this specific group of archers and the man's eyes grew wide with fear as he saw Drathorn's expression. "I'll take care of this." Drathorn said. "Hold all fire from this tower and try and get the others to do the same until I give a signal."

Without checking to see that the archer understood he turned and ran toward the edge of the tower, leaping off as far as he could. As he had hoped; it was barely enough. Drathorn grabbed the dagger strapped to his forearm and stabbed it into the monster's back, barely holding on. He struggled and then pulled himself up on top of the creature.

He left the dagger there and focused on avoiding arrows and balancing on the monster's moving back. The creature's flesh was thick and strong as a rhino's and most of the arrows had only barely pierced it, most had only bounced off or left small scratches. Drathorn's magic arrows appeared to be the only exceptions; they still stuck out at odd angles from the Wyrm's body. Drathorn walked carefully across the creature's back as the arrows began to stop falling on the creature. It was a whole minute of tense balancing and watching as the creature's breath destroyed both friend and foe before he found the miniscule tattoo, still glowing faintly in the darkness of the night. Drathorn pulled a new arrow from his quiver and pulled back the bowstring. He aimed directly at the tattoo, the arrow's tip only inches away. He released the arrow and it collided with a splash of blood and an even greater roar from the creature. "NOW!" Drathorn yelled. Arrows flew from every direction. From one tower the arrows struck its open mouth and wide belly while the other towers struck its eyes and the rest of its body.

Drathorn was never sure whether it was the magic arrow to the symbol or the volley of arrows to the throat that did the job but the roar suddenly became high pitched and then nothing but a low gurgling noise in the back of its throat. The Wyrm swayed for a moment and then fell towards earth. "*Thi Sein Whor!*" Drathorn yelled. The bow disappeared and Drathorn stabbed *Dragontongue* into the creature's head.

Holding on with all his might he braced for the impact. A moment later the dead Wyrm's body struck the ground, flattening at least two hundred fighters and knocking down hundreds more with its earthquake.

Drathorn could hear the cheer from the archers as he leapt off of the Wyrm's limp body. The cheers were numerous but they were soon drowned out as the archers began to shoot at the creature some more, confirming its death, and then at invading enemies again.

It was at that moment that the battle was illuminated from the tower. Orfac's tower glowed suddenly in bright light and seconds later more lights came from it in multiple colours; the battle for the journal had begun. Cursing loudly, Drathorn readied *Dragontongue* and charged forward.

With renewed strength at the Wyrm's and Eldragor's defeat, the soldiers and archers fought harder against the invading foes. Drathorn rushed past them, slashing and stabbing at Vikorgan and Gar as he passed them and even stabbing the giant foot of an Ogre as he dodged its club. He was breathless when he reached the entrance to the courtyard. Argoss and four men were battling valiantly at the entrance to the manor.

Drathorn rushed to their aid. Drathorn had to steer clear of the Dwarf as if he too were an enemy because his swift, powerful, strokes cleaved his every victim in half. The short bearded man had extreme strength for his size. It was only a moment before Drathorn killed one of the attackers and noticed they were humans bearing crude weapons of wood and metal; Cherry's personal thieves had arrived for the battle. It was only due to Drathorn's fire and the arrows from within the manor that the fight was won.

Drathorn decapitated his final foe and threw a fireball at the foe Argoss was fighting and then it was over. Slightly less than fifty bodies lay around them, most with arrows protruding from their backs. Only one of the bodies was a guard. "Argoss, how did this happen?" Drathorn asked quickly.

"What do you mean how'd it happen?" the Dwarf growled. "They came through the gate with tiny weapons and attacked the manor!"

"Alright, go back inside with the king." Drathorn turned his sight to the tower; the flashing lights had stopped. Was the journal safe? Was anyone hurt?

"Three of the men slipped off to the foot of the tower." Argoss answered. "We were too busy with these ones to stop them. Go get 'em Hellbound." With that the Dwarf and his remaining guards re-entered the manor.

Drathorn kept his sword drawn, exhausted from the fight so far, and ran to the tower. Guarding the entrance to the tower were the three men Argoss had mentioned. As he neared, a crossbow bolt flew from the one in the center and the other two charged forward. Exhausted, Drathorn barely slapped the bolt aside. With a quick fireball he destroyed one attacker and then he blocked and stabbed the other.

"It's been a while, Drathorn Teldaga." said the man with the crossbow. "Oh! That's right, its Hellbound now isn't it?"

The sound of the voice was so familiar and angered him so suddenly that he could not stop a fireball from appearing in his hand. The figure stepped into the light; crossbow pointing at Drathorn's bare, unprotected chest. Drathorn growled in acknowledgement as he put two and two together. In front of him stood none other than Mardy Gonvalsen, ex-convict of Greengate.

XXXVII

The Battle for the Journal of the Great Thirteen

Sunday June 7th, 18291; one in the morning. "Surprised to see me?" Mardy asked with a smile.

"Not exactly." frowned Drathorn. "Just surprised you're part of the chain of command in this army."

"Ah yes." Mardy laughed again. "Cherry broke fifty two of us out . . . After our escape I looked to try and find my friends from the orphanage but none had escaped. I demanded they be released and Cherry agreed it could happen, as long as I did him a favour first.

"He knew you were . . . an old friend . . . of mine." Mardy smiled slyly again. "He told me to lead these thieves and thugs to the king and to have them attempt to kill him. Then after the fighting had begun me and two others were to wait to attack you outside the tower.

"I was told to kill you, and allow none in the tower. If I succeeded he would free my friends. If I failed I would not live long enough to tell the tale anyways." Mardy looked at Drathorn, "It seems I'll get my chance."

"Mardy, you could not defeat me way back in the orphanage and I am stronger now. What makes you think you could possibly hurt me?" Drathorn asked.

"Because I'm stronger too." laughed Mardy. "*Proganzak!*" suddenly the flat lands of the courtyard around them turned to ice, making it slippery. "*Proganzak!*" he said again. *Dragontongue* suddenly became extremely heavy in Drathorn's hand and extremely cold. He was forced to drop it before the ice could engulf him as well.

Mardy released a bolt from his crossbow yelling "*Efrall!*" at the same time. The bolt missed Drathorn by inches and exploded into a flash of blinding light. The red light of the flare blinded them both on the slippery ice but Drathorn knew roughly where Mardy was. He slid along the slippery ice and knocked Mardy's feet out from under him. There was a grunt of pain and a short cracking noise of a broken nose.

But suddenly a foot came from the light and caught Drathorn in the ribs. Drathorn doubled over and a fist caught his chest. He landed on his back and rolled over into a kneeling position. There was the sound of a heavily booted foot slamming on the ice where Drathorn's head had been a moment before. Drathorn reached to his belt and pulled the whip from it quickly. As the light slowly began to die away Drathorn saw the figure of Mardy stomping on the ground, trying to find Drathorn.

Drathorn lashed out with the whip as soon as he could see properly. The long weapon slashed across Mardy's back but he only yelped in pain, protected by his leather armour. Mardy turned to face Drathorn and was awarded with the lash of another whip across his face that hurt a lot more than the one to the back had. Mardy fell to the ground, blood streaming from his cheek, and cursed loudly before yelling *"Nervahn Est Mondor!"* Recognizing the words Drathorn dropped the whip and dived forward.

He did so just in time. A giant bolt of lightning fell from the sky and struck the ground where he had been only seconds before, shattering the ice and sending shards of it in every direction. Mardy stood, preparing to say it again but Drathorn was right on top of him.

Drathorn's fist collided with his already broken nose before Mardy could say the second word. *"Nervahn Es-*Uh!*"* was all he managed before he crumpled to the ground but it was more than enough. Around them ten circles of blue light had appeared on the ground. They glowed and grew to the size of a man and then with an explosion that rocked the foundations of the tower ten giant bolts of lightning exploded into the sky from them.

If Drathorn had been only an inch to the left he would have been utterly destroyed. As it was, Mardy's body was gone; his right hand had been in one of the glowing circle's line of fire. All that remained of Mardy was a black mark on the ice shaped like his body.

Ignoring the smell of burnt flesh Drathorn walked across the already melting ice and picked up *Dragontongue* and the fallen whip. He swung *Dragontongue* at the base of the tower and the ice on it shattered, revealing the cold but powerful blade in his hands.

After several quick breaths to steady him, Drathorn began to jog quickly up the steps to Orfac's room where the Journal of the Great Thirteen hopefully still laid waiting.

He barged through the door without thinking, *Dragontongue* still drawn. Four mages lay dead around the room, two were mortally wounded and another seven, plus Orfac and the twins, were bound tightly with magical vines and sitting against the wall, unable to do anything. The table in the middle that had once held the Journal of the Great Thirteen in the sight of the protective mages was shattered on the floor along with a few other bits of furniture.

In the dim light Cherry stood in the center of the room, looking down on his ten captives. "Hello Drathorn." Cherry said warmly without looking up. "I'm afraid you just missed my master. After he and a few followers defeated these mages he took the book and left me in charge. It seems you have lost this one my friend. But you'll not live long enough to regret it."

Cherry turned to face Drathorn, revealing the new sword at his side. It was obviously the sword *Lightningcast*. It was a strange blade. The handle was only long enough for one hand. At the end of the handle the hilt made a "V" shape angling with the two points spreading on either side of the blade. From the center of the strange hilt grew not one strong blade but two thin rapier blades only an inch apart on the sword. Between the two blades electricity danced visibly.

Drathorn summoned his anger at Cherry and a fireball roared to life in his left hand. In his right he gripped the blade *Dragontongue* tighter. "It seems you have acquired a new weapon to test against me." Cherry said. "Very well, let us begin." With a bark-like laugh Cherry leapt at Drathorn, slicing *Lightningcast* through the air.

Drathorn stopped the blade with *Dragontongue* and side stepped as a shower of sparks struck the ground in the collision. "How did you survive, Cherry?" Drathorn asked.

Cherry laughed, repositioning himself between Drathorn and the door. "I transformed as I fell, I died as an animal leaving my human form the only available option." He smiled. "I think you'll notice my necklace is broken?"

Drathorn looked closer and saw that the violet amulet Cherry had once worn was now broken in two. Cherry took his distraction as an opportunity and struck out again. The two mystic blades clashed multiple times, sending a shower of sparks around the room. Drathorn threw a fireball but Cherry's sword absorbed it. They both backed away slightly, panting.

"I am one of the darklord's ten Commandoes." Cherry said. "Unless you remove the shard from my dead body I'll just be reborn anyways." He sneered. "It's only luck that you thought to do that to Bandixi, but you'll not succeed with me!" They both leapt at the same time again, swords clashing.

Drathorn was considered a master of the blade by his fellow fighters, but Cherry was the same and he had been doing this much longer. The two swords collided for the final time and *Dragontongue* flew from Drathorn's hand. Cherry smiled at Drathorn as he backed into the wall *Lightningcast* at his throat. "This will be amusing." Cherry said, stepping forward to slice Drathorn's head off.

Remembering his dream from so long ago Drathorn roared and lunged forward. In mid stance Drathorn morphed into a powerful Weretiger once more. Unprepared for this sudden turn of events Cherry stumbled back and Drathorn's claws slashed at him. Fear showed in Cherry's eyes as he stumbled, fell, and landed on his back.

Drathorn leapt on him, tearing and biting and roaring menacingly. At the last second before he would have died Cherry swung *Lightningcast* and it struck Drathorn in the side. The cut was only enough to make him roar louder but the electric shock knocked him right off Cherry.

Drathorn looked at the thief king, dying with incredible speed as he quickly lost blood from enormous gashes and a missing arm. Pitying the thief Drathorn moved closer, planning to end his life without more suffering. "NO!" Cherry roared. "*Zamjor Kar!*" There was a blinding flash of light and Cherry was gone with *Lightningcast*, the only remains of him were the thick pool of blood and his stub of an arm.

Drathorn stared at the spot where the man had disappeared and then transformed. Shaking his head he lifted *Dragontongue* from the ground and sheathed it. Then he ran and undid Orfac's gag.

"They got the book!" Orfac yelled. "The darklord got the book and teleported away and Cherry killed some and was about to kill us and then you were a Weretiger and you almost killed him but he teleported away to die so you cant take the shard so he'll be reborn and-"

"Quiet Orfac or I'll put the gag back in." Drathorn interrupted. Orfac was silent. "He's gone for now, I'll finish him another time; the important part is that you're safe." He untied Orfac and the mage stood. He muttered a few words Drathorn couldn't hear and the ropes binding the other mages untied themselves and they all stood, stretching cramped muscles. Drathorn looked away from the mages and out into the city. The Vikorgan were everywhere, outnumbering the soldiers two to one in the city and even more were still flooding through the gate.

"You must stop them from entering." Orfac said, following his gaze. "You must give the warriors time to regroup and close the gates." Drathorn nodded and climbed into the window, preparing to jump out. "Once you're at the gate the riders should rally around you and attempt to stop the enemy as you do, use their help. We'll get there as fast as we can to assist from the towers. We saw Eldragor's defeat, congratulations Drathorn."

Drathorn said nothing and stepped out into the sky. As he fell he summoned Ragnarok below him. He landed gently in Ragnarok's saddle as the power erupted from him and hit no one. "*To the gate, we must assist the warriors!*"

"*Indeed, we are losing this battle already.*"

XXXVIII

The Battle for Signaroc

Ragnarok ran on all fours through the town, jumping on and flattening foes where he could. It was only a moment before he had crossed the town and was behind the failing barricade the archers tried desperately to hold. Ragnarok leapt with all his strength over the barrier and unfurled his tiny wings. The wings would not let him fly but for a moment he could glide over his foes. Drathorn threw fireballs in rapid succession from both hands, *Dragontongue* still sheathed at his side. Ragnarok slammed to the ground with a force that knocked a few nearby fighters off their feet again. Vikorgan slashed out at him, their weapons bouncing off his stony hide or shattering, arrows struck him from all sides but did no damage to him. He stood on his back legs for a moment and swiped his powerful front legs in a wide arc, sending enemies flying into each other and remarkably hitting no allies.

Two archers stood in front of him and took aim at Drathorn who was busy firing fireballs at enemies that were trying to enter an archer's tower. Ragnarok roared and spat a gigantic boulder from his mouth that crashed into the archers with the force of a catapult shot and it rolled into a few others. Those few seconds devastated the enemy numbers greatly and turned the odds in the favour of Signaroc for only a moment. Ragnarok took that moment to leap over a group of Signaroc soldiers and into the open gate, tackling forty Vikorgan and four of the Gar to the ground, killing most of them. Two more great leaps and they stood in front of the gate smashing through the numerous enemies.

Drathorn launched two more fireballs at one of the hairy trolls and it screamed in pain. When the Troll fell he leapt off Ragnarok's back and drew *Dragontongue*, slashing through a nearby enemy.

It was only a moment of perilous fighting for their lives before the remaining riders from Signaroc joined them, charging around, stabbing enemies with spears and trampling them with their horses. It was only a moment after that when Orfac and his students arrived and began to assist in garrisoning the archery towers.

The mages helped to stop the enemies within the walls and soon the gates had begun to close and the footmen were repairing it as fast as they could. Although the battle within the walls was done for the time being the battle outside raged on, assisted by volleys of arrows and blasts of magic from the towers. The horsemen still became few quickly because of the great number of enemies. Soon only a dozen and a half men remained on horseback, one on foot had lost his horse, Ragnarok was exhausted as he battled three trolls simultaneously and Drathorn was cornered by a fourth troll, his weapon far from reach.

The troll raised his long arm, preparing to crush Drathorn with it but was stopped as a javelin slid through his head from one of the charging horsemen. Drathorn dived and rolled past the fallen Troll and picked up *Dragontongue*. He looked at Ragnarok battling three trolls and nearly fifty Vikorgan beneath him. It was only luck that the gate was now sealed shut and under emergency repairs.

Drathorn had to decide who to help now; two horsemen cornered by an Ogre or Ragnarok, valiantly fighting a large group of foes. It didn't take him long. He leapt at the Ogre's body and stabbed *Dragontongue* into its back. The Ogre roared in pain and reached for him but he was just out of reach. The cornered riders took the chance to throw their last javelins at the creature's neck. At the same time the creature was struck by a giant spear of ice that flew from Torbille's archer tower and went through its chest.

The Ogre fell and the riders readied spears and began to charge their enemy again. Drathorn turned now to Ragnarok who was still hopelessly fighting against immense odds. He threw a fireball at one of the trolls and it fell from the strength of the blaze. Drathorn ran, picking up a fallen javelin as he went. Ragnarok swept a giant leg in an arc and knocked four Vikorgan aside but the heavily muscled arm of a hairy troll slammed against his armoured flank.

Drathorn launched the javelin as hard as he could and it drove through a troll's chest but failed to kill him. A volley of arrows flew from Zander's tower and struck the worst of Ragnarok's attackers. There was now only a few Vikorgan and the wounded troll left. With one swipe of his leg he killed the troll and then he spat a stone at the Vikorgan. Drathorn killed his last attacker quickly.

"Drathorn!" Orfac's voice flowed from the closest tower. "Get the survivors to back away from the enemy!"

Drathorn didn't have to say anything. The horsemen retreated as a line of ten Ogres charged forward. As the horsemen neared the gate a chorus of *"Lagmenta!"* filled the air. The horses and men were lifted up into the air and carried over the walls, two were shot down by arrows in the process but the rest escaped. Drathorn jumped on Ragnarok's back.

"Get us back over the gate!" Drathorn yelled at him through his mind. *"I'll cover you!"* Ragnarok turned swiftly and leapt at the wall, his powerful arms ploughing through the stone and he began to climb the thick stone wall like a ladder. Drathorn spun in the saddle and began throwing fireballs at random into the crowd below. Ragnarok continued to climb the wall like a ladder and when he reached the top he leapt off and into the city street. They hit the ground, breaking an inch into the cobblestone road.

"Master, I must rest." Ragnarok said. The stone armour the great beast wore was dented and cracked in places from the trolls' arms and he panted furiously.

"Return to the Dragon realm Ragnarok, you have done well." Drathorn said. The great dragon disappeared from under him and he landed gently on the ground. Drathorn looked around.

Archers were gathering arrows and repairing their barricades, footmen leaned against the gate trying desperately not to let the Ogres break it down. Arrows, bolts and blasts of magic fell from the towers and over the walls striking unseen foes. Horsemen gathered new javelins or spears, wounded men retreated inside houses to hide with doctors and watch out the windows with crossbows. There were still many. Salamoray and Argoss suddenly appeared beside him with weapons in hand. "Milord, why have you left the manor?" Drathorn asked.

"Our assistance was required out here so we came quickly." The king answered.

"Yeah, but even with our help the fight is lost." Argoss grumbled. "There are far too many of them."

"Don't say that Dwarf." Orfac said suddenly from behind them, "This isn't over yet."

"No, but it'll only be another hour before it is and I can easily guess the outcome." Argoss grumbled.

"I agree with him Orfac." Salamoray said. "With Zapix gone and the others unable to fight we cannot have help from the dragons. Without them we are doomed." Many of the passing soldiers looked at their king in fear; had they lost many lives for nothing?

"No! Help has arrived!" Orfac said. "Upon the hills are three flags and three armies. The smallest is under two dozen horsemen bearing the flag of Narvahan Shé. The one in the middle is lead by two riders and are just over a hundred footmen bearing the flag of Taldi. The largest is at least three thousand footmen lead by a great brute bearing the flag of Nargak."

"The tribes!" Drathorn, Salamoray and Argoss all said together, all with different emotions in their voices. "They will not help us." Argoss growled. "They hate the emperor and will love to watch us fall."

"They carry weapons of battle, Dwarf, and they move toward us at a quick pace." Orfac added.

"Then they seek to join our attackers and destroy us! As if we're not hopeless already, we should evacuate the city while we can!" Argoss grumbled.

"No." Drathorn said flatly. "The tribes are loyal to me. Taldi and Nargak have joined forces to help the Hellbound, not the empire. They will help you as long as I do. The horsemen of Narvahan Shé must be survivors of the city that have joined with them to help."

"What do we do then, Drathorn?" the king asked; his calm returning and bravery shining in his eyes.

"We wait for the opportune moment and open the gates to join our brothers from the tribes." Drathorn answered. Salamoray nodded, Orfac smiled, Argoss groaned.

Troy sat upon Starcruser at the head of the battle, bow in hand. Thira was at his side on her horse, which she had finally named Riverwind, and held her staff in one hand and fingered her sling in the other. On Troy's other side was Taldi's flag bearer. Not too far to the left was Feronis at the head of the Narvahan Shé riders and bearing the flag of his people. On the far right was Samgarnok standing on his feet with a great battle axe in his hands, his warriors stood behind him wielding rapiers and one with a flag of Nargak.

The army of the darklord was striking the gates of Signaroc, oblivious to the tribal army behind them and the arrows the towers fired upon them. There were still many enemies, at least two thousand. Troy didn't voice his worry that Signaroc would not open their gates and come to their aid; he just pulled an arrow from his quiver and looked at Thira. "Today, we ride for Drathorn!" he called, mainly to the army but also it stated a hidden meaning to Thira. "We have lost friends, brothers, sisters, fathers and mothers because of this foe and Drathorn Hellbound is the answer to that! We *will* save him; we *will* reunite the free peoples! We *will* be VICTORIOUS!"

Troy thundered the last word as the army roared its approval of his short speech. Then he spurred Starcruser forward and toward the army of their enemy. Thira was right behind him, closely followed by the Taldi flag bearer. The riders of Narvahan Shé were faster and quickly passed Troy and collided with the enemy first, Feronis in the lead. Starcruser trampled over a Vikorgan next and Troy released an arrow into the neck of an unsuspecting Troll. Thira came next trampling many warriors on Riverwind and batting aside others with her staff. Then the Taldi flag bearer. It was shortly after that that the footmen of Taldi and Nargak arrived with Samgarnok.

Once the army of the enemy had turned toward the tribes the gates of Signaroc opened. A small group of horsemen flowed from the gates and trampled the enemy from behind. Then came a lone man with long dark hair and a magnificent golden sword. No sooner was that man through the gate was he followed by the King in his golden crown, a short Dwarf with a gigantic axe and the remaining footmen of Signaroc. Arrows and magic fell from the towers and from holes in the wall. It was another two hours before the battle for Signaroc was won.

And that is how Troy and Thira saved Signaroc and were reunited with their long lost best friend.

XXXIX

Reunited Again

Monday June 8th, 18291; "Drathorn, before you leave I must speak to you, it's about your friends." Orfac said. They were in his tower. Drathorn knew Thira and Troy were here and admitted that he was angry they had not listened to him, but he was happy they were here.

"What is it Orfac?" Drathorn asked.

"You remember how we talked about you being able to feel emotions the other Hellbound could not?" he asked, Drathorn nodded. "Well I want you to try not to let that effect you."

"What do you mean?" Drathorn asked.

"Don't . . ." Orfac hesitated, embarrassed. "Don't fall in love, or show too much care for your friends and family."

Drathorn was surprised at first, and then outraged. "Why not?" He demanded.

"To protect them." said Orfac simply. Drathorn's expression filled with confusion. "If the Darklord learns that you feel for your friends in any way, if he learns that you care enough about them to put the whole world at stake to save them, he will use them to get to you."

"They wouldn't betray me." Drathorn objected.

"No, but the Darklord could capture them and use them to lure you into a trap that could kill you and result in the destruction of the world. You mustn't let that happen."

Drathorn frowned, he didn't like the idea of needing to pretend he felt no emotions but it did seem wise. "I . . . understand." He muttered.

"Good." Orfac said. "Now one more thing; since the Hellbound could only feel one emotion they often were overcome by an effect we call the Hell Rage. It is when the Hellbound are so overcome with anger that they can destroy friends, family and enemy alike without so much as a single thought. Since you can feel other emotions this shouldn't be a problem but I still want you to be careful. Now go, your friends are on their way to see you, go and greet them. Come to the manor tomorrow around noon."

Drathorn nodded and left the room, thinking about what Orfac had said. He exited the open door of the tower and walked out into the sunlight of the barren courtyard. He hadn't realised how close Troy and Thira already were.

"Drathorn!" cried Thira. Troy and Thira had been walking slowly toward the tower, unsure of how to proceed. But upon seeing Drathorn emerge Thira had dropped her staff and ran forward. Drathorn caught a glimpse of Troy (limping slowly in their directing and now carrying Thira's staff as well as his own bow) before Thira was upon him. She threw herself at Drathorn with arms spread wide, a smile wide on her face.

Drathorn caught her in mid air and shared the embrace for a moment, enjoying the warmth of having her body so close to his under the mid-day sun. He had expected his sudden growth to make him much taller than her but she too had grown slightly over their separation and he was now only a head taller than her. He held her close in the embrace, all thoughts of his problems gone. Had her hair always smelled wonderfully of pine? Was it always so long and straight and perfect? Were her eyes always so beautiful?

Thira looked up at him, into his eyes and Drathorn saw no fear in her as she looked at the horrible change. There were tears of happiness on her cheek, her leather armour hugged her body almost as tightly as she hugged him and it brought out every curve and muscle in her slender but strong body. It was a moment before he realised he was lifting her unnaturally light body a few inches off the ground. He gently set her to the ground but she didn't let him go. She didn't even seem to mind that he was still filthy with dirt, grime and blood from the battle.

They stayed that way for a moment, just looking into each other's eyes but soon Drathorn felt a pair of eyes boring into the top of his head. He tensed slightly in Thira's hold as he realised Orfac must be watching the embrace with disapproval. Thira appeared confused by his tenseness and looked around; she saw Troy standing close by and must have thought Drathorn was embraced to be hugging her like this in front of him. She released him and stepped away slightly.

Drathorn smiled apologetically at her and looked at Troy. Troy watched him critically for a moment, taking in his greatly changed features and feeling a spark of fear when he looked into Drathorn's eyes. Troy had grown too. His hair was longer now, but clean just as Thira's was. He was a lot more muscular from travel and training just like Thira but he still limped heavily on his wooden leg. "What the hell did they do to you Drathorn?" he asked with mock disapproval.

Thira looked between the boys as though expecting Drathorn to retaliate to the false insult. But both boys suddenly laughed at the exact same time. Drathorn and Troy walked toward each other and hugged awkwardly with the weapons in Troy's hand. "We missed you brother."

"And I you." said Drathorn, taking a step back to look his foster brother in the face.

"Let's never separate again." Troy said.

"Never, for without you I cannot survive." Drathorn answered.

They went back to the Blaygard house in Signaroc and Drathorn quickly washed himself so he was a little more presentable. Then he put on a new shirt and pair of pants but ripped the shirt's left sleeve off and cut it down the middle to resemble his old one. It was now much more comfortable to him in this way. Then he went out to the living room to sit with his friends. They talked well into the night, Troy and Thira told the stories of their adventures first, taking just over an hour and then Drathorn told his own story which took multiple hours. They hid nothing from one another (except the private conversation Troy and Thira had had about him). They were enraged when they learned about the angel sent from the heavens to kill him and amazed that Thira's old amulet had saved him. It was three in the morning when they all went to bed that night and they talked more in the morning. Drathorn even told them about his strange dreams. He told them everything but didn't talk about the Reaper he had seen a few days ago.

Close to lunch Drathorn opened the old trunk he had stored his belongings in. He put Elgard's Ali-Manicota orb in his pocket. He also put Bandixi's shard in the same pocket. Then he changed his mind and put them in his bag with Gradorn's journal, 'The Traveler's Aid', the list of traps, the mysterious puzzle box, and the map of the Home of the

Lone. With all his possessions in the bag he looked at the last item, his Elvin sword.

Drathorn ended up giving this blade to Troy, who tied it to his waist in its sheath and left his old sword behind. They walked to the manor fully armed now. Thira walked on his right with her staff in hand, a dagger strapped to her forearm and her sling and bullets at her waist. Troy carried his bow, the Elvin sword sheathed on his left hip and a dagger hidden beneath his pants, strapped to his boot. Drathorn walked with the whip and *Dragontongue* at his sides, a dagger tied to each his shin and forearm, his feet still bare. The beautiful necklace glinted in the sunlight and the strange Elvin ring was still on his finger.

Thira had seen pictures of both the sword and ring before. And identified the Elvin sword as a common Elvin accessory and the ring as an Elvin engagement ring. Despite not being engaged he still wore the ring as if he were. And so they walked through the town, people waving and smiling at the three heroes of Signaroc. Drathorn told them about Orfac's recent warning from yesterday as they walked. Neither of them had agreed with Orfac's logic.

Soon they entered the study of the manor, a round table was moved into it and it was almost full now. Salamoray sat by the window, on his right was Argoss and on his left was Orfac. On Orfac's other side sat the twins, side-by-side. Next to the twins was the captain and then the bald, dark skinned man named Feronis that lead the Narvahan Shé survivors. After Feronis was Samgarnok, the brutish chief of Nargak. Then there were three empty chairs. After the empty chairs the circle continued with Argoss and repeated. Drathorn sat in the middle chair and was flanked quickly by Thira and Troy.

"I have called you all here to celebrate our victory." Salamoray said. "And morn our defeat . . . Signaroc is saved but the Journal of the Great Thirteen is lost." He looked all around the table at the gathered leaders. "The few living enemies have retreated to Narvahan Shé to heal. Signaroc, Taldi and Narvahan Shé's survivors are too few to remain as their own cities. We must discuss how to proceed.

"I have listened to Feronis and Samgarnok and they have convinced me to abandon the empire and turn Signaroc into a tribal town as theirs are. But further action is required, *what do we do?*" Salamoray looked around the table for an answer.

None came, so Drathorn finally offered. "I will recover the journal before the darklord's cleric can undo the protective spell and use it to end our world. Your fate is in my hands."

"And we'll go with him." Thira said. Troy nodded.

"If the three of you leave there is no one to lead the survivors of Taldi in this discussion." Salamoray said.

"Drathorn is now the voice of Taldi, he'll make all decisions involving their people for you now before he leaves." Troy said.

Salamoray turned to Drathorn. "Our first decision is thus; Signaroc will be helping to wipe out the retreating enemies in Narvahan Shé, will the people of Taldi assist?"

Drathorn thought a moment. "Yes." He finally said. "They will help retake the city."

"My riders will help as well." Feronis said. "But I shall not ride with them. I wish to ride with Drathorn and assist him. Am I welcome to follow?"

Again Drathorn thought for a moment, and then he nodded in agreement. "Then the warriors of Nargak will follow to assist in Narvahan Shé as well." Samgarnok said, "But I shall return home."

"Then Argoss and the captain will lead the attack on Narvahan Shé." Salamoray said and everyone agreed together. "Next we must discuss; Samgarnok has offered to allow all the tribes to come together in his city for protection. There are not enough of us to keep up four cities. Signaroc will accept this offer, what of the rest?"

"Consider all surviving riders as part of Nargak from this moment on." Feronis said. "They will go where Samgarnok commands."

"Taldi will also join Nargak." Drathorn said. "The city is in ruins and the Elders cannot keep it prospering, they will welcome Nargak's help."

"Then the cities will empty and move to Nargak under Samgarnok's rule." Salamoray said simply. "And Argoss will lead the army to join them when the enemy is wiped from Narvahan Shé's ruins."

Again there was a murmur of agreement around the table. "Orfac, a rider has been sent to Signaroc's retreating people; they will soon be sent to Taldi and will use Taldi's ships to go straight to Nargak." Zander said.

"We will go to Nargak with Samgarnok to greet the refugees." Torbille continued.

"I will remain with you, my king." Orfac said. "I will leave Signaroc only when you do."

"Then all arrangements are agreed, Feronis, Troy, Thira and Drathorn will head to Carzak's tower to retrieve the journal. When do you leave?" Salamoray concluded.

"We'll depart two days after Zapix returns." Drathorn answered.

"Drathorn, Zapix in resting in the shade beneath my tower." Orfac said. "He has brought news of our locust crisis meant only for your ears."

Drathorn nodded. "Then I will speak to Zapix and we will leave the hour after the army departs for Narvahan Shé." He changed his mind quickly.

"The army leaves in three days." Argoss said.

"Your horses are being cared for in the stables sir." The captain said to Drathorn. "Should I move Feronis' horse to join them?"

"Yes please." Drathorn said.

With that the captain departed. Samgarnok and the twins followed him out. "I will prepare the troops and gather weaponry to strike the enemy." Argoss grunted. Then the dwarf followed them away.

"I will go to see Zapix." Drathorn said. "Have a good day sire, and you too Orfac."

He left with Thira, Troy and Feronis behind him. "Drathorn, in your goodbye letter before . . . what did F.Y.S. mean?" Thira asked.

Drathorn smiled. "It's something I came up with, my own version of saying lots of love or sincerely. It means 'For Your Safety'."

Feronis grunted. "A fitting slogan for the protector of the free peoples." He said. Drathorn agreed with a nod and smile at the rider.

As they approached Zapix all three of them halted several feet away as Drathorn approached. "*Welcome back, Zapix.*" Drathorn said to the dragon. "*What news do you bring?*"

The dragon turned its eyes on Drathorn and spoke to his mind. "*A cave directly west of the city, on the other side of Hellfire Bay is hiding Paraséect, the king of insects. He is one of the ten Commandoes and is commanding the locusts to eat away the crops in the area to weaken the city. He must be stopped.*"

"*Then we will find him and kill him.*" Drathorn said simply, "*Thank-you.*"

The dragon returned suddenly to the bracelet without answering. Annoyed, Drathorn turned back to his companions. "The locusts are being led by a creature called Paraséect in a cave to the west. He is one of the Darklord's ten Commandoes. We must kill him to stop the locusts."

"Then we'll stop there on the way to Carzak's tower." Troy said. "With any luck we'll gain another shard on our way to the tower."

"So we set out soon huh?" Thira concluded.

"Too soon . . ." Drathorn muttered.

They all began walking slowly back to the Blaygard house where Feronis would be staying with them. Drathorn agreed that if Feronis were to be going with them then he would certainly have to tell Feronis the truth about Icarus and the Commandoes and the current struggle for survival, if he were to come he had the right to know everything. *Except of course the angel and the Reaper.* He corrected himself.

"By the way Drathorn." said Thira suddenly. "If we're leaving in three days that means we'll be on the road for your birthday."

Drathorn was surprised. He had completely forgotten about his birthday. "What's the date today?" he asked.

"Tuesday June 9th, 18291." answered Troy automatically.

"Do you want to stay in town an extra day to celebrate?" Feronis asked in his low voice. He didn't seem the partying type to Drathorn, he didn't even seem remotely interested in Drathorn's answer; he was asking more to inform Drathorn that his decisions were the ones that counted; Drathorn Hellbound was the leader of this group and Feronis would not complain if he decided to stay for his birthday. But Drathorn shook his head.

"I forgot all about my birthday." Drathorn said. "There's no reason to cancel plans for it though, we'll continue on as planned."

Feronis shrugged but Troy and Thira seemed slightly disappointed. He struggled to remember the others' birthdays. He didn't know Feronis' at all but he knew Troy's sixteenth was in another month and Thira's sixteenth was last September. As they walked he cursed himself for forgetting the date. It was June 9th and his sixteenth birthday was June 12th. He smiled as he realised he would live to see that day.

Epilogue;

Don't Fear the Reaper

Icarus waited, watching the man enter his throne room at the top of the Onyx tower. He was furious; not only had Drathorn survived the battle of Signaroc but Cherry was stuck on top of Cryton Perch, unable to leave for fear of being seen by the enemy and Signaroc was joining forces with the tribes! He was so angry that he had destroyed two of his loyal followers without thinking. And now he had received news that someone had demanded to see him. Hoping personally that this man was someone he could reduce to cinders he allowed him counsel.

The man now stood in front of him. His fiery red hair and stunning blue eyes perfectly accented by his flawless face. He was undoubtedly young but somehow old at the same time. The last time he had seen this man he had brought bad news, this time he brought nothing as far as Icarus could tell. The man's plate mail armour clinked quietly as he took a step closer. Icarus' eyes could barely make out the man's two dozen daggers strapped to various parts of his body and the rapier at his side.

"Why . . . have you . . . returned?" Icarus rasped.

"Because my dear lord, you need my help." He said with a sly smile. "Just as you did eight years ago."

"Eight . . . years . . . ago . . . my army . . . was small . . . and . . . there were . . . five . . . of them." Icarus rasped. "And you . . . failed . . . to kill . . . the baby . . ."

"That was my own mistake milord." The man said, bowing low. "But you need me again sire, for an army cannot harm one man as well as one man can harm an army. An army may lose ten men to kill that one, causing more damage to that army than to the man, where as one man against one man one side will lose and the other will win—end of story."

"Do . . . not try . . . and be . . . wise with . . . me . . ." Icarus said. "What do . . . you want . . . in return . . . for . . . killing . . . the boy?"

"My price?" asked the man. "That's simple; to be one of your fabled defenders; to be gifted with the ever lasting life supplied by your shards. I'll take your friend Bandixi's shard for myself when I've killed the boy."

Icarus thought for a moment. "You . . . will be . . . using . . . your . . . fiends again?" he asked.

"The Markolii are my greatest fighters." The man said with a nod. "I will hunt down the boy and use them to kill him; just as I did his mother, father, aunt and grandfather."

"The boy . . . has already . . . killed . . . one of my . . . Commandoes . . . and the . . . king of . . . Wyrms . . . he is . . . not to . . . be trifled . . . with." Icarus said. "Why . . . do you think . . . you can . . . do this . . . when . . . you failed . . . last time?"

The man smiled and reached into a pocket on his cape before pulling out a small vile. "If I die to prove my loyalty to you I will use my last breath to make sure he is infected with this." The man said.

Icarus did not need to ask, did not need to look closer, to know what was in the vial. "That . . . is a very . . . rare . . . substance . . . assassin . . . use it . . . with care . . ."

"I will not fail you master." The man said. "I, Flin Irongaze, *will* bring about Drathorn Hellbound's death."

Wednesday June 10th, 18291; Drathorn, Thira, Troy and Feronis were walking down the street of Signaroc chatting casually after spending the night filling in Feronis. The warriors ran around the city preparing their own belongings for the upcoming battle or running errands for Argoss and the Captain or even the King or Orfac. Drathorn was walking at the back of the group, thinking about the night's conversation while the others talked.

It was then that he caught a glimpse of something moving in the shadows of an alley way. He stopped and looked at the others walking just ahead of him. They had not noticed it. He peered closer and saw his worst nightmare.

He stood in a black cloak, taller than Drathorn even though he was hunched over. A boney hand gripped a towering scythe. Hanging from his wrist was a small hourglass. It was nearly full at the moment but he watched as a single grain of sand fell to the bottom. The Grim Reaper's other hand lifted slowly and put one finger in front of its invisible lips. Drathorn could almost hear a voice in his head say "*Shh* . . ." but it was not one of the dragons . . . it was softer than the wind.

Drathorn already knew that he would tell no one of this vision, he had seen the reaper; death was coming. But Drathorn smiled at Death. He spread his arms wide as if awaiting an embrace and held the smile on his lips. A breeze blew through the alley way and the reaper disappeared. The silent whisper in his mind seemed to laugh evilly and Drathorn dropped his arms to his side and turned to look at his friends waiting for him up ahead. He would not mention this to them for fear of frightening them but as he slowly approached them he whispered to Death, wherever he was. "Bring it on . . ."

End of Book One

Spell in the Language of Magic	Effect
Armondur Nasgoth	Fires a small bolt of lightning from the palm
Balasta Nige	Summons a flying arrow
Efrall	Creates a bright flare when launched from bow or crossbow
Elembrana Siscom Gratmorr	Completely erases the target's soul
Danalas-Vorg	Stops the target(s) heart
Esgatso Monakium	Shoots a blob of acid from the palm
Gortha	Five great pillars are summoned around the target to create a stone prison
Isarmontrol	
Lagmenta	Levitates target
Lipesia	A powerful magical push
Locorman Zang	Creates undead puppet(s)
Lorzore	Launches target forward
Molando	Shoots a small fire blast from the palm
Morfandazman	Launches giant boulder at target
Mort Narven	Creates a weak magical shield
Mozar Notic	Creates a dome of ice around the target(s)
Nervahn Est Mondor	Summons power from the sky to strike the ground in a violent lightning bolt
Nervahn Es-uh	Ten blasts of electricity explode from the ground
Norfal Dorme Hielmore	Puts target(s) to sleep
Nymphorniac	Releases vines that do the caster's bidding
Proganzak	Freezes target(s)
Tela Zrome Larn Sime	Immediately melts ice into water
Thi Sein Whor	Hides a chosen item of the Mystic Dozen
Zamjor Kar	Teleports caster and target(s) to desired location

About the Author

D.Y. Paradis was born in 1994 in Timmins, Ontario, Canada. When he moved to Niagara Falls, Ontario, part way through first grade, he was forced to make new friends and learn a new language. In September of 2005 he decided to become an author and nearly a year later he came up with the Drathorn Hellbound series. After three years of hard work, dedication and encouragement he has finally completed the first book. He continues to move forward on his next masterpiece with his head held high and the encouragement of his family and friends.

LaVergne, TN USA
03 December 2009
165841LV00001B/1/P